T0354378

Scaring The Kids

BY
JOHN A. REID

Book cover, interior page design, and illustrations by John A. Reid

Scaring The Kids

iUniverse books may be ordered through booksellers or by contacting:

iUniverse
1663 Liberty Drive
Bloomington, IN 47403
www.iuniverse.com
1-800-Authors (1-800-288-4677)

ISBN: 978-1-4502-3063-6 (sc)
ISBN: 978-1-4502-3064-3 (dj)
ISBN: 978-1-4502-3065-0 (e)

Library of Congress Control Number: 2010907561

Printed in the United States of America
iUniverse rev. date: 9/12/11

I N D E X

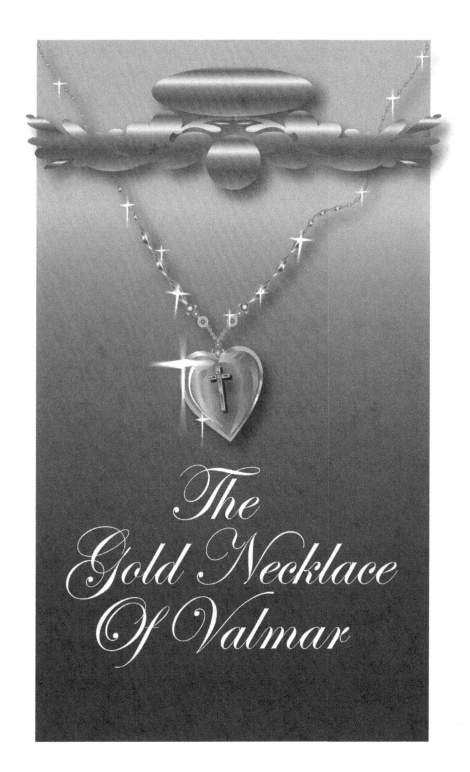

The Gold Necklace Of Valmar

The Gold Necklace Of Valmar

From its vantage point on a dried stem, the grasshopper could see the occasional slow blinking of the bullfrog's left eye as it crouched on the boulder that the sun was doing its best to boil for lunch. Hovering above the frog was a strange appendage that had a quivering glow at the end of it.

As the grasshopper stared longer at it, the quivering glow grew bigger and bigger until a bright ball broke free from the tip of the appendage, hurtled downward, and then shattered when it struck the bullfrog's back.

Lance dipped his index finger into the paper cup of water, raised it above the frog again, then grinned as he watched the next drop fall onto the taut, dry skin of the frog's back, splashing momentary relief from the noonday heat.

"That's slow torture, you know," said Melissa.

"Torture? Naw, no way. It's like a light, refreshing rainfall on a woman's bare breasts on a hot day in the summer," said Lance, then he laughed.

"Oh, that's...it's...Well, it's...Gawwwwd!" she exclaimed.

"Oh, c'mon. Bet you've read even wilder things than that in those romance novels you're always hiding your face with. I read what I just said, somewhere. I think it was in something I had to give a book report on in high school," he said, smiling.

"Hah! I just bet! That'll be the day they let kids read stuff like *that* in school."

"Well, I read it *somewhere*. How else could I know about it?"

"From Cheryl Taylor, or Janet Hendricks, or Kayla Col..."

"Melissa! You don't think I've done that to them, do you?"

"Well, from the way they all slobber over you, I thought you might've. So, have you dated any of them?"

"Uh-uh. Too fast for me, and you know that. I don't know. It's just that I think sex shouldn't take place 'til after you're married. It's something that...Let's take this little guy over to the pond while we're talking, okay? Like, sure, there's lots of girls who want me to ask them out, but the ones that do...Well, I know how far they go from what the guys tell me."

"Very far from what I've overheard in the school washroom. All the girls are always giggling and talking about it. Sex, I mean. And who does what."

"Oh, really? I didn't think little girls your age talked about things like that."

"I'm *not* a little girl! I'm past thirteen!"

"Hmmm, that's still pretty young for that type of talk. *I* hear it, yeah, but from guys my age. They're always bragging about their latest conquests. The only reason I said anything racy to you is because my mother told me she'd read one of the books I saw you reading. Okay? And boy! Was I ever surprised by what she said she read in that book! We'll put our bullfrog buddy in here. There. Look at him go! Right down below the lily pads," he said, smiling.

"I saw him," sad Melissa. "I bet he'll come up later, and sit on a lily pad, and then just sit there for hours and get really dry again. That's sort of weird, huh?"

"Yeah, it is, and yet you told me it was torture when I dropped water on him when we were over by that rock."

"Well, he couldn't plop into any water over there, whenever he felt like it, that's why. Oh! There he is over there! See those lily pads by the branch that's floating in the water? You can just see his head. See him?" cried Melissa.

"By the branch? Oh, yeah! Look, there's another frog at the end of the branch!"

"I see him! That's three bullfrogs we've seen already. That one we had was the biggest. Tyler and Kenny and some of their friends catch them, and then they try to make pets out of them, but their parents tell them to put them back in the pond."

"They're right about that. Things should stay where they live. Just like you and me," said Lance.

"Well, I don't want to live here all *my* life. I'd like to live in a big city, someday, like New York, or maybe even London. I'd love to travel to all kinds of places someday."

"Hmmm, not me. I like it here because you know everybody, but in bigger towns or a city, sometimes you don't even know the people living next door to you."

"Maybe, but with so many people, I bet there's lots of them you can become friends with," she said. "Anyway, *you* go to Valmar every weekend, and sometimes for even longer, so, if you say you don't like to travel, well, you stay there for sometimes up to a week or more."

"Yeah, but I wouldn't go there if I could buy things here like you can in Valmar. Like nicer shirts and jeans, and shoes, too. And besides, if I hung around here on the weekends, then the guys'd be expecting me to start going out with a girl, and you know what most of them want to do on a date. No way I want that."

"Do you know many people in Valmar?"

"Nope," replied Lance. "Just the people in the stores I buy things at. I just stay with my aunt and uncle, and sit around the pool. It's really great. It's a really big pool, and one end of it is really deep, and there's a diving board, too. We have barbecues every day, and some of their friends drop by, so, I *do* get to meet *some* people."

"Do you ever go downtown at night when you're there? I sure wouldn't do that."

"Why not?"

"Because there's lots of crime, that's why."

"Aw, that happens in every city, but nowhere near where my aunt and uncle live. Hey, wait a sec! You just told me you wanted to live in a big city like New York. Think things like that don't happen there? Even more crime there."

"Yeah, I guess I forgot about that. Hmmm, well, when you consider the amount of people to the amount of crimes, it evens out to the same as what happens in a town this size. Not that we've had any murders or anything really terrible, but it could happen, you know, even here."

"In *this* town? No way. I don't know of anybody dangerous. Unless some spooky killer gets off a bus and comes looking for *you*. I can just see him now. Hiding behind some tree, and then peeking out and asking in a very deep, scary voice: 'Where *is* that Melissa? Please! I came here looking for her!'"

"Hah! He'd never get me, because I'd never go anywhere near some strange man I didn't know!"

"Uh-huh, but then what if he was a long-lost relative, and the reason he was, is because he was in prison for maybe thirty years for killing twenty people?" asked Lance, grinning.

"Then I'd run right over to your place and tell you, and then you'd beat him up for me."

"And muss my hair? Sorry," he said with a crooked smile.

"Oh, I know you'd protect me. But your hair always *does* look nice, though. I mean, all the girls say that. Not just me, and you *are* the nicest-looking boy in town. That's why Janet and so many other girls want to date you," said Melissa, blushing.

"Aw, golly, shucks and gee whiz! It's hell being so purty! Hey, you're blushing!" he said, laughing.

"No, I'm not. I'm just getting a sunburn, that's all. Anyway, I've got to go home for lunch. So, um, are you going home, too?"

"I'm just going to sit here and watch the bullfrogs for awhile. Sometimes I think they lead such a useless life. The slimy things just sit around burping all day because they're so fat. Bloated, ugly gluttons. Hmmm, I've lost my appetite for now, but that's okay because my mother won't have lunch ready for maybe another half hour. But you'd better run along now, or you'll be late."

"Okay. Maybe I'll see you later, okay?"

"Sure, you bet," said Lance, smiling, then he winked at her.

"I had a great time! The frog and everything! Bye!"

· · · · · ❖•••••❖ ★ ❖•••••❖ · · · · ·

She turned away from him to go home for lunch, and as she walked, she quickly imagined the start of a romantic fantasy, then she smiled while looking down at her imaginary, gold-embroidered, crimson shoes below her full-length, blue and red-striped dress.

Melissa looked back at the pond and saw Lance's spectacular ship with the two dozen deep orange sails billowing in the breeze, and the ship was docked at the shore of the pond.

She then saw Lance run down the gangplank, then wave at her as he shouted something she couldn't quite discern, so, she closed her imaginary, beaded, red parasol, and began running to him.

As she neared him, Melissa noticed that his white shirt was open to the waistband of his black pantaloons that were tucked into his knee-high, brown boots, and his amazing, jeweled scabbard was sparkling in the sunlight.

Lance held out his arms to her as she ran toward him, then reaching him, he closed his arms around her, and kissed her for a very long time.

"Oh, Lance! Are you leaving for Arabia as you told me you had to, so that you can realize your dream? Your fate to become emperor? Please don't leave me, darling!"

"Leave you? Hah! Never! My future has no meaning without you, my princess-to-be. If you will come with me, I will give up all the riches of the world just to know I would be able to kiss if only your delicate hand once each day."

"Our love is greater than all the riches of the world, so, you need not give up everything for me. I will come with you, my darling. Yes, I would go with you to the ends of the earth. Until the end of time."

"You would give up your great inheritance for me?"

"Yes! Yes, yes, yes, my sweet! Now!" cried Melissa.

"Oh, happy day! Come! The ship is ready to sail! I had only hoped in my wildest dreams that you might say yes, so, I dared! I took the liberty of having my ship laden with gowns, daring lingerie, a year's supply of your favorite bubble gum, and many, many jewels for you, so, you need not pack a suitcase, my beauty."

"Oh, darling! Then let us away!"

Lance swept her up into his arms, and laughed as he carried her up the gangplank to the cheers of the crew and all the townspeople. Bells pealed throughout the countryside as the ship slowly sailed off toward the pink and mauve clouds kissing the horizon that Melissa gazed at with Lance's arms around her while a scented breeze fluffed her glorious, shining hair.

She looked back to wave farewell one last time to her homeland, and Melissa saw the front steps of her porch, and then her romantic fantasy ended, and she heaved a big sigh before slowly walking up the steps on her way into the house for lunch.

· · · · · · ◇••••••◇★◇••••••◇ · · · · · ·

Melissa ate her lunch, feeling so embarrassed for having told Lance that he was the nicest-looking boy in town. He lived next door to her, and every girl she knew had told her how handsome he was. Melissa had had a crush on him since the time he'd started babysitting her when she'd been a small girl.

Now that she was in her teens, she fantasized about marrying him someday because Lance was not only handsome with a wonderful personality and sense of humor, he also had very high moral standards.

He was considered the most eligible bachelor in town, as well, because Lance had a very good position already and a promising career working for his father who owned three of the largest businesses in town.

They'd formed what Melissa felt was a close friendship because at least twice a week she accompanied Lance to the convenience store at the far end of the street, and then after they'd return, they would often sit on his porch, talking for almost half an hour.

She always made sure to be out on the porch, or by a window facing it every day to wave goodbye to him as he left his house in the morning to go to work, and to wave at him again, when he returned from work.

Melissa talked so much about how much time she spent with Lance, that some of her friends had mistakenly presumed, to her delight, that they were dating.

Lance rarely associated with the other young men in town, and he never dated any of the young women, and Melissa felt that he never dated because he hadn't found a girl as interesting as her, and that's why he liked talking to her occasionally.

She felt so proud of him because her parents and every other adult in town admired him, which made Melissa even more attracted to him. However, he still looked at her as the young girl he'd babysat, and Melissa hoped that one day soon, Lance would see her for the young woman of thirteen that she had now become.

From the time she'd been a small child, Melissa had gone next door to chat and to occasionally have lunch with Lance's mother, and then eventually, Lance had let her play his video games in his bedroom during the times he wasn't home.

Whenever he left town to spend a few days with his relatives in Valmar, Melissa would either sit at the computer in Lance's bedroom, reading the poetry he was presently composing, or wander around his room, looking at favorite items he'd collected.

There were dozens of sea shells on shelves, mounted on walls, and several large, beautiful ones on the windowsill in his bedroom.

She loved lying on his bed, and reading one of the many fascinating books she'd taken off one of the four, long shelves in his room.

Lance had a jewellery box in which he kept cufflinks, tie pins, and pieces of jewellery he'd bought in secondhand or antique stores. Melissa appreciated his sense of beauty, and she'd put on lovely earrings, interesting brooches, rings with colored stones imbedded in them, and necklaces.

Last Christmas he'd given her a small piece of his jewellery collection, and Melissa realized that if he continued giving her some of his beautiful jewellery every year, then she'd have an impressive collection, too.

She'd never tell any of the young people in town, especially the boys at school, about Lance's hobby of collecting women's jewellery because she knew that they'd think he was effeminate, regardless of his strong masculine air.

Melissa was at an age where she understood that people would find it odd that Lance loved to collect women's jewellery, nor would they understand his sense of good taste and appreciation of finely crafted jewellery.

Men's jewellery was rather plain, except for a few pairs of cufflinks and some tie pins Lance had that were very old and very beautiful.

She dreamed of the day when he'd ask her to accompany him to Valmar, then they'd stroll along streets, looking through shops, and buying unusual and beautiful jewellery together, and then eventually, they'd shop together as a married couple.

Melissa was too shy to tell him that while he was away in Valmar, she stood in front of the mirror in his bedroom, admiring herself as she wore many pieces of his jewellery.

◇••••••◇★◇••••••◇

Joline noticed her daughter sighing as she sat at the kitchen table, wistfully looking out the window, and she knew that Melissa was thinking about Lance because she'd just returned from a walk to the pond with him.

She was quite aware that Melissa was deeply infatuated with Lance who was more interested in his father's business than he was in dating any of the young women in town.

He was ten years older than Melissa, and Joline knew that one day, Melissa would be heartbroken when Lance took an interest in a young woman closer to his own age, and then married her.

"How long will Lance be gone this time?" asked Joline.

"He said he'd back Monday night."

"I was speaking with his mother, and she told me that Lance's aunt and uncle are actually hers, as well, so, I imagine they'd be the same age as his grandparents. Did he mention that he knew other people his age in Valmar?"

"Well, not really, but he must know some because Lance told me that his aunt and uncle have a big swimming pool in their backyard, and that people come to visit."

"Hmmm," murmured Joline.

"What does *that* mean? Oh, I bet I know. You think he's got a girlfriend in Valmar. He'd tell me if he had. Lance is too serious to date right now, and besides, most of the girls around here, and probably in the city, too, expect more than just kissing and things. Lance is waiting 'til he gets married before he does...Well, does more with a girl. And I know he's not gay, either, if that's what you're thinking. He just has old fashioned values."

"Yes, he does. *Very* old fashioned values. Oh, now don't look at me like that, dear. I just meant that it's a rare quality in a young man today to have values like Lance's. And I'm not saying that young men today are immoral, either. Okay?"

"He's got so many other qualities, too," said Melissa. "He's sweet. Gentle. He's also lots of fun. He's like those fine gentlemen you read about. You know the ones I mean? In romance novels? He treats a woman like a lady."

"Yes, he *is* very polite and very well brought up. Lance'll make a fine catch for some woman, someday. Handsome, nice, and well-situated. I think you have many fine qualities, too, and I just know that one day you'll marry a wonderful young man who appreciates all that you have to give."

"But not Lance, right? You think he's too old for me, but lots of men marry women ten years younger than them. Even fifteen or more. If I get contacts someday, I'll look really pretty."

"You're very pretty *now*, dear. Your glasses are like a beautiful frame for your lovely eyes. Just like a painting that looks even better when it's framed. But I know how you feel, and you know we promised to get you contacts on your next birthday."

"Yeah, I know. Thanks, mom. But another year almost."

"I don't see any reason why we can't get you new frames for your glasses 'til you get your contacts."

"Yeah? Oh, that'd be so great, mom! Hey, can we go into Valmar to get my new frames? There's so many more stores there, so, there'd be a bigger selection of frames. Can we? Please?"

"Sure we can," replied Joline, smiling. "Besides, if you find frames you really like, you can wear them when you're not wearing your contacts. Something chic. Perhaps slightly jeweled, too."

"Oh, yeah! Maybe a real nice red. Or green. Yellow, even."

"Keep in mind that you should think about a color that'd go with the clothes you have. Well, if you find a pair of frames you really love, then I suppose we could buy you a dress and a few blouses to match them."

"Aw, mom, you're the greatest! I can't wait 'til next week!"

"I've got an idea. After you choose your frames, we'll buy a couple of things you can wear with them, but I'll shop alone for a few items so that they'll be a surprise for you. A gift each week for a few weeks. How's that?"

"Yeah, that'd be so great! Um, mom? I was wondering if we could get something else, too."

"Such as?"

"Well, they've got three newspapers in Valmar, right? Two of them are really big, and on the weekends, they've got a big entertainment section and others with, like, one for the arts. Books and paintings and that. And there's other smaller newspapers, too, so, I thought that while we're there, well, I could look at all of them, and the one we like best, we could have delivered. Even just the big Saturday or Sunday one. That wouldn't be expensive, and you and dad'd like it, too, because they've got so much more in them than our local paper. Like, a bigger news section, and more sports coverage, and a cooking section. All kinds of sections."

"All right. When we're in the Roseville Mall, you can visit that magazine and newspaper store on the main floor while I shop for a few things to go with your new frames. That should keep you occupied for awhile," said Joline, smiling.

"Oh, thanks, mom! But I'm not going to tell Lance we were in Valmar 'til after he sees my new frames and asks me where I got them. But if I see him there, maybe he'll come with us and tell me which frames he likes the best. Yeah, that'd be even better. We could even have lunch together or something like that. Maybe he might invite us to his aunt and uncle's home."

"Honey, I...Well, promise me you won't be too upset if we see him in Valmar, and he has a young woman with him. You know that's possible, don't you?"

"Oh, uh, maybe we might. But I just know if he had a girlfriend there, he would've told me."

"Yes, I'm sure he would have, dear. Are you ready for some dessert, now?"

"Yeah, I am, thanks. I'll cut the pie, okay? Wait'll everyone sees me after I get my new frames because they'll be nicer than anything you can buy here," she said, smiling.

. . . . . ❖••••••❖ ✮ ❖••••••❖ . . . . . .

After lunch, Melissa went next door to see Lance, but his mother told her that he'd gone out, so, she decided to walk down to the pond to see if he'd returned and was waiting to spend perhaps the rest of the afternoon with her.

She was halfway to the pond when she became lost in another of her romantic fantasies, and in this one, she imagined hearing musical chimes coming from a small distance behind her, then looking back, Melissa saw a very long, silver limousine moving slowly toward her, then it came to a stop beside her.

One of the doors opened, and a man in dove gray livery stepped out and held open the rear door of the limousine. Lance then climbed out, dressed in a yellow tuxedo and holding a yellow top hat in his white-gloved hands.

"Lance! What a surprise! I was just on my way to the pond!"

"Wonderful! I am, as well, beauty. I'm taking a few visiting presidents from various countries for a tour, and I'd hoped that by including the pond in the itinerary, that you might be there, and here I find you on your way there, now. I just can't believe my luck. I thought you might still be lunching. I'll go on ahead, my lovely, and have my servants set up a table with cold champagne, chocolates, and fresh strawberries by the water's edge. Don't keep me waiting. Promise me, darling. Seconds are eternities when I'm not with you to admire your breathtaking beauty. Please promise me you won't change your mind?" asked Lance, holding her hands.

"Yes, I promise you, as always. But my dress."

"A cabana will also be set up so that you can change, and there'll be a blue evening gown hanging up inside it. The color of the gown will accent your amazing azure eyes that enrapture me so, sweet beauty. And of course, every dress designer in the world knows your size. Oh, and there's also a pink fur stole for you, too," he said, then he kissed her hand.

"Drive on, and I promise not to tarry over a wild flower, my love. I shall quicken my step. Until then, dear one, farewell."

"Adieu, my shining star. Now I feel so soothed, knowing you'll be there," he said, then he blew her a kiss as the car sped away.

· · · · · ❖•••••❖★❖•••••❖ · · · · ·

Melissa's romantic fantasy faded as she hurried onward to the pond while hoping that Lance would be waiting there. She saw Tyler Crawford, one of the boys she went to school with, and a few of his friends riding their bicycles away from the pond and coming in her direction. They called out: "Hi!" to her as they sped by, laughing.

She tensed up when she reached the pond, and her face drained of color, and she felt nauseated by what she saw on the ground near the pond. Torn body parts of bullfrogs were laying everywhere, and

Melissa burst into tears while thinking of how cruel the boys were. For the past five years, dead cats and dogs had been found laying along the sides of the river, and all of them had been mutilated.

Melissa hurried away while vowing to herself not to go back to the pond until the bullfrogs' bodies had been disposed of in some way. She had immediately blamed the boys, however, she would've been much more upset if she'd known that it had really been Lance whom had viciously killed the frogs, as well as all the cats and dogs.

She told her mother about the bullfrogs as she brushed tears from her cheeks, then Joline explained to her that many boys did terrible things like that when they were young, but as they grew older, they regretted what they'd done. Joline also told Melissa that when she'd been a young girl, she'd seen boys pull the wings off insects out of gruesome curiosity.

All Melissa could think of for days was the horrible sight of scattered, gory parts of bullfrogs, and then the next time she saw Lance, she told him about the awful things somebody had done to the frogs at the pond. He'd then told her that it was difficult for him to understand how cruel young boys could be because he'd never had feelings like that when he'd been their age.

As she'd sat on the porch steps with her head resting on the side of his shoulder, Melissa had felt that the only thing that could cheer her up would be to talk about her new eyeglass frames. But then she'd decided not to tell Lance about them because she wanted to surprise him when she wore them with a new dress.

Melissa tried concentrating on new eyeglass frames and new clothes instead of thinking about what she'd seen at the pond, and she hoped it would help her, but she knew she'd always remember the disgusting sight she'd seen.

After she'd told Lance about the dismembered bullfrogs, she had almost swooned when he'd smoothed a few strands of her hair back with his fingertips while telling her that he hated to see her so upset.

Even though the contact had only been for a few seconds, Melissa's heart had beat faster as she thought that this could be the start of the greatest romance the world had ever known.

⋅ ⋅ ⋅ ⋅ ⋅ ❖••••••❖★❖••••••❖ ⋅ ⋅ ⋅ ⋅ ⋅

She felt certain that by wearing a new dress to match her exciting new eyeglass frames, Lance would notice her as more than just the young girl next door, and soon she'd be going into Valmar to select her beautiful new frames.

Melissa laid in bed, finding it difficult to fall asleep that night because she felt excited about going to Valmar to select beautiful eyeglass frames. She suddenly imagined herself as a wealthy young woman, living in a castle, and looking forward to the next morning when she would be driven to Valmar in her ornately gilded coach.

In the sudden fantasy scene she created, Melissa saw herself as the wealthy young woman beginning to awake the next morning, and then there it was, the morning sun, and she slipped out of her huge, magnificent bed, ran to the window and blew a kiss to the new day.

On the road to Valmar, she gazed out the window of her gilded coach, and everything looked more beautiful than ever before. All that was green appeared like emeralds, jade, and other exotic, green jewels. Even the green fields looked like plush, magical carpets that would carry her up and away to marvelous and mysterious lands.

Suddenly, the brakes were abruptly applied, and she jolted forward, and then after leaning her head out the coach window, she saw that a man all dressed in black and wearing a mask was threatening her driver with a pistol.

He saw her, and then after hurrying over to her, the masked man ordered her to step out onto the road, which she reluctantly and haughtily did.

"Your purse, my lady, or a certain and untimely death!"

"Here! Take it, foul oaf!" she cried, hurling her purse at him.

"I love a beautiful woman with spirit! Now, let's see what lies within your purse! Aha! The Ethiopian Eagle! This diamond is the biggest in the world, and it's placed on the famous gold ring with the six black pearls. Hmmm, ah, and a package of my favorite bubble gum. Fifteen gold coins. Oh, this bracelet is worth millions. Hmmm, and *this*. Ah, so priceless. Oh, and here! A silver cellular phone!"

"Take what you want, knave, and leave us!" she exclaimed.

"Not without a kiss!"

"Never! Stand back, rogue!" shouted Melissa, scowling at him.

The masked man made a move toward her, then suddenly, crashing through the tall bushes beside the road, was Lance on a magnificent black stallion.

He was dressed all in red, with a long red cape, and as the masked man stood gaping, Lance leapt off his horse, drew his sword, and before the robber could raise his pistol, Lance held the point of his blade against the man's throat.

"Mercy, my lord!" cried the bandit.

"Only for the sake of Melissa! Give her back her purse, then kneel, bow, and apologize to her, you scum!"

The bandit fell to his knees, then after he handed Melissa her purse, he bowed with his hands on the road, and begged her forgiveness.

She accepted his apology as she smiled at Lance and threw him a white rose, which he caught, then after placing it in his clenched teeth as he grinned, he leapt back up onto his horse.

He leaned over, bound the masked man's hands together with golden rope, and then after he told the bandit to get on his own horse, Lance blew a kiss to Melissa.

She waved her embroidered, lace hanky while watching them riding away; the masked man riding a small distance behind Lance whom held the golden rope that was attached to the robber's wrists.

Melissa smiled as she climbed back into her gilded coach, then sat back against the padded, silk upholstery, and sighed as her fantasy ended. She reached over and turned off the lamp on the bedside table, hugged her pillow, and then fell asleep while thinking about waking on Saturday morning, and going to Valmar.

*   *   *   *   *   ❖•••••❖⭐❖•••••❖   *   *   *   *   *

Saturday arrived, and after they drove to Valmar, Melissa was so excited as she and her parents went to several stores, looking at frames for her glasses.

They went into a big store in the Roseville Mall, and Melissa finally settled on a pair of frames that were slightly narrow and they swept up just a bit into a point at each side.

Instead of a color, they were black and white with a tiny rhinestone star at the top corners of the frames. Her mother agreed that the frames were not only rather fashionable, but that Melissa could wear any color of clothes with them.

Joline then told her that she was going to buy her some black and white clothes to accent the new eyeglass frames.

Melissa browsed through the magazine and newspaper shop while her father strolled around the mall, looking in other stores. Joline shopped for a few other clothes besides the dress she and Melissa had chosen together to accent the new eyeglass frames, and then they met at the fountain forty minutes later.

While her parents were talking, Melissa observed other shoppers in the mall, then she noticed a woman with twin, redheaded girls. She felt sure that the twins were the same age as her, and she liked the clothes they were wearing.

When Melissa brought them to her parents attention, Joline excitedly exclaimed: "Carol? Carol Silverman?"

The woman looked at Joline for a moment, then she laughed and walked over to her and said: "Joline! I haven't seen you in years! You look wonderful!"

"You have twins! They're very pretty," said Joline.

Introductions were made, then after they chatted for awhile, the adults agreed to have lunch at a restaurant that had a section for young people close to the area they'd be sitting.

◦　•　•　　•　•　❖••••••❖★❖••••••❖　•　•　　•　•　•

Melissa loved the booth in the restaurant section that she, Linda and Lee sat in. All the booths were designed like antique cars, and they were seated in one that was representative of a Ford Model T.

Their booth was black, with a white vinyl upholstery, and the top of the table had a black and white checkered pattern. Melissa then wished that she had on her new, black and white frames, but they wouldn't be ready for two weeks.

She felt so pleased that her parents had agreed to spend more money so that she could have the frames, and Melissa thought it would be wonderful to wear them some other time that she'd be here at this restaurant and seated at the same booth.

The girls waved up at their parents who were seated at a table on the mezzanine that had been designed to look like a garden with many white pillars and statues.

Melissa and the twins chatted as they ate their hamburgers with French fries while they sipped on delicious milkshakes in containers that looked like pineapples.

"Your dad had a lot of newspapers," said Lee.

"Yeah, they were the big Saturday ones with lots of sections in them. We're going to subscribe to one of them after we decide which one we like the best," Melissa told her.

"We get the Valmar Voice every day. The Saturday edition's huge. It's got lots of comics in it and all kinds of puzzles, too. The TV guide is really big, just like a magazine with pictures of movie stars in it, so, we think that's the best one," said Linda.

"You're lucky to live here. Back home we haven't got even one movie house, but there's so many here. We rent videos, though. Do you go to a lot of movies, here?" asked Melissa.

"Sometimes, but mostly we rent videos, too. We like that better because you have to pay so much money to see a movie, and then if you want popcorn and pop, that's really expensive, and the worst part is that after paying all that money, you can't hear half of what the actors are saying. That's because there's so many people in the audience talking loudly or shouting across to their friends. The ushers won't tell them to be quiet, either, because all the people've bought tickets and so the ushers say those people can do whatever they want. It's so stupid," said Linda.

"Yeah, and most of them are just hanging out in there 'til they go somewhere else, later," said Lee. "We can't afford to waste lots of money like them, so, I guess they're all rich, and they don't care how much a movie costs. It's so stupid."

"Yeah, I know what you mean," said Melissa. "We came into Valmar to see a big Disney movie and it was very expensive because of the cost of parking the car, too, and you're so right about the noise. Kids running up and down the aisles and shouting. It was like being at a six-year-old's birthday party. My parents told me it's like that sometimes at night, too. Adults yak loudly and just as much. My dad says there's always two or three girls who think they're impressing their boyfriends by pretending to be really stupid and he's so-o much smarter. All the way through the movie, those types of girls keep asking stuff like what's she mean by that, and gee, I don't get it, and other things like that. Like, all she has to do is watch the movie instead of asking her boyfriend all kinds of stupid questions."

"If my boyfriend wanted me to be stupid, I'd tell him to drop dead because boys aren't any smarter than girls. Why do you think those airhead girls do that?" asked Lee.

"Obviously because they have a very low opinion of themselves and other females," replied Melissa. "That's what my dad said. He told me he couldn't stand to be married to a doofus, and that's why he married my mom because he says that she's smarter than him. He said if you're going to spend your life with someone, you should be able to talk intelligently with them, and they should be like your best friend, too. My dad spends lots of time with his men friends, but he told me he loves being around my mom a lot, too. They always talk about really interesting things, too. If I got married and my husband started having no respect for me, and he thought I was stupid, then I'd get a divorce before he knew what was happening."

"Have you got a boyfriend?" asked Linda.

"Um, well, sort of. I don't usually talk about him because people would be shocked," lied Melissa.

"Yeah? Why?" asked Linda and Lee in unison.

"Hmmm, well, you live here, so, I guess I can tell you. I wouldn't tell my friends back home, though. Okay, he's very handsome and...well, he's ten years older than me."

"Yeah? Really? Wow! What do your parents think about that?"

"Of course, they were surprised at first, but we plan to marry when I'm eighteen. It's a sort of platonic affair right now, because he has very high moral values."

"Wow! Ten years older than you! Our boyfriends are the same age as us!" cried Linda, wide-eyed.

"Yeah, they are! Of course, our affairs are platonic, too. But sometimes Bobby wants me to show him things, but I won't. You know what I mean," said Lee, smiling.

"Not mine. He appreciates my mind," said Melissa.

"Yeah? That's so great. Our boyfriends like us, but they spend more time fooling around, or at video arcades and things, instead of with us. So immature," Linda said, then she heaved a big sigh.

"What's your boyfriend's name?" Lee asked Melissa.

"I'd tell you, but...well, because not many people would approve of our relationship, and because he has many friends here in Valmar, and they might think the same way, we'd like to keep it private for maybe another few months. You know how some people aren't so understanding. Maybe if I start coming here more, and I get to know you better, then I'd tell you his name, then. Okay?"

"Sure, okay. My mom hasn't seen yours in a long time, like, not since they went to school together, so, I'll bet they're going to start keeping in touch more now. I heard them say that, so that means we'll get to know each other a lot better, and then you can tell us his name. And I'm going to tell my boyfriend that he should start appreciating *my* mind more, too," said Linda.

"Me too," said Lee. "But I've heard there *are* some men who never appreciate women's minds, so, they beat them up, and sometimes they rape them."

"Yeah, and murder them, too," Linda added. "Did you know there's lots of women murdered here in Valmar, all the time?"

"No, I didn't," replied Melissa, wide-eyed.

"Well, I guess not lots, but there's been *some*. That's why you've got to be very, very careful who you're dating when you get older. Of course, I might stick with Bobby if he smartens up, because he's really cute," said Lee, smiling.

"Yeah, Bobby needs to smarten up. Of course, he's not really dumb, but he's just not too serious about love. Same as *my* boyfriend, Brad. I call him, 'Bad Brad,'" said Linda.

"Well, I don't have to worry about dating men I don't know because I'll be married when I'm eighteen. After that, I told him that I'd like to live in New York City or maybe London, and he sort of likes that idea, so, we might move there."

"Yeah? New York's so big and exciting!" exclaimed Linda.

"We think so, too," said Melissa.

"Wow!" cried Lee and Linda together.

The girls chatted until it was time to leave the mall, and their mothers promised to phone each other more often, and Joline and Jonathan promised to visit Carol and her family the next time they were in Valmar. They said goodbye and left the mall as they talked about the wonderful time they'd had that day.

Melissa felt relieved that the twins hadn't ask her parents about her boyfriend, but she'd loved how Linda and Lee had been so impressed when she'd told them that she was dating a man ten years older than her.

Before they left Valmar, they visited Melissa's aunt and uncle, Joanne and Wes, and had dinner with them, and then her parents promised Wes and Joanne that they'd visit them again in two weeks when they returned to pick up Melissa's new eyeglass frames.

Melissa worried that when they returned to Valmar, her mother would want to see Linda and Lee's mother. If that happened, would their mother ask her mother if the Melissa and Lance romance would be announced in all the newspapers soon?

Then more 'what ifs' tumbled through her mind as she thought of that sly lie she'd told Linda and Lee. Now she wished she'd never begun her wishful ruse of Lance and her saying their 'I do's.'

She kept thinking many 'Oh, noes!' and 'What have I dones?' followed by a few 'Who knows? This might make Lance more aware of me,' then hopefully before her lie was realized by everyone, he'd propose to her on bended knee.

· · · · · ❖•••••❖ ★ ❖•••••❖ · · · · ·

When Lance returned from Valmar, he smiled and waved at her, and Melissa blushed, she felt sure, from her cheeks to her toes while wondering if by some awful stroke of fate, he knew Linda and Lee and their parents.

"Hi, Melissa! Boy, you look like you've been running a race!"

"Hi, Lance. Um, just feels hotter than usual today, I guess."

"Well, come on inside where it's nice and cool. I'll get you something cold to drink and we can talk. Okay?"

"Oh? Yeah, I'd really like that. Hot and all, you know."

"You should go swimming later to cool down."

"Yeah, maybe that's a good idea. So, did you have a nice time in Valmar this time?" asked Melissa.

"Yep. I spent most of my time in and around the pool. It was so quiet and relaxing."

"I'm glad. You work so hard all week, so, it's nice that you can get away from work for more than just a weekend sometimes."

"Aaaaa, I don't work *that* hard. Boss's son, and all. I'm lucky that I don't have to work full weeks during the summer. That's why I don't take a vacation because I can have extra days off whenever I want. Fridays and Mondays. Here we are," said Lance, looking into the fridge. "So, what would you like? Coke, ginger ale, root beer, or orange? Or...Hmmm, there's..."

"I'll have a Coke, please. Thank you," said Melissa.

"One Coke for the little lady. I *love* root beer, so, that's what I'll have. Mmmm, icy cold. That should cool you down. So, what did you do this weekend?"

"Oh, all kinds of things. The usual things. You know, swimming, and all that."

"No, I meant in Valmar. My mother told me that you and your parents went there on the weekend."

"Oh? Oh, *that!* Oh, just for the day. Saturday. Mom wanted to do some shopping, and so did dad. We went to a really neat restaurant, and some of the booths were shaped like cars."

"Oh, yeah, I know that one. It's inside Roseville Mall, and it's called Blinkie's. Fun place, isn't it? Great burgers. Yeah, I've been there a few times."

"You have? Oh. Well, I had a banquet burger, fries, and a really delicious milkshake. It came in a container that looked just like a real pineapple. Mom and dad liked the place, too, and they sat upstairs, and they could see down where I was sitting. Um, I might've run into you there."

"Uh-uh, not me. I don't go downtown that often on weekends. Too many crowds."

"I like being in crowds, sometimes, and there's lots of malls in Valmar because it's so big. Isn't it a strange coincidence that we went to the same mall as the one you've been in? Sort of like fate, or what some people call kismet," said Melissa.

"Kismet? Oh, you and your romance novels."

"Oh, stop grinning. Some of those books are very exciting. Just like a movie. There's lots of big movies playing in Valmar, but we didn't go to any of them. After we shopped around in lots of different stores, we went to my aunt and uncle's home and we had dinner with them, then we came back here late at night, so, I had a lot of fun."

"I'm glad you did. Oh, by the way. While I was there, I bought two new shirts, a great pair of pants and a bathing suit. Do you want to see them? I'd like to know what you think of them because you've got very nice taste in everything you wear."

"Yeah, sure, I'd like that. And thanks for saying I've got good taste. I think everything you wear looks perfect on you, so, your taste is very nice, too," she said, smiling.

· · · · · ❖••••••❖★❖••••••❖ · · · · ·

They went upstairs to Lance's bedroom, and he opened packages and boxes, then he held up a short-sleeved, cream-colored shirt that had a print of big, pale olive green leaves on it.

"Oh, Lance. That's a really nice shirt. It'll look great with your blond, curly hair and great suntan. And your eyes are green, so, it'll accent them."

"Do you think these pants'll go with the shirt?" he asked.

"Sure. It's a very nice tan color. Not too dark and not too light. What some people'd call a sort of light sandalwood color. That shirt'll look great with them. So perfect," she said, smiling.

"And!...Ta-da!" exclaimed Lance, holding up another shirt.

"Oh, wow! That's such a beautiful, rich yellow! That shirt's really beautiful, too. It'll go with almost anything. Oh, yeah. That's one of the nicest yellows I've ever seen in my entire life."

"Thanks," he said, with a crooked smile, then he opened another bag, and removed a bathing suit, which he held up to show her.

"I don't know what you'll think of this. I can wear it to swim in my aunt and uncle's pool in Valmar, but I can't wear it at a beach. It might be considered a bit daring. What do you think?"

"No, not really. Well, it's small, but it's not really that small. The bright green, white and yellow stripes are great. The stripes aren't too broad, either."

"It's the same style as the red bathing suit I wear when I'm at my aunt and uncle's. So, would you like to see a fashion show?"

"Really? Okay. I'll wait out in the hall."

"No, you just sit there. I'll take these things and change in the bathroom. I'll move this table out of the way. And the chair. There. Okay, get ready to applaud, now," said Lance, grinning.

"I'll clap my hands 'til they hurt!" cried Melissa as she laughed.

Her heart had kept pace with her quick laughter when Lance had told her that he'd be modeling his new clothes for her.

* * * * * ❖•••••❖★❖•••••❖ * * * * *

Melissa walked over to the window, hoping she wouldn't blush when she saw him in the bathing suit. She'd seen him in a bathing suit many times before, but not in the confines of his bedroom.

She wandered slowly around his bedroom, and then noticed a folded, flowered kerchief, so, she picked it up to see what it would look like on her head.

A thin, gold necklace with a small, heart-shaped pendant fell out of the kerchief, and Melissa held it up, admiring the little gold heart that had a tiny sapphire cross in the center of it. She undid the clasp, and put it around her neck, and then looked at her reflection in the mirror, and smiled while thinking that the necklace was both unique and beautiful.

Lance yelled that he was almost ready, so, Melissa quickly took off the necklace, dropped it into the kerchief, and refolded it. She hoped that the kerchief looked like it hadn't been unfolded because she didn't want Lance to think that she was a snoop.

She wondered if he'd had her in mind when he'd bought the necklace because her eyes were blue. She then thought that if he decided to give it to her at Christmas, or on her birthday, then the next time she saw Linda and Lee, she could boast about her older boyfriend giving her the necklace as a pre-engagement present.

She then decided she'd better not tell the twins that because it would be adding a bow to her fib.

Lance returned, wearing the new, yellow shirt with the light brown pants, then he grinned as he turned around several times with a flourish. Melissa applauded him as she laughed and said: "You should model clothes for a living because you're so handsome."

"What? You want to turn me into a coat hanger?"

"Well, I think you'd make a great model. Even a famous one, and then you might get an offer to star in movies," she said.

"Naw, I hate the smell of too much popcorn and watching hundreds of people stuffing it in their mouths while they watch me fumble my lines in a movie. Next! The leaf shirt! Be right back. Get out your flash camera," said Lance, then he laughed.

· · · · · · ❖•••••••❖ ★ ❖•••••••❖ · · · · · ·

He modeled his other new shirt, then said he'd return wearing the bathing suit, and Melissa took deep breaths as she looked in the mirror and smoothed out her hair.

Lance returned wearing the bathing suit, a straw hat, a towel around his neck, and he was holding a bottle of suntan lotion as he smiled at her and turned around a few times.

"So? Too daring?" he asked, grinning.

"No! It's...um, it's really, really nice. Yeah. I mean, it's not like a bikini bathing suit, or even anywhere close to one. I don't see why you should be shy about wearing that to any beach because I've seen lots of guys wearing small bathing suits like that. The green, yellow and white stripes are really nice, too. It looks wonderful with your tan. The white stripes bring attention to the sun-bleached parts of your blond hair, too. Yeah, I really like it. So, uh, is that everything? I mean, is that *all* you bought?"

"*All* I bought? You mean, I should've bought a shirt to go with this bathing suit?"

"No, I just thought you might've, like, bought another piece of old jewellery for your collection," said Melissa.

"Oh, I forgot. Yeah, I did. Just a sec. Here it is. I found this in an antique store about ten blocks from my aunt and uncle's. I was going to give it to my aunt, but she said she didn't like jewellery with anything religious on it. It's got a little, blue cross on it. The man I bought it from wasn't sure if the stones were real sapphires or not, but he's sure it's very old. Maybe a hundred years or a bit more. It was a bit pricey, but I've always liked one-of-a-kind things. Here, take a look at it," he said, handing it to her. "Isn't it interesting?"

"Oh, yes. The gold chain is very delicate. I wonder if...hmmm, nope. I thought it opened up like a locket, but I don't think it does. It's very pretty," she said while handing the necklace back to him.

"Man, I must have pieces of jewellery from my grandparents' time to way back to Queen Victoria's time."

"It's a beautiful collection. You know, you should look for a really interesting old pocket watch, sometime. Like, one with jewels on the face of it, and maybe some on the cover of it. Do you ever see real old ones like that?" asked Melissa.

"I've seen old ones, but nothing that interests me so far. As usual, the only nicely crafted pieces of jewellery I see are made for women.

Nothing really nice for men. You go into a jewellery store, and all they have is one small part of one small counter with a few things for men in it, and it's all plain and boring crap. It's like going shopping for clothes. Ninety-five per cent of the stores are for women. I spent most of one whole day, going from store to store looking for those shirts and pants, but almost all the stores carry the same damned thing with the designer labels plastered all over the front and back of every piece of clothing. And that's the only thing different about them is the designer's name. Like Tommy trash and Gap crap. But women. Oh, no, not them. They have tons of selection, and without designers' names all over their clothes, either. It makes me so God damned sick that there's so little choice for men. It's just women, women, women. That's why I just have women's jewellery because it's all made for them. Whoever said it's a man's world? Must've been a woman whining and bitching that she hasn't got anything to wear and yet she's got ten closets full of clothes and dozens of boxes filled with jewellery. But she still wants men to buy more and more for her."

"Well, um, I guess that's because women like lots of different styles of clothes, and men are more interested in different styles of cars. Like, they're always talking about their cars, and fixing them up, right? But your clothes are always really nice, though. But like you said, there's not too much to choose from, and that's why I know it must've taken you a long time to find what you liked."

"Right," he said. "Like this bathing suit I'm wearing. It took me over two months to find it in a store. Like, why *is* that? Don't you think men's clothing stores would carry a bigger selection of bathing suits? But they don't. Just long, baggy shorts. Makes you look like a little kid. And the waistband's so high, too. How the hell can you get a tan like that? But some women's bathing suits are way beyond what you'd call, 'skimpy.' I've heard lots of people saying that men's bodies are ugly. That women are disgusted by them, so, men should cover as much of their bodies as they can at a beach. It makes me sick that women get sick looking at guys wearing small, but nice bathing suits. It's more than simple prejudice. Does it make *you* sick to see me in this bathing suit?"

"Oh, no. No, it doesn't," replied Melissa. "Um, like I said, it shows off your tan. And it's not as small as a lot I've seen."

"A lot? Like, where have you seen guys wearing something like this? Not around here, you haven't. Or at almost every beach I've been to. Guys wear those big baggy shorts for bathing suits, but they're with a girl who you have to look at twice to see if she's really nude or not. Teasing the hell out of guys, and then they say no. No? After wearing something like that in public? Go figure. I mean, why are they wearing something like that for in the first place? It doesn't make sense. They tease and tease and just keep on teasing, and then they say no. It's like when you spend so much money on a girl when you date her. Flowers. Cocktails before dinner in a — has to be expensive restaurant. Wine with dinner. Liqueurs after dinner. And while you're having dinner, she talks so sweet and sexy, building you up, and then after all that, she has the bloody nerve to say no. No! No, to *me*! Hah! They keep saying they won't do this type of sex, or that type of sex with me," he said, scowling.

"But you wouldn't want that anyway, though, because you said you want to wait 'til you're married before you...Well, you know."

"Mmmm? Yeah, I did," said Lance. "But just the same, it's still that way with women. All of them. When you get older, you'll be doing the same thing."

"If you mean I'll still be telling you that you look very nice, yeah. And I'll still like everything you wear," said Melissa.

"I don't mean that. I meant you'll be flaunting yourself in front of other guys. Getting them all worked up, driving them crazy, and then after they try to impress you by spending all sorts of money on you, you'll say no, and then laugh at them. I know. I know how women are. And what they are."

"If I was your girlfriend, I'd never treat you bad because I like everything about you. Everything. Your hair and your smile. I think you're the handsomest man I've ever seen. Honest."

"You like everything about me? You're sure?"

"Yeah, I really mean that. Really."

"Even if I was nude, it wouldn't bother you?"

"Um, well, I guess that depends."

"We'll see about that," said Lance, smirking.

He took off his bathing suit, but before he did, Melissa had gasped and quickly turned her head away. Lance then sat beside her on the bed and took a firm grip on her arm, as Melissa tensed up.

"So, look at me if you're not disgusted," he said.

She looked down, but away from his genitals, and she felt both confused and scared.

"Well? Are you devastated?" asked Lance.

"Uh, no. I, um, it was just so sudden, that's all."

"Are you disgusted? Are my genitals ugly? Are they?"

"Well, I...I've never seen a man's bare things before, so, I'm sort of surprised seeing them for the first time."

"First time? Really? I thought you might've seen some of the boys skinny-dipping once or twice. How do you feel about me baring myself like this?"

Melissa was still staring away from his genitals because she felt too embarrassed to look at them.

"It...well, it's like being at a nude beach, right?"

"Yeah, that's right. You know about erections, don't you?"

"Um, uh. Yeah, sort of," she replied, tremulously.

"Would that make you sick?" asked Lance.

"Um, I...I guess it's a natural thing that happens."

"That's right. You know, this isn't fair. Like, I'm nude and you're fully dressed. You don't have to take off all your clothes, but why not show me your breasts? That way, we've both shown something to each other. We *are* close friends, aren't we? You told me you liked my body. That you wouldn't say no to me. We're all alone in the house, so, we can show each other our naked bodies."

"I don't...I, um, like, um, I've never...I, um..." she stammered.

"Is that a no? You're going to tell me no? You...you little..."

"Hello?...Hello!...I'm home!...Where are you?"

"My mother's home! Stay here!" exclaimed Lance.

He quickly put on his pants and shirt, strode out of the room, over to the staircase, and then leaned over the banister, and called down to his mother: "What're you doing home so early? I thought you said you wouldn't be home 'til four!"

"Barry called Marie and asked her to bring some papers to the office! So, I came home! What're you doing?" she shouted.

"A show! A modeling show!" Lance shouted back.

"A what? Just a minute! I'm coming up!"

Melissa heard Mrs. Johnson coming upstairs, so, she hurried out of Lance's bedroom and stood at the staircase railing.

"Oh, hi, Melissa," said Mrs. Johnson as she smiled.

"Hi, Mrs. Johnson."

"Lance? What's this about a modeling show?"

"Melissa wanted to see how I looked in the new clothes I bought, so, I was acting like a professional model. It was so funny. It made us both laugh so hard," he said, laughing.

"In your bedroom?" asked his mother.

"No! I'm using the bathroom as a changing room, then I walk into the bedroom and pose in something."

"Sometimes I think you're still a little boy."

"The fashion show's over now, so, we're going to have some pop. Do you want one, too?" Lance asked his mother.

"No thanks, dear. I'm going to do some work on the computer. Will you be staying with us for dinner, Melissa?"

"No, thanks, Mrs. Johnson. Mom's already made plans for us to eat together. We're having roast beef."

"Oh, that sounds wonderful, honey," she said.

"Melissa? You go ahead and get a couple of cans of pop, okay? Don't forget. Root beer for me. I'm going to put on my jeans, and then I'll meet you out on the porch, okay?" said Lance.

"Yeah, sure, okay," replied Melissa, going downstairs.

* * * * * ⬩•••••⬩ ★ ⬩•••••⬩ * * * * *

She had almost reached the bottom of the stairs, when the shocking experience she'd had only minutes earlier with Lance caused Melissa's vivid imagination to create an immediate, very dramatic fantasy scene of Lance and his mother.

This fantasy scene began with her imagining that she heard Mrs. Johnson gasp loudly, so, Melissa let herself believe that Lance's mother might have gasped because of a sudden heart attack. She started rushing back up the stairs, then stopped when she saw the look of shock on Mrs. Johnson's face while looking at Lance whom was now wearing just his new bathing suit.

"She bought you that in Valmar? Melissa! Why on earth would you buy a bathing suit like that for my son?"

"I didn't! Lance bought it!"

"You don't like it mother? I think it looks marvelous."

"Yes, it does, but don't you think it's a bit daring, *considering*?"

"Melissa doesn't think so, and she insisted that I try it on to see if she'd bought the right size for me," said Lance, smiling.

"But I *didn't* buy it for him, Mrs. Johnson!" cried Melissa.

"Lance just told me you did, and I don't see why you'd deny it, my dear. What a wonderful gift. He looks sensational in it, but how did you know?"

"Melissa thought I'd look even more sensational out of it. She became so excited when I modeled it, that she begged me to take it off. I was so astonished when after I said I was too shy to do that, she pulled it off me. I couldn't stop her."

"Oh! Oh, Lance! Mrs. Johnson, I *never* did that!"

"Oh, no?" Lance retorted. "You're denying *that* now, too? Then tell me that you don't remember seeing me like *this!*"

In Melissa's wild imagination, Lance suddenly took off his bathing suit, and then both she and Mrs. Johnson gaped at him because instead of genitals, there was a green, white and yellow striped bullfrog.

"She saw that? Oh, no! Melissa! Promise me you won't tell anyone that you saw my son's frog!"

"What astounds me, mother, is how did she know? The bathing suit has the same colors and stripes as my bullfrog. Not unless...! No, she couldn't have! Oh, Melissa! You must've peeked in my bedroom window! I'm shocked!"

"No! I never did that!" exclaimed Melissa.

"You didn't? Then *somehow* you saw my son's frog! Did you tell anyone else?"

"No, I didn't! And I didn't know about his bullfrog! Honest!"

"Lies. So sad. I'm disappointed in you, my dear. Well, Lance, the family secret is out. I suppose she'll blackmail us now, and we were so close to paying off the mortgage, too. Oh, God! No! No, no, no! I'm going to commit suicide!"

"No! Mother please don't do that! I know Melissa has a good heart. She just wanted to let me know, by buying the bathing suit, that she understood how strangely different I am. Isn't that right, Melissa? Tell her. Tell her, please! Mother? Mother! Oh, God! Don't throw yourself down the stairs! Stop! Please! Melissa! Tell her you won't blackmail us! Oh, God, please!"

"I won't! I'd never do that! Honest, Mrs. Johnson! Never!"

"You won't? Oh, thank you so much, dear, sweet Melissa! We're saved, Lance! Thank God!"

"Melissa? Would you run and get my mother a root beer, please? Our whole family drinks root beer. That's another family secret. But please run! My mother's so weak! Please!"

"Yes, of course I will! I'll run all the way! Give her mouth-to-mouth resuscitation, Lance! I'm so sorry, Mrs. Johnson!"

Melissa raced back down the stairs, hoping they hadn't run out of root beer, and that she could convince Mrs. Johnson that she wasn't going to blackmail her because of seeing Lance's bullfrog.

Melissa's shocking fantasy ended as Mrs. Johnson followed her downstairs, and went into the den. Melissa began walking to the kitchen to get the soft drinks while recalling that she'd told Linda and Lee that Lance was her boyfriend, and now she'd suddenly and unexpectedly done something almost sexual with him.

Lance had gripped her arm so tightly that she'd become quite disoriented and frightened, but she now realized that he'd only done that because he had been so eager to know if she'd be shocked by looking at a nude man.

She wondered what would've happened if they had kissed. How much further would Lance have gone? She knew with all her heart that he would be her future husband, but this had been such an astonishing turn of events that Melissa was still trembling and feeling very confused.

She pulled the tabs off the soft drink cans, and pressed the side of one of the cold cans against her hot cheeks and forehead while wondering why Lance had such a low opinion of women.

Melissa then wondered what his opinion would be of her if she told him that she wanted to kiss him right on the lips. She knew that he had very high moral standards because he'd told her how almost every girl disgusted him for having so much sex with so many guys.

She wished that she could discuss her feelings with her mother, or with some of the girls she knew. But she felt that if she told her mother what had happened in Lance's bedroom, then her mother might think that Lance had done something bad.

All the girls knew that she and Lance were together sometimes as much as three times a week, so, if she told them that an older guy had tried to show her his genitals, then they'd certainly conclude that it was Lance whom she was talking about.

She carried the soft drink cans out to the porch, and sat down to wait for Lance while hoping he'd never ask her again to look at him when he was nude because it had sort of terrified her.

As she sat out on the porch, waiting for him, Melissa felt uneasy about doing something sexual again with him. But she thought that if she didn't, then Lance might feel that she was disgusted by what they'd done together, and think that she was like other girls that he knew who couldn't stand the sight of a nude man.

She also hoped he hadn't noticed that she hadn't looked at his genitals when he'd taken off his bathing suit because if he knew that, then he'd think she was repulsed by his nudity.

Melissa quickly smoothed her hair when she heard Lance's footsteps nearing her, then she smiled up at him when he walked out onto the porch.

"Ah, here you are!" he exclaimed, smiling.

"Here's your root beer. You look really nice in your jeans and T-shirt, too, besides your new clothes," said Melissa.

"Thanks. We won't be able to get together again 'til after next weekend, and then we'll take a walk far away from everybody else, and then we'll take off our clothes and have fun. Okay? You told me you wouldn't say no, right? And when we play with each other's bodies, it'll be just fun, and nothing ridiculously serious because we're good friends, and we don't have to kiss before we do it. I can't stand all that slobbering kiss crap. I hate kissing, but we're friends, so, we don't have to do all that kissy-kissy shit. I'll bet you hate it, too, because you're a nice girl. A decent girl. Not like all those other girls I've met who say no to me unless I pay them."

"Oh, sure. Kissing's so icky," she said, feeling so disappointed.

"Yeah, I thought you'd agree, and that's why I like you so much. Next time, we'll make sure we've got plenty of time to be alone together so that we can be nude. We could have a lot of fun, believe me. You know what I'd really like you to do with me?"

"No, what?"

"I love playacting. Like, you keep your clothes on when we start, and then you pretend you don't know me. I come into my bedroom and pretend it's yours, then you act shocked and ask me what I want. I tell you I want to have sex with you, but you say, 'Oh, no, never, you bad man,' and then while I'm trying to pull your clothes off, you keep struggling and trying to stop me. That's so hot. We'll just do that 'til I see your tits, and then you take off the rest of your clothes while you're telling me how much you love my body, and how much you want to have sex with me. Do you like that? Won't it be fun?"

"Um, sure," replied Melissa, blushing.

"Great! But remember. Nobody's to know, okay? Because this is something very personal. People have sex in private. Our friendship makes it private. Just you and me. There'll be no secrets between us when we play around, but it'll be a secret to everybody else. Okay? Besides, this way you'll learn how to please a man. I consider you my best friend, and you really *are* my best friend, you know. I've never done anything like that with anyone else, Melissa. You know, I just thought about that gold necklace I bought on the weekend. Your eyes are a beautiful blue, and I think the blue sapphire cross would really enhance them. I'd really like you to have the necklace."

"Really?"

"Yes, really. It'd be a token of our first time nude together. Well, I was totally nude and you weren't, but it was still a wonderful bond. You could wear just that necklace the next time when we're alone together, and you'd look so beautiful like that. Stay there, and I'll go get it, okay? Be right back," said Lance.

"Oh, um, thanks. I loved that necklace."

It was difficult for her to believe that Lance was giving her the gold necklace, and then feeling so excited about it, she tilted her can of Coke before it got to her mouth, so, it spilled down her chin, and onto the front of her dress.

She felt so clumsy as she tried brushing most of the spilled Coke off her dress before it soaked in. Melissa hoped that Lance wouldn't notice that the front of her dress had been dampened when he returned, and gave her the necklace.

Her thoughts whirled into another fantasy scene that made her imagine herself being so surprised when she lifted her hand to cover the damp spot on her dress, and Melissa found that she was suddenly wearing a magnificent evening gown.

Then raising her other hand, she felt a tiara on her head just as Lance returned with the gold necklace, accompanied by his mother. In this fantasy, he placed the necklace around her neck, then as he was fastening the clasp, Melissa heard his mother heave a great sigh.

"That necklace looks so pretty on you," said Mrs. Johnson.

"Oh? Why, thank you. And thank *you*, Lance. I love it."

"You know, I wanted that necklace. It was the most beautiful thing I've ever seen. Lance had promised it to me, but he told me he'd changed his mind and wanted to give it to you. That's all right, though. I understand. You're far more important to him than I am. I'm nothing. A nobody. Now you have the love of my son. All his love. There's nothing left for me. No love left. He'll leave home now and marry you, then I just know I'll never see him again. I can't travel, you know, and Lance tells me you have decided to live in London, so, I'll never see my son again."

"Mother, please. I told you I'd try to write. You have to learn to adjust to life without me."

"Life? Hah! I have no life, now. But if I don't accept this marriage, then I know that Melissa will never let me see my grandchildren."

"That's not true, Mrs. Johnson! I'd never do that!"

"She's right as always, mother. She told me that she'd send you photos, and I believe her. Melissa would never lie to me because her heart is pure as fresh-fallen snow and filled with so much love," he said, smiling at Melissa.

"Love for you, yes, but for me? And for your father? I can't believe that. No. Photos of my grandchildren are mere pieces of paper. That's all. But I wanted to look into their smiling faces as I held them in my arms and thrilled to hearing them call me 'grandmother.' Lance, I...I want you to tell your father when he comes home that I loved him, dearly. I'm going now, Lance. I'm going to overdose on my sleeping pills."

"Oh, no! Mrs. Johnson, you can't do that! Stop her, Lance!"

"Let her go, Melissa. I know my mother. She could never go on living as a mere shell of her former self. She's right. You now have all my love."

"But Lance! She doesn't have to die! Your mother and I can share your love!"

"Oh, I wish that could be, but sadly it can't. You see, she's made up her mind not to live unless she has all my love, and so we have to face that fact, my darling. It's kismet."

"I never wanted this. Oh, God! Goodbye, Mrs. Johnson!"

"Yes, a very, very long goodbye. There she goes to that eternal sleep. Oh, well. Thank God I have you, Melissa."

"Go to her and hold her hand. I'm going home to weep. Thank you for this beautiful necklace. I had no idea it would bring such tragedy, but as you just said, it's kismet. Goodbye for only a few hours, Lance. I hope I'll see you after dinner. We're having roast beef. Goodbye, darling. Goodbye."

A few moments later, Melissa's fantasy ended just as Lance walked back out onto the porch, and gave her the necklace. He then told her that he had a few things to take care of, so, they said goodbye, and Melissa walked home, smiling down at the necklace in the palm of her right hand.

* * * * * ❖•••••••❖ ★ ❖•••••••❖ * * * * *

Melissa sat in front of her dresser mirror, wearing the necklace, and she wanted so much to confide in somebody about the sexual occurrence with Lance that afternoon.

He'd told her not to show anyone the necklace because it was a very personal souvenir of their first sexual time together, and he wanted her to wear only the necklace when they played the sexual game that Lance had suggested.

The only problem was that Melissa didn't want to be that intimate with him even though she'd fantasized for so long about marrying him. She felt that Lance might lose control when he became highly aroused, and then he might want to go even further than they already had, and that wasn't something she felt she was ready for.

Melissa took off the necklace, and hid it at the back of her dresser drawer, and then she went downstairs. While walking toward the living room, she hoped that she didn't look any different to her parents, now that she'd done something sort of sexual with Lance.

Her parents were reading some of the newspapers they'd bought in Valmar, so, Melissa picked up the entertainment section and tried to concentrate on what she was reading. But she kept thinking about Lance and the sexual act.

"That's disgusting! Awful!" exclaimed Jonathan.

"What do you mean?" cried Melissa, blushing and panicking because she thought he'd found out what she and Lance had done.

"This item in the paper. Sickening," said Jonathan.

"What's the story about, dear?" asked Joline.

"Four employees of a store were shot to death by two men."

"How awful. I feel so much safer living here," said Joline.

"Hmmm, horrible. There's a story about a break-in where they tied the woman up, but before they did that, they slapped her and pistol-whipped her. Her husband came home while they were still there and they shot him to death. Terrible."

"Oh, my God! Did they kill *her*, too?" asked Joline.

"No, fortunately. It must've been terrifying for her to see her husband killed right there in front of her. Awful. Hmmm, oh, here we go again. Gawwd! Another serial killer running rampant. A young woman was raped and murdered. She was the tenth one in Valmar. Shows a photo of her. She was such a lovely young woman, too. Not that that should make a difference. Twenty-two years old. So young. She was a top student, too. Much promise. It says here that she was engaged to be married, so, her fiancé must be extremely distressed. Hmmm, tenth woman. Of course, they'll make a movie out of this terrible tragedy and make this guy into some sort of cult hero. And I'll bet that someone'll write a book about it, and then it'll become a gruesome bestseller. Here's another article about a robbery, and five people shot during it. Seems like Valmar's getting quite a reputation for crime. Oh, and listen to this. A store was robbed at gunpoint in Roseville Mall. Hell, it could've happened while we were there because the robbery took place in the late afternoon. Different day, though, but still, when you think about it, it's rather frightening," said Jonathan, slowly shaking his head.

"For God's sake, you'll have nightmares if you read any more crime reports. Here, I'm finished with the editorial page, so, read that. Where's the life section?" asked Joline.

"Oh! I've got it. I wasn't really reading it," said Melissa.

"No, you continue. I'll look for the life section in another newspaper. Have you had time to look through the papers and decide which one you like the best, honey?"

"No, but Linda and Lee said they thought the Valmar Voice was the best one. You take this section and I'll look through that one."

"All right. Thank you," said Joline, smiling.

Melissa found a few sections of the Valmar Voice, and sat down to glance through them. She noticed the cost of theatre tickets, and she knew that she could never afford to see one of the live performances until she was a working adult.

There was a page with four or five puzzles on it, so, Melissa reached for a pencil and worked on the puzzles for almost an hour before she decided to look through the rest of the newspaper sections. Joline interrupted her when she handed her a mug of hot chocolate and a piece of cake.

"Darn. I forgot the ice cream," said Joline.

"That's okay. I like it just like this. They were right, mom. This is a great newspaper. It's got really interesting things in it. Dad? Do you want the news section?"

"No thank you. I've read enough about crime for one night."

"It's on TV, too," said Melissa. "All kinds of TV shows have Mafia gangsters in them, and they show action movies, too. Doing karate to kick somebody through a window."

"Yeah, but you know that's acting. Sure, it's violent, and I don't like you watching it at anytime, okay? But the real thing is far more frightening. Real crimes that are happening close to us. Valmar's less than fifty miles from here," said Jonathan.

"Yeah, I guess it seems closer when you think about scary stuff happening in Valmar," said Melissa. "Mmmm, this cake tastes so great. Lots of butterscotch stuff in it, and I like the crumble coating on it, too."

· ·   ·   · · ❖•••••••❖ ★ ❖•••••••❖ · ·   ·   ·   ·

Later in the evening, Joline began turning off the lights before they went upstairs to bed, and she suggested that Melissa take the newspaper sections that she was reading, up to her bedroom, and read them until she was ready to sleep.

Melissa got ready for bed, then she sat up in bed with the newspaper sections around her as she looked through one of them. She found the news section, then read about the armed robbery in Roseville Mall.

She then imagined herself with Linda and Lee while one of the robbers pointed a gun at them and asked for her small purse with two dollars in it.

Melissa wondered why the men who had robbed a store in another part of the city, had shot the people when they'd handed over the money, even though the robbers had been wearing masks. She thought it was quite frightening that the robbers were so insensitive to harm people who couldn't be witnesses.

She saw a small headline directing readers to the rape and murder on page six of the section she was reading, so, Melissa leafed through the paper to page six.

The young woman in the photo accompanying the article was smiling and wearing a graduation robe. Melissa thought the young woman was rather pretty, and that it was awful how she'd been murdered at such a young age, and engaged to be married, too.

She started reading the article, and when she learned of how the young woman had been murdered, Melissa shivered. The young woman had been stabbed and beaten so badly that she'd been unrecognizable when her body had been found.

Halfway through the story, Melissa felt like she almost knew the murder victim, so, she stopped reading, and after neatly folding the newspaper sections, she turned off the lamp on the bedside table, and hoped that she wouldn't dream about all the crimes in Valmar, especially the rape and murder.

Because it'd been a sexual crime, as well, Melissa started thinking of what had transpired that day with Lance. She felt so embarrassed, and then she wondered how much more embarrassed she'd be if they now started to become far more intimate.

She couldn't imagine being nude with Lance because it seemed much too personal, and what he wanted to do with her wasn't anything like she'd thought lovers would do in bed together, especially with no kissing.

Melissa had so often dreamed about Lance swooping her up into his arms, and then kissing her, and kissing her again as he carried her to safety from some disaster. And occasionally kissing her as they danced in some magnificent ballroom as everyone applauded them, and kissing him during many other imaginary situations.

But he'd told her that he hated kissing. Lance had said that they'd be having sexual trysts, and that those furtive meetings would be fun as well as very satisfying.

She wondered if he'd ask her to dress up in various costumes, such as a nurse or doctor, or perhaps a policewoman, and then maybe he might want to be arrested by her and handcuffed. Did he have handcuffs, Melissa pondered?

She thought of him nude and in handcuffs, and Melissa felt sure that she could never play any games like that with him because they would be so unromantic and rather sordid. One of the games Lance wanted her to play with him was for her to pretend she was protesting his advances by trying to fight him off before they did anything sexual, so, she wondered if he'd want to handcuff *her*, too.

And the necklace. Lance wanted her to be nude with him, except for the necklace he'd just given her. The necklace representing their first sexual experience together.

Melissa thought of these things as she became drowsy, then she tried to think of flowers, fountains, and colorful birds, instead of the crimes in Valmar, and the overwhelming and somehow frightening sort of almost sexual experience she'd had with Lance.

She tried thinking about so many things that were beautiful, such as the lovely necklace that Lance had given her, and she'd been so disappointed that he hadn't given it to her with a kiss.

As she imagined herself wearing only the necklace, it seemed to dominate the rest of her body. In her thoughts, the gold strand began to grow longer and longer, and the heart pendant started to increase in size until it slowly covered her nudity.

Then in her half-dream state, she pictured herself hiding behind the huge gold heart, and the now massive, blue sapphire cross on it was reminding her of her sinful rendezvous with Lance.

Suddenly, she saw the necklace in black and white, and she bolted upright in bed. Melissa gasped, then turned the lamp back on, and grabbed the newspaper. She quickly turned to the page with the story and photograph of the young woman whom had been viciously raped and horribly murdered.

Melissa had noticed something before, but it hadn't quite caught her complete attention because in the black and white photo, the young woman had been wearing a black graduation gown.

Now, as she looked closer, she could see that the necklace that the young woman was wearing, looked almost exactly the same as the one that Lance had given her.

She got out of bed to get the magnifying glass out of the top drawer of her dresser, then she picked up the necklace and hurried back to her bed to compare the necklaces under the light of the lamp. She saw that the necklaces were indeed the same, right down to the small scratch on them. But it just couldn't be, she thought.

She read the newspaper article again, and then felt relieved when she read that the pendant in the photo was a locket that opened, with a picture of the murdered young woman on one side, and her parents on the other side of the locket. But the heart pendant on the necklace Lance had given her, didn't open like a locket.

Melissa studied the gold heart, turning it side to side, and over and over in her hands while feeling so relieved that it wasn't a locket. Then her heart leapt when he saw a tiny nub on it.

She began picking at the tiny nub with her fingernail, then suddenly, the gold heart fell open, revealing two photographs; one of the murdered young woman, and one of her parents.

Melissa dropped the necklace and it fell into her lap, then she stared down at it as her fright grew. She picked up the newspaper again, and read that the killer took a souvenir from each victim he'd murdered, and it was always a piece of jewellery.

She burst into tears, trying not to believe that gentle, sweet Lance whom never dated girls would commit such horrible crimes. But how did he get the necklace?

She then realized that the man who had sold Lance the necklace was the killer, and that's how he added to his jewellery collection in his store, and she knew that she had to take it to the police. But she didn't want Lance to become frightened because he'd bought the necklace and the police could accuse him of the crimes.

Melissa decided to ask her parents if she could take the bus into Valmar after telling them that she'd decided against the black and white frames for her glasses and that she wanted to choose another color of frames in the same style.

The following day, she told her mother that she wanted the same frames, but in some lovely color, instead, and Melissa asked her if she would call the store to tell them that. Melissa also asked her if she could take the bus into Valmar on Saturday morning, and then return in the afternoon.

"Well, I suppose that'd be all right, but I'll call Joanne and Wes, and ask them to meet you at the bus," said Joline.

"Aunt Joanne could go to the store with me, too, mom, so, I'd be okay. She'd know how to get to it."

"Yes, and you could have lunch with her and Wes, then they could take you to the bus station to come back here."

"Oh, great! Thanks, mom!"

Melissa felt so excited as she waited for Saturday to arrive, then she held the necklace in her hand as she sat on the bus. She knew that her aunt and uncle would be surprised that she wanted to go to the police headquarters in Valmar, so, she had to think of a reason for wanting to go there.

After much thought, she decided to tell them that she wanted to get some photos of wanted criminals for a school project that was about crime.

Joanne and Wes thought it was an odd request, but they drove her to police headquarters after Melissa had looked at eyeglass frames and decided that she wanted the black and white frames, after all.

She felt nervous when she asked to speak to a detective, after telling her aunt and uncle it was another part of the school project, so, they waited for her as she went alone into the detective's office.

Melissa hedged around the subject for a few moments, then laid the necklace out on his desk, and told him how she'd acquired it, and how Lance hadn't known that the jeweller he'd bought it from was the serial killer.

After the detective had closely examined the necklace, he smiled at her as he made a phone call, and then two plainclothes policemen came into the office, took the necklace, and Melissa was asked to stay until the men returned.

The detective was very nice to her, and then after he spoke with Joanne and Wes, he told Melissa that her aunt and uncle were taking her to lunch, but that they'd be bringing her back after that.

Two hours later, she saw Lance being escorted into the police station, and before she could wave at him, he'd entered an elevator with several policemen. Melissa then wondered if she and Lance would get a reward for solving the crimes. She decided to tell the police that she didn't want a reward because it was reward enough to have stopped further killings of young women in Valmar.

She had thought over Lance's proposal about doing sexual things together, and she'd decided that after his interview with the police, she'd tell him no. But in a way that he wouldn't think she was being like all the other girls who had told him no.

She'd also decided to tell him that she wouldn't say no to him if he wanted to kiss her at anytime, and then if they kissed a few times, he might get to like it.

She felt sure that because she had read so many romance novels, and watched many movies, that she could kiss better than other girls, or just as well as more mature women.

The detective talked with her aunt and uncle before they took her home with them until it was time for Melissa to take the bus home. Less than an hour later, she was surprised when her parents arrived, then said that they were taking her back home immediately. Melissa was even more surprised when they told her that Lance would be remaining in Valmar to talk with the police for a bit longer.

Jonathan began driving back home, and Joline sat beside him, with her arms crossed, hugging herself tightly, and then she exclaimed: "He might've killed *her*, next! Who would've known? Right next door to us!"

Jonathan glanced into the rear view mirror at Melissa whom was sitting in the back seat of the car, and then he exclaimed: "She could've been the eleventh victim! Oh, God! It was Lance! And

Melissa spent so much time with him! Thank God she told the police where she got that necklace!"

Melissa then realized that her parents were proud of her for taking the necklace to the police, and that Lance had told them where he'd bought it.

But she knew there was no need for her parents to have thought that either she or Lance were ever in any danger, because they lived far away from Valmar where the serial killer lived, and by showing the necklace to the police, the killer was now caught.

She'd already decided not to accept a reward for solving the murders, and she felt sure that Lance wouldn't accept a reward, either, because he had such high moral standards that he didn't even like to kiss before he married the right girl.

The End

Eyed To Death

Birgitta sat on the moonlit dock, sipping cognac from a large glass while thinking of her plans for the following day. She'd been so deep in thought that she hadn't paid attention to how much darker it became occasionally, and then the next time it happened she looked up at the sky.

She was surprised that she'd never noticed before that there were clouds at night. She'd thought that they simply dissolved in the late evening, then formed again with the rising sun.

Birgitta raised her glass, swallowed another mouthful of cognac, then looked back up at clouds drifting over the moon, making everything darker around her again.

She wondered if, because of all the clouds, that it meant tomorrow would be a rainy day. The dark cloud mass slowly drifted past the moon again, then a few minutes later, more dark clouds blocked out the moonlight before drifting slowly away.

She began imagining that the moon was very annoyed at the clouds for blocking its view of the land far below, and that eventually, the moon would get so angry it would shove the clouds out of its way.

That imagined scenario made Birgitta suddenly giggle while recalling the time she'd stood behind Keith, moments before she'd shoved him off the cliff.

The seven months she had waited before murdering Keith had seemed like an eternity to her, but now, Birgitta smirked as she thought about her new status as a young and very wealthy, recently widowed woman.

She took another sip of her cognac, laid back on the dock, then chuckled as she recalled Keith loading a new roll of film in his camera after he'd taken photos of the mountain across from them, and the town far below, and then he'd uttered a cry of surprise when she'd shoved him off the cliff.

She then recalled the expression on Keith's face while he'd pleaded with her to throw him a rope before he had lost his grip on the small branch below the cliff.

She had shouted out for help as she'd watched him fall to his death, then two tourists had hurried around the mountain ledge just after she'd thrown the rope over the cliff.

Birgitta had wept as the tourists had tried to console her, and she'd continued her performance for the rest of the day. She smiled when she thought of how she'd pretended to be deeply in love with him during their brief marriage, so, when she had returned from their tragic vacation, weeping constantly, everyone they knew had tried their best to console her.

Now that Birgitta was a very wealthy widow, there was only one obstacle standing in her way to get her hands on the rest of Keith's fortune, and that was his ten-year-old daughter from his previous marriage. His first wife had died of breast cancer, and because Keith had loved her so much, he had vowed never to remarry, however, four years later, he changed his mind when he met Birgitta.

He had hired her as a nanny for his daughter, and during the time she'd been employed, she had acted quite demure, but she'd found ways to let Keith find her almost nude on many occasions.

Birgitta had always had a cocktail waiting for him when he arrived home from work each day, and then every morning, she had complimented him on his attire, and often adjusted his tie before he left the house.

Keith had begun noticing that she was taking his daughter to amusement parks and other places that he knew children loved, and Birgitta was paying for those treats with the salary he paid her.

He'd been delighted when Birgitta had asked his opinion of another dress she'd bought for Suzanne. Whenever he'd offered to pay her for one of the dresses, Birgitta had firmly declined his offer while telling him that it gave her so much pleasure to bring happiness to a child whom she adored.

Keith had thought he'd startled and embarrassed her one day when he'd returned home to find her lounging by the pool with the top of her bikini off. Birgitta had then sat up, gaped at him for a moment, and then covered her breasts while hurrying over to a deck chair to retrieve the bra of her skimpy bikini.

Birgitta had begun attending social functions with a gay man, and she had worn very revealing dresses whenever she'd said goodbye to Keith on her way out for the evening with her supposed date.

She had pretended to be quite forlorn for over a week after she'd told Keith that she hadn't known that her boyfriend had been cheating on her, and was now marrying that other woman.

To lift her spirits, Keith had bought Birgitta flowers every day, and while she cried on his shoulder, she'd thanked him for his sensitivity toward nothing more than a lowly employee.

Two months later, Keith and Birgitta started dating, and after she'd done her utmost to sexually arouse him, she'd pretended to come to her senses, then told him that she didn't want to ruin her reputation by having a sexual relationship outside of marriage.

Keith had found her to be very beautiful and his friends had agreed, and said that she was also a wonderful, caring woman, so, he'd married her. He had then begun to notice that although Birgitta treated his daughter so well, Suzanne didn't seem to like her.

He'd assumed that Suzanne felt that Birgitta was going to replace her mother, so, Keith had assured her that he'd always love her mother just as much as Suzanne did, and that no one could ever take her place.

Keith had then told Suzanne that Birgitta loved her just as much as he did, and that Birgitta had told him that she didn't expect to be referred to as Suzanne's mother, but as her dearest friend.

He'd been relieved when Suzanne eventually began to smile and talk to Birgitta again, and Keith had been so pleased to see that his daughter was happy again.

Birgitta raised her glass of cognac, and clenched her teeth as she thought of ways to kill Suzanne and make it look like an accident. Almost a year had passed since she'd murdered Keith, and for the past few weeks Birgitta had been plotting Suzanne's death.

She felt quite impatient because she still hadn't thought of a way to kill Suzanne and make it look like an unfortunate accident. Birgitta then sneered while thinking about her closest friend, Lana. She had helped Lana murder her father five years ago, then two years later, they'd murdered Lana's brother, and the police had been satisfied that he'd died in a fatal car accident.

Lana's mother was quite frugal, so, Lana had been asking for money, which Birgitta willingly paid, but she thought of it as blackmail and she felt certain that after she murdered Suzanne, Lana would then demand higher monthly payments from her.

Lana had told her that after her mother was dead, she'd repay all the money, however, Birgitta didn't trust her, therefore, she'd decided to murder Lana soon after Suzanne was dead.

She'd been lying on her side, gazing up at the stars while devising deadly schemes, then smiling, she sat up, swung her legs over the edge of the dock, and looked for the reflection of the moon in the dark water. Birgitta's heart leapt and her jaw dropped when she saw a large pair of eyes staring up at her through the water.

She quickly stood up, and stepped back away from the edge of the dock. She waited a moment, then knelt near the edge of the dock, and looked back down into the water again, and saw that the large, glowing eyes were still there, staring up at her.

Birgitta rushed to the rowboat that was tied at the end of the dock, then she grabbed an oar, and hurried back, intending to poke at the eyes, but when she looked down at the water, she saw that the eyes had vanished.

She stared down into the water for almost a minute before she drank the rest of her glass of cognac, and then she walked back to the house. She felt certain that somewhere hidden inside her, were feelings of guilt for murdering Keith, and she was determined to rid herself of her hallucinations caused by some scant traces of remorse.

From the time she'd been a small girl, Birgitta had been both repulsed and frightened by people who had something seriously wrong with their eyes, and she felt that her slight sense of guilt had caused her to think of enormous, bulging eyes.

Her fingers trembled as she lit a cigarette, poured another large, strong drink, then smirking, she went upstairs to her bedroom suite.

．　．　．　．　．　❖•••••❖★❖•••••❖　．　．　．　．　．

After taking off her robe, Birgitta sat on the bed, and chuckled after thinking of how a breeze had probably rippled the water's surface, making the reflection of the moon appear like two separate images. She felt certain that the moon's distorted image had made her think she'd seen a large pair of glowing eyes beneath the water.

She finished her drink, turned off the bedside lamp, then lying on her back, Birgitta stared at the ceiling as she imagined Suzanne plummeting to her death after toppling off the edge of some tall building, or out of a very high window.

She yawned, looked at the alarm clock, and saw that it was only a little after eleven o'clock, but the large amount of alcohol she'd consumed had made her drowsy.

Birgitta closed her eyes, and just as she was drifting into sleep, she heard what seemed to be someone throwing small stones at her bedroom window.

She struggled to sit up, then she looked over at the window, and saw a very big pair of glowing eyes suspended in midair. She cried out, turned over in bed, turned on the lamp, then looking back at the window, she saw that the eyes were gone.

Her thoughts whirled as she got out of bed, put on her dressing robe, then hurried downstairs to pour another large amount of cognac. Her hand was trembling as she lifted the glass to her lips, so, she drank half the glass at once, and then she heaved a great sigh.

She finished drinking the glass of cognac, then Birgitta refilled the glass two more times before the alcohol began soothing her jangled nerves.

By the time she went back upstairs to bed, she was quite inebriated, so, she fell asleep moments after she laid on the bed.

The following morning, Birgitta felt quite hungover as she showered, and she felt certain that the large amount of alcohol she'd had the night before had caused her to see imaginary things.

She looked forward to her appointment at the beauty salon where she'd be lounging in the sauna, then having a long, soothing massage, and then a manicure while her hair was being styled.

Birgitta scowled when she thought about having to drop Suzanne off at school on the way to the salon and spa because she hated having to play mother to a child whom she detested.

Her spirits had lifted, slightly, after she'd had her shower, and put on one of her favorite dresses, then setting her coffee cup down on the bedside table, she smiled as she thought of how wonderful it was to have maids to make her bed.

She went downstairs to the living room, asked a maid to summon Suzanne, then she forced a smile when Suzanne entered the room, wearing her backpack, then she smiled, and said: "Good morning, Birgitta. You look really pretty, today."

"Thanks. Now let's get you to school."

* * * * * ❖••••••❖★❖••••••❖ * * * * *

Birgitta tried to show interest in everything Suzanne pointed out on the way to school, then after she watched Suzanne running into school, Birgitta swore and sped off to the salon.

She loved the attention from the staff as she walked into the salon, and then she luxuriated in the sauna, and sighed with pleasure from the massage. While having a manicure and her hair styled, Birgitta talked on the phone to her friend, Lana.

"No, I'd prefer going to Silver Seas, instead, because the seafood is wonderful there. Oh, of course it'll be my treat, Lana. Well, I thought we could have cocktails at Cicero's first, then have dinner. I'll pick you up at...hmmm, let's see. How's six-thirty sound? Fine. All right then. No, it's a deep mauve dress. Oh? I'm so glad you liked the dress I gave you. Yes, I think it looks marvelous on you, too. See you at six-thirty. You bet. All right then, Lana. Bye."

While driving back home from the beauty salon, she thought about dinner that evening with Lana. She loved being able to buy expensive gifts for friends, which made them so envious of her. Although, Lana had sort of almost demanded that Birgitta buy her not only the dress, but a rather costly bracelet to go with it.

She entered the house, and her heart leapt with joy when she saw the very concerned expression on a maid's face, and Birgitta hoped that it was news of Suzanne's death after she'd been struck by a car on her way home from school at lunch hour.

She was bitterly disappointed when she saw Suzanne smiling and waving at her from the dining room as she ate her lunch. Birgitta then became slightly annoyed when one of the maids told her that because the staff had been so busy that morning, they hadn't had time to tidy her bedroom suite.

She swept by the maid while telling her never to make that mistake again, then Birgitta went upstairs to her bedroom suite. She loved the power she had over servants, and she grinned as she sorted through her closet for the dress she planned to wear that evening.

Birgitta admired her new, deep mauve dress that she'd laid out on her bed, then she sat on the bed, and reached for her package of cigarettes, which were in her purse on the bedside table.

After she lit a cigarette, and inhaled deeply, she slowly blew out the smoke before phoning her lover, Kirk. He didn't know her real name or where she lived because their sexual trysts took place either in hotels or at his apartment.

Birgitta didn't want Kirk, a garage mechanic, to spoil her image as a wealthy, grieving widow; nor did she want him know that she intended to marry another very rich man once she had gained control of all Keith's money.

"Hello, darling. It's Carolyn," said Birgitta. "Oh, thank you. I don't often have a handsome man telling me I'm not only very beautiful and sexy, but that I have a voice to match. You do, too. I thought we could get together Friday evening about eight. Oh? Why, you're more than welcome. I knew you'd love the watch. Listen, my mother is just on her way into the living room, so, I have to hang up. You'll meet her in good time. Oh, Kirk. Oh, really? Oh, stop! Gotta go. Friday. Eight. Bye."

While she'd been sitting on her bed, and talking on the telephone, Birgitta had been dropping her cigarette ashes in the coffee cup on the bedside table. She sneered at the cup she'd drank from that morning, and then at her unmade bed as she decided to make certain that the maids cleaned her bedroom suite first, before anyone else's.

She stood up, took a long, last toke of her cigarette, then looked down at the cup where she intended to douse the cigarette in the remains of the coffee. Birgitta then gasped and staggered back with her thoughts swirling.

She felt nauseated and her hands trembled as she looked back down into the cup at the pair of bloodied eyeballs staring up at her. It took her a few moments before she was able to regain her composure, and then her anger surfaced.

* * * * * ⬧••••••⬧ ★ ⬧••••••⬧ * * * * *

She stomped down the long, marble staircase, and she'd just reached the bottom of the stairs when the chauffeur opened the front door, and he frowned as Birgitta glared at him while asking where the hell the maids were.

He told her that he'd seen them in the garden, gathering flowers to put in vases to be placed in the living and dining rooms, then Birgitta loudly and angrily told him to tell the maids to come back into the house, immediately.

The chauffeur rushed out the door, then Birgitta strutted outside, and stood on the porch, with her hands on her hips while clenching her teeth as she watched him hurrying over to one of the front gardens where the maids were gathering flowers.

As the chauffeur talked to them, the maids looked over at Birgitta standing on the porch, then as they began rushing toward her, she turned around and strutted back inside the house.

The maids hurried into the house, then Birgitta started shouting at them, and then the maids, Marie and Colleen, began trying to tell her that they didn't understand what she was accusing them of, and that only made Birgitta angrier.

Suzanne heard Birgitta shouting at someone, so, she hurried over to the living room entrance, and stared wide-eyed at Birgitta, whom was loudly admonishing the maids.

"Well, one of you is a liar! A liar with a very sick mind! Which one of you did it?!...Tell me!" shouted Birgitta.

"Not I, ma'am," replied Marie.

"I have no idea what you mean, ma'am," said Colleen.

"No idea? Hah! Liars! You think you can fool me? Come with me! Immediately!"

The two maids and Suzanne followed Birgitta upstairs to her bedroom suite, and when they entered, she told the maids to look in the cup on the bedside table.

Colleen and Marie walked over to the table, looked down into the cup, then frowned as they looked at Birgitta, and then Marie said: "I'm sorry, ma'am. I'll remove the cup right away, and then we'll tidy your room."

"To hell with tidying my room! I want to know who put those disgusting eyes in my cup!"

"Eyes, ma'am?" asked Colleen.

"Yes, eyes! Which one of you put them in my cup?"

"Ma'am, there aren't any eyes in your cup."

"Don't you dare lie to me again!" exclaimed Birgitta, as she strode over to the maids, looked down into the cup and saw that the bloodied eyeballs were gone.

"They're gone, now! But one of you pulled this disgusting prank! Which one of you did it? Well? Don't just stand there gaping at me! Tell me!" she shouted as she glared at them.

"Honest, ma'am, I didn't do it," said Colleen.

"Neither did I," said Marie. "I wasn't near your bedroom suite this morning. I only just passed by it. We both did, but I never went in, ma'am."

"Liars! This was unforgivable! Stupid! How dare you? Well, if neither one of you will own up to this...this horrible joke, then you're both fired! Now! Get your things and get out of my house this minute!...Go!"

"But, ma'am, I..." Marie started to say.

"I said get *out!* Imbeciles! Such a sick joke!"

"Yes, ma'am. I'm sorry about that, ma'am," said Marie.

"Sorry? Did you think it was funny? Now you've made me fire Colleen, too! I want you both out of this house within half an hour, and if either one of you even step onto this property again, it will be constituted as trespass! Now leave me alone! I'm sorry I shouted like that in front of you, Suzanne, but the maids played a very terrible trick on me. Go back downstairs and get ready to go back to school."

"Okay, Birgitta. You know what? I'm making a paper butterfly at school and I colored it all myself, and the teacher's going to hang it up in our classroom."

"That sounds so lovely, dear. I'm so happy for you. Now run along like a good little girl."

"Okay. Bye, Birgitta. Oh! Your hair looks really nice."

"Yes, well, thank you."

Birgitta closed the bedroom suite door, and then took a few deep breaths. After she hung her mauve dress back in the closet, she went downstairs, poured a large cognac, and glared at the maids as they hurried out the door with their suitcases.

* * * * * ❖••••••❖★❖••••••❖ * * * * *

Birgitta parked her car in the garage after she'd returned from having dinner and going to a nightclub with Lana, and as she walked toward the house, she was thinking about the audacity of one of the maids to have put the eyeballs in her coffee cup.

Something flew past her, and then she saw a small, heavy stick fall to the ground ahead of her. She looked around, trying to discern in the darkness, whom had thrown the stick.

Birgitta suddenly tensed up, and her hand flew to her open mouth when she saw a pair of large, glowing eyes drifting through the trees above the row of bushes near her.

Her shock slowly turned into anger, then after picking up the stick, she hurried over to the area where she'd seen the very big, glowing eyes. Birgitta stepped through the bushes, looked around, and then not seeing anyone, nor the floating, glowing eyes, she hurried back to the house.

She called the police and demanded that they immediately send at least two officers over to her house to search the grounds for an intruder. Birgitta hung up the phone, lit a cigarette, poured a large glass of cognac, then she stood by the window, peering out as her hands trembled.

She had smoked almost the entire package of cigarettes, and she'd drank three large glasses of cognac by the time the officers finished searching the property, and then told her that they hadn't found any sign of an intruder.

She thanked the policemen, and then after they left, she poured another large glass of cognac and thought about what she'd seen. The glowing, floating eyes had been much too large for any animal she could think of, unless they'd belonged to a prehistoric monster.

Birgitta realized that it was silly to think that a prehistoric monster was prowling around the outside of the house, and that instead, what she'd really seen had been the headlights of a car passing by in the distance.

She was becoming quite inebriated, so, she stumbled a few times on her way upstairs to her bedroom suite, then after turning on the light, she swayed over to the window, carrying her half empty glass of cognac.

Her window overlooked the area where she'd seen the glowing eyes, and she sipped on her cognac and smoked a cigarette as she gazed over at the trees and bushes.

She was just about to turn away from the window, when she saw the floating eyes again, and she dropped her glass as she leaned closer to the window.

Birgitta watched the large, glowing eyes drift back and forth above the hedges for a few moments, then move slowly away out of sight. She hurried downstairs, and checked to make sure all the windows and doors were locked.

She then poured another large glass of cognac, and carried it back upstairs. She thought about the big, glowing eyes as she finished her drink, then she laid down, and tried to concentrate on falling asleep.

. . . . . ◇•••••◇★◇•••••◇ . . . . .

Birgitta tried not to think of the glowing eyes, then she concentrated on nicer things, such as buying an emerald necklace and bracelet to wear with the beautiful, pale green dress she'd seen in one of the most fashionable stores downtown.

She heaved a big sigh, then snuggled down in bed while feeling sure she'd now get a good night's sleep. Moments later, she was just starting to fall asleep, when there was a loud bumping sound on her bedroom suite door.

She frowned while listening to the loud bumping on the door, then Birgitta turned over onto her side, reached out and clicked on the lamp, and then looked at the clock on the bedside table, and saw that it was a few minutes before midnight.

The bumping stopped, then she sat up, and looked around the room, wondering if she'd only imagined hearing odd bumping sounds on the door. She then frowned when she noticed that her bedroom window was wide open.

Birgitta felt groggy and slightly confused as she stared at the open window, then her heart leapt when she again heard what seemed to be heavy, muffled beating on her bedroom door.

She slowly got up off the bed, then swayed from the effects of the large amount of cognac she'd consumed, and then she glared over at the door while loudly asking: "Who is it? Is that you, Edna? What do you want? Answer me!...Edna?"

She thought that perhaps the new maid, Edna, was suffering from an illness that Birgitta hadn't been aware of when she'd hired the woman earlier that day.

She didn't care if the maid died of a heart attack, but she was very annoyed when she imagined having to step over Edna's dead body in the morning on her way downstairs for breakfast, so, she walked over to the door and opened it.

There wasn't anyone in the hall, so, Birgitta began walking to the main staircase to look over the banister railing to see if the maid was lying on the floor below.

She noticed something white sitting on top of the newel post at the edge of the staircase, and then walking closer to it, she saw that it was an eyeball that looked as if it had been freshly gouged out of somebody's eye socket.

Birgitta gasped and felt nauseated. She took a few steps closer to the newel post, stared at that gruesome glob, then she quickly turned away from it.

She grabbed onto the banister for support, and while feeling the perspiration on her forehead, she began slowly walking back to her room with her confused thoughts pounding in her aching head, and she wished that she hadn't consumed so much cognac.

She cried out when her bare, left foot came down hard on a cold, damp, slightly spongy ball, then looking down, she saw that she'd stepped on another eyeball. Birgitta screamed as she rushed back to her bedroom suite.

She hurried to the phone on her bedside table to call Lana, then reaching for the phone, she saw two more eyeballs laying beside it. She shrieked, then snatched the phone off the table, and then Birgitta looked away from the gory eyeballs as she called Lana.

* * * * * ❖•••••❖★❖•••••❖ * * * * *

Birgitta trembled while pleading with Lana to rush right over to the house, then she hung up the phone, dropped it to the floor, and backed out of her room as she stared at the horrible eyeballs on the bedside table.

She staggered downstairs, and her hands shook as she lit a cigarette. Birgitta paced the living room and occasionally glanced out at the driveway as she waited for Lana to arrive.

She threw open the front door when she saw Lana's car driving up to the house, then she hurried down the steps to meet her.

"Birgitta! You sounded so terrified on the phone!"

"Come into the house! Hurry!"

"My God! What is it? Has something dreadful happened?"

Lana was quite worried as she looked at the expression of terror on Birgitta's face, and felt her hands gripping her arm as they went inside the house.

"Yes, something's happened! Something...I can't...I want you to see something! It's horrible! I keep seeing them! In the halls! In my bedroom! Everywhere! I told you about that awful phobia I have! About all those awful nightmares I've had for years, every time anyone talks about them! But this time, it isn't a nightmare! It's real! I know it is!" Birgitta excitedly exclaimed.

"Phobia? I think I remember you telling me about how upset you got when Karen told you about a medical procedure she was having done, but I don't remember what it was, exactly. Hmmm, and it has something to do with a phobia you have?"

"Yes! I've had it ever since I was a child! The only person I've ever mentioned it to, is you! I'd never tell anyone else about it because they'd think I'm mentally unstable! But I'm not! I'm perfectly sane! You know that!"

"Are you sure you just didn't have another nightmare, and then you thought it..."

"No, I didn't! Just come up to my bedroom! You'll see! Oh, God! It's so terrifying!"

"You're shaking like a leaf!" exclaimed Lana.

They went upstairs to Birgitta's bedroom suite, and then she pointed to her bedside table without looking at it, as she asked Lana to please cover the horrible things on the table with something so that she didn't have to look at them again.

Lana walked over to the bedside table, looked at it, saw nothing unusual, so, she told that to Birgitta, whom hurried over and stared down at the table.

"They were there! They were there before I came downstairs to meet you at the door!"

"*What* was there?" asked Lana, frowning.

"It was a pair of..." then Birgitta suddenly realized that if she told her what she'd seen, Lana would think she was losing her mind, so, after thinking quickly, she said: "My purse and matching change purse. I fired two maids because money had been stolen from my purse, and now I've been robbed again, and I was asleep when it happened. That means that someone came into my room, and they might've attacked me while I slept. Probably the disgruntled boyfriend of one of the maids. They knew I kept my purse close to my bed, so, I'll have them arrested."

"Yes, you should, and immediately, too. Is there anyone else in the house, right now?" asked Lana.

"Of course, you idiot! The new maid is in her room at the rear of the main floor, and Suzanne's asleep up on the third floor, and the butler has his quarters in the coach house. He *is* the chauffeur, as well, you know."

"I'm sorry I didn't think of that."

"Oh, sorry for calling you an idiot. It's just that I'm so outraged with all that's happened today. I called the police earlier this evening because I saw a man at the far end of the property, but by the time the police got here, he was gone."

"Maybe he hid somewhere, then after the police left, he found a way into the house and came upstairs to your bedroom suite and stole your purse," said Lana.

"Daddy?...Birgitta?" cried Suzanne.

"Now we've awakened the brat. Just a sec," said Birgitta.

She went into the hall and over to the staircase to the third floor, then Birgitta forced a smile as she looked up at Suzanne standing at the top of the stairs, holding a doll while asking: "I heard some people shouting. Is daddy back home?"

"No...dear," replied Birgitta. "A friend and I were laughing loudly at a joke. You go back to bed now. That's a girl."

"Okay. G'night, Birgitta."

"Goodnight, Suzanne. Sleep tight. Let the bedbugs bite."

Birgitta walked back to her bedroom suite, closed the door, sat down on her bed, then said: "She still thinks her old man's coming home again. Stupid little wretch. I mean, the bitch is over ten years old now, and she was holding a doll, for God's sake. At *her* age. My nerves are shot. I need a drink."

"I'll get you one while you call the police."

"Thanks. And you can get one for yourself, too."

"Oh, thanks. That's *so* kind of you," said Lana, sarcastically.

When the police arrived, Birgitta slowly recalled noticing that the eyeball on the floor of the hall and the one that had been on the newel post were gone when she and Lana had hurried to her bedroom suite.

As she talked with the police, she glanced at the newel post and saw that it was gleaming. She had expected it to be sticky from having the gooey eyeball placed on it, but the post looked as though not even a finger had touched it.

Birgitta wondered if she had somehow dozed off for a few moments, and then had another nightmare similar to the ones she'd had so many times when she had been a child, and on several occasions throughout her teenaged years.

She'd stopped having the terrifying nightmares over five years ago, and Birgitta felt certain that she had been wide awake when she'd seen the very big, glowing eyes.

The police wrote down the phone numbers and addresses of Marie and Colleen, and they promised her that they'd speak to the maids within an hour after they left Birgitta's home.

After the police questioned Edna, the new maid, they went to the coach house to speak with William, the butler, whom was also the family chauffeur, and then the police officers walked back to the main house to speak with Birgitta again.

She waited until the police car had driven away, then she thanked Lana for coming over, and then after waving goodbye to her, Birgitta went back inside the house and poured another large glass of cognac.

She finished drinking the cognac, then refilled her glass with more cognac before walking over to the staircase. She giggled each time she stumbled on her way upstairs, and she stopped a few times to rest and admire the grand rooms below.

Birgitta had felt so pleased when the policemen had gaped around at the fine furnishings and the large chandeliers. One of the policemen had been talking with her at the top of the staircase, then he'd looked over the banister and smiled while saying that if he had lived in the house when he'd been a child, he would probably have been able to hang glide over the great expanse of the main floor.

She had been thrilled to see the envy in the lowly paid policeman's eyes when she told him that she was having an antique elevator installed to service all three floors of her palatial home. She had tapped his shoulder while the police officer had been looking down at the rooms below, then Birgitta had winked and smiled at him, and thanked him for his earlier compliment on her beauty.

She had then had felt excited when the handsome policeman had smiled while saying goodnight to her, and she now toyed with the idea of asking to speak with him when she called the police station the following day.

She reached the top of the long staircase, looked down again at the rooms below, and then smiled as she thought about standing there at the top with the handsome policeman's arm around her as they gazed down at the enormous, elegant rooms.

Birgitta swayed along the hall, stopping occasionally to take another drink of cognac, then she reclined on her bed and fantasized about the policeman disrobing across the room from her.

She finished drinking the cognac, placed the empty glass on the bedside table, and then she giggled as she laid back on the bed.

． ． ． ． ． ❖••••••❖★❖••••••❖ ． ． ． ． ．

She turned off the bedside lamp, closed her eyes as she smiled, and snuggled down in her bed. Less than two minutes later, Birgitta heard the front door of the house slam shut.

She sat up in bed, wondering if Lana had returned because she'd forgotten her purse. Extremely annoyed as well as dizzy from drinking so much cognac, Birgitta put on her robe, stepped out into the hall, then after taking a few unsure steps, she almost stumbled into the wall across the hall from her bedroom suite door.

She tried to stifle a giggle while hoping that she wouldn't appear too drunk when she saw Lana. Birgitta swayed along the hall, then stopped before reaching the top of the staircase, and then she looked over the railing to see if Lana was searching for her purse in the living room.

Although she couldn't see Lana down in the living room, what did catch her eye, was a huge paper butterfly gliding through the air. Birgitta gaped at the large, colorful, paper butterfly while wondering how it could fly.

She then noticed that the paper butterfly was attached to a long line on a fishing pole, and Suzanne was running back and forth, holding the pole as she laughed.

She shouted down at Suzanne to stop playing and go to bed, but Suzanne ignored her request and told her to go to hell. Birgitta was shocked that Suzanne had sworn at her and disobeyed her.

She scowled while yelling down at her again, but Suzanne just kept running back and forth, and then she told Birgitta to fuck off. Telling her to go to hell was bad enough, but using even worse language infuriated Birgitta.

She stumbled back away from the railing and hurried toward the staircase, glaring down at Suzanne laughing as she ran back and forth while watching her butterfly kite flying through the air.

She'd gone down eight steps when Birgitta stepped on something cold, hard and moist, and then looking down at her feet, she saw several eyeballs.

She staggered away from the eyeballs, and then saw that all the way down the staircase, there were many more eyeballs on the stairs, some of them with the socket cords still attached to them as if they'd just be torn out.

Birgitta shrieked while whirling around to go back upstairs, then stepping on another eyeball, she screamed in terror, lost her balance, and fell backward. Her head hit a marble step, knocking her unconscious, and then by the time she had tumbled down to the bottom of the very long, marble staircase, she was dead.

Edna jolted awake when she felt somebody shaking her shoulder, and then after quickly removing her sleeping mask, she saw Suzanne looking down at her, wide-eyed and obviously frightened.

"Suzanne! Oh, sweetheart! What's wrong?"

"It's Birgitta! She fell down the stairs!"

"Oh, dear! I'd better go help her!"

"She won't wake up! I tried to ask her if she was all right, but she wouldn't answer me!" exclaimed Suzanne.

"Hmmm, drunk ag...Oh, uh, she's probably just fine, dear, so, don't you worry. She must've fallen asleep before she went upstairs. Wait 'til I put my robe on. There. Now, let's go wake up Birgitta, shall we?" said Edna, smiling.

She had learned through gossip that Birgitta had often passed out from too much alcohol, so, Edna felt sure that because Birgitta had been drinking heavily that day, she'd passed out on the floor at the bottom of the staircase.

When she saw Birgitta's eyes staring up at her, with blood trickling out of her mouth, Edna hugged Suzanne close to her and told her not to look.

She put her arm around Suzanne's shoulders, and led her upstairs to her bedroom suite on the third floor, and then Edna told her that Birgitta had been drinking a bit too much, but she was just fine, so, Suzanne should go back to sleep.

Edna forced a smile as she turned off the light, said goodnight to Suzanne, closed the door, and then she hurried downstairs to call the emergency operator.

Suzanne stood at Birgitta's gravesite, staring at all the people dressed in black, and she wondered if she would be punished for upsetting Birgitta by using such foul language, which had caused Birgitta to become so furious that she'd fallen down the stairs.

She had told Edna that she'd used the words, "damn and hell," in front of Birgitta, then Edna had assured her that those two words wouldn't have shocked Birgitta so much that she'd fallen downstairs.

Of course, Suzanne didn't mention that she'd also used the "F" word, because she knew that she'd be in really big trouble. Nor had she mentioned that she'd used those bad words in defiance to Birgitta's demands that she stop playing with her butterfly kite and go to bed.

The day before Birgitta's funeral, Suzanne had been introduced to her widowed aunt whom would be moving into the house to care for her, and take on the late Birgitta's responsibilities of directing the household staff.

Her aunt, Hanna Clifton, held Suzanne's hand as they walked away from the gravesite to the car, and then the chauffeur tried his best to look sad as he held the door open for them.

Suzanne sat leaning against Hanna and they held hands as they were driven back to the house, then she mustered up a faint smile for her aunt before she walked slowly upstairs to her bedroom suite.

She watched Suzanne going upstairs, and Hanna slowly shook her head as she thought of how much grief her niece had had to endure in one year. First her father dying, and now Birgitta, and

Hanna thought how horribly coincidental it was that both Keith and Birgitta had fallen to their deaths.

. . . . . ❖•••••❖ ✦ ❖•••••❖ . . . . .

The following afternoon, Suzanne stood by the window of her bedroom, recalling the day when she'd been told that her father had plummeted to his death, and then she thought about the day she'd almost been caught snooping around in Birgitta's bedroom.

She had been trying to find Birgitta's personal phone book so that she could discover more about a friend of Birgitta's. But before she could find that small book, she'd heard Birgitta talking to a maid as they came up the stairs, so that had ended her search.

Suzanne, to Birgitta's great misfortune, was a very bright child, therefore, she'd been aware of Birgitta's flagrant flirting with her father, even though Birgitta already had a steady boyfriend.

One day, she'd been playing in the gardens at the rear of the house, when Suzanne had decided to have a cold soft drink, so, she began walking to the patio off the kitchen.

She knew that Birgitta was upstairs getting dressed while her boyfriend, David, waited for her downstairs, and he'd arrived with a friend named, Michael.

Suzanne had been rounding a tall hedge at the far end of the patio, then she'd been quite amused when she'd seen David and Michael kissing while hugging one another.

She'd waited a few minutes after the two men had walked back into the house, then Suzanne had followed them inside, and then gone to the fridge to get a soft drink.

During the next two weeks, she had followed David a few times and seen him enter a well-known gay bar that was situated ten blocks from her home.

She'd seen his name and photo on a poster outside the bar, and learned that he was one of the drag queen stars who performed on weekend nights. Suzanne had then realized that David and Birgitta's romance was a sham, and that her sorrow, a few weeks later, over David running off and marrying another woman, was a big, fat lie.

That was why Suzanne had been searching Birgitta's bedroom suite for that small, personal phone book so she could get David's phone number and address. But when she'd heard Birgitta coming upstairs with a maid, she'd quickly slid under Birgitta's bed.

She had then hoped that Birgitta would simply walk into the room to get something, and then leave again. Suzanne had laid under the bed, waiting for Birgitta to leave, but instead, she'd started talking to a friend on the phone.

Suzanne had been both shocked and angry when she'd heard Birgitta telling that person about the progress of her seduction of Keith. She had then listened to Birgitta talking about her plans to marry Keith for his money.

Later that day, she had tried to tell her father of Birgitta's plans, but Keith had thought that Suzanne was inventing stories because she didn't want anyone to replace her mother.

After her father's death, Suzanne had hidden under Birgitta's bed again, and heard her laughing as she talked on the phone to a friend and bragged about at long last being a wealthy widow. Suzanne had then felt certain that Birgitta had caused her father's death.

She hid under Birgitta's bed another time, and became quite frightened, and then angry as she listened to Birgitta on the phone, talking to somebody by the name of Lana.

"I highly doubt that, Lana. I mean, after all, no one even suspected that I'd pushed Keith off the cliff. I know. Even them, and they were his closest friends. No, I haven't yet, but I'll think of some way. Perhaps accidentally bumping Suzanne off a sidewalk just as a huge truck is coming along. What? You'd better come up with better ideas than that, Lana, old gal. Okay, so, my idea of pushing her into traffic might not work, either, but I'll think of some way to kill the little bitch and make it look like an accident. Once Suzanne's dead, then I'll own everything. If I'd known that eighty percent of his estate was going to her, then I would've made sure that Keith changed his will before I killed him. No, I didn't know! He never told me a thing! Nothing. I presumed that as his widow, I'd get most of the money, as well as custody of his brat. Anyway, we can discuss this tomorrow afternoon. Uh-huh, yes. Two o'clock at Cicero's and don't be late. No, I can't do that. I have to pick up that little bitch, Suzanne, after school. No wait. Fuck it. The school's not *that* far away, so, she can damn well walk home after school. Well, I *have* to drive her *to* school because the other mothers do, and I have to play the part. It's like some God damned tradition. Oh, you are? That looks so nice on you.

No, not that one. My red and blue dress. That should cause attention at Cicero's. Listen, I have to go. Okay, then. Yes. All right. Bye."

Suzanne had held back her tears until Birgitta left the room, and then for the rest of the day, she'd thought about how to keep Birgitta from killing her.

She had been called intellectually gifted by teachers and other people she'd met, and Suzanne felt rather thankful when she realized that Birgitta wasn't very much smarter than her.

Birgitta was more experienced than her, however, Suzanne felt certain that once she was Birgitta's age, she'd be far more intelligent than her. The only problem she'd had at one time, was reaching adulthood before being murdered for her money by Birgitta.

She had one thing in her favor, which was that Birgitta was a heavy drinker. Suzanne smiled as she gazed out her bedroom window while recalling how she'd put her now successful plan into action.

She remembered the first day her war with Birgitta had begun, and Suzanne's smile broadened as she started to envision it clearly.

She began sneaking into Birgitta's bedroom suite, and hiding under her bed whenever she knew that her awful stepmother was on her way upstairs, and then she would eavesdrop on Birgitta's phone conversations.

One phone conversation in particular sparked Suzanne's imagination, and it was this one: "It's her second operation, and the bitch won't shut up about it, and I've told her so many times I don't want to hear about it," said Birgitta. "Oh, you know what I mean, then. Horrible, isn't it? Why would I want to hear about the surgery they're doing on her eyes? It makes me shiver and feel nauseous. I've always had this awful revulsion to anything that has to do with eyes. I used to have terrifying nightmares when I was a child because some idiot boy living near me had one of his eyes poked out in some sort of accident. I was told he'd been taken home by his friends with his eyeball hanging out on his cheek. Horrible! And ever since then, whenever I hear someone tell me they had something wrong with one of their eyes, I panic, and feel...well, terrified, and I have to rush away from whoever it is telling me about it at the time, if they won't shut up about it, after I've told them a few times that I definitely don't want to hear a word about it. No, it's *not* a fetish, Lana! It's called a phobia! Anyway, anyone with bulging eyes, or anyone with some sort of eye problem makes me so scared and extremely queasy. That's why I wish to God that stupid bitch, Karen, would stop talking about her disgusting eye operation when she's around me. God! Well, I'm sorry to go on and on about it, but I just spoke to her this morning, and my nerves are a mess! That's why I've been drinking a bit more than usual. Anyway, enough of that. Let's meet at...Oh, say, at five, then we'll have plenty of time to chat, and do something before we go to the theatre. Fine. All right then, Lana, see you then. Bye."

Suzanne waited until she saw Birgitta go into the bathroom to shower, then she wriggled out from under the bed, ran out of the bedroom, and then spent the next few hours, recalling Birgitta's phone conversation with Lana.

·   ·   ·   ·   ·   ❖•••••❖★❖•••••❖   ·   ·   ·   ·   ·

Near her school there were several streets with many small stores, but the one that had caught Suzanne's attention the most was a joke store, which was crowded with many fun things.

When she'd gone into the store, she had felt excited while looking into the large aquarium that had a huge pair of glowing eyes submerged in it, and there were also battery-operated toy sharks moving slowly back and forth in the water.

The store owner had laughed when he'd told her that the big eyes in the aquarium looked even spookier when placed at the bottom of a shallow river, and he'd said that a customer had told him how he had spooked his buddies on a fishing trip.

Suzanne had rushed home to get some of her savings, run back to the store, and then grinned all the way home after she'd bought the very big, waterproof, battery-operated, plastic eyes.

One evening, she had overheard Birgitta telling a maid that she was going down to the dock after she had her shower, and that she didn't want to be disturbed.

Suzanne had quickly rummaged through her closet, found her snorkel, put on her bathing suit, tied the eyes to a very long string, and then waited beneath the dock for the slightly drunken Birgitta to walk down from the house.

She was beginning to have doubts about scaring Birgitta with the eyes because after waiting almost fifteen minutes, Suzanne was starting to shiver in the water under the dock.

Suzanne could see her through the cracks of the wooden boards, then she was delighted when Birgitta finally saw the eyes beneath the water, and then she had screamed while quickly stepping back away from the edge of the dock.

Suzanne had then pulled the eyes back under the dock, turned off the light, and then waited to see if Birgitta was going to run away, or take another look down into the water.

Birgitta had rushed to the boat at the end of the dock to get that oar, and then on her way back to where she'd looked down at the glowing eyes, Suzanne had started swimming underwater away from the dock.

When she'd reached big bushes far from the dock, Suzanne had then resurfaced, taken off her snorkel mask while looking back at the dock, and then under the cover of darkness, she'd run back to the house, and hurried up the rear staircase to the second floor.

Suzanne had then rushed along the second floor corridor to the stairs leading up to the third floor, then into her bedroom suite, quickly taken off her bathing suit, dried off, and put on her pajamas.

She had then turned off her bedroom light, then stood out of sight at the top of the stairs to the third floor, and then waited until she'd seen Birgitta pass by on her way to her own bedroom suite.

Suzanne had then gone back into her bedroom suite, and leaned out the window, looked down and waited until she'd seen the lights go out in Birgitta's bedroom suite. She had then hurried away from the window to get the fishing pole.

She'd previously tied a pebble to the fishing line, so, she hurried back to the window, and unreeled the line until the pebble was level with one of the windows of Birgitta's bedroom suite. Suzanne had then started swinging the line out away from the window, then each time it had swung back, the pebble had tapped the window pane.

When Suzanne had seen a bit of light in the window, which had been caused when Birgitta had turned on a bedside lamp, then she'd reeled in the fishing line, and then quickly tied the very big, plastic eyes to the end of the line.

She'd turned on the switch to make the eyes glow before lowering them down to Birgitta's window, and she'd almost giggled aloud when she'd heard Birgitta's startled cry of fright.

Before Suzanne had started using the big, glowing eyes to frighten Birgitta, she had looked through the phone book for an abattoir, and then she'd called one of her friends.

She asked her friend, Judy, if it wouldn't be fun to really scare people next Halloween, which was several months away. Suzanne told her about the abattoir, and Judy thought it was a great idea.

Two days later, after Judy had had her elder brother write a note for her, she and Suzanne were driven to the abattoir by Judy's family chauffeur, and then she handed the note to a supervisor.

The supervisor had noticed the Rolls Royce parked outside his office window, the chauffeur standing beside it, smoking a cigarette, and the crest on the girls' school uniforms indicating that they were students at the most prestigious private school in the city.

The note was a request for items needed for a school project, so, as the girls waited, the supervisor left his office and returned fifteen minutes later with a small cardboard box.

Judy and Suzanne thanked the supervisor of the abattoir, then once they were seated in the back of the car, they opened the box, and after staring wide-eyed for a moment at the contents inside a clear plastic bag, they giggled. Inside the bag were over thirty eyes of varying sizes taken from slaughtered cattle, pigs and lambs.

The girls had previously agreed that Suzanne would hide the gruesome bag at her home until Halloween, so, they stuffed the cardboard box into Suzanne's backpack, then chatted about how shocked people would be next Halloween when the girls left eyes on the doorsteps of neighbors' homes after they'd been given candy.

Suzanne was dropped off at her home, then she laughed as she said goodbye to Judy, and then she kept her backpack on while waiting for an opportunity to go down to the basement when the household staff wouldn't notice.

There was a big, walk-in fridge in the basement of the house, and Suzanne had found a place inside that fridge to hide the plastic bag of eyeballs. She especially liked the eyes that were slightly bloodied and had bits of socket cords hanging from them.

The morning after Suzanne had hidden under the dock to frighten Birgitta with the very big, plastic, glowing eyes, and then dangled them from her bedroom window down to Birgitta's window at night, Birgitta had dropped her off at school on the way to a beauty salon appointment.

Suzanne had gone into school, then asked her teacher if she could leave half an hour earlier at lunch hour, then at 11:30 a.m., she walked out of school, and hailed a cab.

Suzanne knew how to enter the house without being seen by the household staff, and then after she sneaked up the rear staircase, she went into Birgitta's bedroom suite, and she'd been so pleased when she'd seen the coffee cup on the bedside table. Birgitta had only taken a few sips of coffee before hurrying around the room to get dressed for her appointment at the beauty salon.

Suzanne rushed out of the room, down the rear staircase, and then after hurrying into the kitchen, she opened a cupboard, and got a small, plastic sandwich bag. She had hurried down to the basement, entered the large, walk-in fridge, and then taken two eyeballs out of the big plastic bag.

She had then rushed back up the rear staircase, into Birgitta's bedroom suite, then carried the cup of coffee into the bathroom, emptied most of the cup, then placed the eyeballs at the bottom of it, making sure that the pupils were facing upward, so that they'd be staring up at Birgitta. She put the cup back on the bedside table before rushing down the rear staircase, then out the side door.

Suzanne checked her wristwatch, then ten minutes after noon, she walked in the front door of the house, and smiled at the maids as she greeted them. She was served lunch at the dining room table, then she suppressed a grin when Birgitta arrived back from the beauty salon, and became very annoyed while the maids told her that they hadn't had time to tidy her bedroom suite.

The maids had then gone out to the garden to gather flowers, and then minutes later, Birgitta had shouted at the chauffeur to fetch the maids back into the house, and it was then that Suzanne knew that Birgitta had found the eyeballs in the coffee cup.

Birgitta had been so angry while standing outside on the porch, glaring at the maids, and waiting for them to return to the house, therefore, she hadn't noticed that Suzanne had left the dining room.

Suzanne had raced to the rear staircase, gone up to Birgitta's bedroom suite, taken the eyes out of the cup, dropped them into the plastic sandwich bag, then raced back down the rear staircase. She had run back into the dining room just moments before the maids had hurried back into the house to be shouted at by Birgitta.

Suzanne had then accompanied Birgitta and the two maids upstairs to Birgitta's bedroom suite, and stood gaping at the them as Birgitta accused the maids of trying to frighten her by playing an awful joke on her.

Although she'd felt sorry about Colleen and Marie losing their jobs, Suzanne had been quite pleased at how the animal eyeballs at the bottom of the coffee cup had visibly shaken cold-hearted and murderous Birgitta.

Birgitta had been rather annoyed after she had fired the two maids because she'd had to spend the next two hours making phone calls to have prospective maids sent over. After interviewing maids for over an hour, then finally hiring one of them, Birgitta had felt quite relieved in the evening when she'd driven away from the house to have dinner with Lana.

Suzanne had waited in the darkness outside the house, and then smiled when she'd seen Birgitta drive up to the side of the house, and then park the car. She had then tossed a stick in Birgitta's direction and it had landed on the ground in front of her. Birgitta had looked around the grounds, trying to determine which direction the stick had come from.

Suzanne had then raised the glowing, plastic eyes, and then crouching behind a long, high hedge, she had walked slowly back and forth, making it look like the eyes were floating in midair.

When Birgitta started walking slowly toward the bushes, Suzanne had quickly lowered the long fishing pole she'd attached the lit eyes to, clicked off the light, then crouching low to the ground, she had run behind the garage.

Birgitta had stepped through the bushes, looked around, and then not seeing anyone, nor the floating, glowing eyes, she had hurried back to the house.

Suzanne had then run around the house to the back door, then up the rear staircase, along the second floor to the main staircase, and then stayed out of sight at the top of the staircase, listening to Birgitta talking loudly on the phone, demanding that policemen be sent immediately to the house to search the grounds for an intruder.

She had been so pleased to see Birgitta drinking heavier with each passing hour because she'd been shocked by the big, glowing eyes outside her bedroom window, then floating in the air.

Suzanne thought it was hilarious when she'd placed two, big eyeballs by the telephone on Birgitta's bedside table, then later, she'd placed more eyeballs in other places for Birgitta to find.

Birgitta had been so drunk on the night she'd died, that Suzanne had been able to enter her bedroom suite, without awakening her, and then open the window.

She had then started knocking very hard on the closed door with a shoe wrapped in a towel, and then after hearing Birgitta asking who was knocking on her door, Suzanne had run to the far end of the hall.

She had peered out from the side of an armoire, and seen Birgitta stumble out into the hall, then begin walking along it to the main staircase. Suzanne had then smiled as she'd listened to Birgitta's screams at finding more eyeballs; one of which had been placed on top of the newel post.

Almost an hour later, she'd tried to contain her laughter while listening to Lana and Birgitta talking excitedly as they'd hurried up the main staircase.

While Birgitta had been pacing the living room, waiting for Lana to arrive, Suzanne had had plenty of time to pick up all the eyeballs, put them in a plastic bag, and polish the top of the newel post.

After noticing how terrified Birgitta had become from seeing the very big, floating eyes, as well as all the eyeballs in so many places, Suzanne had decided it was time for the finishing touch that would ensure that Birgitta would never be able to murder her.

Suzanne placed many eyeballs on the main staircase before slamming the front door, knowing that Edna wouldn't hear because her room was at the far end of the house, and the door to the long hallway leading there was closed.

She then began running back and forth with the butterfly kite attached to a long length of line on her fishing pole. She'd known that blatantly ignoring Birgitta's demands to stop playing and go to bed, would seriously upset her, and Suzanne had also known that using bad swear words would enrage Birgitta.

Suzanne had never used foul language before, nor had she been disobedient before, and her sudden, very rude, disobedient behavior had confused, shocked, and infuriated Birgitta.

Just as Suzanne had hoped would happen, Birgitta had glared down at her while staggering and swaying down the staircase. Suzanne had stopped running with the butterfly kite when she'd heard Birgitta screeching after stepping on an eyeball, and then screaming when she'd seen many more eyeballs on the staircase.

She had watched Birgitta stumbling and staggering, losing her balance, and then screaming before her head had hit one of the steps, and then she'd fallen down the very long marble staircase.

Suzanne had looked at Birgitta's sprawled body for a few moments before she began picking up all the eyeballs off the staircase, and placing them into the plastic bag. She then hurried downstairs to the basement and placed the bag back in the hidden place inside the large, walk-in refrigerator.

She'd stopped for a moment to look down at Birgitta's body before she had walked slowly to Edna's bedroom where she had given a performance every bit as good as the one Birgitta had given after she'd murdered Keith.

For a week after Birgitta's funeral, Suzanne often dabbed water around her eyes and on her cheeks to make people think that she'd been crying. But she really hadn't shed one tear over the death of the deceitful woman whom had murdered her father, and had planned to kill her, too.

The End

Ripping Out
The Heart
Of Innocence

Ripping Out The Heart Of Innocence

Sunlight slowly replaced moonlight, awakening the colors of the land as flowers tilted back their heads to let the morning sun dry the dew on their faces.

Ants began their daily treks to and from their tiny hill homes while birds took flight from an astonishing array of clustered greens while singing many morning songs.

Before noon, only the buzzing of a bumblebee, or the kerplunk of a frog leaping into the water had broken the silence until the laughter and tittering of children titillated the hot summer day.

Heavy tree limbs arcing over the river were draped with clothes and scrambling children who screamed or shouted as they dove and jumped from the branches.

Instead of swimming, Justin and Matt busied themselves with their raft they'd been constructing for the past two weeks. The idea of building a raft had come to them when they'd seen two logs laying along the riverbank, then it had taken them several hours to search the fields on both sides of the river for more logs.

Each time they'd found a log, Justin and Matt had lifted it onto Matt's wagon, tied it in place, then pulled the wagon to the river. After most of the logs were bound together, the boys had then started making trips every day with their wagon across the field to pull planks off the walls of an old, deserted barn.

Today, they'd brought back two more, long planks from the barn, then after they'd sawn them to the size they needed to span the bound logs, Matt had started nailing the planks in place while Justin began binding more logs to extend the length of their raft.

"It was really great of Mr. Fulford to give us all the rope."

"Yeah, he said he'd sharpen our knives for us, too, so, you give me yours when we go home and I'll ask him if he can do it for us before we come back tomorrow," said Justin.

"Okay. How many nails are left in that jar?" asked Matt.

"Just a sec. There's only about eight or ten left, so, we better get some more."

"It's gonna look great with sides on it. Okay, you keep tying the ropes around those logs, and I'm going over to the barn and get some more boards," said Matt. "I'll see if I can find a long pole, too, to make the mast."

"Okay. I'll bring my dad's saw with me tomorrow because it's a lot better than that one. Y'know what? I think we should tie four more logs together. Okay?"

"Yeah, okay. I'm going to the barn, now."

"Hey, and don't climb up near the top of the barn to get boards, okay? Remember the last time we tried to do that. I reached out to get a loose one, and I almost fell off that beam we were standing on."

"I'm not *that* dumb. I'll walk along the beams to where they're close to the walls, and then see if there's any loose boards there."

"I wonder what Star's doing? She's been gone a long time."

"Yeah, she has," said Matt. "She's probably playing over near Gibson's farm. She likes it there because of their apple trees. I saw Star walking along the fence to where some branches hang way over it, and she picked some apples off the tree, and ate them."

"She sure likes apples, and nobody cares how many of them she steals off those trees," said Justin, smiling.

"She really likes watching us building the raft, huh? Maybe she thinks we'll build it big enough for her to ride on it, too."

"Maybe. We'd need a really big raft, then, man."

"If I see her, I'll tell her to get on over here."

"Okay. Y'know what?" asked Justin.

"What?"

"I was talkin' to Mavis and she told me her mother told her that she's gonna have a new baby maybe by Christmas."

"Yeah? Gee, she gets a new brother or sister every year, so, I bet when she's twelve, she'll have twelve brothers and sisters."

"Maybe," said Matt. "My mom can't have anymore. Not since after I was born."

"My mom and dad told me they wanted to get a brother or a sister for me, but they said they still can't get one yet because they can't get a consection."

"What's that?"

"I don't know. But Mavis's mom sure has lots of those."

"Yeah, for sure," said Matt. "When my dad told me about the facts of life, he didn't tell me anything about consections. I'll ask him or my mom about that."

"When we get this raft all fixed up and ready, I bet everyone'll wanna go for rides on it," said Justin. "Carol said it looks real good already, and she's the first one I'm gonna ask to go for a ride on it with me."

"I know why you *really* want her to be the first one on our raft."

"So do I. It's because she comes by all the time to watch us making it, and she always says it looks real good, and so that's why I'm gonna ask *her* first."

"Nope. That's not why," said Matt, grinning.

"Oh, yeah? Then why else do y'think I'd ask her first?"

"Because you like her, that's why."

"So what? So do you and so do lots of other kids."

"Yeah, but they don't give her things. And you ask her all the time if she'll have a milkshake with you, and you're always talking to her and stuff. You got the hots for her."

"Get real. I do not," said Justin, scowling. "I just like her a lot. She's nicer than the others, and she's really pretty, that's all."

"She's prettier than any of the other girls. Bet that's why you think she's nicer and you hang around her a lot."

"Aaaaaa, gimme a break. Carol's got personality and so that's why I like her more than the others. It's not just 'cause she's prettier than them."

"That's what *you* say," said Matt, then he snickered.

"Yeah, that's what I say, and that's what I mean, dummy."

"I just bet."

"Get real," said Justin.

They heard squealing, so, they looked over at the other children, and saw five of them throwing clumps of mud at each other as they laughed while running around in their wet underwear.

"There's Brett," said Justin. "He's just getting ready to dive off a branch. It's so funny how his face gets so red every time you ask him if he's gonna marry Linda."

"Yeah, he gets really mad, too, when you ask him that."

"He says he doesn't like girls and he doesn't like hanging around 'em," said Justin, smiling. "But he sure looks at Linda a lot. I know he's got a crush on her."

"Yeah, I know he has, too, and that gets him so mad every time we tell him that. Hey, I got a great idea! Let's ask Brett in front of all the other kids why he blushes so much every time he talks to Linda! And then we can ask him if he's got a big crush on her! Whaddaya think? Wanna do it?" asked Matt, laughing.

"Yeah! That'd be so cool," replied Justin, grinning.

"Then after that, I'm going over to the barn. If we do this, man, he's gonna get really, really mad at us, so, if Star comes, and you go off with her, make sure you tie the raft up good with lots of knots 'cause Brett might let the raft float away. He better not, though."

"If he did that, then we won't let him on the raft when it's ready. Man, is he gonna be mad when we ask him if he's got a big crush on

Linda, because all the other kids'll really laugh. Okay, let's go ask him, okay?"

"Yeah! This is gonna be great!" exclaimed Matt, grinning.

• • • • • • ❖•••••❖★❖•••••❖ • • • • • •

They laughed as they ran back to the raft, and then talked about how embarrassed Brett had been, and how the girls had giggled when they'd asked Brett if he had a big crush on Linda. A few minutes later, Matt headed off to the barn far across the field to get more boards for the raft.

Justin then began lashing two logs together with pieces of rope, and then he thought about Matt, and he hoped that he wouldn't fall off one of the barn rafters. He'd just finished binding the logs together, when he saw Carol walking along the riverbank toward him.

"Are you going home, already?"

"Yeah, I am," she replied. "My parents are going into town to do some shopping, and Sara's coming with us, and then we're going to have a milkshake while they're shopping."

"Whaddaya think of the raft, now? It's almost finished."

"It looks really, really great. Matt said you guys are going to make a sail for it."

"Yeah, we are, and we're gonna make a mast for it for it, too. When we're ready, we'll take you for a ride on it, okay?"

"Sure, but I better warn you. Brett's really mad about what you said, so, he might do something to your raft," Carol told him.

"Oh, yeah? He better not, man. Naaaa, he won't do that. He's too chicken. Hey, you're going by the old barn on your way home, so, will you see what Matt's up to? He was going to get some more boards and most of the loose ones are way up high, so, I thought he might've fallen or something. Maybe not, but like, if he has, maybe he might be hurt."

"Okay, I'll take a look. You sure that's going to float okay?"

"Sure. We're nailing a tarp on it after. That'll keep the water from coming up through the cracks."

"Oh, I see. Where's Star?" she asked.

"I don't know. But she'll be back. So, um, like, wanna go for a milkshake tomorrow afternoon?"

"All right. I'd really like that. Thanks," said Carol, smiling.

"Yeah? Great! I mean, I like talking to you when we're having a milkshake. Other times, too. Uh, I like your tan. So, um, anyway, I was wondering if Matt's okay. You know? 'Cause he's getting boards over at the old barn," he said, blushing.

"Yeah, you told me. I'll walk over that way on my way home and see if he's okay, and then I'll go across from there to the ridge, and go up it and along to the other side. I like going that way sometimes because you can see a long way from up there."

"Yeah, I know," said Jason. "You can see your place and lots of other places from up there."

"Yeah, and it's like a forest on top of a mountain."

"But I don't think real mountains have lots of trees along the top of them."

"That's because there's lots of snow on top of mountains, and also because trees can't grow up that high," said Carol.

"Yeah, I never thought of that. You know lots about just about everything, and that's because you're so smart. I think you're smarter than all the other girls. Lots of guys, too. So, um, anyway, I guess I'll see you tomorrow when we have a milkshake. Right?"

"Yeah, I like having a milkshake with you. If I see Star on the way home, I'll tell her to come back here. Okay?"

"Thanks a lot. That's really great of you."

"Okay, see you tomorrow. Bye," she said, smiling.

"Bye. Oh! And I hope you have a good time in town!"

"Thanks, Justin! I hope so, too! Bye!"

- - - - - ❖•••••❖★❖•••••❖ - - - - -

At least half an hour had passed by and Matt still hadn't returned, so, Justin decided to go for a swim. He folded his clothes, placed his shoes on top of them, then after tying the pile with rope, he hid it in the bushes so that Brett wouldn't find his clothes and shoes, and then he waded into the river and started swimming downstream.

The water only came up to his chest, so, he could rest once in awhile along the way, and then Justin decided to float on his back and look up at the clouds as he drifted with the current.

He wondered if the shapes and vague, bumpy faces formed by the clouds were ghosts of people who had lived in far away countries, and now they were being carried past the horizon to fade into endless space beyond the stars.

Two birds swept by, flapped their wings rapidly, and sloped downward as they turned right before swooping up again, then a large bird glided slowly into view above him just as he heard a faint, rumbling sound coming toward him.

Justin stood up in the river to see Star racing along the field toward the forest, and he thought that she was the most beautiful white mare in the whole world, and the smartest one, too.

He put two fingers in his mouth and whistled. Star came to an abrupt stop, then shook her head before galloping toward him, and then after she stood by the stream, she whinnied and nodded her head as she looked at Justin.

He waded out of the water, and stroked her snout as he talked low to her, then led her over to one of the large boulders along the side of the river. Justin leapt from the highest boulder onto Star's back, then shifted himself toward her shoulders.

After Star began trotting quickly forward, he held his arms high in the air as he whooped and laughed. He lowered his arms when he saw a movement far off to his right, then squinting his eyes, he could see Matt far across the field, walking back to the river, and pulling the wagon that he'd tied a few boards onto.

Justin shouted and waved at him, then realizing that he couldn't be heard because of the distance between them, he decided to spend some time with Star, knowing that Matt probably wouldn't miss him for a long time, once he became preoccupied with the raft.

He wondered if Matt had found a pole to use for a mast, because if he had found one, then they could look for metal braces to attach the mast to the raft.

Jason felt sure they'd find some metal braces in somebody's garage or barn, then he gently kicked at Star's sides again, and she began to gallop faster toward the ridge in the distance.

The river curved around the ridge and flowed through the densest part of the forest, and Justin laughed as they raced along the field while following the course of the river.

· · · · · · ❖•••••❖★❖•••••❖ · · · · · ·

After reaching the ridge, Justin guided Star along the base of it to where the ridge sloped at a steep angle, and ended close to the river. He hopped off Star, reached up, and held a hank of her mane, urging her forward as they made their way around the ridge until the riverbank widened.

Looking ahead, he could see how the river seemed to disappear as it flowed by huge bushes and very big, old trees growing along the sides of the riverbank. Justin waded into the water, then splashed around in it, and talked to Star while she drank from the river.

Ten minutes later, he saw a tan figure slowly passing by bushes, then he noticed it was a nude man, and he presumed that the man was walking to the river to swim. The man walked clear of the bushes, and Justin recognized him, so, he waved.

"Hi, Todd!"

"What? Justin! What are you doing way over here? Oh, you rode here on Star. She's really beautiful, isn't she? Are you alone?"

"Yeah. Just Star and me. We got here about five minutes ago."

"I see. I was going for a swim."

"The water's really shallow at this part 'cause the river's a real lot wider, so, it's only about up to your knees here," said Justin.

"Well, I'm just going to rinse off a bit."

He watched Todd wade into the river and begin splashing water up onto his chest, then Justin knelt in the water to watch him bathe as he talked to him.

Todd turned around to face him, and Justin noticed that he had dark pink streaks on his shoulders and arms, so, he asked: "What are those stains or whatever on you?"

"Huh? Oh, these. Well, I was walking along the top of the ridge, and you know how there's so many big trees up there? Well, there I am walking, and suddenly, I feel drops hitting my shoulders. I'd taken off my shirt, so, I just had on a pair of shorts, so, I could feel the drops falling down on me. Anyway, I thought it was starting to rain, then I look up and see a dead rabbit."

"In a tree?"

"Yeah, some kids must've just killed it, and then strung it up on a branch of the tree I passed under. So, it turned out that it wasn't raining, after all. It was blood. Yuk!"

"That's really awful. They must've really cut it up," said Justin.

"It looked like it'd been gutted and a couple of legs were hacked off. Good thing I was only wearing shorts or else I would've got it all over my shirt. It's a bitch to get out. That's if it *will* come out."

"It's coming off your skin okay with the water."

"Yeah. I'm glad I didn't get any on my shorts. Star's a big horse. I've heard that horses are very protective of their owners. Would she protect you if a bunch of the guys ganged up on you?"

"I'm sure she wouldn't hurt any kids. Like, she'd just nudge them away from me, and then they'd go away 'cause her nudges are pretty strong," said Justin. "But I don't know what she'd do if it was any of the really big kids, but they wouldn't come after me, anyway. But yeah, I'm sure she'd do all she could to protect me if any big kids ever did come after me."

"I thought so. Horses really scare me."

"Aw, you don't have to be scared of her. She's really nice."

"Hey, have you started smoking yet? Reason I asked is because I was going to have a smoke, so, you can share it with me."

"Well, not really. Like, I shared half a cigarette with Matt a coupla times, but that's all," Justin told him.

"Did you like it?"

"Not the first puffs because I choked and coughed, but then after that it was sorta okay."

"Oh, yeah? Great," said Todd, smiling.

While they'd been talking, Todd had started wading out of the water, and then he said: "I feel like a cigarette right now. My shorts are over there, so, come on over there with me, and we'll light one."

"Okay. Thanks," said Justin, smiling as he followed him.

"Will Star follow us?"

"Naw, she's having fun walking around and looking at things."

"Yeah, I see. Sorry, but like I said, horses really scare me, and you said that she'd get mad if someone attacked you. Well, she can see that I'm not going to do that, so, I don't feel too nervous."

"Yeah, she's ignoring us, right now," Justin said, smiling.

"You'll like puffing on *this* cigarette."

They walked over to the bushes by the river where Todd had hung his shorts, then he took out a joint of a pocket, lit it, inhaled deeply, and then held the joint out to him.

Justin puffed on it, then coughed out: "Kaaaa! Hhk-k-k! This tastes really strong!"

"Y'have to get used to it. Inhale it slowly. Try it again."

"Okay. Huk-kk-huh! Sorry. It still tastes really strong."

"Inhale it slower, okay? Take a few more puffs 'til it feels better on your throat," said Todd.

"Okay. Mmmmm."

Justin took a much smaller puff of the marijuana smoke, but instead of inhaling, he choked again, so, he quickly blew the smoke out, and then said: "Naw, I better not keep trying to smoke it 'cause I keep gagging on it. Maybe if it was a menthol cigarette, then I could smoke some."

"Keep trying."

"Sorry, but it'll make me sick," Justin said, passing it back.

"Hmmm, okay, your loss, kid."

"Star's walking farther. Maybe she saw a turtle."

"Yeah, so I see. Y'know, I wish I could ride bareback. Bet it feels really great when you can ride like that. Just like a wild savage. You ever fallen off her?" asked Todd.

"I fell off a coupla times when I first started riding horses, but now I never do."

"Y'got good balance. Well, that's the end of the cigarette. I'll light up another brand. It's smoother."

He lit a regular cigarette, passed it to Justin, then asked: "How's *that* taste?

"It's a bit better. Yeah, it's a little bit smoother."

"Good. Let's sit down, okay? Yeah, that's better. Here, have another drag."

"Thanks. This cigarette doesn't make me choke."

"Any of your friends coming to join you soon?"

"Nope. They're way down the river. They'd never come all this way unless they rode with me on Star."

"So, you're all alone. Just you and Star, huh? You really surprised me because I didn't expect to see anyone else around this part of the river. Bet you'd tell all your friends you saw me, and we smoked a cigarette together."

"Oh, I wouldn't tell them you let me smoke."

"Hmmm, I didn't want anyone to see me. I'm very shy about being naked, but I used to go swimming naked when I was your age. Young and small. Hmmm, yeah, so free and so innocent. How do you feel, now?" asked Todd.

"Sorta dizzy from coughing so much."

He felt slightly lightheaded because he'd inhaled a small puff of the marijuana smoke, so, Justin leaned back on his elbows, smiling as they talked.

He giggled a couple of times, but didn't understand what had seemed so funny, and then he realized that he was smiling a lot.

"I feel a little bit dizzy. Do you feel that way, too?"

"A bit. If you'd smoked more of that first cigarette I lit up, then you'd feel a lot dizzier," said Todd.

"Yeah? I wouldn't wanna get more dizzier, so, I'm glad I couldn't smoke more of that other cigarette."

"You're sure nobody else is coming to join you?"

"Naw, I'm pretty sure they won't 'cause like I told you, it's too far away from where they're playing, and it's a long way to walk to that old barn that's rotting on Mr. Lougheed's property."

"Oh? Glad to hear that. Must be nice to have a horse so you can go where y'want instead of using the roads. I drove as far as the end of the old road, and then I walked up to the top of the ridge. Y'can see for miles up there, and I like taking long walks where there's nobody around. So nice and peaceful up there. Nobody usually ever comes way over here, so, I was really surprised to see you."

"Carol Saunders comes this way. Sometimes she likes walking along the top of the ridge to get to her place. That's how she went home today, after she went swimming with the other kids."

"Oh, yeah, I forgot. That's right, the Saunders' property is about less than half a mile from here. Yeah, it runs right up to the ridge. I saw her in town last week with some friends. She's really starting to grow up. I guess she's what? Nine, now?" asked Todd.

"No, she's eleven like me. Carol's birthday is two months after mine, so, she was eleven on March the twenty-seventh, and she had a big birthday party."

"I bet the party was a lotta fun. Yeah, Carol's a nice kid, and she's very pretty, too."

"Yeah, she is."

"Mmmm, I feel so good from smoking that first cigarette. And my dick feels good, too. See? It's hard."

"Oh? Oh, yeah, it is," said Justin, smiling.

"It feels great when I do this. Yeah, mmmm, so good."

"Jeez! Are you going to play with yourself?"

"Yeah, I might. Why don't you feel it? Come over here and feel it, okay? C'mon. Hey! Where are you going?"

"I'm gonna splash some water on my face 'cause I feel sorta sleepy in a way. Maybe 'cause I'm feeling sorta dizzy. Hoo-oo! Oh-Oh! I couldn't stand too good at first. I wanna see what Star's up to, so, I'll be back in a sec, okay?"

"Okay. Hurry back. Promise?"

"Um, yeah. I wonder where Star got to? Can't see her. Guess she decided to go over to the Gibson's orchard. She does that in the afternoon, sometimes."

"She's gone? Will she be coming back?" asked Todd.

"Yeah, but if she doesn't come back here, she'll come home, later. That's okay, though, 'cause I can swim a bit and walk a bit back to where the raft is."

"So, we're all alone. Nobody but us. Yeah, I like that. Y'know, you look really nice in just your underwear. Hey, Justin?"

"Yeah?"

"Come back over here and feel this, okay?"

"Naw."

"Why not? It feels really great," said Todd.

"Hey, y'wanna go farther down where the water's deeper?"

"No, thanks. I wanna play with my dick. Why don't you play with yours, too?"

"Oh, uh...I, well...I'm just gonna stay here in the water."

"Okay. So, go ahead. Play with your dick."

"Naw, I don't wanna do that," said Justin.

"Hey, I asked you nice, didn't I? So, do it."

"Um, I already told you I don't want to."

"You rotten, little...Okay, then just come over here, and we'll talk about it, okay?"

He felt scared because Todd had looked very angry when he'd asked him to touch his penis and Justin had refused. He suddenly recalled in his partially drugged state, that several times before, Todd had looked angry while they'd talked and smoked.

Todd had also stared in a strange way at the front of his underwear, and that had made Justin feel very apprehensive. He now felt more exposed than he'd ever been in his life, so, he began slowly backing away from where Todd was sitting near the river.

Justin had been trying to think of an excuse to get away from him, and then he thought of Star, and he hoped that Todd would believe him if he said that she was nearby.

"Oh, there she is!" cried Justin, although it was a lie.

"Who?" asked Todd, looking around.

"Star. I just saw her walk into some bushes a little way down the stream. Hey, Star! C'mon!"

"Don't get her to come here!"

"Oh? Oh, yeah, I forgot you're a bit scared of her, so, I'll go down there, and shoo her off home. Okay?"

"She'll go if y'do that?"

"Yeah, most of the time."

"Yell at her from here, and see if she'll go back home."

"No, she won't go unless I patted her, then told her to go home. Okay? I'll go do it, and be right back, okay?"

"Hmmm, I don't want her around here because she might get mad at me, and attack me. Okay, go do it, but run right back here, okay?"

"Yeah, sure. I'll be back in a minute. Bye."

He began running along the edge of the river, and he hoped he'd be out of Todd's sight very soon. He stopped to look back, and saw Todd hurrying toward him, so, Justin darted into the bushes at the side of the ridge.

He hoped that Todd wouldn't catch up with him before he had time to scramble up to the top of the ridge, and then if Star was down on the other side of it, he'd be able to run down to her, leap up onto her, and ride away.

. . . . . . ❖••••••❖✸❖••••••❖ . . . . . .

Halfway up the ridge, he stopped and listened, trying to discern whether Todd was in pursuit of him. Justin crouched down as he stepped carefully, trying not to make a sound.

Because he'd been looking in the direction where Todd was, instead of looking ahead, his foot hit a large lump on the ground, and then he stumbled, lost his balance, and toppled over sideways.

He screamed into the hand that he'd quickly clamped over his mouth when he saw Carol lying on the ground with most of her clothes ripped off, and she was staring vacantly at him.

He realized that she was dead, and that Todd had killed her because he felt sure now, that when he'd first seen him, it hadn't been rabbit's blood that Todd had been washing off his body.

Justin tried to catch his breath while he wept and trembled. He brushed matted hair away from Carol's face, and then kissed her forehead. Instead of her lovely smile that Justin had loved so much, Carol's open mouth looked distorted from shock and terror, and he groaned and whimpered when he realized that her jaw was broken.

He wept as he hugged her ravaged body that was streaked with blood, and then he panicked when he heard rustling sounds near him as Todd pushed his way through bushes, looking for him. His heart leapt when he heard Todd shout: "Hey, Justin! Where are you? I wanna talk to you! I saw you coming this way! Justin? I like you, okay? So, why are you hiding from me? Justin? C'mon!"

Justin quickly looked around, then saw a very thick, wide bush close to him, so, he crawled on his hands and knees around the bush and saw another bush close to the one he'd circled.

He winced as his flesh was scraped while he squeezed between the two bushes, then he laid curled up on his side. His trembling increased when he heard Todd shouting out to him again.

He could only see a slight amount of Carol's body through the bushes, so, he knew that Todd wouldn't be able to see him through the thick bushes.

Justin held his breath when he heard Todd's shouts coming closer, and then a few moments later, Todd appeared in front of Carol's body. Justin could barely see him through the bushes, but he was able to see the angry look on Todd's face.

Todd called out to him again as he began hurrying higher up the ridge, and Justin bit down on his bottom lip as he tried to whimper quietly while he felt the stings on his body from the many scratches he'd received while crawling between the two bushes.

He knew that he had to hide somewhere else because Todd had looked for him behind every bush he'd passed, and there weren't that many more bushes around, which meant that Todd would eventually find him.

Justin stood up slowly, and sucked in his breath as the rough branches scratched his body, and then he peered around for any sign of Todd. He gauged the distance from where he was standing to the denser part of the trees, and he hoped he could reach that area before Todd saw him.

. . . . . . ❖•••••❖★❖•••••❖ . . . . . .

He felt so relieved when he reached the trees, and then he stopped hurrying to look up at the top of the ridge to see if Todd had gone all the way up there to look for him.

Justin couldn't see him on top of the ridge or anywhere on the hill leading up to it, so, he turned around to run through the trees, and then he cried out when he suddenly bumped into Todd.

"Todd!"

"Where'd you go? Look at you. You're all scratched up."

"Uh...um...uh...I was...I was feeling dizzy. Um, Star ran away before I got to her, and...and, um, then I had to pee, and then I fell over a bush," said Justin, shaking.

"Why didn't you just piss in the river? Never mind. Let's go back down the hill."

"Uh, I...I was gonna go back home 'cause, um...I...I, uh, I still feel sorta dizzy."

"That's the tobacco. It's foreign. Takes awhile to get used to it. You'll be okay, so, there's no reason for you to go back home, okay? You'll stop feeling dizzy very soon. There's my shirt over there. Get it for me, will you? Thanks. I sure wish I had another of those foreign cigarettes we smoked. Guess we'll have to smoke the other kind. I'm going to wash off when we get back to the river, and you can help me do it. Okay? Well? C'mon! What's wrong?"

"Uh, well, I...you...um..."

Todd glared at him as he gripped his arm, and Justin felt terrified.

"I said, c'mon, Justin!"

"Yeah, sure, okay."

·   ·   ·   · ·   ◇•••••◇★◇•••••◇   · ·   ·   ·   ·

He kept a firm grip on Justin's arm as he led him back down the hill to the river, and then after they'd waded into it, he started laughing, but Justin felt like vomiting from the terror he felt.

Justin couldn't look at him because when he did he felt nausea, and an almost uncontrollable anger because of what Todd had done to Carol. His hands were trembling, his body felt numb, and Justin's head seemed to be crammed with horribly confused thoughts.

"Okay, now let's lay out and dry off in the sun," said Todd.

"Oh? Uh, I...Yeah, okay."

"Good boy. Sit down. I said sit down, okay?"

"Uh-huh. Um, yeah," replied Justin, panicking.

"I'm worried about you telling people you saw me here. I can't let that happen," said Todd through clenched teeth.

"Why would I tell anybody? Bet I forget about it in an hour. I see lots of guys naked all the time, and some of them are about the same age as you, and some of them are even older than you. Okay? They're always laying in places along the river. Besides, I got lots of other things to think about. Honest. Like, I'm making a raft with my best friend, and we work on that all the time. Okay?"

Justin hoped that by telling him the lie about seeing many other nude adult males sunning themselves along the river, it would make Todd let him go.

"Hmmm, I don't think you'll forget you saw me."

"I bet I will," said Justin. "But I won't forget about that rabbit y'saw hangin' up in a tree. I've been tryin' to think who I know might've done that. I bet it's gone now. Like some other animal climbed up that tree and ate what was left of that rabbit. Maybe a raccoon. Right?"

"Yeah, maybe."

"A coupla weeks ago, I was over at the old barn with Matt and we saw a dead raccoon with his paw in a trap, so, I guess he starved to death after he couldn't get his paw outta that steel trap."

"Yeah, he must've starved to death. I don't want to talk about crap like that. I want to talk about sex."

"Oh, uh, sure," said Justin, becoming even more tense.

"What's wrong?"

"Huh? Nothing."

"You look scared."

"No. I'm not. I was just thinkin' about that dead raccoon I saw, that's all."

Justin kept picturing Carol viciously ravaged with her dead eyes staring at him, and then he envisioned Todd in the river, washing streaks of her blood off his body. He knew that he was probably only moments away from death, and he still couldn't think of how to get away from Todd.

"Why are you so uptight? Why?" exclaimed Todd.

"Uh, I'm not. Just feeling sorta weird. Like a bit dizzy."

"Don't worry about that, okay? I told you, you'd stop feeling dizzy soon, right?"

"Yeah, y'did."

"I'd really like you to play with my dick when it gets hard again. You'd make me real happy if y'did that, and you'd like to make me feel happy, wouldn't you?"

"I...uh, I don't know."

"Whaddaya mean, y'don't know? It's a simple question! Do y'wanna make me happy or not?"

"Um, I don't wanna see you *un*happy."

"Neither do I, kid. So, I guess that means y'wanna make me happy then, right? Right, Justin?"

"Yeah, um, sure."

"Tell me y'wanna make me happy. C'mon. *Happy*. Say it!"

Justin winced, then began speaking in almost a whisper as he said: "I...I'd like to make...I'd like to make you happy."

"I knew you did," said Todd as he grinned.

Justin was desperately trying to think of some way to stop Todd from killing him. He noticed that Todd occasionally shrugged his shoulders, then rubbed them, and then Justin suddenly thought of something that he hoped would take Todd's mind off sex until he could think of some way to get away from him.

"Uh, Todd?"

"Yeah?"

"It looks like your shoulder muscles are stiff 'cause you keep shruggin' them and also sometimes rubbin' them."

"Yeah, I get stiff muscles in my shoulders a lot every day. I guess it's because of the way I sleep at night, or maybe my bed's either too hard or too soft."

"Well, uh, when my mom or my dad get tight muscles like that in their shoulders, they really like it when I massage them. Like, they're always telling me I'm really good at it, okay? So that'd be a good way for me to make y'feel happy, too. Okay?"

"Hmmm, yeah, okay, then after that, we'll do some fun things."

"I'm really good at massaging. You'll see."

* * * * * ❖••••••❖★❖••••••❖ * * * * *

Todd sat leaning forward with his folded arms resting on his knees, and then after Justin stood behind him, he leaned over and began massaging his shoulders.

"Oh, yeah, mmmmm, I love getting a massage. Mmmmm, that feels so great. Yeah, mmmmmm."

"It'd feel a lot better if y'laid on your stomach, and relaxed while I did it," said Justin.

"Oh, I get it. You're getting horny, aren't you?"

"Huh? Uh, I...oh, yeah, I guess I am. I like rubbing your back and shoulders. Hey, Todd? Are you ticklish?"

"A bit. In some places. Why?"

"I thought I'd stroke your back and your shoulders really lightly with a branch that has real soft leaves on it."

"You horny little bugger. Yeah, that'd really turn me on."

"Yeah? Great! Just a sec," said Justin.

He began selecting a branch as Todd glared at him, and Justin's hands were trembling because of his building rage at what Todd had done to Carol. He knew, however, that he had to try very hard not to let Todd know just how much he hated him, or how scared he was.

He chose a long, thin branch that had soft leaves on it, then Justin broke it off the bush, and then smiled as he said: "Okay, I'll start on your back first, and then you roll over, and I'll do it to your front. If I do it real slow for a long time on your back, then I bet it'll make you feel real, real good."

"Yeah, I'm sure I will."

"Great. So, lay on your stomach," Justin told him.

"Right. Hmmff. There. Mmmmm."

"Okay, I'll start. You like this?"

"Mmmmm, yeah, it feels great," replied Todd, then he heaved a big sigh, and then lowered his head to rest his forehead on his crossed forearms.

"I'll use my hands to massage you for awhile, okay? Then I'll go back to using the branch, okay?"

"Oh, yeah, go for it," said Todd.

"Now close your eyes so you'll be more relaxed, okay? That's it. Oh, yeah, do y'like this?"

"Mmmm, yeah, that feels great."

He continued lightly massaging Todd as he talked to him, then a few minutes later, he slowed his hand movements and slowly stopped touching Todd's back.

"Just relax. Yeah, that's it. Lay still."

"Mmmmmm, your hands feel so good," said Todd.

"Yeah? I'm glad. Just don't fall asleep, okay?"

"Not a chance. But I'm feeling really relaxed. Your hands feel so fucking great. What are you doing?" asked Todd.

"Moving around you to the other side."

Justin stood up, feeling so scared. His thoughts whirled and his heart pounded heavily, making his ears ring as he looked down at the ground close to the big bush that he'd broken a branch off.

Moments later, he hurried back from that bush, knelt close beside Todd, and then after taking a deep breath, he leaned over, placed his hands on Todd's upper back, and began slowly massaging him.

"Does this feel okay?"

"Mmmm, yeah. Yeah, slow like that. Hey! You stopped! Good, you started again. Yeah, I know what you're up to, you little tease. Mmmmmmmm, yeah."

"It'll be a surprise when I stop, and then start again, and you won't know when," said Justin, then he forced a laugh.

"Teaser. Mmmmm, I like it though. Yeah, mmmm, you sexy kid."

"I like massaging you. This feels really good, doesn't it?"

"Yeah, it does," replied Todd. "Oh, yeah, mmmmm, and we're gonna have so much fun. If you hadn't been so stoned before, then we could've played with each other's dicks. But fucking you'll be better.

I can hardly wait. I'm going to...Huh! Hmfff! Aaaaaaa! Ohhhh! Hmnnfff! Uhhhhh!"

* * * * * ❖•••••❖ ★ ❖•••••❖ * * * * *

Justin sat in the room, staring down at his shoes. He could hear people talking somewhere near him, but he couldn't quite hear what they were saying because his ears seemed stuffed.

He got up slowly with his eyes closed, then knowing the window was behind him, he turned around, walked over to it, and slowly opened his eyes to look out at the landscape.

His heart leapt when he saw Star standing out in the field, and he wanted to run to her, leap up onto her back, race to the horizon, and then leap off the edge of the world into a very long dream.

Star shook her head and trotted back and forth along the side of the fence, then she galloped out into the field, made a wide circle, and then galloped back toward the fence.

Justin began to recall the last time he rode her, and then he panicked when he envisioned seeing Todd at the river. Words tumbled through his mind, and he could hear many voices in the room saying: "It's okay. You had to do it. Are you all right? Justin, it's okay. You're okay." He then imagined seeing red stains on his hands, and feeling wet specks on his face.

He stared out the window, and saw Carol staring at him with her body ravaged and her clothes ripped. Justin slowly looked up at the sky and saw a bird gliding slowly by, and as his thoughts lifted up to it, he felt that he could see what the bird was seeing.

The land sped by beneath him, getting closer to him at one moment, then far away in the next, as he swooped and often soared while flying toward the ridge. He passed over it, and saw the river coming up to him, then spreading his wings, he glided very slowly close the surface of the water toward the place he had sat with Todd.

Nearing that area, his stomach began trembling and his thoughts began slowly swirling, and then getting even closer, his thoughts picked up speed, whirling and making him dizzy. Justin felt a scream rising up in his throat as his gaze swooped closer to where he'd knelt beside Todd and massaged him.

He closed his eyes, and then he could see only the area close to himself and Todd, brightly lit, but the light circling them, faded into a black void. Justin saw himself sliding his hands over Todd's back, and he could feel his mouth moving as he spoke to him, then he saw himself lifting his hands slowly away for a few moments, then lowering them back down on Todd, over and over again.

The reality of what had actually happened shot back to him with horrifying clarity. Justin had turned away from Todd, stood, leaned over, and after leaning back up again, he'd turned back to face him, and then knelt again to begin slowly massaging Todd's back.

He tensed up as he saw himself raise his arms high above his head, and then his recollection of what he'd done made his fingernails cut into the palms of his clenched hands as he watched himself pause and look down in both terror and rage at Todd.

He screamed, and everyone in the room rushed to him as Justin remembered his hands rushing downward, then red blobs and drops flew into the air and onto his face and body.

Jason gripped the boulder in his hands, and he kept raising it high and slamming it down until he'd almost completely battered Todd's head into hideous, gory pieces.

Justin was still screaming as he tore away from the hands that held him, and then he ran out of the house, and toward Star. She whinnied when she saw him running toward her with tears streaming down his face, so, Star trotted quickly over to meet him.

He climbed the wooden fence, leapt onto her back, and after Star whirled around, she galloped off into the field. He tried to get her to change direction as he screamed and cried, but Star refused, and instead, raced toward the river.

She began galloping slower until she came to a stop at the edge of the river, then Star stepped carefully down the riverbank, waded into the river, and then she began moving slowly through the water toward her destination.

Justin bent his head back to look up at the sky as he wept and yelled at the clouds that didn't care about him because they had to carry their ghosts to eternity.

He scrutinized the clouds, then after not seeing Todd's features in any of the clouds, Justin panicked when he thought that Todd wasn't dead, but was instead looking for him so that he could kill him.

His head felt heavy and crowded with pain, then he hung his head, and wept, with his eyes tightly closed, then Star stopped wading through the water, and after she snorted and whinnied, Justin slowly raised his head, opened his eyes, and then gaped ahead.

He became aware that he and Star were in the river and that the lower part of his legs were underwater. Justin fell forward, wrapped his arms around Star's neck, and then he burst into tears again.

He hugged her as he wept, and his swollen, aching heart began slowly deflating as his painfully confused thoughts seemed to separate and float slowly away like the clouds above him.

Star had taken him back to where he'd been so happy. She'd waded through the river and come to a stop in front of his raft that she had watched him and Matt constructing.

Justin slipped off her back and felt his clothes become heavy as the water soaked them as he waded closer to the raft, then he leaned over and touched it.

He then leaned back up and heaved a big sigh before he turned around tried very hard to smile for Star while wading back to her, and then laid his head against her shoulder.

He took a deep breath, then led Star up out of the river, and then after he'd climbed onto her back, she began slowly trotting back to Justin's home.

He cast a wistful glance at the river they were passing and he knew that the raft would lay by the riverbank to rot away; never to carry him, Matt, nor any of his other once carefree friends.

The sound of children's laughter as they played and swam had been silenced after they'd become aware that their almost nude bodies could be fodder for a lurking sexual predator, now that Carol had been raped and murdered.

The beauty of the landscape around Justin and the other children would slowly fade, now that adulthood was being thrust so rudely and too soon upon them.

The trees would never again be places to build imaginary, magical forts in, nor would their branches be high springboards to dive from, or be the exciting steps up to great heights that, once conquered, rewarded one with marvelous views of the landscape for miles around.

Instead, Justin would learn very soon, that trees should simply be things that stood unnoticed when not being harvested for lumber, except for a few weeks each year, when many of them flaunted their magnificent autumn colors.

Innocence had been cruelly torn into tiny pieces to flutter up, and then disappear among the slowly drifting clouds that Justin would never again gaze up at to discern the ghosts being carried beyond the horizon to what brokenhearted and disillusioned Justin now believed was a hopeless eternity.

The End

THE NOVELLA:

Eyes Of
Fire And Water

PART ONE

★

TROY
An Extraordinary Gypsy Boy

At night, when the owl had swooped soundlessly down to clutch its prey, then winged silently up again to perch on a high branch, it had seen many glowing eyes at various levels along the ground and through bushes.

One night, the owl sat wide-eyed in the moonlight, satiated for the moment, scanning the land below while deciding which small pair of glowing eyes would make the next tasty meal, when suddenly, two glowing eyes rose and fell over hill crests. But they were much larger eyes, casting an even brighter glow, lighting trees in its path as the darting black form sped closer.

As the rushing, growling figure whisked by, the owl gaped down in time to see the sudden, tiny glint of two eyes in the belly of the quickly moving black beast. The tiny, dark eyes had opened slightly and quite briefly, then closed again for perhaps hours.

When they'd opened, only the owl and Lena had seen the dark eyes for just over a second, but she had noticed because she'd been cooing down at little Troy while Yuri clenched his teeth and gripped the steering wheel as he sped through the night toward home.

Cradled in her arms was what Lena felt was a darling bundle of joy, which of course, all babies are. But eventually, some people would react strangely to something they'd see in his eyes.

That something would cause Troy to be unreasonably hated by many men, however, there would be many women who would find that mysterious spark in his eyes quite pleasantly stimulating.

Yuri's lips clamped tightly together in a downward curve; his jaw was tense, and he was breathing forcefully through his nose as he stared at the road ahead and listened to Lena cooing to Troy.

For the past year, Craig MacIver, the handsome, rich, forty-year-old man whom drove up from the city to his country home for occasional two-week visits, had been too friendly with Lena, and now Yuri felt certain that Troy wasn't his son.

Yuri was a very jealous and possessive young man, and his doubts about paternity were fueled by his brother, Oleg, whom had never liked Lena, so, now Yuri was livid at the thought of having to support what he believed to be the bastard son of a man he was extremely jealous of.

Troy, at this point in his life, wasn't able to sense that the man driving him and his mother home had such hatred for him, but his first inkling of that would arise very soon when he would learn that Yuri wouldn't hold him, and most often, wouldn't look at him.

Yuri pulled up in front of the dilapidated shack, slammed the car door, strutted over to the shack, then stopped when he realized he had to continue feigning delight at having a newborn.

He then held the door open for Lena, and smiled as she passed him on her way inside. Yuri then told her that he was going to run next door to announce the arrival home of his second son, and then as Lena sat down, smiling and holding little Troy, Yuri strode over to the farmhouse to speak with his brother and their mother, Vera.

.   .   .   .   .   ❖••••❖★❖••••❖   .   .   .   .   .

"The bitch is back and she's got the bastard with her," said Yuri.

"You should've strangled it when she wasn't looking. Sit down and cool your heels," said his brother, Oleg. "I'll get you a drink. She can bloody well wait. She thinks that because she grew up speaking mostly Romany, that she's some kinda rich, hoity-toity bitch from Rome. Fuck her."

"I'm tellin' y'one thing. I'm not about to raise him," said Yuri.

"Now boys, I'm sure you can think of some way to ease the burden. Fatal accidents happen all the time," said Vera.

"Yeah, and we'll make it happen soon," Oleg said with a smirk.

"She's lookin' at it like it was more important than *my* son. She never had that look when she had *him*. Bet Lena thinks he's better than Mark," said Yuri, scowling.

"She's probably gonna spoil him rotten, too. Bet she's tryin' to stuff both tits in his mouth right now. Hey, that's not a bad idea. Smother the brat," said Oleg, then he laughed.

Lena peered out the window through the darkness at the lighted window of the old farmhouse, and she saw Yuri and Oleg sitting at the kitchen table.

She knew how much Oleg hated her, and she felt sure that he'd do his best to keep Yuri away for most of the night, so, Lena sighed, then smiled down at Troy.

* * * * * ❖•••••❖★❖•••••❖ * * * * *

Three weeks had passed by, and Lena hadn't expected Oleg and Vera to acknowledge Troy, but Yuri had started spending every day until late each night with his mother and brother.

Lena felt that perhaps he was having a problem adjusting to the birth of another baby so soon after their first child.

* * * * * ❖•••••❖★❖•••••❖ * * * * *

She was much more intelligent than Yuri, and she had a genetic gift that she'd passed on to Troy, and part of that gift was the ability to sense danger.

For the past several days, Lena had been trying to ignore the feeling of brewing danger, which she'd dismissed as only a natural reaction to Yuri's quite often dark moods, however, this night she felt sure that something terrible was about to happen.

She tried to concentrate on the outfit that she was knitting for Mark, whom Yuri had taken with him to visit Oleg. Lena had told him that Mark would sleep through the visit because it was so late in the evening, but Yuri had insisted, as usual, because he felt so proud of Mark and loved having him nearby.

Suddenly, she raised her chin, sniffed the air, then gasped when she detected the scent of both gasoline and paint thinner. Never one to panic, no matter how dire the situation, Lena calmly set down her knitting, and hummed as she swaddled Troy in a blanket.

She cradled him in her left arm as she began turning off all the lights, and then she stood by the door, peering out the window beside it. When she saw two dark figures disappear around the rear of the shack, she quickly opened the door, stepped outside, closed the door, and then hurried away under the cover of darkness toward the road.

Standing close to the road was the shed that tools and chopped wood were stored in. Lena entered the shed, closed the door, and then looked out the small window that faced the shack.

Moments later, she saw a burst of light at one side of the shack, then within moments, the fire quickly spread all around it. The flames grew into a raging fire, and then Lena smiled, looked down at Troy, and said: "Why, it's a firelight celebration of your arrival. Yes, it *is*, and it was *all* planned by your daddy and your uncle."

Lena saw flames on the ground moving away from the rear of the shack, then she heard excited shouts as the flames picked up speed until they nibbled at the base of the barn.

The flames then suddenly swept up the side of the barn to the roof, and then began spreading over it. Lena knew how devastating the barn fire would be to Oleg and his mother, and she watched them and Yuri struggling to lead horses and prod cattle out to safety, and then they stood waving their arms in grief at seeing the old, wooden barn lost to the raging fire.

Lena smiled as she looked back down at Troy, and said: "And Troy, it's turned out to be a *surprise* party! Aren't you excited and pleased? Mommy's *very* pleased, sweetheart."

She slowly opened the shed door, and stepped outside after a crowd had gathered to watch the fire. Lena smiled because the loss of their meager possessions could easily be replaced by her friends, and she was quite talented at sewing and knitting clothes, or altering those donated to her.

She could also do wonders in the preparation of meals with very little money, and with sparse utensils, as well. Lena and her parents had been able to live reasonably well through the Great Depression on just pennies a day.

Now, three years after WW2, with more job opportunities because the national economy was improving at an impressive rate, Lena felt certain that by the 1950s, she and Yuri would be living in a much better home on their own farmland.

Lena knew that now Yuri and his brother would have to sell the livestock and find jobs in town until they earned enough to build a new barn and replace all the farm equipment that had been lost in the fire they'd set.

She cuddled Troy in her arms as she pushed through the crowd until she was standing beside Yuri, Oleg, and their mother, Vera, then Lena told her bewildered husband that she'd taken a stroll, and how awful it was to return to such an unfortunate incident.

A few months later, when Yuri raised his hand to strike her, Lena astonished him by slamming him back against the wall, grabbing a butcher knife, and holding it to his throat.

That was his last attempt at physically abusing her because he was terrified enough to know, just as Lena had promised him with a smile, that she'd kill him while he slept, and not care if she'd be executed for his murder.

.   .   .   .   . ❖••••••❖★❖••••••❖ . .   .   .   .

Yuri's dislike for Troy intensified when neighbors passed by his new home, which was a converted stable, and they'd unintentionally disregard his firstborn son to marvel at the color of Troy's hair.

At first glance, his hair looked golden blond, then letting one's gaze linger, Troy's hair shone with hues of orange and vermillion. His hair color seemed to reflect the flickering flames of the great fire that had been set with the intent to kill him and his mother.

While nearing his third birthday, the varying flame-like hues in his hair softened to a light brown. By the age of seven, the color of his hair became very dark brown like the burned timbers of the barn that Yuri and Oleg had accidentally set on fire.

His eyes were an even darker brown and Lena was startled one day when she noticed a glint of bright red in Troy's eyes. She'd only seen that red glint for about a second when Troy had turned his head to look out the window, but Lena had wondered if that sudden red glint meant that his eyes would eventually change to a lighter shade of brown.

Moments later, a bird fluttered down onto the outside sill of the window, and when Troy turned his head to look at the bird, there was a sudden glint of very bright blue in his eyes. Lena wondered why she hadn't noticed before that Troy's eyes had occasional flashes of both bright red and blue in his eyes.

In the following weeks, the bright red and blue glints in Troy's eyes happened more often, and then Lena smiled while thinking that the bright, colorful glints in his eyes seemed to reflect fire and water.

When she brought that to Yuri's attention, he'd sneered while saying that the sudden glints of bright red and blue in his eyes meant that Troy had the mind of a violently insane criminal.

Lena told him that was a ridiculous assumption to make, and she said that Troy could never have an evil thought, then she became even angrier when Yuri said that Troy would be thought of as a freak if more people noticed weird flashes of color in his eyes.

* * * * * ❖•••••❖★❖•••••❖ * * * * *

Yuri felt pleased when his friends and neighbors began showing as much attention to Mark as they did to Troy, but he became quite angry whenever Craig MacIver dropped by to dote on Troy.

Craig told Lena that he intended to bequeath Troy a large portion of his estate. Unfortunately for Craig, news of his planned gift of money to Troy reached the ears of Craig's wife and her lover who were acquaintances of Yuri and Oleg.

A few weeks later, Craig's body was found floating in the lake, with a deep gash in the back of his head. The local police determined that Craig had gone fishing out on the lake again, then he'd probably struck the back of his head on a part of his rowboat when he'd lost his balance after he had stood up in his boat for some reason.

The deep gash in the back of his head had really been caused by a tire iron in the hands of his wife's lover after he, Oleg and Yuri had beaten and kicked him unconscious.

Yuri and Oleg had then rowed Oleg's boat far out into the lake, towing the rowboat that Craig always used when he went fishing, then after dumping Craig's body out of Oleg's boat, they untied Craig's rowboat, and let it drift away.

Yuri had then felt sure that Troy would remain as poor as the rest of his family, however, Troy would eventually enrage his father even more by proving that his future could never be controlled by Yuri.

He'd inherited his mother's sixth sense, which, much to the chagrin of Yuri, would become much stronger than Lena's, and Troy's developing psychic powers, as well as his artistic talent, would draw the attention of Hanson and Tanya Willoughby.

He would meet Tanya a month after his twelfth birthday through his odd, humorous friend, Howard, whom was Tanya's nephew.

· · · · · · ❖•••••❖ ★ ❖•••••❖ · · · · · ·

Two years after Troy was born, Lena gave birth to another son who resembled Troy, and she named him, Sasha. Troy would sit on the floor, happily looking up at Sasha in the arms of Yuri whom would also have Mark sitting on his lap.

Yuri had never smiled at, nor held Troy since the time he'd been born, and he often slapped or knocked Troy over whenever Lena wasn't present, as well as making continual snide remarks about him to Lena.

By the age of eight, Troy proved to have much higher intelligence than other children his age, and his schoolteacher told Lena that there was a small school for gifted children in the city. He said that if she could afford to send Troy to that special school, then the local school officials would have him transferred there.

Lena phoned her parents in the city, told them about the special school, then she was elated when her father told her that the lease on their apartment would be ending in a few months, and that instead of renewing it, he'd look for an apartment close to that special school.

A few weeks later, her father called to tell her that he'd been able to rent a small house within two blocks of the school. After thanking her parents, Lena spoke to Troy's teacher, whom then arranged with the local school board to have Troy enrolled in the school for gifted children, starting in September.

Yuri felt pleased that Troy would only be home on weekends and school vacations, but it took Lena several weeks to persuade him to pay for Troy's bus fare to and from the city, as well as giving him an allowance of a dollar per week.

Her parents were so pleased to have Troy living with them, and Troy felt even more pleased to be safely away from the constant verbal and physical abuse from his father.

Part Two

★

Uh-Oh!
Here Comes Howard!

Troy was nearing twelve years old, and about to become close friends with Howard, a boy he'd been avoiding for years. Howard lived just up the street from Troy, and he was ridiculed by all the other boys because of his outrageous lies.

At ten years old, Howard began coming to school dressed in various, very colorful Chinese clothing, and he told everyone that he was the crown prince of China, and he demanded that all the other boys kneel and bow before him.

Of course, the other boys refused to bow to Howard even though he constantly threatened to have his palace guards cut off their heads.

A few months later, Howard began dressing in purple and red costumes while telling everyone that he was the grandson of Tsar Nicholas of Russia. Some of the boys were convinced that Howard was a Russian royal because he'd learned to speak a dozen Russian words, but all the other boys at school told him that if he were really Tsar Nicholas' grandson, he would be dead.

In the following year, Howard pretended to be many characters, including the nephew of Queen Liliuokalani of Hawaii. He then told everyone at school that he was the secret inventor of bubble gum, and then not long after that, he said he was the world's greatest and youngest baseball player.

Then four months ago, Howard decided that when he was in his teen years, he'd become one of the greatest actors in Hollywood. When he read that Kabuki was performed by males, and many of them played female roles, then Howard felt certain that he could play the part of a girl better than any other boy in the world.

That's when he began acting more effeminate than any girl in school and the entire neighborhood. All the boys at school were both astounded and very annoyed by Howard's flamboyant effeminacy, which he played quite convincingly.

He was also rather handy with his fists, as any boy could attest to, after trying to bully him because of the way Howard acted and spoke. Associating with him was considered taboo by the other, supposedly tougher boys, and Troy also avoided him.

Troy was as convinced as most of the other boys at school that Howard's latest facade was indeed his true self, and Howard felt very pleased that he'd convinced just about everyone that he could be more effeminate than any girl.

Adding to his odd, eccentric affectations, Howard seemed to be rather rude and obnoxious, and that was why Troy avoided him like a plague. Troy, however, was going to attract even stranger people, and Howard would be the first.

Howard wanted to make sure he won Troy's friendship, so, one day, when he saw him half a block away, walking home from school, Howard rushed to catch up with him.

"Troy! Hey, Troy! Wait up!"

Troy looked back, and when he saw Howard, he groaned, and began walking faster.

"Hey, slow down! I live half a block away from you, right? So, I'll walk home with you!"

"No thanks!" Troy yelled back to him.

"Oh, I know why! You belong to that gang of jerks who hate me, and *you* constantly ignore me, too! Even though we've always been in the same classroom! Well, I'm going home for lunch and I'm going to walk with you! Fuck them! I, darling, don't give a damn what they think of me because they're jealous! I'm prettier than them! Fuck, darling, I'm prettier than Wendy Lee Lawson! I can sing higher than her, too! Hey! Wait up!"

"No! Bugger off!" shouted Troy, walking even faster.

"Hah! I can walk just as fast as you, so, it'll look like we're walking home together, anyway! So there!"

"Jeez!" exclaimed Troy, scowling.

"Your parents are older than my mother!"

"They're my gramma and grampa. My mom and dad live out west of here. About a hundred miles, okay?"

"Well, I don't have a father! He's dead!"

"Oh, yeah? That's awful. Did he die from your shouting?"

"No! The Nazis killed him in the war! Hey, and the reason I'm shouting is because you're walking too fast, so, you can't hear what I'm saying!" shouted Howard.

"Yeah? That's because I'm trying to lose you, okay?"

"Why? Oh, I get it. Your jerk friends don't like me and they'll hate you for talking to me."

"Jeez! Y'know they hate you, and they know I don't like you, either, so, they'd laugh and stuff if they saw me talking to you."

"Are you scared of them? They don't scare me one bit. My sister told me to tell them to fuck off, and if they don't, I beat them all up, so, now they just swear at me. But that's them, and you're you. I think you're very interesting, besides being really smart, and I like the way your eyes sometimes have flashes of bright red and bright blue in them."

"So what? I bet there's lots of people with almost black eyes that reflect colors in them. Just like feathers on starlings do."

"I've never seen anyone else with black eyes that reflect colors like yours do. Anyway, that's just one of the reasons why I'd like to be friends with you."

"Well, I don't wanna be friends with *you*!"

"Why not?" asked Howard, smirking.

"First off, you don't like most of the things I like, and you don't like my friends, and you don't...Aw, forget it. There's just too many other things I'm sure we don't have in common."

"So what? You can *still* be my friend."

"No! Bugger off!"

"Why? Wait up! Hey! Everybody's going to think we're friends, anyway, because I'm going to follow you everywhere you go! Troy? Wait up! My birthday party's this weekend and I'm inviting all the other guys and you, too."

"They won't come to your birthday party, and I won't, either."

"Oh, no? Sure they will, and so will you. Lots of sandwiches and cake and pop and ice cream, so, all the guys'll be there for sure. Just wait and see. Besides, Wendy Lee's coming, too, and they'll all want to be around her. I just don't know why, darling. I mean, I'm much prettier than she is. I could show them I am, but my mother and all the teachers won't let me wear dresses to school. Much better dresses than Wendy Lee'd wear. She has absolutely no taste."

"Dresses? Jeez! You're *really* weird!"

"I'm not *weird*, darling. I'm dramatic," said Howard, smiling.

"Don't call me darling, okay?"

"Why not? Movie stars call each other darling and I'm going to be a big movie star when I grow up. I can act and I can dance, too. I can also sing, and I can play the harmonica. Well, a bit, but I really don't like harmonicas, anyway."

"So what? I don't care if y'can fly planes. And I can't come to your birthday party on Saturday because I go home to see my parents every weekend," said Troy.

"Not *this* weekend. My mother's already told your grandmother about my birthday party, and she said you'll be going."

"She did? Jeez!"

"Here's my house. I'm going in now. I'll see you at school after lunch hour. Ta-ta, darling," said Howard.

"Don't call me darling! Jeez!" cried Troy, stomping on home.

At afternoon recess, Troy was just about to walk over to a group of his friends, then he stopped when he saw Howard strut over to them, then about two minutes later, he strutted back to the girls he'd been talking with previously.

Troy hurried over to the boys, then asked them: "Hey, what'd Howard want?"

"He asked us to come to his birthday party," said Joel.

"Yeah? You're kidding. You guys aren't going to go, are you?"

"Sure, why not? I'd love t'see what's inside that huge mansion. He's gonna have lots of stuff there. Oh, and hey, he's giving us all a gift, too," said Jimmy.

"Really? For everybody?" asked Troy.

"Yeah, he's getting birthday gifts from his relatives and he's giving them to us. He says he knows he'll hate his gifts anyway, and his mother's rich, so, he doesn't care. Howard said you're going to start hanging around with him, too."

"No way! I hate him!" exclaimed Troy.

"So do we, but why don't *you* be friendly with him? You can get to meet his big sister and she might show you her boobs. Bobby's big brother said she likes to show 'em to guys she knows, so, if you're friends with Howard, she'll maybe show 'em to *you*, then you can tell us what they look like. Okay? Maybe she'll show 'em to us when she knows you're friends with us. Get it?"

"Yeah? Jeez! I didn't know *that!* But all he talks about is girl stuff, and he thinks he's even prettier than Wendy Lee Lawson, so, no way I wanna hang around with him all the time," Troy told them.

"Aw, c'mon. Pinky's boyfriend's kid brother, Sheldon, works at the drug store, right?"

"Yeah, so?" asked Troy.

"Okay, so, he always gives free Cokes and sometimes ice cream cones and chocolate bars to Howard's friends and if you're friends with Howard and Sheldon, then you can steal stuff from the store when they're not looking. Okay?"

"Mr. Dobson'd be watching, though."

"No, he won't. He leaves the store long before it closes, and old Tom locks up after, so, when he goes to the stockroom, you can grab some chocolate bars. Howard says he does it all the time."

"But I can't grab tons of chocolate bars because then how do I get them out of the store if Sheldon's watching?" Troy asked them.

"Bet Sheldon steals 'em, too. Just grab a few of 'em for awhile, then after maybe a coupla weeks, start taking more. They keep lots of boxes of 'em downstairs in the stockroom, so, you can put lots of 'em in your pockets when you're downstairs using the bathroom."

"Well, I don't know," said Troy. "What if I get caught?"

"Y'won't! Don't be so chicken!" exclaimed Jimmy.

"I'm *not* chicken! But Sheldon's over eighteen, and if he saw me stealing, he'd beat the crap outta me."

"So, steal things when he's not around, dummy," Joel told him.

"Aw, heck. Okay, I'll start talking to Howard. Jeez!"

The next day, he saw Howard a few yards ahead of him, so, Troy ran to catch up with him, then grimaced as he exclaimed: "Hi!"

"Troy! Hi! You wanna come to my house and have a Coke?"

"Yeah, okay," he replied, forcing a smile.

"Good! We can have cookies, too. There'd *better* be cookies, or *else*. Mother was supposed to buy more."

They entered Howard's huge home and Troy gawked around at the many strings of colored paper lanterns, paper butterflies and birds hanging from the ceilings, and long swags of brightly colored material sweeping up and down around every room.

He then gaped at the big, black dog sitting on one of the couches, wearing a small, frilly dress as it bared its teeth, then Troy frowned as he said: "He looks mad. Does he bite?"

"Nope. He's just smiling. Mother?...Mother!...I'm home!"

"I thought she had a job."

"She does, but she owns several companies, so, she's always home before I get back from school. Mother! Come *here!*"

Troy heard quick footsteps clattering down the stairs, then he gaped at Howard's mother when she appeared in the living room. She was a beautiful woman, and her obviously long blonde hair was swept up into a marvelous style. But what Troy found so unusual was her formal, late-afternoon attire.

She had on a purple, strapless evening gown that had huge, magenta bows on it from the waist down, and she was holding a very big, bright blue, feathered fan.

"Good! You've changed! Mother, this is Troy."

"Hel-lohhhhh, Troy. So *nice* to meet you at last, darling. This is that handsome boy I told you I see sometimes, Howard. You have such big, beautiful brown eyes, Troy. So dark and so enchanting. Such marvelous mystery in them. I'm so pleased that Howard finally invited you to our home."

"Uh, hi," said Troy, shaking the blue-gloved hand she held out.

"My! Such a wonderful, firm handshake! It shows you have a politely assertive, confident nature! Oh, yes! One can usually tell immediately by a handshake what type of..."

"Mother, please! We don't need to hear all about the meaning of handshakes, okay? It could go on for hours! Now please get us some Cokes! And are there any cookies left?"

"Oh! I'll dash and see! I'm sure there are! Back soo-oon!"

"Is she going to a party?" asked Troy.

"No, she always dresses like that when she's not driving her employees mad. Did you like her dress?"

"Uh, well, I guess so. It's really fancy."

"I look so much better in it. Do you wanna try it on sometime?"

"No! Jeez! I don't wear dresses!"

"You don't? I don't see why not because they're far nicer than boys' clothes. Mother!"

"She's, um, well...she's very pretty," said Troy.

"And *very* nice. Mother!...Well, it's about time!"

"Thank you, ma'am," said Troy, taking a glass of Coca Cola.

"You're so welcome, darling. Have a cookie. Come-come!"

"Mother! Is that *all* the cookies we have?"

"Yes. Oops on me! I'm sorry, but I forgot to pick up more."

"You're just *too* forgetful! Come here! Bend down!"

"Yes, Howard. Oh, dear. I don't like that look. No, not at all."

She leaned over and puckered her lips, then Howard turned his head away from her.

"No kiss! You forgot the cookies! Don't *ever* do that again! C'mon upstairs to my room, Troy."

"Uh, yeah, sure, okay. Bye, Mrs. Chaplin."

"Have a marvelous time upstairs, now. I'm awfully sorry about the cookies, darlings."

.   .   .   .   . ❖•••••❖★❖•••••❖ .   .   .   .   .

After leading Troy upstairs, Howard smirked as he decided to take him into his elder sister's room, instead of his own, so, he opened the door of Pinky's bedroom suite, and then Troy followed him inside.

He gaped when he saw what he assumed was Howard's bedroom, which looked like it belonged to a girl. On the bed that was covered in a frilly bedspread, there were several different sizes and colors of embroidered and fringed pillows.

An antique doll sat on the wide windowsill, and standing in a row along the top of one of the chests of drawers, were four little dolls wearing native costumes of the countries they represented.

"Lots of dolls," Troy commented as he sat down on the bed.

"Of course there are. When I decided to show everyone that I could act the part of a girl far better than any girl could, then I changed the decor of my bedroom to look more feminine than any other girl could possibly have. Frills everywhere, fluffy bedspread and pillow cases, and so on. I think I've accomplished what I set out to do. I had more dolls than these, but unfortunately I left a dozen in the bathtub one day, and they drowned. I hate dead dolls."

"I hate dolls, dead or alive," said Troy.

He looked at the fancy pillows on the bed, then Troy frowned as he picked up the one that had "Pinky" embroidered on it. He laid it back down with the other pillows, then looked around the room again, and then looked at one of the partly open closet doors.

Troy saw dresses on hangers, and a few pairs of different colors of high heeled shoes on the floor of the closet. He then looked at the other chest of drawers, and saw a big, silver-framed photo of a very beautiful, smiling young woman wearing a tiara and holding a big bouquet of flowers.

Troy felt sure that the photo was of Howard's elder sister, Pinky, after she'd won a beauty pageant, and that this was *her* bedroom.

"Hah! This is your sister's bedroom!"

"No, it's not," said Howard.

"Jeez! What a liar!"

"I *never* lie! Okay, so, this really *is* hers. I didn't want you to see mine because I didn't have time to tidy it up."

"I thought your maids did that."

"No, they clean all the other rooms, but my mother makes *me* tidy up my own room. She can be so cruel."

"She should tell you not to lie, too."

"I just told you I never lie."

"Yeah? Baloney!"

"Hmmmm. Well, think what you want, then."

Howard felt miffed because Troy had seen through that lie, so, he decided to tell him another lie that would sound so true, it'd boggle Troy's mind. While they talked about school, Howard was desperately trying to think up a lie that would both shock and deeply impress Troy. A few moments later, he felt triumphant after he'd thought of a very big lie to tell Troy.

"By the way, Troy, I felt so shocked when you thought I'd actually lied to you. It was just sort of an excuse because I didn't want you to be completely devastated if you saw how messy my bedroom is."

"So what? I wouldn't've cared because I've seen very, very messy rooms before."

"Not as bad as mine, I bet. Anyway, now that you think I lied to you, I guess you won't believe other things I tell you."

"Not if it's the truth," said Troy.

"I told you I never lie. But I bet if I tell you something else right now, you'd be so shocked and you'd think I was telling you another lie. But it isn't. Honest and truly."

"Okay, then tell me. I won't be shocked."

Howard felt sure that his next lie would make him sound more sexually sophisticated than Troy and all the other boys at school and in the entire neighborhood.

"Do you have a heart condition?" asked Howard.

"Huh? No, I don't."

"I see. Have you ever tried to slash your wrists after you've been told something very shocking?"

"I'd never do that, no matter how shocking something was that I was told," said Troy, frowning.

"So, you're saying you haven't tried to commit suicide before after you've heard shocking things."

"No, I haven't."

"Uh-huh, I see. Then how about nervous breakdowns? Have you ever had one after you'd heard something very, *very* shocking?"

"No, and I don't think I'm the type of person who'd ever have a nervous breakdown."

"You're sure?" asked Howard.

"Yeah, I am."

"I had a feeling you were strong enough to withstand any shock to your nervous system, so, I've decided to tell you something that'd shock the average person into heart failure, or even worse."

"Jeez! It sounds really serious."

"To some, yes, but I'm used to very shocking things happening around me all the time. That's why I'm sure nothing could ever shock me. Okay, now are you ready for what I'm going to tell you?"

"Sure, go ahead."

"Okay, before I tell you my shocking secret, I'll start off by telling you that I have many uncles, but very few of them are actually related to me. You see, my mother wants me to call them my uncles when she brings them home to fuck her."

"To *fuck* her?" asked Troy, incredulous.

"Of course. I've peeked into her bedroom lots of times and seen them doing that, and in all sorts of ways, too."

"Jeez! That's amazing!" exclaimed Troy.

Howard felt so pleased that he'd shocked Troy by telling him the lie about seeing his mother having sex on many occasions. Now he felt sure that Troy would be even more impressed when he told him the biggest lie that he'd just thought of a few minutes ago.

"I'm so relieved that you didn't pass out when I told you that about my mother," said Howard. "I'm now sure I can tell you the biggest and most shocking secret, and I won't have to worry about you committing suicide or having a heart attack. Wait! What am I thinking? If I tell you my secret, I might shock you so badly that you could die! Are you absolutely sure you're strong enough both mentally and emotionally to hear my most shocking secret?"

"I'm sure I am because I'm still okay after you told me what your mother does with all those men," said Troy.

"Well, okay, then. You do know that men produce semen during sexual intercourse?"

"Yeah, I know that, dummy. You produce semen at puberty."

"I bet you've never seen it, though," said Howard.

"No, but I know it's to get a woman pregnant."

"Everyone knows that, but I see it all the time."

"You do? When?"

"That's my big secret."

"Really? You mean you've reached puberty?"

"No, of course not, but I see semen all the time because I'm having an affair with my uncle."

"*What?*" exclaimed Troy, wide-eyed.

"Shocking, isn't it? Are you going to have a heart attack?"

"No! But jeez! I didn't know you were having an affair with your uncle. So, um, that means you have sex with him all the time, then?"

"Of course not! I'm not a homosexual. I'm an actor. Only homosexuals have sex with each other."

"But I thought...But how? What I mean is, I thought if you were having an affair with your uncle, that meant you were...uh, well, like, you know, doing something sexual with him."

"There *is* something sexual between us, in a way. You see, the reason I asked you if you'd ever seen semen was because my uncle can't control when his semen will suddenly appear."

"Jeez, that's too bad. I guess it's sort of like how some kids wet the bed at night," said Troy.

"Oh, but worse. It happens at any time of the day to my uncle, and when it happens while he's visiting us, then I have to run and get a broom and start hitting all the bubbles to break them before they float up all over the ceiling and on the walls and furniture. It's lucky that we have five brooms so that I can get help sometimes breaking all the bubbles that float out of his shirt cuffs and his collar and out of the cuffs of his pants and so many other places on him."

"Does that happen a lot?" asked Troy, wide-eyed.

"All the time," lied Howard. "That's the sexual part of our affair because he has an orgasm when all his semen bubbles float out of him, and then many times they fall down all over me, too."

"Yeah? All over you? Jeez! Is it icky, or what?"

"No, it's slippery. You know there's millions of seeds in sperm, right? Well, each seed is enclosed in a bubble, so, millions of colored bubbles of many sizes drift out. It's quite spectacular. They float everywhere around the room, and if you're there at the time he has one of his accidental orgasms, all those bubbles cover you from head to toe, and that's how I get all slippery. The bubbles have to be slippery to get inside a woman, but only if he's lying on top of her at the time he has one of his orgasms. So, that's why I call him 'Uncle Slippery' sometimes."

"Guess y'*would* if he gets people all slippery like that."

"Sometimes when the bubbles start, he has time to run to the nearest bathroom, then he takes a shower with all his clothes on before the bubbles start floating up everywhere and all around the place. That's why he calls them: 'Bubble Troubles,'" said Howard.

"Yeah, I guess he *would* call them that. I never knew that some guys had that problem."

"Now you know why girls feel so lucky that they don't produce semen when they're in puberty. But they have to keep buying bigger and bigger bras if they're the types of girls who grow really big breasts. My sister has big breasts, and I've been thinking that I might decide to grow big breasts, too."

"Boys can't grow breasts, dummy," said Troy.

"*I* might. After all, I have nipples, but if I can't grow breasts, then I can wear falsies. I wear them now whenever I wear one of my mother's dresses. Wanna see me wear one now?"

"No, I gotta go home soon."

"I'll put one on the next time you're here. Maybe next time my sister might be home, and then I'll ask her to show you her breasts, okay? Have you seen a girl's breasts, yet?" asked Howard.

"Uh, no, I haven't. Not yet, but I'd sure like to."

"By the way, today's my birthday, but I'm having it on Saturday because there's no school. There's going to be lots of kids here. What are you doing after school on Friday?"

"Nothing. Why?"

"Good. Then you can come to the store with me where Sheldon delivers things from."

"Yeah, okay. I really like Sheldon's motorcycle."

"He takes me for rides on it sometimes, so, I bet he'll take you for a ride on it sometime, too. Let's go back downstairs."

"Yeah," Troy said as he stood up.

Howard felt elated now that Troy had believed both of his huge lies, and he also felt sure that Troy now thought that he was very sophisticated. When they opened Pinky's bedroom door, Troy heard music coming from downstairs.

When they reached the main floor, he saw Mrs. Chaplin with her head thrown back and her arms stretched out, swirling around the room and dipping occasionally as she sang.

The music changed, then she began tap dancing as she grinned and twirled a closed umbrella. Troy was astonished when she jumped up onto the coffee table to dance, then she danced around the room for a few moments before jumping back up onto the coffee table, and continued tap dancing while singing.

"Mother thinks she dances as good as Ginger Rogers, but I think she dances like Dumbo. Awful voice, huh? Don't forget about Friday after school, okay?"

"Uh, yeah, sure, okay. Um, has she ever fallen off the table when she's dancing?" asked Troy.

"Lots of times. But who cares? She doesn't. Bye, darling."

"Yeah, okay. I mean, bye. Jeez! I don't like being called darling! I told you that before, so, don't ever call me that again!"

"Of course not, darling. Bye-bye!"

Troy was about to yell at him again, but before he could, Howard slammed the front door shut.

* * * * * ❖•••••❖★❖•••••❖ * * * * *

As he walked down the sidewalk, Troy thought about his visit to Howard's enormous home, and meeting his mother, then he saw five of his friends waving at him as they walked toward him.

"Hey, Troy, was Pinky home?" asked Joel.

"No, but their mom was. She likes to dress up and dance and sing. She wears lots of lipstick and makeup, too."

"Yeah, I know. I see her lots of times when I deliver the paper."

"She looks like a really beautiful Hollywood movie star, and she dresses up like one, too, but my mom says she bets that she's balmy, and that her brain's the size of a bird's," said Keith.

"Maybe it is, but I don't care because sometimes she gives us Cokes and cookies," Lloyd said as he smiled.

"Hey, Troy. What about the store where Sheldon works? Is Howard going to show you how to steal stuff?" asked Bobby.

"He didn't say anything about that, but he wants me to go there with him on Friday after school," replied Troy.

"Yeah? Cool! Don't steal any candy the first time. Wait 'til you start going there a coupla times, okay? Hey, did you ask him about his sister's boobs?" Keith asked him.

"No, but he told me he's going to ask her to show 'em to me."

"Yeah? Cool!" exclaimed the boys in unison.

"Jeez! He talks a lot about sex. He told me he sees his uncle's semen because his uncle is always having accidental orgasms, and Howard said the semen floats out in thousands of colored bubbles. But I think he's lying," said Troy, scowling.

"So who cares about his uncle's orgasm accidents? I'd rather see a big pair of boobs," said Jimmy. "Hey, Troy, did fruity Howard ask you to bring a birthday gift on Saturday?"

"Nope. But my gramma'll probably say I have to. Bet she'll buy him a T-shirt, but I bet he'd rather have a blouse. Jeez! And you should see his dog! *He* wears a dress, too!"

"Yeah, I know. I've seen his dog in the backyard. He sits on their back porch and he grins a lot. Bet he's a fruit, too."

"No, he's not," said Lloyd. "I know that because I saw him screwing Mrs. Wilson's dog in her backyard."

"Oh, so *that's* why Cuddles has black puppies," said Keith.

"Yeah, he chases after lots of girl dogs all the time, so, Louise must be the father of over a hundred pups now," said Joel.

"Louise? Jeez! That's a girl's name!" exclaimed Troy.

"No, it's not," said Keith. "Howard said he named him after three French kings called Louis. Okay? And French people pronounce 'Louis' like 'Loo-ee.' Right? So, more than one Louis is pronounced 'Louise.' Right? That's what Howard told us, and he said lots of people in France call their boy dogs, 'Louise,' so it's not really a girl's name. See what I mean?"

"Hmmm, well, Howard's studied more French than I have, so I guess he read about that pronunciation for more than one Louis," said Troy. "But even if he named his dog after three French kings, that doesn't explain why he puts those dresses on him, or why his dog doesn't mind Howard dressing him up like that."

"Because Louise is just as weird as....Aw, no! Coming! My mom's hollering for me to come home for dinner, so, see ya."

"Yeah, I've got to get home, too," said Troy. "I'll see you guys after dinner, okay? We'll play baseball in the schoolyard, okay? I'll bring the bat."

"Yeah, okay. See ya."

Troy felt secretly happy about going to Howard's birthday party because it meant that he didn't have to go home that weekend. His father always found some excuse to beat him when his mother wasn't present. But his brothers, Mark and Sasha, were never slapped or beaten, no matter what bad things they said or did.

* * * * * ❖•••••❖✹❖•••••❖ * * * * *

On Saturday, Troy sat at the kitchen table in his grandparents' home, wrapping Howard's birthday gift while thinking about how much he'd miss seeing his brothers that weekend.

His grandmother walked into the kitchen and saw Troy sticking so many bows on the birthday gift, that it was beginning to look more like a pile of bows than a gift.

"That looks lovely, dear. Hmmm, if you put more bows on it, it'll look like the package the bows came in."

"Well, I'd never put lots of bows on any other gift, but I gotta put lots on this one because Howard likes really fancy things on everything, and his mother's crazy about bows, too. Like, she has them all over her dresses, and Howard's dog likes bows, too," said Troy, putting another bow on the gift.

"His dog?"

"Yeah. Well, I think that's enough bows for his gift. Now I'll tie more ribbons on it. Bet he'll think it's not fancy enough even with all this junk on it."

"Oh, not at all, dear. I'm sure he'll love it," said his grandmother.

"I bet you haven't talked to him, except saying, hi. Howard's a lot like a girl," he said, tying more long ribbons on the gift.

"Well, he *is* a pretty boy. I imagine he takes after his mother, but that's a bit difficult to tell because of all the makeup she wears."

"She wears big gowns at home, and she dances and sings, too."

"Oh? She sounds very talented."

"Guess that's why she has so many boyfriends. I wonder if *they* can tap dance, too?" Troy pondered aloud.

"I'm sure they must do, dear. You know, I've often wondered why a woman like her with so much money wouldn't want to live in a wealthy neighborhood with...Oh! Look at the time! You'd better get on your way to the party, dear. Comb your hair before you go."

"Yeah, okay," said Troy, then he went over to the kitchen mirror, took his comb out of his back pocket, ran it through his hair, once, and then he scowled.

"There. Now you look perfect," she said, smiling.

"The wind'll probably mess it up again, anyway."

"Then comb it again before you knock on their door. Bye now. Have a nice time, dear."

"Yeah, I'll try, gramma. See ya. Jeez!"

Mrs. Chaplin greeted him at the door, wearing a massive red hat and a red dress that fitted her tightly down to her knees, then it flared out, and the ruffled hem extended two feet behind her.

"Oh! Oh, it's Troy! What a delightful surprise! Come-come! Entres vous, darling!"

"Um, your lipstick's a bit smeared, ma'am."

"Oh? Why, thank you, darling. Oh! What a simply magnificent gift! How sweet! The other kiddies are gathered in the back gahr-den. Mingle, darling. Howard will be joining you soon. Such a gift! Bows! Ribbons! Ohhhh, what creativity! Oh, yes! Howard will absolutely *adore* it!"

"So, um, I'm going out to the back, now, ma'am."

"Of course you are, darling! Ta-ta!"

He walked to the back of the house and saw that the entire backyard was decorated with helium-filled balloons, massive paper flowers, and many strings of colored lights.

At the far end of the backyard, there was a large, high-backed, very ornate chair that resembled a throne, and it was situated in the middle of a big platform.

There were two, four-foot-wide steps at the front of the platform, and long spears at each corner of it held up a huge canopy that had broad white and gold stripes.

Howard's sister, Pinky, rushed over to him, grabbed his hand, and led Troy over to one of the long tables lining the backyard. She then plopped a piece of cake on a small paper plate, and handed it to him along with a plastic cup filled with Coke.

Troy hadn't stopped gaping at Pinky since he'd first seen her. She had on a pink bikini, which displayed her quite ample breasts, admirably, and there was a little pink bow at each side of her head.

Pinky was wearing pink, high heeled shoes, so, she had to stoop slightly to hand Troy the cake and cup of Coke, and he gasped as he looked down inside her bikini bra while he said: "Uh, thanks. Is this Howard's birthday cake?"

"Why, no, that'll be brought out, later. Would you like ice cream on your cake?"

"Sure. Thank you. My name is Troy."

"I know, and I'm Pinky. I'm so pleased to meet you. I see you all the time, and now we've met face-to-face."

"Face-to...Yeah, sure. Jeez! So, um, lotta people here."

"Yes, Howard has so many friends, hasn't he? Well, at this party, but of course, they hate him something terrible the rest of the time. Isn't it hilarious? Howard just loves riling everyone. For the past few months, he's taken on the role of a girl, and he's much too good at it. Now all the boys think he's gay, and Howard loves how much *that* riles them. So many adults are so against people with different sexual preferences, too, aren't they? And Howard knows that all too well. He just love shocking people by acting and dressing the way he does. I often wonder what he plans to do next. You know, I sometimes toy with the idea of shocking people, too, although I realize I might not ever shock anyone as much as Howard does. You see, I've been thinking of dressing like a butch dyke or perhaps a diesel dyke for a week or two. That just might shock my boyfriend, but then so many men fantasize about watching two women making love. Odd in a way, isn't it? I wonder if dykes know that? Do you know what a dyke is, darling?" asked Pinky, leaning over and smiling at him.

"Um, no, I don't," replied Troy, looking at her cleavage.

"That's a lesbian. A girl who likes other girls. But I'm not a lesbian. Well, not yet, darling, because I haven't found a girl yet to try it with. But I find men so terribly sexy, so, I wouldn't want to be a lesbian all the time. Oh, no, no, no. Just now and then. Hmmm, it's hard to decide, though. Butch or fem? Oh, well."

"Oh? Well, thanks for the cake and the pop, Pinky. I'm going to say hi to the guys, now. When's Howard coming outside?"

"Soon, darling. Enjoy the party," she said, smiling.

"Thanks. So, see you later. Jeez!"

Troy backed away from her, smiling and trying to keep his eyes on her face as he walked mostly backwards over to a group of his friends, then he bumped into them.

"Hi, Troy! Great bathing suit on Pinky, huh? Big boobs."

"Yeah, they look really nice. So does she," said Troy.

"What're y'eating that cake for? There's tons of sandwiches and other stuff. They're even having a barbecue, later. That's what I'm waiting for. Are you going to eat that cake?"

"Pinky shoved it in my hands, so, what was I gonna do?"

"So, dump it in the garbage can. She gives cake to everyone when they come here, and she knows they all dump it. She doesn't care. I'd rather get that than a party hat. Y'can't dump a party hat. Hey, and watch out you don't step in any dog shit. Louise is out here somewhere. Unless he's next door visiting Cuddles," said Joel.

"So, Howard's going to sit on a throne, huh? Jeez! I wonder if he's going to wear a dress, too. Think he will?" asked Troy.

"Bet he is," replied Joel. "If we boo him, his mom'll kill us."

"If they light all those torches that they stuck in the ground, bet the flames'll start burning all these decorations," said Keith.

"They put the torches all along the ground to make it look like a path going up to the platform," said Troy. "There's sixteen torches on each side of that path, but there should only be twelve on each side of it because he's twelve years old now. Well, not today, because Wednesday was his real birthday."

"So who cares? Wendy Lee looks really pretty, huh? I'd go talk to her, but she's with all the other girls. No way I'm going to be around all *them*. Bet Howard'll want to, though. That's why he invited them all here," Bobby said, scowling.

"At least they've got really great music playing. Hey, I hope they don't try to make us dance with the girls to the slow music."

"Hey, Troy, you should've seen his mother dancing to all the slow ones, and by herself, too. She was running up and down the backyard, and turning round and round, and curtsying, and swinging her arms all around," said Lloyd.

"Yeah, I figured she might do that out here in the backyard, too. The first time I was here, she was tap dancing all around the living room and on top of tables," said Troy.

"Oh-oh. Mrs. Chaplin and Pinky are lighting the torches. Guess Howard's ready to come outside."

"Come-come, everyone! Gather round! Howard is about to come outside, darlings!" cried Mrs. Chaplin.

Large curtains had been hung along the edges of the back porch, then drawn back to expose just the front of it, and then Mrs. Chaplin and Pinky quickly closed the curtains to hide the porch.

All the guests murmured when the bottom of the curtains began moving, but instead of Howard appearing, Louise stuck his head out. The dog pushed through the curtains, trotted over to one of the tables, put his front paws up on it, and grabbed a sandwich off one of the plates before he walked away.

Mrs. Chaplin changed the music, and now Sir Edward Elgar's "Pomp and Circumstance" was playing loudly from six speakers, which made the guys groan at Howard's arrogance.

Pinky and Mrs. Chaplin hurried up the porch steps again, and as they pulled on braided gold rope to slowly open the curtains, they threw back their heads and cheered.

Whispers of goshes and gollies tumbled from the guests up to the slightly parted curtains that revealed Howard standing with his arms stretched up above his head, and he was clad in a clinging, pale blue satin gown.

Three, very long, pale blue ostrich feathers were attached to the front of his tiara, and he was wearing pale blue, long gloves that reached up almost to his shoulders.

He slowly lowered his arms to shoulder level, so that his hands disappeared behind the partly open curtains, then a moment later, he began slowly raising his arms again.

Pinky and Mrs. Chaplin opened the curtains wider, then the guests gasped when they saw two heavily muscled men standing at

Howard's sides, and holding his raised hands. The men were painted gold, and they had on astounding gold masks.

The men were wearing pale blue satin loincloths to match Howard's dress, and they had on wide gold wristbands, gold Roman sandals, and hanging from their waists were big scimitars in jeweled, gold scabbards.

"Those guys are wearing blue skirts!" exclaimed Joel.

"They're not skirts. They're called loincloths," said Troy.

"Yeah? Well, they *look* like skirts."

"Wow! Their swords look like they're real! Bet they cut off heads with them!" Jimmy whispered loudly.

"Jeez! Howard *did* wear a dress," whispered Troy.

"Told ya he was a real fruit. Oh, no! Look at that!"

The men knelt, lifted Howard onto their shoulders, stood back up, and then began slowly walking down the steps and along the path of lit torches as Howard blew kisses to his guests.

They walked up onto the platform, then the two musclemen shrugged Howard up off their shoulders and sat him on his throne, and then they stood at each side of him.

The guests, except for Troy and his friends, had been speechless while watching the procession and the seating of Howard on his throne, and they stood gaping at the two gold-painted musclemen flexing their muscles in various professional bodybuilder poses.

Mrs. Chaplin then used a pair of scissors to cut loose many of the helium-filled balloons, then she opened two boxes on a table, and white doves flew up into the air to follow the colored balloons.

She then grinned at everyone before changing the music, and then she started her strange, whirling dance around the backyard.

"This is like being at a weird, crazy circus!" whispered Joel.

"Yeah! Louise is gonna rip Mrs. Chaplin's dress to pieces!"

"I didn't know you could rent musclemen," said Jimmy.

"They're bodyguards to protect Howard because he's wearing a dress, and they probably thought we'd beat the crap outta him for doing that."

"He's a really good fighter, though. Well, if we ganged up on him I guess we could pound him out," said Joel.

"No way. That's cheating. But I bet there's one of us he can't beat up, though."

"Oh, Louise! No-no! Bad boy! Stop it! Louise!" shouted Pinky.

"Louise is humping her leg! Cool!" cried Jimmy, grinning.

"C'mon! Let's rescue her and maybe she'll show us her boobs!"

Unfortunately for the boys, one of the musclemen rushed over to pull Louise off Pinky, and carry the dog into the house, so, the boys groaned out: "Awwwww, darn."

When the man came back out of the house and closed the door, he walked to the platform, then Howard stood up, raised his chin, and then the musclemen escorted him back to the house.

Howard stood on the porch, facing his guests for a moment with his hands on his hips, then he whirled around, and strutted into the house with the golden musclemen.

Almost an hour later, Howard came back outside, dressed like a boy, and after pouring himself a paper cup of Coke, he walked over to Troy and the other boys, and he smirked as he said: "Well? Bet that pissed you guys off, *royally*. That's why I wanted the throne."

"Yeah, it did because y'wore a weird dress and all the foo-foo crap was a hoot, too. Knew you'd wear a dress," said Jimmy.

"Thank you, darling. My mother had it altered for me. Any of you boys want to dance?" asked Howard.

"What? No way!"

"Okay, then I'll dance with Wendy Lee. Oh, Troy? Why don't you ask my sister to dance when she comes back out?"

"Me? I, um, well...I don't know. Maybe," he replied.

"I'll ask her!" exclaimed the other guys in unison.

"You'll have to wait a few minutes, because she's talking to her boyfriend. He was one of my palace guards. The other one is that uncle I was telling you about, Troy. Slippery?"

"Yeah? Oh, uh, the bubbles guy," said Troy.

"That's right. He shaved off his body hair to look like the other guy. Well, I'm going to dance. Enjoy the party," said Howard before strutting away to talk with a group of girls.

"I wonder what Wendy Lee'll tell him she thought about him wearing a dress? Yuk!" exclaimed Joel, grimacing.

"He was wearing fake boobs, too, and he'll probably ask her if she wants to borrow them," said Keith.

"Yeah, maybe he will. I hope they start the barbecue soon, because I'd sure like t'have a hamburger. Hey, Troy, are you really going to ask Pinky to dance with you?" asked Jimmy.

"If you do it, first, I'll ask her after. Jeez!" he replied, blushing.

He never got the chance to work up the courage to ask Pinky to dance with him because she came back out of the house, wearing a dress, and Troy found out that she was leaving with her boyfriend.

* * * * * ❖•••••❖★❖•••••❖ ∙ ∙ * * *

The birthday party continued until an hour after the barbecue, then grandly wrapped gifts of socks, T-shirts, comic books, and little dolls were distributed to the guests on their way out of the house.

On their way home, guests chattered about Howard's bizarre birthday party; the efforts of which had made Howard the center of all the girls' attention, and he received more hassles from the boys.

But Howard loved both riling and shocking everyone, and he was always thinking of other ways he could get all the boys to hassle him even more.

The boys' code of honor to only fight one-on-one also assured Howard of being able to defend himself when confronted by a boy whom refused to accept Howard's pompous attitude.

Troy hadn't been perturbed when Howard had told him about his affair with his uncle because he'd been too preoccupied by his first experience of visiting Howard's home and gaping at the very strange things he'd seen during that visit. And as he matured, he would continue to accept odd social and sexual practices.

* * * * * ❖•••••❖★❖•••••❖ ∙ ∙ * * *

Troy learned again that there was something that some adult males mistakenly found mistrustful about him when his teacher informed the students that permission had been granted by their parents for her to take them to a planetarium and a tour of a museum in a small city across the border.

The children were quite excited because the Mexican city of Esperanza was a tourist attraction, and there were many game arcades as well as a wonderful amusement park close to the museum.

It was three hours by bus to the border where the bus stopped, then the teacher and the bus driver showed documents to the border guards, and they explained their reasons for the brief trip as the children looked out the windows of the bus at the border guards.

The guards smiled, waved at the children, but just as the teacher and bus driver were getting back onto the bus, one of the guards shouted at them to halt.

"Wow! Y'think they're going to shoot Miss Canfield and the bus driver? Maybe us, too, because they're looking at us like we're weird!" exclaimed Keith. "Boy, does that one guy ever look mad!"

"Oh, no! They're looking at *our* window!" exclaimed Troy.

They watched the teacher trying to calm the one guard, then after a few minutes, she and the other guard had been able to assure the angry guard that it was all right to let the bus cross the border.

The children excitedly asked their teacher what had made the man so upset, then she looked at Troy as she talked to them.

"It seems, for some odd reason, the guard felt that Troy wasn't part of our group because he looked different from the rest of you, but everything's just fine now, so, please take your seats, and we'll be on our way" said Miss Canfield, smiling.

The bus began moving slowly toward the border, and then many of the children stared at Troy.

"That's weird! Y'don't look different to me!" cried Keith.

"Uh, well, other men've acted that way to me, too. A dentist I went to said he didn't want to work on my teeth, and he was sorta real angry at me like that guard, too. Same with a doctor, and some of the men teachers. Even men I met with my parents. But I don't know what makes them act that way," said Troy.

"Do you think maybe it's because your eyes are so black?"

"No, I don't because some of the other kids have got very dark brown eyes."

"Maybe he saw your eyes flash red or maybe blue and he thought that meant there's something bad about you."

"Yeah, maybe he thought that," said Troy frowning.

"Have your brothers got eyes like yours?"

"No, they've got blue eyes and their hair is a lighter brown than mine. Their hair gets even lighter in the summer. But I don't think that border guard could've seen any red or blue in my eyes from where he was standing. Besides, the sun wasn't shining in my eyes when he was looking at me."

"Hey, maybe your eyes are like that because you're a Gypsy, and that border guard doesn't like Gypsies!"

"No, I don't think so because people don't act that way to other Gypsies," said Troy. "Sure, they don't trust some of us because they think we're all robbers and stupid, but that's not true. I'd never steal all the time like some of the other guys I know who aren't Gypsies, and I'm a lot smarter than a lot of people who aren't Gypsies, too. That's why I go to a special school."

"Bet that's it, though, but your eyes don't bother me, and they don't bother anybody else I know. That's the first time I ever saw somebody act really weird when they saw you. I sure hope that guy's not there when we come back because he might start shooting at the bus. Wow, was he ever sorta real mad at you!" exclaimed Keith. "If more guys like him get mad at you because of your eyes, then maybe it'd be better if you started wearing sunglasses."

"I'm not going to start doing that," said Troy. "Besides, he was probably upset because his wife's so sick."

"Yeah? I didn't see her," said Keith.

"That's because she's in the hospital. I sort of saw her there."

"Yeah? Then she must be really sick if she's in the hospital. Hey, y'know what I wanna buy when we get to Esperanza?"

"What?"

"The last time I was there with my parents, I saw a store with souvenirs in it and all kindsa other great stuff, and they had statues of naked women with big boobs and everything."

"Even if you found that store again, and they let you buy a statue like that, I bet you won't get it across the border."

"I bet I can," said Keith. "I'll put it in my haversack when I get back on the bus," said Keith.

"Where're you going to put it if you get it home?"

"At the back of my closet. I'll show it to all the guys when they come over to my place."

"I might get one, too, but my grandparents wouldn't care if I put it right on top of my dresser because they don't think there's anything dirty about a naked person. Neither do I, so, it's too bad you think you have to hide your statue if that store lets you buy it."

Keith bought a statue of a naked woman, but after he got home from the bus trip to Esperanza, he had to give it to Troy after his mother found it in his closet.

Howard bought a big pair of hoop earrings, an ankle-length, flowered, wraparound skirt and a matching handkerchief-style blouse, and he told the boys that he was going to wear that outfit, with a tall hat that he'd make out of glued-together plastic fruit, then he'd look like Carmen Miranda.

Howard then told them he was going to have a mariachi band perform at his next party while he was singing and dressed like Carmen Miranda.

The boys hadn't known whom Carmen Miranda was until Howard brought a photograph of her to school, then all the boys groaned when they saw that Carmen was a woman, instead of what they had thought would've been a Mexican clown who was the lead singer of a small circus group that performed at beach parties.

PART THREE

Troy Meets The Startling Tanya

His grandparents held a party for him on his twelfth birthday, and when he unwrapped their gift to him, Troy felt so happy and pleased when he saw that his grandparents had bought him the baseball glove that he'd been admiring for months in the store.

Many young people arrived before Howard, whom then handed Troy two, very creatively wrapped gifts, then told Troy to open the bigger gift first.

Troy unwrapped it, and then became excited when he saw a T-shirt with a big picture on the front of it, and it was a color portrait of his favorite baseball player, Hank Aaron.

After opening Howard's second gift, which was in a small, square box, Troy was both astonished and ecstatic to find a baseball signed by Hank Aaron.

The following weekend, Troy took the bus home while looking forward to the birthday party his mother had arranged for him. He'd been calling home three times a week, and he spoke with Lena and his brothers, but Yuri always refused to speak with him.

He arrived home to find a table set outside on the lawn with food and drinks, and about a dozen children waiting to greet him. He felt relieved that his father wasn't there because Yuri had decided to visit some friends for most of the day.

After the birthday party and before dinner, Troy was sitting in the living room with his mother and brothers, talking about the party, when he tensed up, and then stared at the door.

"Troy? What is it?" asked Lena.

"It's dad," he replied. "He's really mad about something. He's coming down the road right now."

Lena went to the window, looked out, then not seeing enough of the road, she went outside and peered in both directions for as far as she could see, then she went back inside, and said: "I'm sure he's still at the Colson's, honey, because I didn't see him on the road."

"He's coming, though. I know it. I see him," said Troy.

"Just a minute. I'll call Doreen."

She called Doreen Colson, and was told that Yuri had just left their home five minutes ago, and Lena knew that it would take another fifteen minutes before he could be seen rounding the bend in the road, which was quite a distance from the house.

"He just left their home five minutes ago, dear."

"I know that, mom. I gotta run, okay? Tell him I went to see somebody. Anything. Please. I see him, mom."

"Oh, no. Oh, Troy. When he gets here, I'll ask him why he's so upset with you."

"He keeps telling me I'm not welcome here, that's why. And that's why he hits me all the time when I come home."

"Well, he'd better not try that while *I'm* around. On second thought, you stay here, and then so help me, if he raises a hand to you, I'll...Well, don't worry," said Lena, scowling.

"Yeah, but he'll get me sometime, though. Sometime when you're not looking. Okay, I'll stay here in the house."

.   .   .   .   .   ❖•••••❖★❖•••••❖   .   .   .   .   .

Yuri arrived home, and when Lena asked him why he was in such a bad mood, he forced a smile as he walked to the bathroom while telling her that he had a hangover, but that he was starting to feel much better.

After dinner, Troy and Sasha went to the far end of the property where there was a small brook because Sasha wanted to show him a little boat he'd made.

They played with the boat for awhile, and then Sasha said he had to run back to the house to get a toy that he wanted to place on the boat to see how far the boat could carry it downstream.

Sasha had been gone two minutes when Troy heard a faint voice that he always sensed before any serious accident he'd experienced. He slowly stood up, looked around, and saw Yuri running toward him, holding a thick, wooden pole.

Troy turned and ran, but moments later, he stumbled over a rock, and fell to the ground, then Yuri was suddenly standing over him, beating him with the pole. Troy grunted loudly in pain, then rolled over onto his stomach, covered his head with his arms, relaxed, and let his thoughts carry him away from the awful pain.

He wasn't sure how much time had passed before he heard his father shouting out in pain, then his mother pulled him up to his feet and began leading him away as she wept.

Lena put him in the truck, then drove him to the hospital where he received stitches to gashes on his arms and back, and it wasn't until almost four hours later, that Troy let himself feel the fear and pain, and then he burst into tears.

Troy stayed with friends of his mother's until he'd calmed down, and then Lena told him that she was going to divorce Yuri whom had been sentenced to three weeks in jail for his drunken abuse of Troy.

Sasha told him in private that their father had stopped beating Troy when Lena had started hitting Yuri over the head with an iron frying pan until she'd knocked him unconscious.

· · · · · ❖••••••❖ ★ ❖••••••❖ · · · · ·

Troy didn't go back to school for a week, and when he did, he was asked if he'd been in a car accident, then feeling embarrassed, he told his friends that he'd fallen out of a tree onto some rocks.

Howard said he didn't believe him because he'd seen bruises on him before when he'd returned from visiting his parents, but this time, they were far worse. He then said his cousin had been beaten by a man, and it looked like the same thing had happened to Troy.

Troy told him that he was right, but not to tell anyone because he didn't want his friends to know that his father had been sent to prison for beating him up, so, his father was a jailbird, now.

"He went to jail?" asked Howard.

"Yeah, he did," replied Troy, frowning. "For three weeks. My mom told me she's going to divorce him."

"Good for her! Fuck him! Now when you go home, he won't be there to beat you up. He sounds demented. Did he beat up your brothers, too?"

"No, just me. He's always done that, but I don't know why."

"Keith's father beats up all his kids, but not as bad as your father did to you."

"He does? Keith never told me that."

"Well, maybe I shouldn't say he *beats* them, but he spanks them. If mother tried that with me, I'd take all her dresses and burn them in the backyard. Well, the ones I don't like."

"So, don't say anything to the other guys, huh? Promise?"

"I promise, but I don't know why you don't tell them. I've heard about lots of kids getting beat up by their fathers, so, it's nothing new, so, if I know that, sure as fuck *those* jerks know it. And it's not *your* fault, either. So *what* if your father's in jail? Jimmy's father was in jail for a year for some reason and none of the guys care."

"Yeah? Jimmy never told *me* that," said Troy.

"Probably because he thought you already knew. Ask him when you see him. Oh, I almost forgot to tell you. My aunt's having a birthday party for my uncle, and she told me to bring you with me, so, do you wanna come?"

"She invited *me*? But how did she...I don't know. When is it?"

"Two weeks from Saturday. She's having it in the afternoon. They don't have any kids, so, I'll be the only one there, and Pinky's spending the weekend with her boyfriend. Besides, mother asked me to ask you, too. She really likes you."

"Yeah? Well..."

"Tell your mother you don't want to go home on weekends for awhile because of what your dad did to you. He might be out of jail by the time of the party, and he might beat you up again because he's mad that he had to go to jail for beating you up. You never know."

"Well, I don't want to see him for a long time because he's acting really strange for the past year. He's been getting drunk all the time. Okay, I'll go to the party with you."

"Good! Oh, and you know how the teachers got upset by those drawings and paintings you had at the school art show because they thought a few of them were sort of sexual?"

"Yeah, but my grandparents didn't think so, and that's why I brought them to school for the art show."

"I thought they were great. Anyway, my aunt bought one. It was one of the paintings that you got two dollars for, and my other aunt bought one of the drawings when mother told her about them. She went down the next day and bought it. She's very excited about the drawing, and she said it was the work of a budding genius. Or a bloody genius. Whatever, darling."

"Yeah? That drawing was the same price as the paintings. I made ten dollars by the time the show was over. That was really nice of your aunts to buy my artwork."

"Aunt Margaret has your painting in her living room, and Aunt Tanya had your drawing put in a nice frame and she has it in *her* living room, too."

"Wow! I've never had anything of mine framed before."

"Tanya thinks you're very, very talented. So do I. She wants to meet you. You might be shocked when you see her, though."

"Why?" asked Troy.

"She's got what people call an odd side to her."

"They think that?"

"Yes. Her wedding for example. Her taste is astonishing at all times, and her wedding dress was sensationally beautiful. I've never seen any other dress like it. She has the finest designers creating her clothes, and they design clothes for Hollywood stars and some of the wealthiest women in the world. Royalty, too."

"Oh, so that's why people think she has an odd side to her?"

"No, it was because of the way she appeared at her wedding ceremony. We were in the church, the wedding music began, and Tanya began walking down the aisle in her magnificent white wedding gown, but she did her usual black thing for her wedding."

"Her black thing? What's that?" asked Troy.

"Black face. Tanya blackens her face. Quite often, too."

"Huh?"

"Yes, odd isn't it? It's a thing she has. It shocks most people."

"Yeah, I guess it'd shock *some* people, but it wouldn't shock *me*. After your birthday party, not much could."

"Wait'll my next one," said Howard. "Where are you going?"

"I'm playing baseball with the guys."

"Okay. When you see Keith, tell him what really happened to you. Tell *all* the guys. Don't make it such a big secret, okay?"

"Yeah, maybe I will. You're right. I shouldn't be embarrassed. My dad's the one who should be. See ya," said Troy, smiling.

"Bye, darling."

"Jeez! Stop calling me that!"

"Sorry! Bye, darling!"

"Wait! I told you to stop call..." he started to say, but Howard had started running home before Troy could finish telling him again to stop calling him "darling."

* * * * * ❖•••••❖ ★ ❖•••••❖ * * * * *

Troy told Keith and his other friends that he really didn't have an accident, and that his father had beaten him, and now his father was in jail because of that.

The boys called his father a jerk and they were very sympathetic to Troy. And just as Howard suggested that he do, he told his mother that he didn't want to come home for perhaps a month, and she agreed with him.

Two weeks later, he asked Howard what time the party was being held, and he was told it was at three o'clock on Saturday afternoon.

Howard told him that his mother wouldn't be going to the party because she had a charity benefit to attend, and that he had an appointment to have his hair cut at two-thirty.

"I tried to get an earlier appointment, but I called the barber shop yesterday and they had so many customers scheduled to have haircuts for Saturday," lied Howard.

"Yeah, Saturdays are busy at barber shops. I'll go with you, then wait while you get a haircut," said Troy.

"Oh, I was counting on you going on ahead to the party because I thought that way, at least one of us wouldn't be late. They live just ten or fifteen bus stops from here. Would you mind? Please? Then you can tell them I'll be there a little after three. Okay?"

"Yeah, okay."

"Great! I'll give you the address, and if you take the bus at two-thirty, you'll get there a bit before three."

"Okay. Your hair doesn't look like it needs to be cut."

"That's what I told my mother, but she said it's a bit too long at the back. I didn't want to argue with her because she might've collapsed in tears.

"Hmmm, I bet she wouldn't've done that."

"Okay, maybe not, but I decided to get a haircut, anyway, just to please her. Okay, here. I've written down the address, and I hope I get there soon after three," said Howard, smiling broadly.

.   .   .   .   . ❖•••••❖★❖•••••❖ .   .   .   .   .

Troy dressed in a suit and tie, then took the bus to Mr. Denning's birthday party. He was astonished to see that their home was crowded with antiques, and many guests were wandering from room to room through the great amount of ornate furniture.

He gaped around at tables piled high with plates on display stands, and four or five ormolu candlesticks of varying heights up to five feet tall.

He introduced himself to the Dennings who gave him a small plate of fancy party food and a soft drink, then Troy gently pushed his way through the crowded rooms.

There were heavy curtains, either hanging straight down or draped in different ways on the windows, so, most of the light came from glass shades on many of the bronze statues.

He was fascinated by statues that were taller than him, and he liked all the gold-framed oil paintings that were hung so closely together that in some rooms, the walls couldn't be seen.

People sat on odd-shaped Victorian couches, others on love seats, and some guests were sitting in chairs that had very ornately carved backs that were almost as high as the ceiling.

Troy thought it was like being in a packed antique store as he squeezed his way past guests, some of whom were wearing kimono-like, satin, floor-length gowns that reminded him of Howard's conservative lounging drag.

Troy was talking to an elderly couple who were admiring the small painting he'd done, and he felt rather proud that such wealthy people as the Dennings had bought it.

He heard murmurs ripple through the room he was in, which was near the entrance to the apartment. After several adults had stepped out of his way, Troy was able to see what had caught everyone's attention, and then his eyes widened when he saw the latest arrivals.

The couple caused quite a stir because the man was wearing a bright red shirt, yellow tights with little, chrome studs all over them, a pair of black riding boots, a black sequined bolero jacket, white bow tie, and a red cowboy hat.

When Troy saw the man's white, close-fitting, narrow mask, he thought it very much resembled The Lone Ranger's mask. The petite woman with him had on a goldenrod-yellow dress with a slit up one side to her thigh.

Her wide-brimmed red hat had a thick, red veil that covered her face, and she was wearing red, elbow-length gloves, and she carried a red purse to match her red shoes and other red accessories.

Troy felt sure that the woman's favorite color was red because even her yellow dress had a three or four, big, red hibiscus flowers printed on it, then he overheard women close to him, remarking on what marvelous taste the woman had.

Troy wondered if the recently arrived woman in yellow and red was hiding her face with the thick veil because she was famous movie star, or someone as equally well-known.

He watched the couple walk slowly through the room, and the man stopped to speak briefly to some of the guests, then Troy heard him ask where Mr. and Mrs. Denning were. They met the Dennings, chatted for a few moments, then the striking couple began moving among the guests.

Shortly after his arrival at the birthday party, he had noticed that one door in the huge living room was kept closed, and sometimes Mrs. Denning would open it slightly, look in for a few moments, then close the door, and resume chatting with her guests.

But whenever a guest opened that door, they'd look in, frown, then quickly close the door, and walk away. Troy had initially thought that the room was a bedroom, then after seeing Mr. Denning sometimes come out of the room with a couple of bottles of liquor, he presumed it was a storage room of some sort.

He then overheard some guests excitedly saying that the room was a small den with a bar, and Troy couldn't quite hear the rest of their conversation, but it sounded as if they had said there was something sort of unusually dark or black inside that room.

* * * * * ❖•••••❖★❖•••••❖ * * * * *

Troy began thinking that Howard had changed his mind about coming to the party because he'd said that they'd be the only young people there.

He asked a guest what time it was, and learning that it was nearing four o'clock, he made his way to the front door to wait there and greet Howard. He decided to wait twenty minutes, and if Howard didn't arrive, then he'd return home.

Moments later, Troy heard deep laughter, and then looking through the crowd, he saw that the laughter was coming from the man wearing the red cowboy hat and Lone-Ranger-style mask.

He watched the masked man holding his escort's arm while leading her through the crowded room to the entrance door where Troy was standing, so, he assumed that they were leaving the party.

He stepped away from the door so that they could leave, but they stopped close in front of him, and then the petite woman with the red veil covering her face, suddenly exclaimed: "Hi, Troy! Scott and I've been looking for you!"

"Howard? Jeez!" cried Troy in a loud whisper.

"Well, my aunt and uncle *did* tell me some of the ladies were dressing up for the party."

"Yeah, but that meant the *ladies*, man!" exclaimed Troy.

"So? Scott's a ladies' man, and besides, it's about time that men's fashion started to have more flair. Obviously, most of the women here at this party need even *much* more flair. Just look at the boring gowns on them. No oomph."

"Howard," said Troy, heaving a big sigh.

"Oh, yes. Troy, Scott. Scott, Troy. Smile! Flash pearls!"

"Hi, nice to meet you, Scott. You look, um...great."

"Thanks. Nice meetin' you, too, Troy. Yeah, I'm gettin' lots of compliments on what I've got on. I don't usually dress up like this unless I'm going to a party at one of Howie's mom's friends or relatives. She gets all the clothes made for me and some of them are pretty wild. This get-up is sorta a bit more conservative than mosta the things I'm asked to wear. Man, sure is a weird crowd here at *this* party, huh?" he said as he looked around the room.

"Scott's planning to leave home soon, and it's about time, I say. I plan to leave home when I'm eighteen. Scott's been asked to share an apartment with a New York financier who has a great house on Fire Island. Scott adores beaches, *and* being adored *on* the beaches. Anywhere, darling," said Howard, smiling.

Troy gaped up at Scott and he wondered how many guys with astounding physiques Howard knew. He estimated Scott to be over six and a half feet tall, whereas the tallest guest in the room was about five-foot, six inches tall.

"Uh, so, I see you've met some of the guests," said Troy.

"I smile, Scott talks. I'm still practicing my Talullah Bankhead voice. I saw your painting on the wall. Not as interesting as your sex drawings, but I like the colors you used. I've got a dress in those colors. Very pretty," said Howard.

"I'll bet. You know, if you keep dressing in women's clothes, a lot more people are going to think you're really gay."

"Good! Then that'll mean I've convinced more people that I'll be a great actor. Well, I already am, in a way."

"Hey, if you think these guests are weird, well, I don't think so, but something's weird around here," said Troy.

"Oh? The statues *are* rather garish. I can't see where that fat woman with the cigar over there is dropping her ashes, so, is it onto something you think is weird? Like an ashtray that a dead, stuffed midget is holding with his teeth?"

"No, there's a room down there, and they keep the door closed, and I heard some of the guests say not to go in there because of something strange and dark or black in there."

"Aha! I know what it probably is. Their collection of leather drag. Scott looks very fine in black leather."

"Thanks, Howie," said Scott, grinning.

"Jeez, Howard! Your voice keeps changing from deep to high, so, if any of these guests hear you talking like that, they'll know you're really a boy," Troy told him.

"I know what you mean. The onset of puberty is unpredictable. I'm just another innocent struggling up the high hill to adulthood."

"Innocent? You? In what way?" asked Troy.

"Never limit yourself, darling. Always aspire. Scott started having sex at a very young age. Mother dragged him home from some playground or gym, but I rescued him from her so that he could add to his repertoire."

"Pardon? Sorry I didn't hear you. I was listening to those people over there. Add to my what?" asked Scott.

"I was just telling Troy that it was my idea to add the mask to your ensemble. Scott relies on my good taste. Don't you think he looked great at my birthday party?"

"He did? Scott? Sorry, I don't remember seeing you at his birthday party."

"I was one of the gold-painted palace guards," said Scott.

"This is that uncle I was telling you about," whispered Howard.

"Slippery?" asked Troy, gaping.

"Yes. In the flesh, so to speak. And a wild lover, too. The day my mother broke up with him, I watched as ten huge men tore him off her while he was making wild love to her."

"What'd you say, Howie? Tore me off what?" asked Scott.

"I said you tore yourself away from those very boring guests at that party you went to last week."

"Oh, right," said Scott, looking around at the guests.

"Was Howard's mom with you at that party?" asked Troy.

"Hmmmm? No, but I've been to a few parties with her, and I've always had a great time with her," replied Scott, smiling.

"Yes, and in more ways than one," said Howard. "Mother has a big collection of interesting dildos."

"Howie. Stop telling lies," said Scott, scowling at him with a slight smile.

"Well, she might have at least *one* dildo!" exclaimed Howard.

"Howard! Shhh, people can hear you," whispered Troy, trying not to laugh.

"Only if their hearing aids can tune in this far. Well, let's mingle, darlings. They absolutely *love* our drag," said Howard.

· · ·   · · ❖•••••❖ ★ ❖•••••❖ · ·   ·   ·   ·

Almost an hour later, Troy looked around, and he was surprised to find that almost all the guests had left while he'd been talking to a couple in one of the smaller rooms, then returning to the room he'd just been in, the people he'd been talking with, told him that they were leaving, too.

Troy strolled from room to room, looking into them, and when he saw that they were empty, he walked to the far end of the enormous apartment and saw four guests talking with the Dennings, then he wondered if Howard and Scott had left, too.

Mrs. Denning passed a plate of sandwiches to him as she talked with her friends, then Troy took a few of the small sandwiches, smiled, and thanked her.

He decided to look at more paintings, then leave the dwindling party, if he found out that Howard and Scott had already left. He walked by a room, noticed the door was slightly open, then looking inside, he couldn't recall being in that room before.

Troy walked into the room, then his eyes widened when he saw a woman with long, wavy blonde hair, sitting on a couch. She had her long, beautifully shaped legs crossed, and her forearms were folded across her knee.

She was leaning over, with her head bowed so that her forehead rested on her wrists, therefore, her long, wavy blonde hair hid her face, then Troy presumed that she was either inebriated or very tired.

He was just about to step back out of the room, when she threw back her head, leaned back up, and sighed. Troy sucked in his breath when he saw how very beautiful she was.

He realized that she must be well over six feet tall when she was standing, and with the very high heeled shoes she was wearing, he felt sure that she stood as high as seven feet.

They stared at each other for a few moments, and then a lovely smile crept wonderfully across her face, and Troy gaped when he realized that she was Tanya because she'd slightly blackened her face, and then his heart leapt when she spoke.

"Darling, you must forgive me, please. I've stayed in here since I arrived because I found the other guests incredibly boring. But I *did* tell Margaret and Tom that I'd drop by because I just *had* to meet you, darling."

He was mesmerized by her low, lilting voice and alluring way of forming every word that she spoke very slowly; pronouncing her words in a way that captivated him.

Troy felt sure that she was the most beautiful woman he'd ever seen, and he estimated her age at somewhere around twenty-five, but he'd learn months later, that she was thirty-six.

Something akin to a gentle, but powerful electrical sensation tingled throughout his body and mind, and he felt as though he'd known her and sensed the serene comfort laying within her for a very long time.

Tanya and Hanson Willoughby were childless, but soon Troy and his brothers would become their adopted sons. His father and his accomplices had made certain that Troy would never benefit from Craig MacIver's estate, but eventually, Troy, Mark and Sasha would inherit the immense Willoughby fortune.

"You're Tanya. You bought one of my drawings."

"Yes, I did, you sweet, charming, wonderfully talented child."

When Tanya talked, she often pouted and raised her eyebrows, as if she were expressing a surprised: "Oh!" and that added even more excitement to her beauty. Troy was dazzled by her big, sparkling, violet-colored eyes, and he thought that everything about Tanya was far more than wonderful.

"I'm shocked! From what I was told of you, I expected to see simply another very clever child with an endearing smile, but you're such a handsome young man. Your eyes are as exciting as your aura. Eyes of fire and water. So rare a gift to have eyes such as yours that reveal the hidden now and faint glimpses of the future. Your psychic powers will grow stronger through the years. People must find that alarming about you. Well, *some* people. Idiots most that do. Your marvelous attributes, as well as your brilliant, artistic talent will draw many women to you when you are in the eligible years for romances. But *I*, fortunately, have a romance that I know must stir great envy in countless women. I am deeply in love with my husband. He is my greatest sexual desire, darling. I lust for him. Hanson is fiddling with some sheikh or emir in Saudi Arabia at the moment. Something to do with oil, I imagine. It's always some dull thing or other. My love Hanson finds our various oil businesses fascinating, whereas I do not. The only oil of interest to me is the most recent scented oil at my spa. But enough about my tiny, temporary tribulations regarding Hanson. You're twelve, are you not?"

"Yes, I am. My birthday was almost a month ago."

"Would you like a martini, darling?"

"Uh, no thanks, ma'am. I don't drink."

"No? I'm relieved to know that. I'd be even more relieved with a martini in hand. Make one for me, please do."

"I don't know how. I'm sorry," Troy said as he smiled.

"Then I'll teach you. There is the gin, and there is the vermouth. It's rather simple, darling. Six or seven drops of vermouth, and you fill the rest of that silver container with gin. There is ice in that silver bucket. Then you..."

Troy stood at the small bar, following Tanya's directions, then he poured some of the ice cold martini mixture into a crystal glass that Tanya had selected by pointing to it with her long, beautiful finger.

Tanya excitedly told him about her newest home, which was a replica of Mespelbrunn Castle in Bavaria, replete with a moat and swans. She went on to tell him how long she and her husband had searched for the perfect spot to have their new home built, and that it now stood amidst a forest-like setting close to the central part of the city's vast ravine.

He listened, fascinated, as she told him that they'd had their new home decorated by her favorite interior designer whom had flown over from Italy, however, Troy wasn't listening to much of what Tanya was saying because he was entranced by her thrilling voice.

He was lost in her strange and astonishing beauty as she continued talking, then Tanya was standing before Troy was aware that he'd been in a daze. She thanked him for coming to the party so that she could meet him, then she leaned over, kissed his forehead, smiled at him, and then she seemed to float out of the room.

Troy couldn't move for a moment, then he walked to the door, and saw her leaving the immense apartment. When he'd regained his senses, he asked Mr. and Mrs. Denning if they'd seen Howard, and they told him that he'd had to leave in a hurry.

He thanked them for inviting him, and then after he left, he thought about Tanya all the way home. Troy was in love.

. . . . . ◇••••••◇★◇••••••◇ . . . . . .

He got off the bus, then started walking home while smiling and thinking about the time that he'd spent with Tanya. He saw Joel and Keith walking toward him, so, Troy grinned and quickened his steps, and then told them about the birthday party, and meeting Tanya whom was extremely beautiful.

"Yeah? Did she show you her boobs?" asked Keith.

"No! She's not like that! Jeez!"

"Who's birthday was it?" asked Joel.

"Howard's uncle's," replied Troy.

"Yeah? I didn't think you'd go with *him*. Well, this time he couldn't wear a dress, though," said Joel.

"Well, he...It was an okay party. But it was even better when I met his Aunt Tanya. She's so amazingly beautiful and she's really, really nice. I hope I see her again."

"Maybe next time she'll show you her boobs," said Joel.

"Jeez! You guys!" exclaimed Troy.

"Hey, we just came back from your place because we wanted to tell you that Joel's mom and dad are having a big barbecue for dinner and we're all going. We just asked if you were home, and your grandmother told us you weren't, and then we asked her if you could come, too and she said it was cool," said Keith.

"Yeah? Great! Can Howard come, too? I mean, he invited me to his aunt and uncle's place, so, I just thought it'd be sorta nice to ask him to come to your barbeque, too."

"Yeah, okay," said Joel. "Hey, I can ask Pinky to come, too, and you never know, she might show us her boobs."

"She's gone away for the weekend," said Troy.

"Aw. Hey, you know when you went to the store with Howard, and then he stole chocolate bars for us? Well, he gave us a whole box of 'em this morning when we were going by his house. We're going to pass 'em out at the barbecue."

"You can't do that because your mom and dad'll ask you where you got them. Right?" said Troy.

"Oh, yeah. So, we'll see y'later, okay?"

"What time should I come over?" asked Troy.

"As soon as your ready, okay? And we'll play catch for awhile. We're having the barbecue after six, and guess what? We're setting off fireworks when it starts getting dark out."

"Yeah? Then I better tell my grandparents that I'll be staying out 'til after dark."

"We already told her that," said Joel. "She's cool. So, later, okay? See ya."

"See ya," said Keith.

"Yeah, see ya, guys," Troy said as they parted company.

He felt so pleased that he'd been invited to two parties in one day, then he suddenly remembered that Joel and Keith had said it was okay for Howard to come to the barbeque.

When Troy returned home, he told his grandparents about the birthday party and Tanya, and then he phoned Howard to tell him not to wear a dress to the barbecue at Joel's.

Howard asked him if a simple plain pair of slacks and a pretty, floral, off-the-shoulder blouse would be acceptable. Troy then said definitely not, so, Howard heaved a huge sigh, and promised that he'd think of something more boyish to wear.

Troy thanked him for the invitation to the birthday party, and told him how much he'd enjoyed meeting Tanya. He also said that he didn't think her habit of wearing black on her face was odd, and that it just made her unique.

"*Unique*? Do you know how she met her husband?"

"No, she didn't tell me," replied Troy. "She just said she really loved him a lot, and that he was away on a business trip."

"Well, I'll tell you how they met. She was invited to her best friend Laverne's place because Laverne wanted her to meet the man she was going to marry. She wanted Tanya to be her maid of honor. Laverne and her boyfriend had been going out together for months and she wanted to have a little party to announce their wedding."

"Oh, so Tanya met her husband at her girlfriend's."

"Yes, she did. Laverne asked her to come over early and help set up things. Like, put candles around and place all sorts of vases of flowers everywhere. Tanya has fabulous taste."

"I know she does," said Troy, smiling. "I mean, I'm sure she does because she looked really great when I saw her. Sorta far more than really great."

"The party wasn't 'til that evening, so, they had lunch together after they decorated the place. Well, Tanya did most of the decorating, as usual, because Laverne has absolutely no flair. I don't know what she would've done if Tanya hadn't come back from her vacation in Paris. So, anyway, they had lunch and Laverne calls the caterers for the twentieth time, as usual, because she's very, and I mean *very* insecure. She's won the Miss Neurotic pageant every year since her teething days. Anyway, so then she gets a phone call. Tanya told mother all this, and I secretly listened on the extension phone, so that's how I know. It turns out that it's her fiancé calling, and he's coming right over, so, Laverne says: 'Oh? Why? Uh, well then, please do.' Can you believe she'd ask her boyfriend that? I mean, if the guy hasn't seen her for almost a month, don't you think he'd be horny, and *that*'s why he wanted to run right over to see her?" asked Howard, then he heaved a big sigh.

"Well, maybe. Yeah, I guess so."

"Tanya guessed so, too. I mean, after all, she *is* my aunt. So, she tells Laverne she'll come back later, but oh, no, Laverne tells her she simply *must* stay. After all, Tanya's her very best girlfriend and she's going to be her maid of honor, so, Tanya says okay, darling, sort of thing. Well, Laverne being so insecure, when the doorbell rings, she runs to the bathroom to pee because she's so excited and she has to check her makeup and hair again for the umpteenth time. Right? So, she asked Tanya to go to the door and invite her boyfriend in. Now they're not friends anymore."

"Yeah? Why?"

"Well, as Tanya says, she just doesn't understand why Laverne feels that way about her. She said it wasn't her fault for opening the door because Laverne had asked her to do that."

"Oh, I see. She had her face done black, right? And her boyfriend sees Tanya and he freaks out?"

"Well, I suppose you can say that he freaked out. Tanya explained it all to mother. Tanya went to the door, she opened it, she sees him, he sees her, they gawk at each other, then they grabbed each other and fell down on the floor and started fucking like crazy. Laverne walked out of the bathroom and sees them fucking on the floor in the hallway, and she goes into hysterics. Tanya thought Laverne was overreacting because they were supposed to be best friends and there's Laverne so upset just because Tanya had fallen in love with Hanson, and he'd fallen in love with her."

"*What?*" cried Troy, wide-eyed.

"I mean, how was Tanya to know that she was going to fall in love? Or Hanson? He hadn't married Laverne yet, anyway, so, things change. People change. Laverne even refused to be Tanya's maid of honor. Not much of a best friend, huh? And after all the nice things that Tanya had done for her, like helping her set up the party for Hanson and her friends. Laverne was so ungrateful. Well, she sure showed *her* true colors, and she didn't go to their wedding, either. It was fabulous. I loved it. To hell with Laverne. I'm glad she's not friends with Tanya anymore. I *never* liked her. She was always whining about something. So, you don't think I should wear something with a little flair to Joel's barbecue, huh? Oh, well, I'll just wear my black and white striped T-shirt, and of course, I have a matching pair of pants. So, what do you think of that? Too much like a prisoner? Prisoners are tough-looking."

"Uh, I...hmmm. No, wear something like jeans and a T-shirt."

"Well, all right then," said Howard. "See you there, darling."

"Hey, and don't you start calling everyone darling when you get there, okay?"

"Who me? I'd never do that. Okay, I'll go get ready. See you at the party, darling. Bye," said Howard, hanging up the phone.

"Wait! I told you...! Jeez!" exclaimed Troy.

PART FOUR

The Horrific, Senseless Tragedy

As Troy got ready to go to the barbecue at Joel's home, he thought about what Howard telling him how Tanya and Hanson had met, and then he realized that there was a lot he didn't understand about adult relationships.

He had a wonderful time at the barbecue and the biggest surprise was Howard. He arrived wearing jeans, a torn T-shirt, black leather boots with chains on them, and he'd drawn fake tattoos on his arms. He also had a heavy chain around his neck besides the studded dog collar, and he'd mussed up his hair to make himself look scruffier.

All the boys gawked at him because Howard looked and acted much tougher than any of them, and he also made sure he used his lowest voice when he talked. In the following year, Howard would surprise them even more by becoming quite masculine and the top athlete in school, after deciding that he had explored his feminine side to the nth degree.

Howard, Troy, and the rest of the boys laughed and talked, and they loved the fireworks and the marshmallow roast at sunset, and then everyone began saying goodnight and thanking Joel and his parents for the party.

"The guys asked me to join the baseball team," said Howard.

"Yeah? That'll be great," said Troy. "Hey, wait a sec. Are you any good at baseball?"

"Of course, I am. In fact, I can play baseball better than you or any of the other guys."

"Hmmm, this I gotta see. Hey, and while we were at Joel's, y'didn't call anyone darling, did you?"

"No, of course not. Just his parents."

"His father, too? Jeez!"

"Oh, I'm just kidding. Let's have some cocoa before we have to go to bed, okay? Your place or mine? As they say."

"Okay. We'll go to your place because my grandparents'll be watching their show on TV, and I don't wanna have cocoa and watch it with them because I don't like that show," said Troy.

"You can call them from my place when we get there. No, *I'll* call them and say you're in the bathroom because they might ask you to come right home. Okay?"

"Yeah, okay."

They walked into Howard's home, and as they passed the living room, Troy looked in and saw Mrs. Chaplin standing behind a tripod with a big camera on it. She was wearing another of her huge gowns that looked like a wedding dress, and she was singing. Her big, fluffy gown was tinted in shades of yellow, black, blue, and pink. She said a hello, darlings, to them before she leaned over, and threw a large black cloth over her head to look through the camera.

Troy and Howard went to the kitchen, put the kettle on, and talked about the barbecue as they waited for the kettle to boil.

Howard went to the wall phone, then just before he called Troy's grandparents, he said that he shouldn't lie to them, so, he told Troy to go upstairs to the bathroom while he made the phone call.

Troy waited in the bathroom for a few minutes, then as he began walking to the door to go back downstairs, he experienced a sudden tingling sensation rushing through his body. He then envisioned himself standing in a strange, sunlit place that was surrounded by high walls of flowers in many shapes and colors.

He smiled when he saw his mother and his grandparents lying on their backs as they floated slowly through the air toward him. When they'd floated closer to him, Troy's smile broadened when he saw that they were smiling as they slept, and they had their hands placed neatly over their waists.

He watched them slowly rising higher and higher as they floated by him, then it suddenly became darker and cold when he detected a movement to his left.

He turned his head, then panicked when he saw Yuri five times bigger than he really was, and wielding a huge baseball bat as he shouted and swore at him.

Troy spun around, and as he began running away, he darted left and right to avoid being struck by the baseball bat, then the terrifying vision of Yuri disappeared at the same time his hand touched the doorknob of the bathroom door.

Troy relaxed and heaved a big sigh when he realized that the vision he'd seen had probably been a comparison of the pleasantness and serenity of his mother and his grandparents to the frightening abusiveness of Yuri. To soothe his jangled nerves, Troy concentrated on his sudden realistic vision of his mother and his grandparents smiling and asleep while floating slowly up to the clouds.

They'd also been wearing their best clothes, so, Troy felt sure that in his vision, they had been rising to a prayer meeting inside a magnificent cathedral in the sky.

He decided not to tell Howard about his vision because he didn't want him to think his visions were becoming so realistic that he would soon be able to read minds.

* * * * * * ❖••••••❖ ★ ❖••••••❖ * * * * *

He went back downstairs to the kitchen, and Howard told him that he'd called Troy's grandparents. They then prepared the hot cocoa and decided to go into the living room to see what Howard's mother was photographing.

Troy almost spilled his mug of cocoa when he saw that she was taking photos of Scott as he reclined on a couch across the room. He was nude and smiling, and there was a very long, wide, red woolen scarf wrapped around his neck, and the rest of the scarf hung all the way down the front of his body to cover his genitals.

"Hi. More photos? What for, this time?" Howard asked her.

"Hi, Howie! Hi, Troy! How was the barbecue?" asked Scott.

"Okay to ho-hum, then on down to a yawn," replied Howard.

"Aw, don't listen to him," said Troy, smiling. "We had a great time. There were lots of fireworks and we had a marshmallow roast."

"Sounds great," Scott said as he grinned.

"Mother. The photos?" asked Howard.

"Why, for Christmas cards, darling. Okay Scott, now tug the scarf up over your chin a bit so that it looks like winter and it's oh, so frightfully frosty out. Oh, I should've had you wear a tuque or some other sort of winter hat. Diddly drat! Oh, well, I can just paint a hat on you after the photos are developed," said Mrs. Chaplin, smiling.

"Do you like the way I've got the scarf now? Or is it covering too much of my chin?"

"No, it's perfect, but I might want you to arrange the scarf differently in a few moments."

When she said that, Troy turned his head away to look at a picture on the wall, because he thought that Mrs. Chaplin was going to ask Scott to wrap all the scarf around his neck.

"Oh, yes, Scott! That little sprig of mistletoe taped over your navel looks so Christmasy! Flex the biceps now! Bend your leg a bit! Hmmm. No, darling, the *other* leg. Just a little more, please. Aha! Marvelous! Now the clickies!"

"I certainly hope you're adding a bit of spice to at least *some* of the Christmas cards," said Howard.

"Of course, I am, darling. As soon as I take five clickies of him like this. Pearls, Scott! Lovely. Three...four...five! There! No more clickies. Now for the spicy ones."

"Coming right up, Joanna. Hand me that towel, please, Howie."

Troy choked on his cocoa when he wondered if Scott was suddenly going to have another of his accidental orgasms.

Scott thanked Howard for the towel, and then as Troy kept staring at the framed landscape painting on the wall, he detected some movement out of the corner of his eye, so, he turned his head further away from them.

"Troy? Do you wanna help me, too?" Scott asked him.

"Me? Oh, um, no. No thanks," he replied.

"Okay. I'll give you some you can have with your cocoa."

"Huh?" gasped Troy.

He heard footsteps coming toward him, so, Troy put his left hand over the top of his mug of cocoa, then Scott walked past him, wearing a towel around his waist. Howard walked by him seconds later, and Troy watched them heading for the kitchen.

"I'm in a bit of a hurry, darling, so, would you help them clean up after, please?" asked Mrs. Chaplin.

"Uh, I...oh...um, well, I..." stammered Troy.

"Thank you. Wait, wait, wait. Tick-tock, tick-tock, tick-tock, tickety-tock. Oops! Tick-tock, tick-tock...Aha! Wonderful!"

Troy gawked as Scott and Howard came back into the living room, carrying trays piled high with various sizes of Christmas cakes, bowls of colorfully wrapped candies, and plates of cookies.

The bigger tray Scott was carrying also had a larger bowl containing Christmas tree ornaments and many strings of brightly colored beads.

Scott reclined on the couch again, waited until Howard, Mrs. Chaplin, and Troy had turned their backs, then he unfastened the towel, and left it covering himself while he placed the red scarf back over his genitals, and then he removed the towel.

Howard and Mrs. Chaplin then began placing the contents of the trays around and over Scott as he grinned. They then turned their backs to Scott again while he slid the scarf away, and placed the biggest Christmas cake over his genitals.

"Ready!" Scott exclaimed.

Mrs. Chaplin and Howard turned around to look at Scott, then she hurried over to the camera on the tripod, and then ducked back under the big black cloth.

"Oh, yes! Yes, yes, yes!" she exclaimed. "Biceps, please! So spicy! Just Perfect! Ready, aim, *fire*, darling! Keep flashing the pearls! Yes! Yes, that's it! Marvelous smile! Hmmm, perhaps ten clickies. Click...click...click...and so on, darling. Whew! All done! I'll have Edward develop them, and I do hope they turn out all right, but if they don't, then the next time I'll make sure I have a hat for you to wear. Hmmm. Oh, of course! Skis, too! Damn! Now that I think of it, the photos would look more authentic with skis. Scott, darling, would you mind sitting through another photo session next Saturday?"

"Hey, no problem, Joanna," he replied, smiling.

"Wonderful! Thanks so much! Well, I must away. I'm off to Blanche's, well, party, and I'm late as it is, darlings. Where's my handbag? How-*word*?"

"It's in the entry hall by the door. I didn't borrow it for the barbecue. It wouldn't go with *this* ensemble. I mean, *really!*"

"All right then, ta-ta, everyone! Thank you again, Scott!"

Mrs. Chaplin threw a jade green fur stole around her shoulders, then she hurried out into the entry hall, grabbed her purse, and left the house to be whisked away in the family limousine.

"Good grief! Green fur with *that* dress?" exclaimed Howard.

"Uh, so, I was wondering if he, um...if he..." stammered Troy.

"If Scott *what?*"

"Um, like, when you were in the kitchen, did he say he felt like he was going to...um, you know? Like, have another one of his bubble accidents?"

"Wanna help me out here, guys?" asked Scott.

"Of course, we will," replied Howard, smiling.

"So you *are* going to...um...go get a broom and help Slippery, I mean, Scott...uh... I have to go to the bathroom," said Troy, blushing.

"Hurry up. You've got to see his bubbles," Howard told him.

Troy hurried upstairs, and stayed in the bathroom, then hearing Scott laughing, he felt sure that Scott had had one of his accidental orgasms, and now he and Howard were holding brooms to hit and burst all the colored bubbles in the room.

He waited another five minutes before going back downstairs, then as he neared the living room, he saw that Scott and Howard had piled most of the food and decorations back onto the trays, and Scott had his trousers on.

"Howie! Come on. Tell Troy," said Scott.

"Damn! Okay, then I'll tell him the absolute truth. Troy? I just thought I'd let you know that before we loaded the trays, I helped Scott get rid of all his bubbles that floated around the room."

"You little bugger!" exclaimed Scott. "Troy, I wondered why you ran upstairs. He told me about telling you that I had sudden, accidental orgasms, and that millions of colored bubbles floated out of me, then all around the room, so, now I know why you ran away. That's got to be one of the biggest lies Howie's ever told, and one of the most amazing ones. Bubbles. Man, what an imagination. Just for that, brat, I'm not going to dress up for you anymore."

"Okay, okay. I lied, okay? Satisfied? And Troy! Don't you *dare* tell the other guys that I lied! Okay?"

"Jeez! I thought...Howard! Aw, forget it. I'll get you for this. You just wait. Here, I'll help you carry all this stuff out to the kitchen. Jeez! What a liar!" exclaimed Troy.

"I'm not. I mean, what's wrong with a very tiny fib? Ow!"

"I'll slap your bum harder next time," said Scott, smiling.

"Um, and, uh...the dildos Mrs. Chaplin has?" asked Troy.

"More of his big, fat lies. And no, there's no financier or Fire Island cottage, either. And I met Howie's mom when I began dating Pinky, and since then, Joanna and I've been good friends. Okay? No sex. Not ever, because she's still very much in love with Howie's dad, so that's why she never accepts dates from other men. Howie sure has told you some wild stories, man, but he's not really a bad guy. He's just like the rest of his family. Wonky, witty and wonderful. A bit more than shocking, but really great, and far too intelligent," said Scott as he smiled.

"Don't tell him *everything*!" cried Howard.

"Oh, not now, but eventually. Quiet! Don't say another word! I'm having a drink, so, are you guys making another mug of cocoa before I send Howie up to bed?"

"Yeah, sure," replied Troy, smiling.

"I think I've *already* been sent up," grumbled Howard.

"Aw, too bad," said Scott, smirking. "Man, this babysitting gig sure is hell, especially taking care of Howie."

"I don't need taking care of! I am *not* a child!" exclaimed Howard. "I'll be in puberty at any moment."

"Scary thought, isn't it, Troy?" said Scott, grinning.

· · · · · ❖••••••❖★❖••••••❖ · · · · ·

They laughed and talked while drinking their beverages, and at one point in their conversation, Troy playfully punched Howard's shoulder and called him a fibber for telling him about the semen bubbles, then Howard scowled at Scott for making him tell the truth.

"Guess I better get on my way home now," said Troy.

"You don't have to hurry because there's nobody home. I called there, remember?"

"I thought they were home when you called to tell them I'd be home later. They never go out on Saturday nights because of their favorite TV show."

"As I said before, things change, people change. Oh, unless I dialed the wrong number. Will you call Joel and ask him if he found my dog collar? A few of the guys wanted to try it on, but I didn't see who the last one was, wearing it. Please, darling?"

"If you promise not to call me darling again," said Troy.

"Oh, all right then. It's going to be *very* difficult, though."

"Goodnight, Scott."

"Goodnight, Troy. Nice seeing you again."

"Don't forget to call Joel for me!" cried Howard.

"I won't forget. See ya," said Troy as he went out the door.

He wondered if Howard had also lied to his mother about those many thousands of colored semen bubbles floating out of Scott, then after thinking about it for a minute, Troy felt sure that it wouldn't shock Howard's mother at all, considering how shocking she was, too, much of the time.

While approaching the house, Troy noticed that the lights were off in the living room, so, he presumed that his grandparents had gone out, after all.

Stepping onto the walkway leading up to the house, he hesitated when he heard his strange whispers swirling louder through his thoughts until he heard the voice that always heightened his senses and warned him of imminent danger. But he dismissed those electric feelings as being simply a reaction to the exciting events of the day.

He unlocked the door, turned on a lamp in the hall, then went into the dark living room to phone Keith. Troy noticed his grandfather lying on the couch, sleeping, so, he turned around and tiptoed out to the kitchen to call Keith on the extension phone.

He stopped walking, and gasped when he saw his grandmother lying on the kitchen floor, and then he hurried over to her, and fell to his knees.

Troy shook her shoulder, and when he couldn't waken her, he rushed to the phone on the kitchen wall to call the emergency operator, then suddenly, he was kicked in the back, and he fell forward onto the floor.

He quickly turned over onto his back, looked up, and saw Yuri holding a baseball bat in the air, then just as it swung down, Troy rolled over and the bat missed him.

"You rotten little bastard!" shouted Yuri, swinging the bat down at him again as Troy scrambled toward the kitchen door on his hands and knees, and then he stood up, and ran for the front door.

Troy fumbled in his pocket for the key, and just as he inserted it into the lock, Yuri swung the bat down onto the doorknob above the lock, and Troy jumped back away from him, and darted from side to side as Yuri swung the bat at him.

Yuri was between him and the front door, then Troy suddenly thought about jumping from his bedroom window onto the roof of the front porch, and then jumping to the ground, so, he whirled around, and raced for the stairs.

Troy's thoughts spun, and his ears were ringing from the pounding of his heart as he ran upstairs while hearing Yuri's rushing footsteps on the stairs behind him as he yelled and swore at him.

Troy ran into his bedroom, slammed the door shut, and he hoped that the small, flimsy hook and eye latch would be strong enough to keep Yuri out until he was able to get the window open, and then jump down onto the porch roof.

He struggled to lift the window as he heard Yuri smashing at the door with the baseball bat, and throwing all his weight against it, then the hook and eye latch broke off, the door burst open, and then Yuri rushed in, wielding the bat.

Troy knocked over a chair, and other pieces of furniture in a vain effort to make Yuri stumble over them, and he'd also been trying not to let panic dominate his sense of self-preservation.

He threw everything he could find that was heavy at Yuri as he looked around his bedroom for even heavier objects to throw as he dodged the baseball bat.

Troy looked over at his wardrobe cabinet, and he kept dodging the bat as he made his way over to it while throwing his heaviest books at Yuri's face. He then grabbed onto the back of the cabinet, yanked it forward, and leapt out of the way as it toppled over against Yuri, causing him to lose his balance and stumble backward.

Troy leapt over the fallen wardrobe cabinet, ran to the bedroom door, and then back downstairs. He didn't have his front door key because Yuri had grabbed it out of the lock after he'd struck the doorknob with the bat.

Troy thought of the basement window that opened onto the walkway at the side of the house, so, he raced toward the kitchen just as Yuri reached the bottom of the stairs and began chasing him.

He opened the basement door, slammed it shut behind him, then Troy began running down the stairs while desperately hoping that he could get to the basement window, open it, and struggle through it before Yuri found the light switch for the basement stairs.

The only light in the basement came from a bulb that hung by a long cord from the ceiling, and he knew that Yuri had never been in the basement before, which was to Troy's advantage.

He reached up, unscrewed the bulb, then threw it against one of the brick walls to smash it, and then he jumped up onto his grandfather's workbench below the small window.

His heart was beating very fast as he fumbled with the lock on the window while listening to Yuri coming down the stairs. Troy hoped that he could get through the window before being beaten to death with the bat. His heart leapt when the window swung open, then he jumped from the workbench, and began squirming out through the window that was just a few inches wider than the width of his body.

He then yelled when he felt Yuri's hand grip one of his ankles, and begin pulling him back through the window as Troy shouted for help and frantically kicked Yuri's hand with his other foot.

Yuri kept holding Troy's ankle, as he grabbed Troy's belt with his other hand, and began yanking him back through the window. He then grunted loudly when he was kicked very hard in the face, then Troy heard him swearing loudly as Yuri let go of his ankle.

Troy scrambled away from the basement window, then he stood up, and began running down the narrow walkway between the houses, and then he ran out onto the street.

He looked around at the neighboring houses, and then realized that by the time someone answered his urgent pounding on their door,

Yuri would have killed him with the baseball bat, so, Troy began running toward Howard's home while listening to Yuri shouting and swearing far behind him.

He ran up onto Howard's porch, then he looked back at the street and saw Yuri running across the lawn toward him, so, Troy ran to the end of the porch, jumped over the railing, down to the ground, and then he began running to the back of Howard's house.

He reached the backyard, and saw Scott smoking a cigarette and talking to Howard, so, Troy began shouting at them: "Get into the house! It's my dad! He's after me! He's got a baseball bat! He wants to kill me! He's gone crazy!"

"Troy! Howie! Get inside!" shouted Scott.

They ran inside the house, but Scott stayed outside after he told them to shut the door, lock it, and then call the police.

Howard hurried to the phone and called the police as Troy peered out the window at Scott whom was standing close to the side of the house, with his back pressed against the brick wall of the house.

The instant that Yuri appeared, Scott whirled around to face him, then Yuri crouched over from the impact of Scott's fist slamming into his stomach.

Scott then smashed his fists into Yuri's jaw, several times, and Yuri fell to the ground. Scott leaned over, yanked up Yuri's head, and then hit him in the jaw again, before he leaned back up and kicked him a few times in the ribs.

Yuri was unconscious by the time Howard opened the door to tell Scott that the police were on their way, then he said: "Well! That'll teach *him* never to come here without an invitation! Of all the nerve! Scott! He beat up Troy! Look at the size of *him*, and look at the size of Troy! I hope you killed that rotten jerk!"

"He...he...uh-huh-huh-a-a-a-aha-haaaa!" Troy burst into tears.

Scott hurried to Troy, picked him up, carried him into the house, and sat him down in the living room.

•   •   •   •   • ❖•••••❖★❖•••••❖ •   •   •   •   •

The police arrived minutes later, then they handcuffed Yuri, and then he was starting to regain consciousness as two policemen dragged him to their car, and drove away. Two more policemen had stayed to ask Troy what had happened, then he told them that he'd returned home to find Yuri waiting for him with a baseball bat.

He also told the officers about the severe beating he'd received from Yuri, whom had then been incarcerated for three weeks. The policemen told him to stay with Howard and Scott while they went to his home. Troy then felt embarrassed when he started to cry again, but he couldn't stop because he felt so terrified as he wondered how badly hurt his grandparents were.

•   •   •   •   • ❖•••••❖★❖•••••❖ •   •   •   •   •

Troy thought his head was going to split open in several places, and that he was going to die because his body shook so much from his sobbing. He fell to his knees, and his heart seemed like it was going to explode as he listened to the people around him.

He could vaguely hear somebody telling him that Yuri had been in a drunken rage when he'd murdered Troy's mother and her parents. After he was able to stop sobbing and he'd caught his breath, Troy excitedly asked the people standing around him if Sasha and Mark were all right, then he burst into tears of relief when he was told that they were unharmed.

An hour later, his mother's elder sister and her husband hurried into the house, and held him in their arms as they all cried together.

·   ·   ·   · · ❖••••••❖★❖••••••❖ · ·   ·   ·   ·

Days after attending the funeral of their mother and grandparents, Troy and his brothers still found it very difficult to speak or eat. Mark sometimes stared out a window while saying they shouldn't be at their aunt and uncle's home, but instead, back at their own home so that they could make sure it stayed just as nice and clean as their mother had always kept it.

Two weeks later, the boys were told that they'd be living permanently with their aunt and uncle, and that Troy would be attending one of the local schools.

·   ·   ·   · · ❖••••••❖★❖••••••❖ · ·   ·   ·   ·

He sat beside the phone, hoping he wouldn't start crying when he told his friends that he wouldn't be seeing them again, then he began wondering which one of them he should call first.

He decided to phone Howard first because even though Howard

told huge lies, and he could be quite eccentric and very annoying at times, Troy now felt that Howard was his best friend.

Howard interrupted Troy's emotional farewell call by asking if he could speak to his aunt, so, Troy handed the phone to her, then he watched her facial expressions as she began saying: "Oh? I see. Well, Troy can't leave here and come live with you without your parents' consent, and even then, he'd only be able to visit you for a day. Yes, that's right. No, I just told you that's out of the question. *What?* May I speak to your mother, please? Oh! *What?* I want to speak to her! *Why?* Never you mind, *why!* Just put her on the phone! My God! Hello? Mrs. Chaplin? I've never heard such language from a boy his age. Well, I hope you do. Yes. As I told your son, we'll have to discuss that. Oh? Are you sure you want to do this? Yes, I know. Yes, he loves that school. Well, I...He wouldn't? Well, yes, it could be. As I said, we'll have to discuss it. I'll ask him, but I'm not sure if he'd want to do that. Terrible, yes. Just awful. Yes, he's very upset. I'm sure it'll be quite some time before he feels better. Yes, I will. This is quite generous of you, Mrs. Chaplin. And you've thought it over very carefully? I see. Well, I'll talk it over with him. Yes. All right then, thank you for calling. Oh, I *will* tell them. Poor children. Awful. Thank you again. Goodbye, Mrs. Chaplin."

She hung up the phone, and slowly shook her head, then she sat down beside Troy, and scowled as she said: "My word! That friend of yours used awful swear words. I told his mother, and she was shocked. Mrs. Chaplin said she's going to have a stern talk with that boy. Does he swear all the time?"

"Well, just a couple of times," replied Troy, trying not to smile.

"Mrs. Chaplin feels it would be quite upsetting for you to stop going to that school because of all the friends you've made, and then, too, it's also a special school for advanced children. High school included in the agenda. I suppose you'd feel a little out of place going to the high school here, and being in a classroom with students much older than yourself. Mrs. Chaplin thinks that because of that, it would help if you continued going to the same school instead of having to make new friends. She sounds like a very nice woman. I imagine she must be very upset to know her son uses such language. Troy, how do you feel about going back to the city and attending the same school?"

"Uh...well, I don't know. All my friends are there, but I can't go...I mean, where would I stay if I went back to school?"

"Mrs. Chaplin said she's quite willing to have you stay with her. She said she has five extra bedrooms, and she said she expects her daughter will be getting married soon, so, I imagine you being there'll help her feel less lonely with one less child soon."

"Yeah?"

"I heard a dog barking in the background, so, you'd have a pet to help take care of, too."

"That was Louise. Sort of an unusual type of dog," said Troy.

"How nice. Has Louise ever had any puppies?"

"Quite a few litters. Constantly," he told her.

"Oh? Well, from what I understand, they're well-equipped to take care of them 'til they find homes. I was surprised to find that the Chaplins have so much money. She told me that her sister would be offering all financial assistance to ensure that you're well-taken care of. She must be a very generous woman. A Mrs. Willoughby."

"Tanya! Her name's Tanya Willoughby and she's so nice! She's very beautiful, too. I really, really like her. I never thought she'd want to help pay for me living with Howard and his mom because they've got lots of their own money. Maybe now I'll get to see Tanya a lot more! That'd be great!"

"Oh, and Mrs. Chaplin told me that with the extra bedrooms, your brothers can visit as often and as long as they like on weekends and school holidays. If you do decide to accept their offer, I think it's only proper that you help with the housework. Don't *you*?"

"Yeah, sure, I'll help do some of it, but they have several maids come in twice a week to do everything."

"I see. With their money, I can see how they can afford such a luxury. She also said you can wear some of the clothes she bought for that Howard of hers. And a gown. Well, I suppose that's for graduation. That means she wants you to stay with her for a long time. Well, you think about it, and let me know, okay? I'm so happy to see you smiling, dear. Now you think about this very carefully, and if you decide you want to live with them and go to school there, I hope you don't pick up any swear words from that Howard. He sounds a bit rough. Like a bully. I hope he doesn't cause trouble at school, too."

"Yeah. Yeah, I'd like to live with them. And all my friends'd be at the same school," said Troy. "Oh, and Howard's really not that rough. Honest. But I'm not going to wear any gowns."

"Why, everyone wears one at graduation, dear."

"Not Howard," said Troy. "He'd *never* wear what everyone else wears at graduation. Uh-oh! Knowing *him*, I bet he *will* wear a gown, and it'll be...Jeez!"

The End

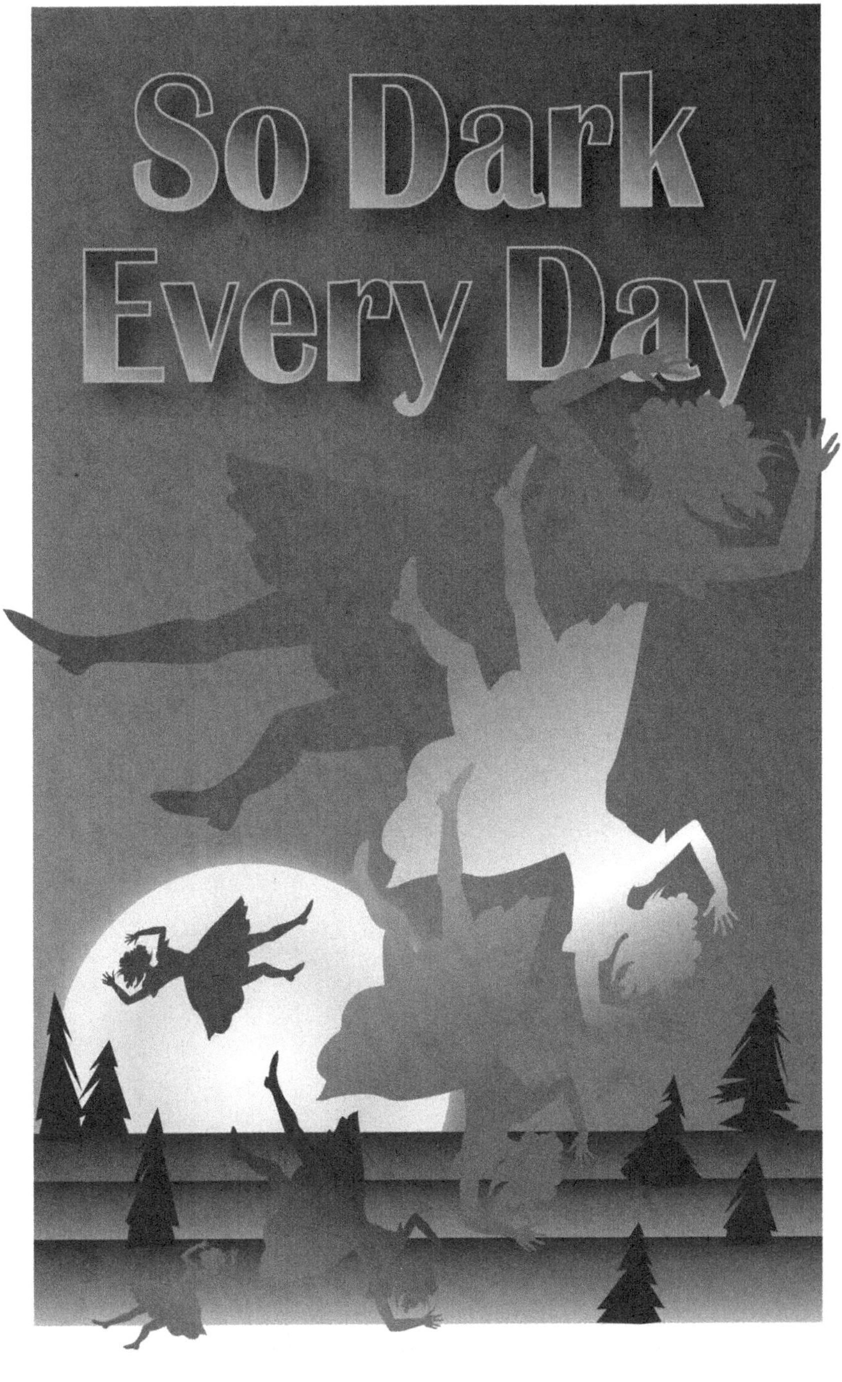
So Dark
Every Day

So Dark Every Day

Viola picked up more dinner dishes and cutlery off the kitchen table, then while carrying them over to the sink, she heaved a sigh as she looked at her daughter, Zeina, standing at the window again.

"Not again! Stop staring out the window and help me clear the table! Please!"

"Oh, okay! I was just seeing if anyone was hanging around near the barn," said Zeina.

"Hmmfff, if it's not the barn, it's somewhere else. I don't know what you expect to see. You're always so jumpy. You see a shadow and you think it's somebody lurking around and about to attack you. I'm sure that's because you spend far too much time daydreaming."

"It's just that it's so dark every day and sometimes I think I see things, but when I look again, it's not what I thought it was."

"Just *sometimes*? You think you see things *all* the time. If something's not in the usual place, you panic and think it's something it's not. Yesterday, when I left the kettle on the sink counter, you thought it was a gray cat. Then last night your father hung his coat up on the coat tree for the first time in ages, and you thought it was somebody standing by the door," said Viola.

"That's because he hardly ever hangs up his coat there, and he put his hat on the top of the coat tree, right above his coat, and the hall was sort of dark, so, that's why I thought it was somebody standing close to the door."

"Yeah, *you* would. Everything's starting to look like something it really isn't to you. You're not a little kid anymore. You're almost eleven years old, so, it's about time you acted more grown up."

"Sorry. It's just that sometimes I think I see spooky things."

"Well, you better make sure you never tell your father about seeing things that aren't really there because he'd make very sure you never imagined seeing things again."

"Uh, yeah, I know. That's why I only tell *you*."

"I have enough to put up with as it is, so, I don't need you telling me about seeing things that aren't really there. You've got a wild imagination even when you see real things happening. Like last week when your father got into a rage again, and he grabbed that knife and stabbed me in the back, near my shoulder, then you thought he'd killed me. But you should know by now that he'd never stab me where it'd be fatal. But you got hysterical."

"It's just that that time he beat us up more than he usually does, and so when he got the butcher knife and he stabbed you, I thought he wasn't going to stop stabbing you, and then he might start stabbing me, too," said Zeina.

"Well, he *did* stop, didn't he? The trouble with you is that you don't go out enough."

"Sometimes I don't want to. Like, especially when I've got more than two bandages on me, then people stare at them, and they ask me what happened, and then I have to try thinking of something else to say for *that* time."

"Well, you look okay now, so, there's no reason for you to hang around the house again tonight. Why don't you go over to the dance at the town hall again?"

"I hate going there alone, and nobody's going to ask me to dance because most of the boys don't want to dance, and the ones that do are a lot older than me and they only like dancing with girls a lot older than me, too."

"Yes, well, unfortunately, boys your age don't want to dance with girls. But you never know, Zeina. If one or two boys your age saw you at the hall, one of them might ask you to dance with him."

"I suppose so, but I just feel funny going by myself. Besides, most of the boys like doing other things than going to dances at the town hall at night."

"Well, the longer you stay home by yourself, the more jumpier you'll get. Why don't you just walk by the hall, and maybe you'll feel like going in?"

"I don't know. Well, maybe I will. It's just that I feel a bit nervous walking along the road at night."

"Why? You know everyone around here and in town, too, and it's not as if you were in some big city where there's so much crime. I can finish these dishes myself, so, you go upstairs and get ready to go out. By the time you have a bath, and fix your hair, I'll bet you'll feel a lot better, and you'll want to go to the town hall."

"Okay, mom. Are you sure I can't help do..."

"Go on! I want you to enjoy yourself."

"Thanks, mom. I might go. Yeah, okay, I *am* going. I'll be back downstairs in less than an hour."

Zeina slowly climbed the stairs and began filling the tub before she went to her bedroom to look through her closet for something pretty to wear.

⬩   ⬩   ⬩   ⬩ ⬩ ◈•••••◈ ★ ◈•••••◈ ⬩ ⬩   ⬩   ⬩   ⬩

She had laid out three dresses on her bed, and Zeina was still trying to make a decision when she suddenly remembered the tub, so, she hurried back to the bathroom to turn off the taps.

On the way back from the bathroom, she noticed that the door to her parents' bedroom was halfway open, then as she began passing it, she looked in, and then her heart leapt when she saw a large man combing his hair in the dresser mirror.

She opened the bedroom door wider, and sighed with relief when she looked into the dimly lit room and saw her father asleep on the bed, and the man she thought she'd seen had only a figment of her overactive imagination.

The bedroom was slightly lit by the spotlight on the barn across from the house, and the shadows of swaying tree branches made some objects in the room appear to be moving.

Those slowly moving shadows were also on the dark-patterned quilt hanging on a hook attached to the front of the closet door that was close to the big mirror on the dresser.

That big, dark quilt with slowly moving shadows of tree branches on it had caused Zeina to think for a moment that she'd seen a large man standing in front of the mirror, combing his hair.

One of the other closet doors was open, and she saw her mother's dress that had broad, dark blue and white stripes on it. Viola hadn't been allowed to socialize with her friends and neighbors for the past year, so, she hadn't been able to wear that dress.

Zeina felt sure that her mother wouldn't mind her wearing it to the dance hall. She took the dress out of the closet, then took some of her mother's cosmetics, and a pair of black, high heeled shoes before she hurried to her own bedroom.

She undressed, put on her bathrobe, walked to the bathroom, then after hanging the robe on the hook on the back of the door, she slowly lowered herself into the tub.

For the past week or so, she had felt a bit more nervous than usual, and she often imagined seeing somebody lurking not only inside the house, but everywhere around it.

Zeina then wondered if she'd feel confident enough to walk into the dance hall unescorted, regardless of how much effort she put into looking her best.

She was skimming her hands across mounds of foamy bubbles as she smiled, when a sudden movement beside her made her panic and cry out.

She quickly squirmed around in the tub, cowering to the other end of it, away from where she'd seen the darting movement, and her heart was pounding as she looked around the bathroom.

She then realized that she was alone in the bathroom, and the darting figure had really been her bathrobe when it had slipped off the hook on the door and fallen to the floor. Now Zeina knew she definitely had to start getting out of the house more often.

·   ·   ·   ·   ·   ◇••••••◇✦◇••••••◇   ·   ·   ·   ·   ·

She returned to her bedroom, put on her mother's dress that fell quite loosely about her body and hung down to her feet. She smiled as she watched the dress swirling and billowing as she turned side to side, then she imagined the dress swirling and billowing as she waltzed around a magnificent ballroom with a handsome prince.

She loved applying makeup, and the different looks she could achieve by making her lips smaller or bigger with lipstick. Zeina decided to make her lips almost twice as big with the lipstick, because then her smile would be more noticeable to the boys at the dance, and then one of them might want to kiss her cheek.

She carefully patted rouge on her cheeks until they looked almost like round, red apples. Zeina then fastened several big, red bows at the top of her head, then put five butterfly and four floral clips close around the red bows, and then she felt pleased while thinking it looked like she had on a pretty hat.

She studied her reflection in the mirror for over a minute before she heaved a big sigh, and left her bedroom.

She clomped downstairs in her mother's high heeled shoes, which were about two sizes too big for her, then after entering the kitchen, Zeina uttered a slight cough to get her mother's attention.

"You look wonderful," said Viola, smiling.

"Thank you. Yes, I *do* feel much better. Hmmm, but I still don't know if I'm going to the...Oh, what the heck. By the time I get there, I might feel more different."

"I'm sure you will, and it's a lovely evening."

"But I always feel nervous because there's no lights on the road 'til I'm almost at the town hall."

"Oh, now c'mon, Zeina! I think you're just trying to make up another excuse for not going out again. Now you stop that, and get on your way before your father gets home. You never know what sort of mood he'll be in, so, stay away 'til around midnight."

"Okay. I'll go now."

"Bye. Have a nice time, now," said Viola, smiling.

. . . . . ❖•••••❖★❖•••••❖ . . . . .

She left the house, and as she walked toward the gate that opened out onto the road that ran by her home, Zeina saw a man passing slowly by the gate.

She was startled for a moment because he looked similar to the man she thought she'd seen combing his hair while looking in the dresser mirror in her parents' bedroom.

The man on the road was the same height and weight, and dressed exactly the same as the man she thought she'd seen in her parents' bedroom. Moments later, Zeina relaxed when the man disappeared around the corner of the road.

She felt determined to stop letting her imagination frighten her every time she saw a sudden movement or something that was just an ordinary person or thing.

Zeina began walking up the incline of the road, and she knew that after she'd walked down the other side of the hill, and then up and down over the next hill, she'd see all the little, colored lights strung around the outside walls of the town hall and in the trees in front of it.

Nearing the crest of the first hill, Zeina saw a man sitting on a big boulder at the side the road, and she couldn't see him clearly enough in the dark to make out his facial features.

She felt scared while thinking he'd been waiting for her, and now that man was going to attack her. Zeina then concentrated on not being scared because she felt sure it was just her vivid imagination again, and that the man seated on the boulder had no intention of harming her.

But he did seem scary because he was the same height, weight, and he had on the same clothes as the man she'd seen on the road, walking slowly by the front gate.

When she was nearing him, Zeina's eyes widened and her heart began pounding because the man seated on the big boulder by the side of the road looked so much like the man she'd thought she had seen combing his hair in front the big mirror on the dresser in her parent's bedroom.

But it seemed impossible to her that the man sitting on the boulder was the same man she'd seen on the road, and the man she'd thought she'd seen in her parents' bedroom.

She hugged her mother's spare handbag tightly to her chest, then after moving to the opposite side of the road, she tried to remain calm as she walked onward to pass by the big man seated on the boulder.

He stood up, turned around, and walked out of sight, then Zeina felt so relieved. She thought it had been ridiculous to have been frightened because the man had started walking along the side road that led to Mr. and Mrs. Bellamy's farmhouse.

She then felt sure that it'd probably been either Mr. Bellamy or his elderly brother whom had stopped to rest before continuing on down the road to the farmhouse.

She reached the top of the hill, and looked down the road to the Bellamy property, but because the road curved past a large grove of cedars, whoever she'd seen was now out of sight.

She looked around for a few moments to be sure that man wasn't coming back, then Zeina hurried along the road and stopped again at the top of the second hill when she saw all the cars parked around the town hall and several couples walking toward it.

She smoothed out her hair, and then after taking a deep breath, she started walking down the hill. Zeina had intended to linger outside the town hall until she felt confident enough to go inside, but after seeing another car arriving, she began walking toward the open door of the town hall.

Zeina entered, and looked around the poorly lit room, then smiled when she saw a vacant table at the far end of it. She draped her sweater over the back of the chair before she went over to the bar to order a soft drink.

Returning from the bar, she saw a few of her friends seated at the table next to the one she'd chosen, and they waved to her as they smiled. Zeina sucked in her breath and smiled as she neared them while hoping they wouldn't ask why she was alone again.

"Hi, Zeina! You look great!" cried Marianne.

"Yeah, you do," said Barry, grinning. "C'mon and join us at our table. You can't sit over there all by yourself."

"Hi, Marianne. Hi, Barry. Hi, Peter. It's okay. I don't mind sitting by myself. Anyway, it's great seeing you guys, but I'll..."

"Don't be silly, Zeina. We'd like you sit with us. Grab your things and join us. Please," said Marianne, smiling.

"Well, okay. Thanks, I will."

As Zeina picked up the handbag and sweater, she also gathered the hope that Peter would ask her to dance with him because he hadn't brought his girlfriend, Lorna, to the town hall. But after a few pleasantries were exchanged, Zeina learned that Peter was leaving soon to meet Lorna at her home.

"I haven't seen you for so long, Zeina! Almost a month, but then, I can't blame you though, considering. So, anyway, how's your mom and dad?" asked Marianne.

"Mom's fine. Dad's still got problems with his asthma. I think he has so many nightmares because he has trouble breathing at night."

"Gee, that's too bad," said Barry. "I bet your mom gets really worried when it's hard for him to breathe like that."

"Yes, she does. Dad tells her to stop worrying about him, but she can't. She was sitting up half the night until dad told her that if she didn't stop worrying, he'd have *more* trouble sleeping. A few nights, mom's laid on my bed with me, pretending she's sleeping, but I always know that she's awake so she can get back off my bed if she heard dad start wheezing real bad again, or shouting stuff if he's having a nightmare."

"She must be so tired," said Marianne.

"Mom never shows it because she's always busy all day, and then she...Anyway, you didn't come here to listen to my dad's asthma problems. So, anyway, will Benny and his band be playing here tonight?" asked Zeina.

"They might be, but that's only if they finish playing over at Clapton's. There's a banquet there for the lodge tonight. Benny told me he might make it here before closing time to play some music, so, that'd be great," said Peter.

"Even if they can't make it here, there's already some great music being played here," said Marianne. "Zack's the DJ tonight, and he's been playing some really great dance numbers."

"I love the one he's playing now," said Zeina, smiling. "But he's got the volume turned down so low that I can't tell what song's on the record he's playing."

"But it's loud enough to dance to," said Barry.

Zeina felt rather pleased and almost like an adult because the friends she was siting with were eighteen years old.

Every time she'd attended a dance at the hall recently, the music had been played so low that sometimes it was difficult to determine what type of music was being played.

But Zeina felt sure that was because most of the people who attended the dances were senior citizens, and they'd probably requested that the music be played very low.

* * * * * ❖••••••❖ ★ ❖••••••❖ • • • • •

She found it odd that whenever she looked at a very dark area of the room, it would light up more, and then she could see people in that area, looking at her, and frowning.

It seemed that those people were upset or very worried about something they saw somewhere behind her, or close around her. She assumed that was why they'd chosen to sit at tables in the darkest areas of the room that were only momentarily lit up the instant she looked at that one particular area.

She quickly turned her attention back to her friends when Peter began getting up from the table while saying: "Speaking of dancing, I'm dancing out of here. Enjoy yourselves, kiddies. Nice seeing you again, Zeina."

"Oh, you're leaving. It was nice seeing you, too, Peter. Say hi to Lorna for me. Goodnight."

"Bye, Peter. Too bad Lorna couldn't make it. Tell her I'll call her tomorrow around noon," said Marianne.

"Yeah, will do. See you, Barry."

"Bye, Peter. Take care, man."

Zeina looked around at the unusually sparse gathering, and wondered if most of the people were attending the lodge banquet, then she said: "Clapton's must be packed tonight because there's usually so many people *here*."

"Yes, there usually is," said Marianne. "But you know, I think many of them are still quite shocked about what happened, so, they're in no mood for fun."

"Shocked? About what?" asked Zeina.

"You mean you haven't heard?"

"No. What happened? Was there a fire in somebody's home, and somebody got hurt?"

"Oh, I forgot you don't have a television set, and I guess with your father's breathing problem, you haven't been listening to the radio, either," said Marianne.

"It was the strangest thing, Zeina. I thought you would've heard about it, somehow," said Barry.

"Some people were murdered."

"No! Really?" cried Zeina.

"Yes, and there was an autopsy on the bodies. They always do that when there's a murder."

"Yeah, I heard they do that. When did the murders happen?"

"Oh, about...well, a few days ago," said Marianne.

"I didn't know that. Gee, murders. Right here in town, too."

"The funeral's taking place tomorrow," said Barry.

"Yeah? I don't like funerals. I mean, I've never been to one, and I don't think I'd want to, but I'm sure my mom'll go to it. Maybe my dad, too, if he's not in a very bad mood again," said Zeina.

"We'll be going. Lots of other people, too."

"Oh? Um, I feel so awful now," said Zeina. "I don't want to...I mean, I think I'll go home now. Thanks for letting me sit with you, and it was great seeing you again."

"We're leaving, too, as soon as we finish our drinks. I don't feel like staying, and I really didn't want to come here, either, but Barry thought it'd take our minds off the murders," said Marianne.

"Well, I can see I was wrong," he said. "I feel just as bad about them as you do. Goodnight, Zeina. If you want, I can drop you off at your place because it's on my way."

"Thanks, anyway, Barry, but I think I'd like to walk back home, now. Goodnight."

"Goodnight, Zeina," said Barry and Marianne.

* * * * * ❖••••••❖★❖••••••❖ * * * * *

While walking along the very dark road on her way back home, Zeina thought about the murders that she'd been told had happened a few days ago.

She then began thinking of the clothes in her closet, and she wondered if her mother would have time to dye one of her dresses black before the funeral. She thought that instead of asking her mother to dye one of her dresses, she could wear her mother's black skirt, with her own black, three-quarter length, fall coat.

She'd reached the top of the first hill when Zeina thought she saw something moving to her right. Turning her head quickly, she saw what looked like several people running over the tops of huge boulders that were part of the many hundreds of other boulders that formed the high ridge in the distance.

She stopped walking, and watched the people disappear into to the tall trees at the other end of the rocky ridge. Zeina thought it had been quite reckless of those people to have run across the high ridge at night because they could have tripped over something in the dark, and then she continued on to the next hill.

She felt less nervous when she saw a few lit windows in her home, then Zeina walked faster, and then she began running. She stopped when she reached the front door, then she took a big breath.

She bit down on her bottom lip, and her hand trembled as she slowly turned the doorknob, opened the door, and then she felt both very surprised and scared when she saw her mother.

"Well! This *is* a surprise! You're home sooner than I expected. I thought you might've stayed much longer," said Viola.

"Um, well, that's because there weren't many people there, and the ones that *were* there, were mostly old people. But Marianne and Barry and Peter were there, and they asked me to sit at their table with them, and I really liked that. And guess what? They told me that some people were murdered!"

"Murdered? Who?"

"I don't know. But that's what they told me."

"My God! That's awful! When did it happen?"

"They said a few days ago. I know how you feel because I was really shocked, too, when *I* heard about the murders."

"I haven't listened to the news for almost a week. If I'd only known, I could've tried to...No, I suppose not. There's not much I could have done, anyway, is there?"

"Are you going to the funeral?"asked Zeina.

"Well, I'd like to go, but I don't think your father's up to it."

"Oh. If I go with you, I thought I'd borrow your black skirt. I can wear that with my black, fall coat."

"What time's the funeral service?" asked Viola.

"They didn't tell me."

"I see. Well, then we might have time to go by the florist's and pick out some flowers. After we do that, we could have an early lunch at Lindstom's."

"Yeah, sure, that sounds nice. I'm so glad I decided to go out tonight. If I hadn't, we might not've heard anything about this. That's why I didn't stay. How's dad doing?"

"Not too good, I'm afraid. If he gets any worse, I want him to see a specialist. But at least he still has a good appetite. He's been eating much more than usual, but that extra weight he's put on lately doesn't help with his breathing," said Viola.

"Laying around so much isn't healthy for him, either."

"I know, and I keep trying to get him to exercise. Even if he went for a long walk, but he just gets so grouchy when I suggest that. His moods are bad enough as it is, so, I don't want to upset him more than he already is."

"Hmmm, I'll see if dad'll go for a walk a couple of times a day with me," said Zeina.

"I hope he'll do it. Anyway, I'm feeling tired, so, I'm going to bed. I might be bunking in with you again tonight for a few hours. Your father sits up, coughing and gasping for air, and he gets so mad when I have to ask him so often if there's something I can do to relieve his discomfort."

"I know. I'm going up to my room. Goodnight."

"Goodnight, dear," said Viola.

The top two buttons had fallen off the black skirt she'd borrowed from her mother, but Viola had solved the problem by giving her a big, black silk scarf that Zeina could wrap around her waist, then fasten it with a brooch, which they both agreed looked very pretty.

When they left the house to go to the funeral service, Zeina noticed that it was an unusually dark day again, but she thought it was rather apt, considering that there was a funeral in town.

During the funeral service, she looked around at the people seated in the chapel, and she noticed that many of the men appeared quite similar. All of them were wearing black suits, which wasn't unusual, considering the sombre occasion, but they looked so much alike.

What seemed even more curious to her, was that when they'd entered the chapel and started looking for a pew to sit in, Zeina had noticed that all the men were the same height, and they also had the same builds.

She wondered why she'd never noticed that before, but she supposed it was because she'd never seen so many of the townsmen gathered in the same place before.

Zeina kept looking at them, then she quickly turned her head away when one of the men whom had noticed her looking at him, smiled and winked at her.

She hadn't paid attention to the funeral service because she'd been looking at the people around her, then Viola nudged her when the service was over, and they moved out into the aisle.

The small chapel was at the south end of a shopping mall, so, Zeina and Viola chatted with neighbors about the funeral service while they examined sale goods in stalls placed along the center of the wide hall.

Zeina wished that they lived in a larger town because of the lack of choices in clothing they had at the town's mall. Even the florist shop had a poor selection of flowers, and she and her mother had bought the last of the flowers, which were two, very pale pink roses and half a dozen white ones.

She slowly shook her head while thinking of how all the clothing on the sale tables lacked color. Every skirt and blouse, and even all the men's shirts were pale gray to match the suits they wore.

She stood beside her mother, and nodded her head whenever she heard someone ask if they agreed with something that Zeina wasn't paying attention to as she looked around the mall at the people who were dressed in either black or gray clothing.

A group of what looked like over a dozen men and women entered through a side door of the mall, and they began taking shoppers by the hand, then leading them out of the mall.

Zeina hadn't had time to see the faces of the people who had guided the other people out of the mall. She suddenly wondered if it was her wild imagination playing tricks with her eyes again because it seemed as though the men who had led those people out of the mall, bore a striking resemblance to one another.

All those men had been heavyset, wearing gray suits, and from what Zeina had been able to determine, they'd had their same gray hair that had been cut in exactly the same way. The women had been almost the same height as the men, and they'd also been heavyset, and dressed in gray clothing.

"Zeina likes that, too. Don't you, dear?" asked Viola.

"Yes, I do," she replied, unaware of the topic.

"We should be getting back, now. Did you want to do some shopping, Zeina?" Viola asked her.

"Mmmm? Oh, no, thanks. I'm just looking."

"We're leaving, now, too," said Dorothy. "I noticed that you and Zeina walked here, Vi. We can drop you off at your place."

"Oh, thanks. Are you sure that won't be a problem?"

"Nonsense! It'll give us more time to chat."

· · · · · · ◇••••••◇★◇••••••◇ · · · · · ·

Ken and Dorothy Gladstone gave them a lift home, and after they'd thanked the Gladstones and said goodbye to them, Zeina saw her father sitting on the porch, and she thought it was rather surprising how she'd never noticed before how much he looked like most of the other men she'd seen at the funeral and in the mall.

Now that he'd gained more weight, he looked just as hefty as the other men that she'd seen that day, and his facial features were so much like those other men, too.

She went upstairs to change, then passing her bedroom window, Zeina glanced out, and saw her father walking to the barn. She hoped that he'd decide to go for a long walk after he left the barn because he'd spent the early part of the day, sitting on the porch.

She then began hurrying to change out of the clothes she'd worn to the funeral, so that she could rush over to the barn and suggest to her father that they walk down to the lake.

Zeina looked out her bedroom window again as she quickly undressed, and saw he father walking past the closed barn doors, instead of opening one of them and going inside.

She began dressing as fast as she could while looking out the window and seeing her father begin walking out into the pasture, and she kept looking out the window as she finished dressing, while watching him walk far across the pasture.

Zeina took one last glance out of the window, saw her father walking into the trees at the far end of the property, and then she hurried downstairs.

Viola was pouring three cups of tea when Zeina rushed by her to go out the door to catch up with her father.

"Why are you in such a rush, Zeina? I was hoping you'd have a cup of tea with your father and me."

"Oh! Thanks, but I'm going to catch up with him. I saw him way over at the far end of the field."

"Now why didn't he tell me that he was going for a walk? Well, I'm glad to see he's getting some exercise. If he's on his way to the lake, I'll join you two down there."

"All right! Bye!" cried Zeina, rushing out the door.

She hurried down the porch steps and began walking quickly toward the area she'd last seen her father. Zeina stopped when she suddenly recalled seeing what seemed to have been somebody on the porch when she'd rushed out of the house.

She turned around, and gaped when she saw her father sitting on the porch, his head resting on the back of the rocking chair, and he had his eyes closed.

"Dad?"

"Hmmfff?"

"Dad! I thought I just saw you way over at the other end of the field less than two minutes ago!"

"Mmm-hmm? Wasn't me."

"But I was sure I saw you way over at...Hmmm, if you're here on the porch, then who could that've been?"

"Hmmff. Mmmmm, I'm *trying* to have a nap! Damn it!"

"I'm sorry. Uh, I'll let you sleep."

Zeina walked back inside the house and told Viola that she'd been mistaken about seeing her father going for a walk.

"I *thought* you were wrong about that, dear. Your father's been so weak lately, and that's because he's not getting enough sleep. Too much coughing and gasping. Hmmm, would you look at that? It's getting even darker out. The days are so dark lately, that there's only about half an hour of light each day, and even then, it's not much, at all. I have to carry a flashlight around with me all day long whenever I'm outside. It's a wonder you could even see anyone near the barn, let alone way out in the field. Are you having a cup of tea, Zeina?"

"No thanks. I'm going around to the back of the house and sit on the swing for awhile. I love watching the sunset, but I haven't been able to do that for over three days because it's been so dark all day, and so many big, dark clouds, too."

"Yes, I know. Almost like night every day. This lack of light every day is so strange, isn't it?"

"Yeah, it sure is. Well, because it's so dark out, I've changed my mind about playing on the swing, and instead of doing that, I'm going to bed early. Goodnight."

"Goodnight, Zeina."

She'd been asleep for what seemed to have been only five minutes, when she awoke. Zeina sat up, reached for her robe, then while slipping it around her shoulders at the same time she was shuffling her feet into her slippers, she became aware that the side of the bed she was sitting on was much higher than usual.

She turned her head, then gasped when she saw a very big man lying on the other side of her bed, with his back to her. Zeina's hand flew to her mouth, and her eyes widened as she quickly got off the bed, and stared at the man on it.

There was only a slight amount of moonlight coming through the window, but it was enough for her to see the man on her bed. She struggled not to panic while hoping it was just her overactive imagination making her see things that weren't really there.

Leaning closer to the bed, Zeina's heart pounded so heavily as she looked at the man while trying to determine in the dark if it was a stranger, or her father.

Her eyes widened even more when she saw that he was wearing a black suit, and he looked almost exactly like those men she'd seen on the road on her way to the dance hall, and at the funeral service, and in the mall.

The man on her bed had a hefty build like all those men, too, but she knew it was impossible for the man she'd thought she'd seen combing his hair in the mirror in her parents' bedroom to have so many male relatives who looked almost exactly alike.

Zeina backed away from the bed, then tiptoed toward her bedroom door. She tried not to make a sound while very slowly opening and closing the door, and then she hurried down the hall to her parents' bedroom, and opened the door.

She looked in, and saw that her parents were asleep in bed, so, Zeina felt scared while wondering whom that man was on her bed. She gently shook her mother's shoulder until she'd awakened her.

"Zeina? What are you doing up at this hour?"

"Shhhhhh! Mom! There's somebody sleeping on my bed! A huge man!" she whispered loudly.

"On your bed? Are you sure you weren't just dreaming?"

"I'm sure I wasn't!" whispered Zeina.

"Hand me my robe. Thanks. Your imagination has been running wild, lately, but I'll come see what you're talking about."

"Wait! We should wake up dad first, because this man could be very dangerous if he's broken into the house!"

"Shhhh. Zeina, let's you and I have a look first, all right?"

"But what if he...Well, okay then, but let's be very quiet when we get close to my room. Okay?"

"Of course, but I still think you had a bad dream."

They went along to Zeina's bedroom, then she told Viola to stand beside the door and just have a peek into the room, then if the man made a move, they could hurry back and rouse her father.

Zeina slowly opened her bedroom door, then Viola poked her hand inside and flicked on the light switch that was just inside the door. The small lamp beside the bed lit up, and Zeina was shocked to see that there wasn't anybody on her bed.

"There, you see what I mean? It was just a bad dream."

"But he was a *really* big man, so, I couldn't have been wrong about seeing him!"

"You probably just dreamed that. Now try to calm down."

"But he looked so real! He could've..."

"Could've *what*? Left? You were only in my bedroom for less than two minutes, so, if there'd been a man on your bed, and he'd got up, and then gone downstairs to leave the house, then he would've had to walk by us in the hall to get downstairs, and your window's locked from the inside. See?"

"It's...it's just...I'm sure I saw him."

"It was that funeral today. It's got your nerves all on edge. Hmmm, I think I'll sleep with you for the rest of the night. Would that make you feel better?"

"Would you mind? I feel so nervous," said Zeina.

"I can see that. Well, just to make you feel even better, I'll sleep on *that* side of the bed, so, if you wake up, you'll know it's me, and not some stranger. Okay?"

"Yeah, thanks, mom. Gee, now it might take me a long time to get back to sleep."

"Just close your eyes, dear. Now that you see that everything's okay, you'll soon be asleep."

Viola got onto the bed, moved to the far side of it, then Zeina reached over and clicked off the small bedside lamp, and snuggled down, closed her eyes, and hoped that her nerves would settle enough for her to sleep.

It seemed like only moments later, when Zeina awoke, then smiled when she realized that she'd fallen asleep quicker than she'd thought she could have, after such a scare.

She closed her eyes again, and became aware that her side of the bed had risen higher, then moments later, she realized that her mother wasn't heavy enough to weigh the other side of bed down so much.

Her heart leapt when she suddenly thought that perhaps the big man was back on her bed. Zeina held her breath as she turned her head very slowly to look at the other side of her bed, and then she panicked when she saw the huge form lying beside her.

She trembled while staring at the very big man lying beside her, and because he had his back to her, she couldn't see his face. Zeina took a few deep breaths before slowly turning over onto her other side to reach out for the bedside lamp, but it wasn't close enough for her to turn it on.

She slid herself very slowly to the edge of the bed, then she slipped off it and stood beside it, then she turned on the bedside lamp, and then she rushed away to the door.

Zeina opened it, then looked back at her bed, and then her jaw dropped when she saw only her mother lying on her bed. Her thoughts swirled as she tried to make sense of what she'd seen before she'd turned on the bedside lamp.

Zeina trembled as she tried to convince herself that she had only dreamed about seeing a very big man on her bed. But the weight of him. She could recall how realistic it had felt to be elevated on her side of the bed because of the supposed man's great weight.

Her paranoia was growing as she recalled seeing her father walking out of sight across the far end of the pasture, and the man sitting on a big boulder at the top of the hill.

Hearing about the deaths in town had also made her feel scared, and then on her way back from the dance at the town hall, she had seen those people running across the rocky ridge.

She'd also noticed how almost all the men she'd seen that day, including her father, had looked so much alike, and they'd all had grey hair, too, and they'd all had on identical clothing.

Adding to that odd coincidence, during the past two days when she'd looked out the living room window and seen men walking along the road, they'd looked so much alike that it had seemed as though the same man was passing by every ten or fifteen minutes.

And those men whom had escorted people out of the mall had been the same height and build as all the other men she'd seen recently, and she wondered how that could be possible.

As Zeina was thinking about how all the men she'd seen recently looked like carbon copies of her father, she saw her mother awaken. Viola smiled as she slowly began to sit up in bed, then she turned sideways, and placed her feet on the floor. She then looked at Zeina again, and smiled.

"Are you going back to your bedroom? Are you? Mom? Say something. Why are you smiling like that? Mom?"

Viola slowly stood up, then very slowly walked around the bed, and began walking toward her as Zeina backed away from her.

"Mom! Stop smiling like that! Please! You're scaring me! Say something! Mom? Stop!"

Zeina's heart was pounding faster as she darted sideways to avoid being bumped into by her mother who, although she was smiling oddly, she seemed to be either sleepwalking with her eyes open, or in a strange trance.

Viola slowly turned to watch her rushing toward the bedroom door, then Zeina rushed out, and down the hall. She was just nearing her parents' bedroom, when she saw the door slowly opening, and her father stepping out into the hall.

He had a cryptic smile, too, just like her mother, and he wouldn't answer her when Zeina asked him why he was looking at her in such a strange manner.

He reached out and held her arms, then she began struggling out of his grasp as she fought her way to the staircase, and then she stumbled several times as she ran downstairs.

Zeina ran to the front door, threw it open, and then gasped and uttered a cry of fright when she saw four men who looked so much alike, standing on the porch, smiling at her. She slammed the door shut, turned around, and then began running to the back door.

After running out the back door, and then a few yards away from it, she stopped to look back at the house. Zeina then saw even more identical men, as well as heavyset women who looked so much like the men, gathering around the back of her home.

She ran to the front of the house, then toward the road, and then stopped when she saw more men walking from both directions along the road.

Zeina looked around and saw dozens more people in the darkness; some leaning against trees, seemingly chatting, some seated on the ground, and others slowly walking toward her.

She then saw many cars appearing over the hill, and from the other end of the road, and when they stopped, the people getting out of the cars were wearing very dark clothes and carrying black wreaths with big, white bows on them.

More cars were arriving and Zeina realized that for some unknown and frightening reason, almost all the townspeople had decided to come to her home.

She began whimpering when all the people noticed her, and started walking slowly toward her. Zeina gauged the distance between them and herself, then she began running toward the trees off in the distance while hoping all the people wouldn't follow her into the very dark forest.

By the time she reached the trees, her heart pounded heavily and she was gasping for air, then Zeina began crying out each time a sharp branch scraped her flesh as she fought her way farther into the trees that she could barely see in the darkness.

She screamed whenever she felt hands grabbing at her from somewhere amidst the trees that she kept bumping into as she stumbled and ran through the dark forest.

She panicked when she heard her name being called out by people she couldn't see in the dark. Then she saw it. A clearing far ahead of her, and lit by moonlight.

A distant memory was beginning to form as she fought off the branches and the hands that were reaching out for her. She was beginning to recall that if she could reach that barely discernible clearing in the forest, that she'd be able to find refuge from the terror around and behind her.

Zeina tripped, fell to the ground, then screamed as she fought off the hands grabbing at her legs and arms. She kicked, pounded, and clawed at the hands until she was free, then after quickly crawling away from them, she staggered to her feet and began running again.

Suddenly, somebody stepped out in front of her, so, Zeina gathered all her remaining strength, and rammed her fists into the person's stomach, toppling whoever it was over onto the ground.

She began running again, groping out in the darkness to make sure she wouldn't bump into a tree, and she felt her nightgown clinging damply to her body because of all the perspiration from her trembling body.

Zeina thought about the people pursuing her from all sides, then knowing she had to somehow distract them from her goal, she took off in another direction, and felt only slightly relieved that she could hear the now faint pounding of their footsteps near her.

She stumbled down a hill, tearing her nightgown on bushes she skirted as she made her way around again to where she'd led the people away from.

She then stopped for a moment, listening for any nearby footsteps. She couldn't hear any sounds near her, so, Zeina hurried toward the moonlit clearing in the forest.

She reached the clearing, then started running toward the door that was wedged between two trees. She slowly turned the doorknob, then cried out when it came off in her hand.

Zeina cried and whimpered as she jiggled the doorknob back into the door, hoping that she could get it back into position before dozens of hands started grabbing at her again.

Her ears were burning as she jiggled the loose doorknob while listening for any sounds of rushing footsteps behind her. She felt dizzy, then she realized that she'd been holding her breath too long, so, she blew out a great breath, and then inhaled deeply.

The stem of the doorknob clutched the ridges inside the slot after she'd wobbled it side to side, then Zeina slowly turned the doorknob while hoping it would keep turning, then she heaved a big sigh when the door clicked open.

She flung the door open wider, rushed through it and into total blackness, then she slammed the door shut, leaned back against it, and then closed her eyes tightly while panting heavily.

Zeina was leaning back against the door, with her thoughts whirling as fast as the red and white lights she could see with her eyes tightly closed.

She then worried that somewhere in the blackness she was now standing in, somebody might be groping around in the dark, trying to grab onto her.

She turned around and slid her hands over the door until she found the doorknob, and as she began to very slowly turn it, Zeina hoped that when she opened the door, all the people who had been chasing her, would have run past the door and farther into the forest.

She slowly opened the door just enough to poke her head outside, and when she didn't see anyone lurking in the trees nearest to her, she stepped outside the door.

Zeina moved away from the closed door while thinking that if she saw anyone, she could turn around and run back to the door. She took a few more steps away from the door, then screamed when someone standing close behind her, gripped her arms, and she began trying to struggle away from whomever held her so tightly.

Suddenly, many of the trees ahead of her began fading, then moments later, her thoughts spun as she stared wide-eyed at dark figures silhouetted by the light from the open front door of her home.

She could vaguely hear the man gripping her, telling her to relax because now she was safe. Her terror and her race through the almost pitch-black forest suddenly made her feel overwhelmingly tired, then her knees buckled.

The man gripping her quickly caught Zeina before she slumped to the ground, then after he picked her up and began carrying her away, she began falling asleep while feeling soothed by the man telling her that she'd feel much better when she awoke.

Moments later, her heart leapt when she realized that she was still running through the dark forest while heading for the door wedged between the two trees.

Zeina grabbed the doorknob, opened the door, and rushed through it again into the total darkness. She slammed the door shut behind her, then leaned back against it, with her eyes tightly closed, and then she panted heavily.

She took a long, deep breath, exhaled slowly, then after opening her eyes, she winced from the bright light. She gasped at finding herself in the kitchen of her home, leaning back against the door, and her thoughts swirled as she gaped at her mother.

"Zeina! You're going to break your neck one of these days racing downstairs like that! Now you go right back upstairs, and I'll tuck you into bed. That's a good girl," said Viola.

"I'm so scared!"

"Then turn on all the lights upstairs, dear. Either your father or I'll be up shortly. Go on."

"Okay. You're coming up soon, right? Promise?"

"I promise, Zeina. Very soon, dear."

She climbed the stairs, then Zeina turned on all the lights in the hall as she walked to her bedroom, and then she turned on all the lights before getting back into bed.

She began to relax when she saw that the curtains on the window were closed, and she was glad they were because she didn't want to be frightened by seeing the tree branches swaying and casting eerie shadows across the ceiling and walls of her bedroom.

Her father opened the door, entered, and then stood by the door, smiling at her. She felt a little frightened because he now looked so similar to all the men she'd been seeing recently. Zeina then felt so relieved when her mother came into the room and closed the door. Zeina sat in her bed, propped up on the pillows she had stacked against the headboard, and she was frowning while looking at her parents as they stood silently by the closed door, smiling at her.

When Zeina asked why were smiling, they didn't answer her, then her parents continued smiling at her as they started walking very slowly toward her. She burst into tears while begging her parents to explain why they just kept smiling at her without speaking, then her father sat down close beside her on the bed.

Her lips trembled into a slight smile after he'd raised his hands and gently cupped the sides of her face. A moment later, her father slid his hands down to her neck, then after baring his clenched teeth, he began strangling her.

Just as she was losing consciousness, Zeina saw herself putting on her mother's dark blue and white striped dress again while trying to decide whether she should go to the dance at the town hall.

She then saw herself walking along the dark road to the town hall, being invited to sit down at the same table, then having almost the same conversation with Marianne, Peter, and Barry.

But whenever they mentioned murder, Zeina would sometimes smile and say she had to leave. At other times, she'd jump up from the table, take off the big, high heeled shoes, and then run out of the town hall.

She often thought that she'd only been dreaming of continually doing almost the same things every day, but Zeina felt sure she couldn't have been dreaming because everything seemed so real.

She reasoned that every day seemed so dark because she'd been sleeping so much, and for what seemed like months at a time.

She awakened, but kept her eyes closed, hoping that her father would think she was dead, because then he wouldn't start strangling her again.

She then heard another man's voice talking low as he said to somebody that it had been two days since the awful incident. Then another man said that Zeina was still in a state of shock, but with his care, and the help of a child therapist, she would slowly begin to accept the deaths of her parents.

* * * * * ❖••••❖ ★ ❖••••❖ * * * * *

Somewhere far back in her mind, and too terrifying for Zeina to comprehend yet, that horrifying memory lay waiting to be awakened to grim reality.

She was in too much shock to dare even a glimpse of that memory of her father repeatedly stabbing and slashing her mother as he shouted in rage.

Zeina had been cowering in a corner of the kitchen, wide-eyed and screaming and aching from the terrible beating her father had just given her.

She had stared up at the knife in her father's raised hand as he'd loomed over her, and then she'd known that she would die when he swung the long blade down at her.

In what had seemed like a split second, her mother had lunged at him, and bashed his hand away to try knocking the knife out of his hand, and then he'd whirled around and started stabbing Viola.

Zeina screamed and sobbed while watching her father slashing at her mother's face and arms. Viola had started staggering backwards while trying to dodge the knife, then she'd turned around, leaned over the kitchen counter, and reached out for the butcher knife.

That was when Zeina had seen her father stab her mother in the back, near her right shoulder. Viola had groaned loudly and almost started falling to her knees before she'd whirled around, and then screamed while plunging the butcher knife into his neck.

Zeina had then watched her mother fall to her knees, topple forward on top of him, and then moments later, it had been so quiet as she'd stared at her parents sprawled on the bloody kitchen floor.

She had then run out of the house, fearing that her father might get up off the floor and start attacking her again. When she'd seen many of her neighbors coming toward the house in the darkness, she had thought that they wanted to kill her, too.

Traumatized by the horror she'd just witnessed, and the brutal beating she'd suffered, Zeina had become terrified and mistrustful of all adults.

When a few of her neighbors had held her and tried to calm her, she had felt sure that they were holding her until her father came out of the house to kill her.

She'd broken away from her neighbors, and then started running into the forest. She had become hysterical when two men had run after her, then managed to grab her while she'd been running through the trees. When they'd held her and tried to soothe her, Zeina had screamed and struggled until she'd fainted.

Police cars and an ambulance had arrived by the time the men had carried her out of the forest, and then placed her in the arms of one of the ambulance attendants.

. . . . . ❖••••••❖★❖••••••❖ . . . . . .

It took Zeina almost a year under the care of a child psychologist before she was able to come to terms with the horror she'd witnessed. But sometimes that terrifying memory flashed back for a few moments, even years later, whenever she treated a terribly bruised child whom had been viciously beaten by a parent.

As a pediatrician, and a survivor of child abuse, Zeina could understand so well the intense emotional damage suffered by physically abused children. Zeina often thanked God that she had such a wonderful, loving and gentle husband whom idolized their two, happy, healthy children.

The End

.

SAND DUNES

.

Sand Dunes

The deer stopped drinking from the river, raised its head to look around, and then lowered its head again to resume drinking. Cole waited until the deer raised its head again, and looked in his direction before he focused on it.

He was just about to shoot when he detected a sudden movement off to his left, so, he lowered his camera and saw his nude father running toward the river.

The deer bolted for the safety of the trees, and then Laura, who was also nude, ran to the river and laughed as she splashed into the water. She and his father then embraced and kissed while unaware that Cole was standing amid the trees and bushes, watching them.

He'd told them that he wasn't hungry because he'd had a big breakfast, and that instead of having lunch, he wanted to take photos of cows at a farm about a mile down the road from the cottage.

A few minutes after he'd told them about his plans, Cole had walked by the partly open door of their bedroom, and overheard their plans to have a picnic lunch by the river.

That's when Cole had started thinking of ways to ruin their picnic lunch. He had walked along the road toward the farm, and then once he'd been out of sight from the cottage, he had hurried off the road and into the trees.

He had waited until he'd seen them appear at the river, and then a few minutes after Laura and his father had run into the river, he crept through the trees and over to the blanket where they'd left their clothes and picnic lunch.

Cole spread out his father's shirt on the blanket, placed a few items on it, tied the shirt around them, then he ran back into the woods and hid the bundle behind some bushes.

After a few more fast trips back and forth to gather more of their items, he carried the blanket over to the bushes, and then he grinned because Laura and his father hadn't seen what he'd done.

Cole put all his loot in the center of the blanket, gathered up the corners, and began tugging the blanket through the trees, then he stopped at the spot where he'd been standing when he'd seen them playing in the river.

They waded out of the water, and Cole's father laughed as he laid on the grassy riverbank, and then Laura ran away, shouting to him that she was going to get cold drinks for them.

Cole sat down, opened the blanket, and began eating one of the sandwiches Laura had made as he wondered where he should hide their clothes.

He watched his father standing with his hands on his hips as he waited for Laura to return. A few moments later, she was running back to him while shouting that their clothes, lunch, and everything else were gone.

Cole waited until they began walking away before he gathered the blanket into a bundle again, and started dragging it through the woods close to the river.

Now that the blanket, clothes, and picnic lunch were gone, his father and Laura would think that the culprits had been some local troublemakers who had seen them coming to the river.

Cole knew that his father would be quite angry, especially because he'd rented a cottage that he had thought was far away from any other one.

. . . . . . ❖•••••❖★❖•••••❖ . . . . . .

He hoped that farther downstream there would be a place where he could hide the bundled blanket, then about ten minutes later, Cole came across a small inlet off the river, and he saw about a dozen boulders laying on the ground near the water.

He undressed, waded into the inlet, and smiled when he noticed that the water only came up to his knees. He pushed the blanket bundle underwater, and stomped on it a few times before he began gathering boulders to place on top of it.

After he finished that shocking prank, he waded back out of the water, and laid on his back, then placed his forearm over his eyes to shield them from the sunlight.

As the warm breeze dried his body, Cole began recalling the

many times his parents had taken him to a resort near the desert, and he'd basked in the sun while lying on a sand dune close to a small pond he'd been playing in.

Less than fifteen minutes later, Cole got dressed, slung his camera around his neck, and then started running through the woods toward the main road.

He reached the road and began walking along it, heading for the farm because he'd seen a few apple trees close to the fence that ran along the side of the road.

He climbed over the fence, and then after he set his camera down on the grass, he took off his shirt, climbed an apple tree, and began dropping apples onto the ground.

Cole then wrapped a dozen apples in his shirt, and then he began walking back down the road to the cottage.

• • • • • ◇•••••◇★◇•••••◇ • • • • • •

Two weeks before he'd accompanied his father and Laura on vacation, Cole had seen a Baptist church a few blocks away from his home, and a few of his friends had told him about the baptismal rites that were performed on new members of the church.

They'd said that a girl who lived on their street had been taken on a bus trip out of the city, and then she and ten adults had been baptized in a river, so, that had given Cole a great idea.

He planned to tell his father and Laura that a big group of Baptists had arrived near the cottage, and they planned to baptize new members of their church.

Laura looked out the window and saw Cole walking shirtless toward the cottage, holding something inside his shirt, and she hoped it wasn't a snapping turtle, or a few frogs, or even worse: a snake.

Cole entered the cottage, walked over to the table, and unfolded his shirt, then said: "I got some apples off a tree down the road."

"Oh, they look delicious, sweetheart," said Laura.

"Yeah, when we were coming here, I saw some apple trees near that farm. They were right close to the road, too, so, I went there and I got some."

Moments later, his father entered the room and saw the apples on the table, then he asked: "Where'd *they* come from?"

"Hi, dad! Guess what? There's lots of kids here now! They're from a Baptist church in the city, and they came here in a big bus, and they've got a camp near the river. That's where they're gonna dunk people in the river, and make them into new Baptists! Oh, and I met Gary and Jack. They're from the Baptist church, too."

"Where did you meet them?" asked Derek.

"Down the road where I got these here apples."

"Hmmm, you know, Derek, I'll bet one or two of those kids are responsible for what happened to us," said Laura.

"What happened?" asked Cole.

"Your father and I went for a swim, earlier, and someone stole a few of our things and the blanket we were sitting on."

"Yeah? I'll ask Jack and Gary if they can find out who did it and then I can get your stuff back."

"I've got a good mind to go over there and..."

"Uh, Derek? I don't think that's a good idea because how would you explain...You know what I mean?" asked Laura.

"Yeah, I do. Hmmm, a big church group, huh? I'd hoped we'd have some time alone, but now I bet a few of them'll be coming around here to peddle their religion. I don't need those types trying to convert us," said Derek, scowling.

"There's that lodge I saw in the brochure. It's ten miles north of the town, and it's situated on a lovely lake. It has a four star rating, too, so, why don't we spend the rest of your vacation there?"

"Hmmm, yeah, you're right, Laura. I'll call the agent in town to tell them we won't be staying here for the rest of the week. Cole, you go to your room and start packing, okay? We'll be leaving here in about an hour or so."

"Yeah, okay, dad."

"Oh, I made some sandwiches for *you*, too, Cole. I'll get them. Would you like a soda pop, or milk?" asked Laura.

"Thanks, I'd like a root beer, but I'll get it," he replied, smiling.

He thought that his lie about the Baptist church group arriving within a mile of the cottage had been a brilliant idea, and now Cole felt so pleased that he'd ruined their vacation plans.

He knew that he'd enjoy staying at the big lodge for the remainder of his father's vacation because there would be other children to play with.

He'd already taken photos and bought souvenirs at places Derek and Laura had taken him on their way to the cottage, and now Cole could take photos of his father and Laura having a nice time at the lodge without being bothered by a religious group.

Cole had pouted and moped around the house for days when he'd heard that his father and Laura were going away on a vacation, and leaving him behind.

He'd refused to eat as the time drew nearer to his father's vacation, and then Laura had suggested to Derek that they take Cole with them.

Cole hadn't eaten any food that he'd been served while he'd hoped to persuade his father to take him on vacation with Laura, but he had sneaked food upstairs to his bedroom, and then smiled as he ate there. He'd been elated when his father had eventually given into his protests, and agreed to take him with them on his vacation.

Cole wanted to make certain that he was always included in his father's vacation plans because he loved finding ways to ensure that Derek and Laura would never enjoy any vacation they went on.

He was as sweet-natured as his mother had been, and Cole felt sure that she would approve of everything he was doing.

Derek had also agreed, in exasperation because of Cole's tantrums, not to send him to a boarding school, so, now Cole was attending a private school and living at home.

He'd been enrolled in a public school when his mother had been alive, but now that his father had married Laura, Cole had had to adjust to an entirely new way of living.

The home he now lived in had servants and a chauffeur, and whereas his mother had prepared all their meals, now maids served him, his dad and Laura at a large dining room table.

Cole had missed his friends when he'd moved away from them to live in Laura's home, but it hadn't taken him long to acquire two close friends.

His mother had died a month after his eighth birthday, then his father had married Laura six months later, and that had greatly disappointed Cole. Most of the time, his parents had seemed happy together, however, there had been other times when Cole had overheard them arguing in their bedroom.

He'd also noticed how his mother had looked very annoyed when she'd asked his father if he'd be working late at the office like he had the night before, then his father would apologize to her, and explain why he had to work late.

To make her feel better, Derek had taken two-week vacations every three months, and they'd spent that time vacationing in various parts of the country his mother had loved, and Cole had always greatly enjoyed those times with her.

Cole had been very withdrawn, and he'd had nightmares for several weeks after his mother had died from a severe asthmatic attack in a desert close to a hotel where they'd been staying.

He often recalled how in the weeks following her tragic death, he'd been afraid to sleep in his bedroom for fear that he might die in his bed during the night.

He had therefore waited until his father had say goodnight to him, then Cole had sneaked out of his room, gone up to the attic, hidden behind some storage boxes, and slept there.

In the mornings, he would awaken with a start, quickly turn off the alarm clock, hurry down from the attic, and then into the bathroom before his father awoke. After he'd get dressed, he would then run downstairs to the kitchen to have breakfast.

When he began having trouble paying attention at school, his father had been advised to send Cole to a therapist who would help him come to terms with the death of his mother.

While visiting the therapist, Cole had quickly learned how to hide his feelings, and to act as if the help he was receiving was beneficial to him. But eventually, his anger at having had his mother taken away from him, had turned into acceptance mixed with much grief.

The therapist had told Derek that his son was intellectually gifted, and she'd said that in many cases, a child with Cole's intellect had a greater sense of loss, therefore, that was probably the reason for Cole's temporary emotional problems.

A few months before he'd ruined their most recent vacation, Cole told his father and Laura that he would like to get a chemistry set on his birthday, which was two weeks away. He explained that he'd met a boy at school whom had a chemistry set, and Cole said he'd been fascinated by all the things that boy was able to do with chemicals.

Cole had been elated when his birthday arrived, and he was given a chemistry set, then Laura and his father told him that a small laboratory had been set up for him in one of the rooms in the house.

Because of his age, Laura had made sure that there were no harmful chemicals in the small glass tubes of his chemistry set before she'd given it to him.

She had put Epsom salts in two of the tubes, and a combination of salt and a slight amount of ground aspirin in the two other tubes, then she'd had small labels made with the names of various chemicals, which Laura had then pasted onto each tube.

Cole was delighted whenever he watched the powdered mixtures fizz after he'd combined them with water, so, he believed that he was working on real scientific experiments.

Laura had been relieved when Cole had stopped having nightmares and had taken an interest in school again, and he occupied much of his time in his little lab.

She sensed Cole's sorrow, and tried her best to be a mother to him, so, she'd been pleased that she and Derek had been able to make Cole quite happy by having a nice birthday party for him, as well as giving him what he wanted most of all for his birthday.

She hadn't realized, however, just how curious children could be, because after Cole had received his chemistry set, he had wanted to experiment with other chemicals besides those in the four glass tubes that Laura had given to him.

Cole had decided that items inside the bathroom medicine cabinet would be safe, after he'd been taught that cleaning solutions were rather dangerous. He'd then started testing the effects that iodine and other items he'd found in the medicine cabinet would have when mixed with the contents of the four tubes in his little laboratory.

He'd discovered that some chemical combinations caused a foam, and others simply blended, so, now he used very small amounts of mixtures that didn't foam in his harmless test studies.

Cole had studied the effects of the concoctions he'd developed by sneaking small doses of them into a cup or a glass his father was drinking from. After learning that Derek often had diarrhea, or sometimes stomach pains for an hour or two, Cole had been delighted that he'd discovered something new in his little lab.

But he'd been smart enough to realize not to put small amounts of his concoctions into his fathers' drinks too often, or else he'd be suspected of being responsible for his father's indigestion or diarrhea.

Cole's mother, Enid, had been a painter and photographer, and he'd always been mesmerized by her creativity. She had loved photographing sand dunes, which Enid, through careful study of their formations, had made some of them appear like nude bodies with flowers strewn over them.

She'd told Cole that she looked at sand dunes in the same way other people looked at clouds and saw shapes of animals and people in them.

Cole had watched her holding her camera at various angles for long periods of time, and although he couldn't see anything resembling an animal or a person in the mounds of sand, by the time his mother had developed the sometimes large photographs and then framed them, he would be very surprised at the results.

The majority of their vacations had been spent near desert locations, and while Derek had amused himself with other things, including gambling, Enid had taken Cole on walks in the desert.

She'd sketch or photograph the landscape while Cole played in a natural pool, and then a few hours and a picnic lunch later, they'd walk back to the hotel, and Cole would then play with other children in the pool at the hotel.

He'd loved those time with his mother, so, he'd been extremely distraught when Enid had died during a vacation close to another desert. Now, Cole convincingly pretended that he approved of his father's marriage to Laura.

* * * * * ❖••••••❖ ★ ❖••••••❖ • • • • •

Cole showered and put on fresh clothes before he phoned Paolo to tell him that he'd arrived back home from the cottage, and he suggested that they go for a hamburger and a milkshake.

"Yeah, great! I'll call Caroline and see if she wants to come with us. Okay?" Paolo told him.

"Yeah, okay. I'm coming over to your place now."

"Okay."

"Oh, and my dad and Laura are going out for dinner."

"Yeah? Why don't you come to my place for dinner, and then sleep over? Do y'want to?"

"Sure, okay. I'll tell them. See ya," said Cole.

"See ya."

He told Derek and Laura that he'd been invited for dinner and a sleepover at Paolo's, and that he was going over to meet him. Cole left the house, hopped onto his bicycle, and then he rode over to Paolo's home.

"Hi! Is Caroline coming?" asked Cole.

"Yeah, she's meeting us at Chubby Chow's. Leave your bike in the garage, okay?" said Paolo.

"I had a really great time when I was away. I took lots of pictures at Ghost Canyon and at Caribou Falls, and then after that, I saw a real live deer right near the back of the cottage where we stayed at, too. But then he saw me, and so he ran away before I could get a picture of him."

"Did y'see any bears?"

"Nope. My dad said there weren't any where we were, but there might've been because he told me there wasn't any deers near there, either, but I saw one, so, if there was deers, then there could've been bears, too. That deer I saw, ran away when I tried to get a bit closer to him, and boy, do they ever run fast."

While walking to the restaurant, Cole told him about all the things he'd seen while he'd been away, but he didn't tell Paolo about stealing the clothes, blanket, and picnic lunch.

Caroline waved to them from the table she was seated at in the restaurant, and the boys grinned as they walked over and sat with her. While they waited for their hamburgers, Cole told her everything that he'd told Paolo, then while they ate, Paolo and Caroline told him what they'd done while Cole had been away.

"And guess what? Splatter IV started last Monday, so, let's go see it on Saturday, okay?" Caroline suggested.

"I thought y'hated horror movies," said Paolo.

"I never said that, okay? I just said I thought most of them were stupid because even if somebody gets killed, they're alive again in the next movie because they were still alive after the explosion or the car accident, or when they drowned, or whatever. Okay? But in the Splatter movies, there's always new people in the house where the murders happen," she said.

"Yeah, I forgot that. They never show anyone getting killed, either, and I bet if they weren't cartoon people, then they'd show them getting killed," said Cole. "They show lots of people getting killed in the movies they won't let us see."

"Hey, Cole, you'll like Splatter IV 'cause there's supposed to be a crazy scientist in it, and he bought the huge, old house, and then he changed it into a hotel, and then some family comes to stay there. Okay? And the crazy scientist has a real spooky lab in his basement, and that's where he boils up something that changes people into zombies and vampires," Paolo told him.

"I already did that to all our household staff, and I'll prove it to you next time you stay over at my place," he said, grinning.

"Oh, yeah, I just bet," said Paolo. "I wonder how this movie'll end? I bet a sheriff goes to that spooky house, and he sees that the front door's open, then he goes inside and he sees someone dead, and then he calls the army and they all come and kill off all the weirdos. Y'think that's what'll happen?"

"Maybe. They couldn't kill off the vampires, though, unless they shot them with wooden bullets," said Caroline. "I saw a movie on TV last week where a lady did a perfect murder. That's what they called it because the police didn't know she did it, and she got away with it. She put a poison in something that doctors can't find inside you after you're dead."

"There's all kinds of poisons like that," said Cole. "I've seen some TV shows with detectives in them, and lots of times people are murdered by all kindsa different poisons. That's why I study chemicals in my lab."

"You're always doing that ever since you got that chemistry set for your birthday, and you keep telling us all about secret potions you make. But I know they're not because if they really *were* secret potions, you would've shown them to us lots of times," said Caroline.

"Oh, yeah? I do so make secret potions, and all the time, too. Okay? But I never show them to you because they're secret."

"I bet they're not," she said.

"Yes, they are," Cole told her.

"Are not."

"Are, too."

"Are not."

"Are, too, forever," said Cole.

"Aw, you beat me again. Sometime I'm going to say *forever* before you do, then I'll win, and then you'll have to tell me I'm right. Anyway, she did the perfect murder, but she was killed in a car accident after," said Caroline.

"Then she didn't get away with it, right?" Paolo said.

"But *some* crimes are perfect. Like pushing someone in front of a subway or hitting someone with your car somewhere far from where you live, so, because the man was a stranger, and you didn't know him, then you'd get away with it. All kinds of things like that. Lotsa crimes aren't ever solved," said Cole.

"That's really scary," said Caroline. "Lotsa kids get kidnapped and the police can't find them 'til maybe after lots of weeks or lots of months or even lots of years later, and they're dead, too."

"Yeah, that's why when you weren't looking, I sneaked a secret poison in your milkshake and so real soon you'll look okay to everyone in here, but you'll be in a trance, and nobody'll know you are, and that's when we'll take you to the forest. When we get there, we'll tie you to a tree, and then after that, we'll blow our secret whistles. They're the ones you can't hear when you blow them, but bears can hear them. We'll blow our secret whistles, and then big, big grizzly bears'll come and get you," said Cole, grinning at her.

"Nope. You can't do that because it'd say on the news that pretty Caroline Fullerton is missing and she's nine years old, and then they'll tell everyone on the TV about my beautiful, black, long curls. They'll tell them that my skin is the color of the most delicious chocolate in the whole world, too. Okay? Yeah, and they'll also say that the last time anyone saw me, I was with two friends who looked really stupid, so, after they tell people that on the news, you guys'd get caught," she said, smiling.

"Darn it! I figured there might be one mistake, Paolo!"

"So, how long will I be in a trance for?" Caroline asked them.

"Not too long," replied Cole. "About three whole days."

"Great. That means I'll be out of it by Saturday, so I can go and see Splatter IV."

"You'll like it even more, too, because that poison I put in your milkshake makes you become a vampire," Cole told her.

"I didn't I tell you my secret, did I? Do you guys know if I'm really asleep at night, or if I'm wearing a big, long, black cape and I'm sneaking around at night?" she asked them.

"What? Oh, no! That means...Yeah! That's not really a strawberry milkshake! It's not! It's...It's...It's blood! Blood! Blahh-ha-haaa! It's blood mixed up in a big glass of milk!" cried Paolo, cowering away from her.

"Your teeth! They're...Oh, no! Look! They're growing longer and sharper! Help! Help! Stay away from me!" exclaimed Cole.

"Your eyes! They're making me go into a weird trance! Aaaaaaa!"

"Yuk! You guys won't win the Academy Award," said Caroline.

Laura smiled when she saw Cole and Paolo come into the house, and then run upstairs. She recalled when he'd been so withdrawn after his mother had died, and how slightly mistrustful he'd been of everyone around him.

Cole had ceased having nightmares after a month of therapy, and after the therapist and Derek had complied with his wishes to have a lock put on both his bedroom door and the door of the small room where he played with his chemistry set.

Laura recalled how she'd suppressed a laugh when Cole had described his therapist as a woman who looked like Roger Rabbit's girlfriend because of the tight-fitting, revealing clothes she wore.

He'd also said that during his first few sessions, instead of talking to him, the therapist had been more interested in putting on even more makeup, or having chats on the phone with all her boyfriends.

Laura had known that wasn't true because Derek had told her that Cole had liked the therapist and he'd said that she had helped him feel better about moving into a new home.

She hoped that with Cole having close friends to play with, he'd become even more outgoing, and Laura had seen a great change in him recently, so, she had a feeling that he was learning to deal with his grief over the loss of his mother.

Shortly before, and during their recent vacation, Cole had been so happy, and Laura felt certain that he would continue to be, then perhaps in another few years, she hoped that he'd begin to refer to her as "mother," instead of calling her by her first name.

Half an hour later, she heard Cole and Paolo running back downstairs, then after they rushed into the room, Laura saw the excited look on Cole's face as he held his backpack and told her that he was leaving now to have dinner and a sleepover at Paolo's home.

"I hope *you* have a great time, too," said Cole.

"Thanks. I'm sure we will," replied Laura, smiling.

"I told Paolo I'm not getting the pictures developed that I took while we were away 'til I get my new darkroom, and then I'm gonna ask Caroline and Paolo to come over, and then we'll read the book on how to develop pictures. After we know all about that, then we're gonna try to develop all the pictures by ourselves, and then I can develop pictures for you and everyone else, and then I'll...Well, that's what I'm going to do."

"You're going to be a very busy boy, soon. I'll bet that Paolo and Caroline and your other friends will want to help you develop their pictures all the time, too," she said, smiling.

"How big can you make them?" Paolo asked him.

"Not as big as a poster, but pretty big, though. My dad hasn't told me yet if we can do that because he says he thinks we're too young to walk around in the dark with just a little red light on inside the room, and because to make pictures you have to use chemicals that he said can burn your hands. But if I can get some big paper, then we can see how big we can make them."

"If you boys start making them as big as posters, you'll be able to open your own store," said Laura.

"Naw, I'd rather be a scientist instead of having my own store. Hmmm, or maybe an astronaut," said Cole. "But I guess most of all, I'd like to be a scientist who works with detectives. Okay. We're going now. I'll see ya t'morrrow. Bye."

"Bye, Mrs. Crosley," said Paolo, waving at her and smiling.

"Goodbye, boys."

* * * * * ❖•••••••❖★❖•••••••❖ * * * * *

Later that evening, the boys played a few video games in Paolo's bedroom suite, then after they'd returned from getting a soft drink, they laid on their beds and talked.

"Hey, Cole? Do you really believe that some people can do the perfect crime just like Caroline said she saw on TV?" asked Paolo.

"Well, yeah, sometimes. Remember what she said about the poison that woman killed her husband with? Well, there's hundreds more, too. Then there's other ways, too."

"Yeah, I guess so, but y'gotta make sure there's no witnesses and you've gotta have a good alibi. Y'know what an alibi is?"

"Yeah, I know. The cops listen to anyone's alibi, and then if it sounds good to them, they say it's okay," said Cole.

"Yeah, I know."

"But the killer doesn't need any alibi if he didn't put any fingerprints on anything because he wore some gloves. That's a perfect murder when you do that, and then besides that, there's all kinds of other perfect murders, too," said Cole.

"When you hit them with a car, right?"

"Yeah, that's one of the ways. If you get a drivers license, then you can kill anybody you want. You ever see any cars ever slow down on the highway? Nope, not ever. They never do that because they've got a drivers license and the man walking across the highway doesn't. You can kill anyone y'want on a street or a highway. Nobody ever slows down their car unless they see an accident and they wanna look at it."

"Yeah, I know 'cause I've seen some movies where some man's running away from some killers on a highway, and none of the cars ever slow down. I know I would if I saw somebody running on the highway," said Paolo.

"I bet y'wouldn't because everyone says that before they get a license, and then after that, they don't care. They can kill someone with a car and never go to jail."

"Except if you're drunk when you're driving."

"Hah! All they do then is tell you that you can't drive for a little while, that's all. That's only if you're poor, though, but rich people don't get their drivers license taken away from them, and they never have to go to jail, either."

"Why not?" asked Paolo.

"Because they're rich, that's why. Cops really like rich people, but they hate poor people. You don't know that because you've never lived in a poor neighborhood. There was one near where I lived before, and I went to school with a boy who lived there. His name's Kevin, and I liked him a lot, and sometimes we used to play at his house after school, and then we went to his house one day, and when we got there, we found out that the cops had come there. His mother was crying 'cause the cops bashed open their door, and then they went inside, and they wrecked almost the whole house."

"Yeah? Wow! Why'd they do that?"

"Because they thought Kevin's big brother had robbed a store, but he didn't because he was almost blind, and he never hung around bad guys, and he didn't even look like the guy who did it, either. The cops didn't even say they were sorry because they'd made a mistake, and when Kevin's father came home from work, he called the cops and they swore at him, and hung up the phone."

"Yeah? That's really mean," said Paolo.

"Yeah, they're really mean to you if you're poor, but if you're rich, you can even murder someone and the cops never care. If lotsa people saw a rich man murder someone, then the cops have to arrest him, but all the big lawyers'll make sure the rich man doesn't have to go to jail, and those lawyers don't even care about the people who get murdered. But the other lawyers who don't like the rich man's lawyers, they don't lie or hate the dead people because they try to tell the judge to put the rich man in jail," Cole told him.

"That's because the rich man pays his lawyer a lotta money to stop him from going to jail. Right?"

"That's right. And all those big, rich lawyers go to church, too, and they even lie to God and all of the angels, too, and some of those angels are ones that the rich man murdered. Those lawyers only care about making lots of money from rich people, so, those rich lawyers are just as guilty as the man who did the murder. But they're too cruel to care."

"There's rich lawyers living around here," said Paolo.

"Yeah, I know, and I bet that lots of the people living around here've killed people, too, but all the cops are too scared to ask them any questions, so, they got away with the murder."

"That's really, really scary. Does that scare you, too?"

"Yeah, it really does," replied Cole. "That's why I hate cops, and I don't ever trust them, and they really scare me because cops only work for the rich people. If we saw a murder, then they'd never believe us because we're kids. Maybe a coupla cops might believe you, but just a bit, but then they'd never arrest the rich man who did the murder."

"But don't they have to ask the rich man if he really did the murder you saw him do?"

"Nope. The cops are so scared of losing their jobs for asking a rich man if he did it," said Cole as he frowned.

"Gee, that's bad. So, does that mean that my dad wouldn't go to jail if he murdered somebody?"

"Well, sometimes they arrest a rich man, but the judge sends him to a special jail where all the rich people go. My dad says it's like a resort, and he said that they can play golf and eat fancy food and all kinds of other fun things like that. Nothing like a real jail where they send poor people, so, the judge and the cops think that rich people are like kings forever and ever, even if they kill people. I feel a lot safer now because I live around here. Well, a bit safer. If I see any cops when I'm downtown, I get really scared because I know that they'd yell at me if I ever told them I saw a murder. But sometime when I'm a bit older, I'm going to try to meet some detectives. They're the bosses over the cops and I know they'd be nice to me. I know I could tell them anything I wanted to, just like the detectives y'see on TV. If I ever met some detectives like the ones on "Law & Order," then I know they'd smile at me and listen to anything I said 'cause I watch them all the time in the afternoon after my dad tapes their show. All detectives are a lot like them. They don't care what the judges or the rich lawyers, or the cops think. Like, all the detectives wanna do is solve the crimes. There's also some people called district attorneys and they work with the detectives, and then they talk to the judge, and they say: 'That man did it, so, I want you to send him to jail, and I don't care if he's the richest man, or she's the richest woman in the whole world because he murdered somebody,'" said Cole, grinning.

"Yeah, I know, but y'gotta sneak by the cops to get to any of those bosses over the cops. Right?"

"Yeah, because the cops don't want you to tell a detective that you saw a rich man or a rich woman murder someone. But I found out that if somebody rich did a murder even over a hundred years ago, the detectives'd still arrest them. Isn't that great?"

"Yeah, it sure is. Hey, maybe you should be a detective when you grow up," said Paolo.

"Naw, I wanna learn all about poisons and things like that, and then I can help the detectives catch the killers 'cause they're too busy chasing all the criminals and asking them all kinds of questions. Like, somebody's gotta stay in the police station to look at all the poisons and chemicals to see which one of them was used to do a murder. But I already know how to make people a bit sick with some chemicals that are in my lab at home."

"Yeah? Have y'done it, yet?"

"No way. Not me," lied Cole, then he giggled into his pillow.

········◇······◇★◇······◇ · · · · ·

They continued talking about crime until they started to get ready for bed, and Paolo began thinking about how every time Cole stayed overnight with him, he'd simply have his shower, put on his pajamas, and then get into bed.

"How come when we're at your place, y'lock the door before y'go to bed?" asked Paolo.

"Well, um, that's because I haven't lived around here for a long time, and so I don't trust all the people living in the house. It was different before. Like, when I lived with my mom, there was just me and her and my dad in the house."

"You don't know the live in staff here, either."

"Yeah, but *you* do, so, if nobody's hurt *you*, yet, or even killed you, then I figure it's safe," said Cole.

"Oh, okay. Hey, did you have your own bathroom inside your bedroom where y'lived before?"

"Nope. There was two bathrooms, though. Oh, and the little one downstairs near the kitchen."

"Who used the two bathrooms upstairs?"

"There was one in my parents' room, and the other one we all used sometimes, but I used the other bathroom all the time. Like, my dad used it if my mom was in the one in their bedroom."

"We've got five bathrooms here in our house, and I'm glad I've got my own," said Paolo.

"So am I. My bathroom's got a window in it, but y'can't see out of yours because they're all big glass blocks. When I was having my shower, I started to think that if someone ever came into your room...Like a killer, right? Then if y'ran into the bathroom to get away, y'couldn't get out the window because there's glass blocks instead of a window. I guess it's okay, though, because you've got burglar alarms."

"Yeah. Think your parents've come back home by now?"

"Maybe. And they're not my parents, either, okay? My real mother is up in heaven."

"Sorry. I just thought that because she was your stepmother, well, y'know what I mean," said Paolo.

"I call her Laura, sometimes, and sometimes I call her Aunt Laura. I don't know much about her, and I don't wanna know. I just care if she's a nice person, that's all. Well, she is. She's a really, really nice person, too, but I don't really care. All she ever cares about is making my dad happy. Laura's in love with him, and lots of other women really like him, too, 'cause they think he's handsome, so, they wanna have an affair with him. Like, do things in bed with him. I know that what they do is called sex, too."

"Yeah? My parents are too old to do any sex 'cause my dad's forty years old, and my mom's getting close to that, now. She's thirty-six years old, already."

"My dad's...hmmm, I think he's forty-two, or about that, but I think he still does sex because he just got married again, and I bet Laura wants to have a baby."

"Yeah, maybe. So, y'think lots of other women think your dad's handsome?" Paolo asked him.

"Yeah, I've seen the way they smile at him all the time. Maybe they like him because he's got lots more money now because he's making more money at his job."

"I've heard some women say *my* dad's handsome, but he says he's not handsome, but my mother's really, really beautiful. I bet she's the most beautiful woman in the whole world," said Paolo.

"Yeah, she might be. My mom was so beautiful, and she was really, really nice, too. I really loved her a lot, and sometimes when I think about her I start crying. I guess I always will, though. When I say my prayers, I promise her all the time that I'm gonna study real hard and maybe when...well, someday. Someday, you'll see."

"That's really sad that your mom died. If my mom died, I'd cry all the time. Yeah."

"Let's not talk about that anymore, okay?"

"Okay," said Paolo, smiling at him.

"Too bad Caroline couldn't sleepover, huh?"

"Yeah. Maybe on Friday night. She's really smart."

"Yeah, she really is. I like her voice the best of all. When she screams at the movies, or when she sees something really scary all of a sudden on TV, she sounds just like a woman insteada like a girl, and I like that," said Cole.

"I never noticed that before."

"I did because I study things like that. Y'have to do that when you're studying crime. Especially murders. I listen to how the women scream in movies, and Caroline screams really close to the way they do. So great. I bet detectives can tell when a woman's screaming 'cause she's mad, or if she's scared. Yeah, I bet. I'd sure like to meet a detective someday. If he...or maybe *she* got...Women are detectives, too, y'know. Anyway, I bet if they got to know me, they'd think of some way to get me past the cops to get me to a district attorney's office. I'm a pretty good detective, now, and I bet all the detectives'd think that, too. I'm thinking I might have to kill someone soon, and that's why I figured maybe I better try real hard to meet a detective before I do that so that he can tell me how good I am."

"You're really thinking about killing someone?" asked Paolo.

"Well, yeah, if I have to. Like I said, though, I'd have to talk to a detective first or maybe even a district attorney, okay? It's just that...well, sometimes some things happen before y'can talk to them. Boy, I'd sure like to meet some detectives real soon."

"What if they tell y'not to kill someone?"

"Like, I still might have to, okay?"

"Oh, y'mean, like, if someone came after you and y'had to kill them before they killed *you*, right?"

"Yeah, that's right."

"If y'feel scared sometimes, then maybe y'should get to know a detective now, so that if it ever happens, he'd know about it."

"Naw, not yet. Maybe in little while because they're really hard to get to meet. But until I meet a detective, I'm just gonna study and take pictures, and then if I...Oh, yeah, I gotta make some tapes, too. Real detectives do that, too. Then if I know a murder's gonna happen, I'm gonna try to meet a detective, and then he might even tell me to stop the murder by killing the killer, myself. Right? And maybe he'll give me a gun, too. Naw, I'm too scared of guns. Like, real ones. Not like the kinds of guns in movies. Then I'd get a...Ahhhhh-ummm. I'm getting tired," Cole said after he yawned.

"Me too. It's gotta be really late. Maybe close to a long time after ten o'clock. Close to that time, anyway."

"Oh, yeah, I forgot to tell you something. Guess what?"

"What?" asked Paolo.

"We're going away on another vacation in I think a coupla weeks, and for two weeks. That's 'cause my dad only stayed away for one week and two days this time. But I know for sure that Laura and him had a really good time. So did I," said Cole, grinning.

"Mmmm, they did? That's good. Mmmm, I'm sohhh sleepy. Goodnight, Cole."

"Goodnight."

Cole waited a few minutes before he said goodnight to his mother and told her how much he loved and missed her.

* * * * * ❖•••••❖★❖•••••❖ * * * * ❖

Laura stopped packing to look through the travel brochure again that Derek had selected, and she hoped that while they were away on vacation, there'd be opportunities for her to bond closer with Cole.

She realized that he probably felt upset because she'd married Derek not long after Enid had died, but she planned to tell Cole, when he was older, that she'd known his father for over two years before Enid had died.

They had been introduced through her father because he was a client of the company Derek worked for, and although Laura had been immediately attracted to him, she had never thought they would ever become more than just friends.

She smiled as she began recalling the sometimes amusing incidents that had occurred after she'd met Derek. The first amusing incident had happened when she had been shopping in a large department store and she'd turned around from a sales counter after making a purchase, then she'd almost bumped right into Derek.

They'd apologized to each other, then she'd recognized him as the charming man whom her father had introduced her to, then she'd asked him about his wife and family.

They'd talked for a few minutes, then Derek had asked her if she had time to have a coffee with him in the department store cafeteria before he was due back at the office.

She had accepted his invitation, and then after they'd sat down at a table to drink their coffee, Derek had taken out his wallet, and shown her photos of his wife and his son.

During the fifteen minutes they'd sat at the table, Derek had talked about Enid and Cole, the fun vacations they'd been on, how well Cole was doing in school, and what Derek planned to buy his son for Christmas.

They'd met by chance again a week later, when Laura had been having lunch in a restaurant close to her father's office where she worked part-time.

Derek had entered the restaurant, sat at a table across the room from her, then a few minutes later, when he'd noticed her, he had smiled and nodded to her, then walked over to her table to greet her.

Laura had invited him to join her at her table, then after Derek had accepted, and after the light lunch he'd ordered had been served, he had shown her new photos of Enid and Cole.

He'd chatted happily about his wife and son for most of the time they'd been in the restaurant. Derek had then looked at his wristwatch, and then apologized for having to rush back to work.

More coincidental meetings with Derek had taken place almost on a weekly basis. At the yacht club, on the street, in restaurants close to her father's office, and at several social events.

One each of those occasions, Derek had always shown her recent photos of his wife and son, then spent a great deal of time proudly talking about them.

Derek had often stopped by her desk to chat with her whenever he'd had a business appointment with her father, which was usually about once every week because Derek managed one of her father's major accounts. She had known how much he had loved his wife, and she'd felt so sad for both him and young Cole when Enid had died.

While Laura and her parents had been attending the funeral, her father had given his condolences to him and invited him to dinner whenever Derek felt he was able to socialize again.

Three weeks after Enid's funeral, Derek had come to dinner, then within a month they were dating, and Laura knew that he needed a woman who could understand the depths of his grief.

Derek had become increasingly dependent on her, and then one day, he'd told her that although he still loved Enid very much, he was falling in love with her.

Laura had initially thought he'd wanted a mother for Cole, but she'd soon realized that Derek would have loved her even if he hadn't had any children, so, she had told him that she loved him, too.

⬧••••••⬧★⬧••••••⬧

Laura felt so pleased when she saw how happy Cole was as he ran to the car, then he grinned and asked her and his father to smile as they posed beside the car, and held their suitcases while Cole took a photo of them.

Their plans were to spend the first week at a resort where there was an amusement park for Cole, then the second week of their vacation would be spent at a cottage near the mountains.

Laura knew that Cole would love taking photos of the mountains, but because he'd said he was terrified of heights, she and Derek had agreed that they wouldn't attempt to take him on a walk near the foothills of any of the mountain in case Cole panicked while thinking they were going to urge him to try walking higher up a foothill.

She felt sure that Cole would have fun playing near the cottage while she went mountain climbing with Derek for about two hours each day.

◦   ◦   ◦   ◦ ◦ ❖••••••❖★❖••••••❖ ◦ ◦   ◦   ◦   ◦

Cole enjoyed the amusement park where his father and Laura took him, and when they arrived at the cottage, he took photographs of the mountains surrounding the cottage, then he asked Laura and Derek which one they were going to climb.

Laura then pointed to a ridge that sloped upward to a high mountain, and then she explained how she and Derek would be hiking along that ridge for about half a mile before they'd start climbing the mountain.

"Wow! That ridge looks really high in some places! Aren't y'scareda falling off it?" asked Cole.

"Oh, no, not at all, because the edge of the ridge is at least thirty feet away from where Laura and I'll be walking to get to the part of the mountain we'll be climbing."

Cole then pointed to a lower part of the ridge, and then he asked his father: "How high is it right there?"

"About as high as a ten-storey building," replied Derek.

"Yeah? That's really high, so, I guess that next part's as high as about a twenty-storey building. Right, dad?"

"Almost, but as I said, there's no danger of falling off."

"Is the ridge really wide all the way along it 'til you get to the part of the mountain where you're gonna start climbing up?"

"Well, no, because it gets narrower, the closer we get to the part of the mountain we'll be climbing, and most of the time, we'll be a safe distance away from the edge of the ridge," said Derek.

"Yeah, but you can fall off the mountain when you start climbing it, can't you?"

"Don't you worry about that, son, because we have all kinds of climbing equipment that makes it safe for us to climb to the top of the mountain if we wanted to."

"Your father's right, Cole. It might look very high and very dangerous, but it really isn't," said Laura, smiling.

"Well, I guess if lots of people've climbed up it, and none of them fell off it, then you'll be okay, but *I* sure wouldn't wanna try climbing up even a little bit of that mountain," said Cole.

"I saw in one of the brochures that there's a lookout about three miles from here where people can take photographs from. There's a railing all around that area, so, there's no danger of falling. Your father and I can take you there if you'd like."

"No thanks. I'd be too scared to do that."

"There's lots of chipmunks and other small wildlife in this area, so, I'm sure you'll have fun taking photos of them," said Derek. "If you follow that path over there for about less than half mile, there's a stream, so, you might find some frogs or a small turtle you can take pictures of."

"Are there any poisonous snakes near there?"

"No, there's not," replied Derek, smiling.

"Oh, okay. Hey, dad, what time are we gonna have supper?"

"In about an hour and a half."

"Yeah? Okay, then I'm gonna go over to that stream you told me about over that way."

"All right. Make sure you don't go too far along the stream because I'll be turning on the barbecue around five-thirty, okay?"

"Okay, dad. Bye! Bye, Laura!" cried Cole, hurrying away.

"Bye, Cole. Have a nice time," she said.

They watched Cole running away, then Laura and Derek kissed before they held hands and began walking back to the cottage.

 .   .   .   . . ❖•••••❖ ★ ❖•••••❖ . .   .   .   .

Cole had run into the trees, then stopped, and peered around the trunk of one of the big trees to watch his father and Laura until they went back inside the cottage, then he hurried through the trees, and then after he'd passed the rear of the cottage, he headed for the base of the high ridge.

Twenty minutes later, Cole had trudged up the incline to the part of the ridge that his father had told him was approximately as high as a ten-storey building.

He walked to the edge of the ridge, looked down, and he could see the roof of the cottage above the trees. Cole saw that the trees ended near the bottom of the ridge, and he felt sure that the distance from the trees to the ridge was only about five feet in some places, and then he began hurrying back down the steep incline.

He walked along the base of the high ridge, looking up occasionally, then he stopped walking when he was directly below the area of the ridge where he'd looked down at the cottage.

Cole stood close to the trees, and he felt quite pleased when he couldn't see the area of the ridge that he'd looked down from, which meant that if someone were looking down at that moment, they wouldn't be able to see him through the branches of the tree he was standing under.

He'd timed his trek up to the part of the ridge he'd looked down from, and then Cole had estimated how long it would probably take his father and Laura to get to that area of the ridge.

Derek had told him that they wouldn't be walking close to the ridge, however, Cole intended to make sure that his father and Laura would have a reason to do that.

He grinned as he began running back the same way he'd come, then after he got to the stream, Cole began looking for small animals to photograph.

An hour and a half after breakfast the following morning, Cole told Derek and Laura that he was going to the stream to take photos of frogs and turtles, and some chipmunks, too. But instead of doing that, he spent that time setting up something that he hoped would seriously hinder Laura and Derek's fun.

About an hour later, he ran back to the cottage, and then walked through to the kitchen where his father and Laura were talking.

"Hi! I took lotsa pictures at lotsa places at the stream, but I only saw one chipmunk," said Cole, smiling.

"Well, maybe you'll see lots more tomorrow. Laura and I are going on our hike in about ten minutes. We'd ask you to come with us, but I know you're scared of heights."

"Yeah, I sure am. I'm going back to the stream and see if I can see some more chipmunks or some other little animals. Bye! Oh! How long'll you be gone?"

"Oh, about two hours. Maybe a bit less. When I get back, I'll start the barbecue," said Derek.

"Great. Are we going into that town tomorrow? Because I'd like to see if they've got a souvenir store," Cole told him.

"Yes, we are. And we're having dinner at a lodge about two miles outside of town," said Laura, smiling at him.

"Yeah? That'll be fun. Hope there's some other kids there. Oh, I almost forgot. When we're in the town, I wanna get some postcards to send to Caroline and Paolo."

"I'm sure they'll like them because the mountains are very beautiful, and so is the scenery around them. Well, are you about ready to leave, soon?" Derek asked Laura.

"I'll be ready in less than five minutes," she replied.

Laura hurried to the bedroom, and returned a few minutes later, and then they picked up their backpacks and headed for the door.

"Have a nice time at the stream, Cole, and you be sure that you don't wander far from the cottage after you come back from the stream. Okay? Promise?"

"I promise. I told you before that I'm going to do some coloring in my book after I take some more pictures."

"All right then. Bye," said Derek.

"Bye, dad. Bye, Laura."

"Goodbye. I hope you have a wonderful time," she said.

"Thanks. I will. See ya," Cole said, smiling at them.

Laura and Derek walked in the direction of the ridge, then after they were out of sight, Cole hurried out of the cottage, and began running toward the ridge in a slightly different direction than the one Derek and Laura had taken.

Cole reached the base of the ridge, then ran along it to the area he'd chosen the previous day, and then after sitting under a tree, he looked up through the branches and he could barely see the part of the ridge that he'd looked down from.

He opened his small backpack and took out his tape recorder, two apples, and a can of root beer, then he munched on an apple and drank his root beer while taking glances at his wristwatch.

Cole tossed the apple core away, looked at his wristwatch again, then he grinned, turned on his tape recorder full blast, and waited for Laura and Derek to appear at the edge of the ridge.

"Oh, my God!" cried Laura.

"It sounds like somebody's in trouble," said Derek.

"Wait! Listen! I think it's coming from over there! Yes, it is! We've got to help! Hurry!"

"Laura! What if it's...Sorry. Okay, I'm coming."

They heard a woman screaming, then sometimes shouting: "Help! I can't hold on any longer! I'm slipping off! I'm going to fall! Help! Please help me! Help!"

⋄•••••⋄★⋄•••••⋄

Cole had laid clothes out on the ground in a way that it would look like somebody had fallen from the area of ridge where he now sat with his tape recorder.

Last Halloween, he had seen a TV program about scarecrows, and he'd thought that they'd looked like real people at night. There had been both male and female scarecrows, so, a week before he'd left for the cottage with his father and Laura, Cole had decided to make a sort of scarecrow that would look like a real woman.

He'd told Caroline that he wanted to scare kids who came to his house next Halloween asking for treats, then he asked her to let him tape her screaming and shouting that she was falling off something very high. Caroline had thought his idea was both very scary and very amusing, and she'd readily agreed to Cole's request.

He'd then bought some women's clothing at the Goodwill store that was situated about six blocks from his home, and then he'd hidden the used clothing beneath other clothes in his suitcase.

After breakfast that morning, Cole had sneaked the plastic bag of used clothing out of the cottage, then carried the bag to the area directly below the high ridge.

He'd then spread out the long sleeves of the blouse, placed the skirt below it, and the pantyhose stuck out from the bottom of the skirt. Cole had then dropped a black sweater at the top of the blouse.

Cole went up the incline, looked down from an edge of it, and he'd been rather pleased that the clothing he'd arranged looked just like a real woman had fallen off the ridge.

He had waited until he'd felt sure that his father and Laura were near the area of the ridge where he'd looked down at the clothes he'd laid out on the ground, then Cole had turned on his tape recorder, with the volume as high as it could go.

Laura had been shocked when she'd heard a woman screaming and shouting for help, then Cole had turned off the tape recorder about five seconds before he'd seen her appear at the edge of the ridge. She'd screamed, then shouted down to the fallen woman that she was coming down to help her.

Laura had then quickly turned around and rushed away from the edge of the ridge, then a few seconds later, Cole saw his father appear at the edge, and then look down from it for a moment before he turned around and rushed away.

Cole ran to the clothes he'd laid out on the ground, picked them up, then ran back into the trees, and crouched down out of sight. Five minutes later, he watched Laura running along the base of the long ridge, looking for the fallen woman, and then moments later, he saw his father reach Laura.

They searched the area for about twenty minutes before Laura suggested that they drive to town and ask for help to find the woman whom had fallen from the ridge. Cole could vaguely hear her telling his father that the woman must have crawled away while calling out for help, then Laura wept as she began rushing back to the cottage.

Cole ran back the cottage, then folded the old clothes, and placed them back under a few other clothes at the bottom of his suitcase. He then went to the kitchen, got a soft drink out of the fridge, and then he stood by a window of the cottage, and watched for Laura and Derek to return.

He saw his father and Laura walking toward the cottage, so, Cole hurried out onto the porch, and when they were closer to him, he frowned while asking them why they'd returned so soon from their mountain climbing fun.

"A woman fell from the ridge," said Laura.

"Oh, wow! That's really scary! Is she okay?"

"We weren't able to find her. There's too much area to cover, but we saw her from where we were standing on the ridge. She was...Oh, it's so awful!" she exclaimed.

"Yes, it is," said Derek. "We're driving into town to see if we can round up a search party."

"So, um, should I go look for her?" asked Cole.

"No, don't do that. She might be...well, sort of...No, you come with us," Derek told him.

On the way to town, Laura kept wiping away her tears as she told them that she hoped the woman wasn't dead, and she said that she felt so terrible because of what she'd seen. They were followed back to the cottage by three cars with three or four men in each one.

Much later in the day, Laura and Derek returned to the cottage with a few of the men, and Laura was visibly shaken. Cole sipped on his bottle of root beer as he listened to everyone talking about the woman who might have fallen to her death.

Over two hours later, the men had called off the search because it was becoming dark. Cole felt pleased that everyone believed that a woman had fallen off the high ridge.

An hour after he'd said goodnight, he sneaked out of his room, pressed his ear against their bedroom door, and listened to Laura telling his father how upset she was, and that she just couldn't remain at the cottage after witnessing such a tragedy.

Cole suppressed a giggle as he tiptoed back to his bedroom, then he suppressed another giggle the following morning as they loaded the car. He'd won another round, so, now he had to think of other ways to ruin any other vacation of Derek and Laura's.

* * * * * ❖••••••❖★❖••••••❖ * * * * *

The day after they returned home, Cole, after thinking about it since the time he'd talked with Paolo when he'd spent the night at his home, decided it was time that he met a detective, somehow.

He asked Paolo and Caroline to ask their parents how to contact a detective, then Cole wrote down the names of several detectives.

He prayed to his mother, asking her if she would approve of him killing someone for a very good reason, and then not getting a reply, he knew that he had to make that decision by himself, after he spoke with a detective.

He now felt sure that he was able to help the detectives stop murders from happening.

Detective Ian Thompson smiled when he read the unsigned note from Cole, and he felt sure that it had been written as a hoax.

"What're you reading that's so amusing?" Glen asked him.

"It's a note somebody wrote to me, saying he or she can help solve some murders," replied Ian. "It's anonymous, of course."

"That's all that's in the note?"

"No, whoever wrote it, is asking for a signal that we're willing to cooperate with him or her," Ian told him with a crooked smile.

"Hmmm, and it was addressed to you?"

"Yeah, it is. Probably found my name listed on the board. I'll bet it was some jerk they brought in for questioning. I'm going to get a coffee. I'll pick one up for you."

"Yeah, sure, thanks."

Ian had crumpled up the note, then tossed it into the wastepaper basket, so, Glen took it back out of the basket, smoothed out the crumpled paper, and read:

"Dear Mr. Thompson. I've seen Law & Order on TV lots of times so I know I can help you solve some murders. Not

ones you already know about, but I know a big secret and

so I know I can help stop more murders before they happen.

I know where you work and so if you come outside where

you work and you wave a red hanky and then you turn

around three times at four o'clock on Thursday afternoon

then I can know you want me to help you stop some more

murders. Your friend. X."

He realized that the note had been written by a child, and whereas Ian had thought it was a hoax, Glen felt that something had motivated the youngster to contact the police.

The part of the note that had been of most interest to him was the statement: *"I know a big secret."* Glen was reading the note over for the third time, when Ian returned with two cups of coffee, and put one down on Glen's desk beside the note.

"You're not taking that seriously, are you? Wave a red hanky and turn around three times?" Ian asked him.

"It's just like in some fairy tales. Make a wish, turn around three times, then clap your hands."

"Yeah, and I'll bet if you went outside and did that on Thursday afternoon, there'd be a few guys across the street, laughing their heads off while one of them caught it on camera."

"Yeah, probably. How's that file on..."

Glen changed the subject, however, he had decided to follow the instructions in the note.

Cole felt frightened as he waited for four o'clock on Thursday afternoon. Before he had gone to school that morning, he'd tried very hard to appear happy when he'd been in the presence of Laura and his father, as well as the household staff.

He stood outside school, watching other children being picked up by their parents, then Cole hid behind a big tree so that Laura would think that he'd been picked up by Paolo's or another friend's parent. When he saw Laura drive away, he walked to the bus stop, and sat looking out the window of the bus on the way downtown, wondering if he'd made a mistake.

Two stops away from the police station, Cole got off the bus and started slowly walking, and then he went into a large, busy department store that had a big window facing the police station.

The growing tension in his stomach made him feel like he was teetering on the edge of a high roller coaster hill, ready to speed down and then up and over the next high hill.

Cole suddenly felt the urge to urinate, so, he rushed away to the bathroom. Minutes later, he flushed the toilet, walked out of the stall, and then while standing at a sink, washing his hands, his fingers were trembling. He closed his eyes and prayed to his mother before he sucked in a big breath, then he dried his hands with paper towels, and then walked out of the washroom, and back to the window.

He kept glancing at his watch as the time moved closer to four o'clock, then he saw a man come out of the police building, wave a red hanky and turn around three times, and then Cole felt unable to move because of both his fright and uncertainty.

342

Glen looked around, and after waiting a few minutes, he waved the hanky again, and turned around three times. He looked very slowly around the street, then saw a small boy standing inside the department store across the street, and looking out the window.

Glen waved the hanky as he smiled and walked across the street, then he began to hurry when he saw the boy turn away from the window, and rush into the crowd inside the store.

He hurried through the store, looking around carefully, and then seeing a display with a mannequin standing among papier maché palm trees and a fake bush, Glen walked slowly toward the display.

Cole was crouched down behind the bush, and after he looked up into Glen's smiling face, he tensed up.

He saw how scared the boy looked, so, Glen continued smiling as he crouched down and held out his hand. Cole stood up very slowly, then suddenly rushed into Glen's arms and began weeping.

Glen patted and gently massaged Cole's back as he carried him out of the store while telling Cole almost in a whisper that he was going to be all right.

. . . . . ❖•••••❖★❖•••••❖ . . . . . .

An hour later, Glen sat in a room, holding him on his lap as Cole slowly stopped crying. Cole told him about his laboratory and how he'd been studying chemicals so that when he grew up he could help detectives solve murders. He then explained how he'd put chemicals in his father's drinks to see the effect they would have, then Cole began to talk about the recent vacations he'd been on.

Glen felt certain that Cole would eventually trust him even more, and when he did, he would tell him the real reason for sending the note. He felt the tension in Cole's body when Glen suggested that he would drive him home, so, he spent the next hour in conference with him and a female detective by the name of Charlene, as they planned an excuse for Cole not returning home.

Laura answered the phone, and then smiled as she listened to whom she thought was Paolo's mother telling her that Cole was having dinner at her home and spending the night.

Charlene told Laura not to worry about pajamas because Cole could wear a set of Paolo's, as well as a change of clothes for school the following day, and then she added that there was a new toothbrush that Cole could use, as well.

Cole looked from Glen's smiling face to Charlene's smiling face while sitting with them in the quiet room, and sharing a pizza. Occasionally, he would set his slice of pizza back down on the plate, and find it difficult to swallow because tears had started trickling down his cheeks, and then Glen and Charlene would soothe him.

He felt terrified at times until they assured him that what he had told them, and whatever they'd told him, would be all right, and that he needn't be afraid anymore.

After Cole told them why he wanted to work in a forensics laboratory when he grew up, he felt emotionally exhausted. Glen and Charlene told him that they felt certain he'd be an excellent forensics expert, and even a great detective.

Charlene then nodded to Glen, and he gently removed Cole's arms from around him, and then Cole fell asleep moments after Glen had laid him on the couch. Charlene hurried out of the room and returned a few minutes later with a blanket, which she then spread out over Cole as he slept.

Glen called home to say that he'd be staying with Cole for a few more hours, and then after hanging up the phone, he slowly shook his head as he looked down at Cole asleep on the couch.

He knew that the boy would need more reassuring when he awoke, and that very soon he would be probably be facing quite difficult times, and Glen hoped that Cole would be under the care of a competent child therapist.

He began reading the notes he'd taken while Cole had been talking to him, and Charlene occasionally looked over at Cole whenever he moaned in his sleep.

Two hours later, Cole tensed up, then relaxed when he opened his eyes to find Glen sitting beside him and smiling at him. He'd only taken a few bites of pizza, so, when Glen asked him if he was hungry, Cole smiled and nodded.

Glen told him that he was just going next door for a few minutes to order in some dinner for both of them, then he would return. Cole nodded his head again, then slowly sat up.

* * * * * ◇•••••◇ ★ ◇•••••◇ * * * * *

After Glen left the room, Cole's thoughts began drifting back to the time when his mother had been alive. He pictured her smiling at him as she told him that they were going for a walk among the sand dunes so that she could photograph and sketch while he played.

He recalled that on the last vacation he'd spent with his mother, his parents had stayed at a big hotel near a desert. In the evenings, after hiring a babysitter for Cole, they would dance in the hotel ballroom, or gamble at the casino.

That had annoyed Cole at the time because he'd been worried that a babysitter might tell him to go to bed earlier than usual so that she could watch television by herself and not be bothered by a kid.

Cole could clearly remember the morning of the day that his mother had died of a severe asthmatic attack, and what had happened before his parents had left the hotel room.

He'd wanted to spend the day at the big pool with other kids his age who had been staying at the hotel, and to play with them on the water slides, and at the small amusement park area close to the pool, instead of going on a boat trip with his parents.

Close to the sand dunes, there was a long, high ridge that had a very sparse growth of trees and bushes on it, and just beyond that ridge there was a small, artificial lake with a boat rental facility.

Cole had told his parents that he'd find it too boring to go on a boat ride, even though they'd told him there were swans on the little lake, and that they'd be renting a rowboat to see the swans up close.

He had awakened very early that morning, and when he'd walked out of his bedroom, he had seen his father on the balcony, looking out at the landscape.

He then recalled going to the fridge in his bare feet. He poured a glass of orange juice, then while passing by the balcony door, the movement of his father's right hand caught his attention.

Derek had been resting his crossed forearms on the balcony railing as he leaned forward to look far in both directions while his right hand kept moving as he held it close to his ribcage.

Cole had been fascinated by the continual movement of his father's hand, then walking closer to the glass door of the balcony, he'd seen that his father was holding one of his mother's inhalers, and he was pumping it.

Cole had then returned to his bedroom to watch television. He recalled turning off the television when his mother had knocked on his bedroom door to tell him that breakfast was ready.

His mother had poured a cup of coffee, taken a few sips, then she had hurried away to take a shower and get dressed for the walk across to the ridge with his father to the little lake.

The hotel suite had been rather large, and Cole had finished his breakfast and was walking back to his bedroom when he saw his father looking through his mother's purse.

Enid had told Cole to take twenty dollars out of her purse so that he could buy lunch at the pool with his friends, so, he was about to tell his father that he was going take some money, too, when Derek walked away to the bedroom to speak with Enid.

Cole went over to the table where his mother's purse had been laying because he was going to take twenty dollars out of it, and then after looking into her purse, he had seen an inhaler in it. He'd picked it up, held it to his ear, shaken it, and noticed that it was empty, therefore, when his mother came out of the bedroom, he told her about the empty inhaler.

She thanked him, but just as she was about to return to the bedroom to get another inhaler, Derek took one out of his shirt pocket and laughed as he said he was one step ahead of her.

His father had previously emptied two inhalers, and placed one in Enid's purse, and the other empty inhaler in his shirt pocket. Derek dropped the empty inhaler into her purse, closed it, handed the purse to her, and told her that they should be on their way.

Cole had felt a strange sensation when he'd seen his father do that, and for some reason he couldn't quite understand at the time, he had decided to follow them.

His parents had made arrangements the day before to ensure that Cole would be under the care of several other parents while he played at the hotel pool and amusement area. He had said goodbye to his parents as they left the hotel, then he'd watched them walking toward the ridge.

There were a few large bushes that were higher than him, scattered along the way to the ridge, so, Cole had run from bush to bush while following his parents.

His father had a leather bag with a long strap slung over one shoulder, and Derek had said that it contained four bottles of water, some sandwiches, and fruit.

Cole sat looking around the dimly lit office, as he waited for Glen to return, then his heart leapt and he suddenly sucked in his breath when he felt that he was right there at the time when he'd followed his parents into the desert.

He saw his father pointing to an area of the ridge, then they changed direction. Cole knew the place that rented small boats was far in the other direction, so, he wondered why his father had suggested that they head the other way.

He kept walking at a distance behind them, and Cole unbuttoned and opened his shirt because it was becoming very warm as the sun rose higher. He was wiping perspiration from his forehead by the time he reached the ridge, and as he stood in the shade of a tree, Cole wished that there were more trees in the area.

He couldn't see his parents because when he'd reached the large ridge, he found that there were many sand dunes of various sizes on the other side of it, and some were quite high.

He caught a glimpse of his mother climbing a sand dune, then after reaching the top, she waved, and Cole looked around and saw his father waving back to her while he held a camera. He could hear the faint shouting of his father, telling her to go to the next sand dune, which was much higher and farther away.

Cole watched her disappear down the other side of the dune, then he tensed up when he saw his father open the leather bag and remove a hatchet. He gaped as he watched his father strip nude, and while Derek was putting on a studded leather pouch, Cole noticed that his father had shaved his chest, stomach, and legs.

He became even more frightened when he saw Derek pull a close-fitting, leather hood over his head, put his shoes back on, pick up the hatchet, and then begin hurrying in the direction where Enid had gone down the other side of the sand dune.

He'd become scared and so confused because of what he'd seen his father do, that Cole couldn't move for a few moments, then he began rushing along the sandy ridge.

He lost his balance and slid down a steep sand dune before he scrambled to his feet and ran to another high sand dune. He was puffing and sweating as he struggled up the shifting sand of the dune, then standing at the top of it, he saw his mother running away from his father whom was far behind her.

Cole plodded as fast as he could over the sand dune, stopping occasionally to see where his mother was in relationship to his father. He then saw his mother disappear down over another high sand dune moments before Derek reached the base of it.

Cole wished that he could move faster along the dune, but his feet kept sinking deep into the hot sand. His heart was pounding when he heard his mother's faint screams coming from somewhere on the other side of the sand dune that she'd just scrambled over, so, Cole tried to move faster.

He had to slide down the high sand dune to reach the next one, and after he'd slid to the bottom, and because he could no longer hear his mother's screams, he knew that neither she nor his father could hear his shouts.

Cole fought his way up the next high sand dune after sliding halfway back down, several times, then standing at the crest of the dune, he gaped at his father closing in on his mother while wielding the hatchet high above his head.

He saw his mother clutching at her throat as she struggled to breathe, and Cole knew that she was having an asthmatic attack caused by the terror of being attacked by some strange, insane killer.

He witnessed his father threatening her with the hatchet by continually swinging it down into the sand close to her head and body as his mother lay on the sand, twisting and turning while trying to dodge the blade of the hatchet.

He watched her coughing and gagging as she held up one of her hands to fend off Derek's attacks, then Cole's thoughts swirled, and his anxiety heightened when he saw her trying to use the empty inhaler that his father had tampered with.

Cole kept crying and shouting out to her as he watched her struggling, then he saw her collapse onto her back, and slowly stop moving. His father lowered the hatchet, and then stared down at her for several moments before he knelt to feel her pulse.

Derek stood back up, turned around, and started running back to where he'd left his clothes. Cole felt terrified as he saw his mother lying on the ground, and he continued his efforts to reach her.

He'd managed to climb over two more high dunes before he let himself slide back down the third dune after he'd seen his father's head rising above a sand dune, so, he knew that Derek was returning to perhaps do something else to Enid.

He wept after he'd slid down the sand dune out of sight from his mother's body, then he waited a few minutes before he wriggled back up the dune, and looked over at her again.

Cole saw that his father had his clothes back on, and then Derek replaced the empty inhaler in her purse with, Cole felt sure, a full one. He peeked over the top of the sand dune, and watched his father hurrying back to the hotel.

Cole began running toward his mother, hoping to reach her before she died so that he could pump some of the full inhaler into her mouth. He worried that his father might return, find him, and kill him, however, Cole was only thinking about rescuing his mother.

Moments later, he crawled to her on his hands and knees, took the inhaler out of her purse, and as he looked down at her, Cole cried out when he saw the agonized expression on his mother's face.

He shook her as he begged her to wake up and take some puffs from the inhaler, then not getting a response after many tries, he held his ear close to her mouth while he held his hand on her chest.

He wailed when he realized that she was dead, then sobbing, he laid his head on her chest. He suddenly thought that his father might have stopped rushing toward the hotel, and started coming back to do something else to his mother, so, he slowly pulled away from her, and stood up.

He knew that he had to hide from Derek, therefore, Cole hurried back to the sand dune where he'd viewed his mother being terrorized by his father. He looked for areas where he could get over the sand dunes faster to protect himself from his father, and then Cole hoped that he'd be safe when he saw smaller sand dunes ahead of him, as well as a sparse growth of trees and bushes.

Cole felt so scared as he ran from tree to tree and bush to bush on his way back to the hotel while hoping that his father hadn't stopped to look back to see if he was being followed.

. . . . . ❖••••••❖★❖••••••❖ . . . . . .

When he reached the hotel, Cole took off his shirt, shorts, shoes, and socks before he ran to the pool in his underwear. After resurfacing, he had water splashed at him by other kids who were laughing and playing in the pool.

They didn't know that Cole's face was also wet with tears, nor did they know he wasn't shaking because of the cold water, but instead from fright and much grief over the death of his mother.

An hour later, Cole listened to the other youngsters asking why an ambulance and two police cars had arrived at the hotel, then he got out of the pool and stood with his arms crossed as he trembled and stared around at the hotel guests who had gathered near the lobby.

He felt so scared that his father would kill him, too, if he found him, but Cole didn't know what to do to protect himself. He walked away from the pool, and then stood where no one could see him.

Cole saw a boy he'd played with in the pool the day before, so, he hurried over to him and asked what had happened. The boy, Jason, told him that he'd heard some adults saying that Cole's mother had become very sick, so, Cole asked Jason if he could come up to his room until his father returned from the hospital.

When they arrived at Jason's suite, his parents told Cole to take a shower, and then put on some of Jason's clothes. After he'd showered and dressed, he told Jason's parents that he had asthma just like his mother did, and that he was going to hurry to his parents' suite, get his inhaler, and then return.

Cole wasn't asthmatic, but he hoped that they'd believed his lie, and then he felt so relieved when they finally agreed to let him go to his suite because it was only one floor up and directly above their suite. But they asked Jason to go with him.

Once they were close to the staircase leading up to the Cole's suite, he told Jason to wait and watch the elevators in case Derek came to Jason's hotel suite to look for him.

Cole then hurried up to the next floor, and then instead of going to his suite where his father might be waiting to kill him, he took the elevator down to the basement of the hotel.

He found a door leading out to the rear parking lot, and then Cole crouched down as he moved among the cars toward the highway. He ran along the side of the highway until he was far from the hotel before he stuck out his thumb to hitchhike.

A car stopped beside him, then a couple with a daughter about the same age as him, asked him why he was hitchhiking, and Cole told them that he'd been visiting a friend, and then Jason's father had suffered a heart attack and had been taken to the hospital.

Cole explained to them that his father had gone to a business convention for a few hours in a city, and that he couldn't remember the name of the hotel where the convention was taking place.

"So, I gotta get back to our hotel because everyone forgot about me when Jason's dad had a heart attack in that hotel back there. I was in the lobby with Jason when they went by us with the stretcher that had wheels on it and his dad was laying on top of it. Jason ran after them, so, I can't go up to his room because I don't have a key, so that's when I figured I'd just hitchhike back to the hotel my dad and I'm staying at," lied Cole.

"You should've asked one of the guests to drive you there because you're much too young to be on your own. Oh, well, you'd better get in, now. No use you walking all the way back to your hotel by yourself," said the woman. "That's so awful. Poor little boy. Your friend must be very upset."

"Yeah, he was. He was crying so much, that I started crying, too. I...I feel really scared and really sad, and...and that's 'cause she's dead. I saw it. I did." Cole began crying again.

"Aw, I'm so sorry, son. We'll get you to your hotel. We'll be there very soon. You ask the desk clerk when you get there, what the name of the hotel is where your father's convention is. Okay? And they'll call him right away."

"Yeah...yeah, okay. Yes, sir," replied Cole as he wept.

* * * * * * ◇•••••◇ ★ ◇•••••◇ * * * * *

The couple dropped him off in front of the hotel where Cole had told them he was staying, then they watched him until he'd entered the lobby before they drove away.

Cole slowly walked through the main floor of the hotel, looking into large, open rooms where people were either sitting at tables and drinking cocktails, or other rooms where they gambled.

He walked into a huge room that was crowded with people who were laughing and talking as they ate food from platters at tables lining the room.

He ate sandwiches and had a soft drink before surreptitiously picking up as many sandwiches as he could without drawing the attention of the usher standing by the door, and then he kept his back to the usher as he left the room.

Cole went out the back door of the hotel, walked to an area where there was some grass, and where he couldn't be seen. He sat behind a high hedge, then the sight of his mother frantically struggling to breathe before she'd died, caused him to weep until he fell asleep.

.   .   .   . . . ❖•••••❖ ★ ❖•••••❖ . .   .   .   .

He awoke late at night, and saw two policemen searching the parking lot and surrounding area. Less than five minutes later, they shone their flashlights behind the hedge and saw Cole sitting on the ground, and then they drove him back to his hotel after the police had called Derek and told him that they'd found his son.

Listening to the police talking on the phone, Cole knew that his father hadn't been arrested, so, he began thinking of excuses for running away from the hotel.

He was trembling and close to hyperventilating as he stood beside the policemen on the way up in the elevator, then he wet his pants when he saw his father standing in the hall, waiting for him.

Derek took his hand as they were escorted into the suite by the police officers, then Cole was led into the bathroom by his father whom helped him undress, and then into the shower.

Cole told him that some boys he'd been playing with had told him that his parents had been killed in a car accident, and that some people were coming to take him away to an orphanage, so, that was why he'd run away.

Derek waited until the policemen had left before he sat beside Cole on the couch, put an arm around him, and told him that Enid had died from a severe asthmatic attack. Cole cried as he pulled away from his father, and then ran into his bedroom.

Derek followed him, then sat on the bed and talked softly to him, but Cole was trembling from fright because his father was sitting so close to him.

The next day, Cole concluded that because his father had a very good alibi, the police would never arrest him for the murder. He grieved for weeks, and then discovering that Derek was dating Laura, Cole slowly reached the decision to try to protect her from being murdered by his father.

Laura was a very wealthy woman, and Derek had received a large amount of money from a life insurance policy after Enid's death. Cole felt certain that Derek would kill Laura for her money, too, therefore, he had started planning ways to ruin every opportunity his father might have to kill Laura while they were away on a vacation.

While listening to Cole explaining how he'd been able to perhaps save Laura from being murdered, Glen and Charlene had been surprised by his ingenuity.

After he'd fallen asleep on the couch inside the police station, the two detectives had whispered to each other about how brave Cole had been, how tragic it was that he'd suffered so much grief, and how clever he was for such a young boy.

* * * * * ❖•••••❖★❖•••••❖ * * * * *

Laura was shocked when the police arrived to arrest Derek for the murder of Enid, then she became very concerned about Cole because she'd learned that he had witnessed his mother's death, and he was now terrified of his father.

She drove to the police station while hoping to convince Cole that that she loved him, that he'd be staying with her, and that she would be caring for him for many, many years.

Later that night, Glen carried Cole to Laura's car, then she drove home as Cole slept with his head on her lap. Glen followed them in his car, then carried Cole upstairs while Laura arranged to have a bed moved into Cole's bedroom suite so that she could be available to him if he awoke frightened.

Laura laid in bed, looking at Cole, and recalling what the police detectives had told her about him trying so hard to save her life, then she knew that now Cole would begin to bond with her.

* * * * * ❖•••••❖★❖•••••❖ * * * * *

Four months later, Cole would tell his friends that he had to hurry home because his new mother was waiting to have supper with him. Now he had two mothers. One up in heaven with God, and one on Earth, and both of them loved him and took very good care of him.

Laura collected many of Enid's art pieces, and learned much about her. She also told Cole quite often that she agreed that his mother in heaven was very talented, beautiful, and a wonderful angel who loved and watched over him every day, and every night while he was sleeping.

The End

A Car For Halloween

Scott waved at Laurie as he walked toward the front door, then after entering the house, he walked to the kitchen, and sat down at the table to have lunch.

"Hi, Scott. Did you see Laurie?" asked Marianne.

"Yup! I saw her leaving the Jenson's. I think she's having lunch today at the Nottenway's."

"Oh, yes, I forgot about that. I baked a chocolate cake this morning because I know that's your favorite. Lemon-flavored icing, and cherry filling between three layers of cake."

"Oh, yeah? Wow! Thanks! Everything you make is really great, just like this chicken noodle soup you made me for lunch. My other favorite soup is tomato. Could I have another glass of milk, please? Oh, and can I please have some chocolate powder in it?"

"Sure. I'll get it for you right away, dear. Oh, and if you're still hungry after you eat that sandwich, I'll make you another one."

"No thanks. Right after I eat my lunch, I gotta run over to the pond to meet up with Laurie and Alfie. We're gonna have lotsa fun."

"Hello there, tiger!" exclaimed Bob, coming into the kitchen.

"Hi! Were you shooting hoops in the backyard?"

"Sure was! Wanna shoot a few with me?"

"Golly, I sure wish I could, but I told Laurie and Alfie I'd meet up with them real soon, like, right after lunch," said Scott, smiling.

"When you see Laurie, tell her not to be late for dinner. I'm making pot roast and scalloped potatoes," said Marianne.

"I won't forget," Scott said as he hurried to finish his lunch.

"I'll be home at lunch on Thursday, so, we can do something together then. Okay?" said Bob, tossing the basketball in the air.

"Sure! That'll be fun!"

"Here's your chocolate milk, dear. Now don't drink it too fast, or you might spill some on your shirt," said Marianne.

"Thanks. Mmmmm, that tasted really, really good. Okay, gotta run. Bye!" cried Scott.

"Bye, dear! Careful climbing any trees!" yelled Marianne.

"See ya, Scott!" Bob shouted to him.

He ran down Baker's Road, turned left at Corley Street, then Scott ran along it to the pond. Alfie and Laurie were sitting on a large boulder, and when they saw Scott running toward them, they waved at him as they grinned.

"Anybody ask where you were going?" Alfie asked him.

"Yeah, and I said I was meeting you guys here at the pond. I sure hope nobody sees us going over to the other end of the ravine.

"Naw. If anyone's looking over here right now, they probably think we're gonna stay around here for awhile, and then go play on the swings in the schoolyard," said Alfie. "Okay, so, you and Laurie go around the end of those trees across the pond, and pretend you're picking flowers, and I'll go over there, and pretend I'm chasing a frog or something. We'll circle around and meet up past the pond. Okay?"

"Perfect! Okay, come on, Scott," said Laurie.

Alfie walked to the brook at the far end of the pond, then he leaned over, and pretended he was making grabs at a frog as he slowly made his way toward the trees.

While he was doing that, Laurie and Scott picked wild flowers as they walked slowly to the edge of the pond, and then they took off their shoes and socks and carried them as they began wading slowly into the pond. Moments later, Laurie stopped, and then frowned while looking down at the water.

"C'mon, Laurie! Let's go! What're you looking at?"

"The shadows in the water. They're so spooky."

"What do you mean by *spooky*?" asked Scott.

"I keep imagining that when the wind blows and the trees sway, then the shadows of the branches in the pond look like long, black fingers. The trees reflected in the pond look like they're all moving shadows of people underneath the water, and their long, ugly fingers are waiting to reach up and grab me. It's so spooky."

"It's just the trees, okay? Stop thinking that way because you're scaring yourself. It's just us here, and there's not lots of spooky people under the water because it only comes up to your shins."

"I guess so, but it's just that it sort of looks like they could be lying on their backs under the water, reaching up for me with their long, black fingers," said Laurie.

"If they are, and you don't wade over here fast, then they *will* grab you with their spooky fingers. C'mon, hurry."

"I'll just keep looking at you until I get to the other side."

"Hurry, Laurie! That's it! There, you made it. See? You didn't get grabbed. Now hurry. We gotta meet Alfie."

They sat on the ground to put their socks and shoes back on, and then before she started following Scott, Laurie looked back at the pond as she bit down on her bottom lip.

* * * * * ◇•••••◇★◇•••••◇ * * * * *

They hurried through the woods, and saw Alfie leaning against a tree, then the trio ran deeper into the forest at the end of the ravine. They'd been warned to never go into the forest without being accompanied by an adult because they could be attacked by one or more of the dozens of big, black bears, or bitten by one of the many deadly poisonous snakes on the ground or hanging from trees.

They knew they would be severely reprimanded for ignoring the dangers lurking in the forest, however, they'd discovered there weren't any big, nasty bears in the woods, and they doubted there were any poisonous snakes, either.

Laurie, Scott and Alfie hurried through the trees, and then about ten minutes later, they reached the abandoned house that sat on the edge of a hill that sloped down to an old road.

They looked in all directions, and then after they were sure nobody was in the area, they pulled a few boards off one of the windows. They'd pried the boards off that window when they had first sneaked into the house, then every time they'd leave it, they would press the boards back over the window.

After they were inside the house, they rushed through it to the rear staircase beside the kitchen entrance, and then they hurried down those stairs.

Half of the basement was the garage of the house, and the former owners used to drive out of the garage, down the slight incline onto the narrow road that led out to the local, two-lane highway.

Scott, Alfie and Laurie had been quite excited when they'd discovered that the previous owners of the house had left one of their cars in the garage.

On shelves against one wall of the garage, there were empty jars, boxes of books and magazines, and in one of the boxes, Laurie, Alfie and Scott had found the owner's manual for the old car.

They had been secretly working on the car for almost a year whenever they weren't doing after school and weekend chores. Those chores were bagging groceries and stacking shelves at the grocery store, and pumping gas and washing cars at "Len & Bob's Gas Station and Garage."

Len Wilson and his father had started the business, then Len had eventually taught his own son, Bob, how to repair cars. Len's father retired when Bob finished high school, then Len and Bob had become business partners.

Now that Len had retired, and Bob was running the business by himself, he appreciated the part-time help from Alfie, Scott and Laurie, who also kept the garage clean and tidy.

Lining two sides of Len & Bob's Garage were many wooden shelves and cupboards stocked with cans of motor oil and other items he sold to his customers. There were also cardboard boxes of many different sizes containing car parts that Bob and his father, Len, had amassed through the years.

Len had often told his son that there was always the chance that someone might stop by their garage for gas someday, and ask if they had particular part for an old car that person was refurbishing for an antique car show.

Scott, Laurie and Alfie had looked through all the boxes in Bob's garage during the time they'd been helping him, and they'd found spark plugs and other items they needed for the car they'd secretly been working on, and they knew that Bob would never miss the items they stole from his garage.

Alfie had been taught how to drive when he'd been ten years old, so, he had taught Laurie and Scott how to drive whenever they'd found a car parked with the keys in it, and at a time when they wouldn't be seen driving back and forth along a driveway.

Laurie and Scott had only practiced driving for ten minutes each time to make sure they weren't caught by the owner of whatever car they'd been able to use for their very brief driving lessons.

To reinforce their supposed inability to drive, they often told an adult whom was driving them somewhere, that they couldn't understand how one little key could make the motor growl, the horn to toot, and the wheels to start rolling. The adult driver would then smile and say that children were so cute whenever they asked questions about things that grownups did.

During school summer vacation, whenever they weren't working part-time at the grocery store, or helping Bob Wilson at the garage, Scott, Laurie, and Alfie had been able to spend up to two hours a few days each week, secretly working on the car.

Every half hour, one of them would run back through the woods to a street, then tell any of the adults they saw, that they were on their way to meet their two friends at either the school playground, or at one of the stores in town.

They now felt sure that the car was ready, but driving it out of the garage could prove to be a serious problem if the car sputtered to a stop right out in the open where anyone could see it.

This was the day they'd dared to take that chance, so, they opened the garage doors, then drew straws to determine which of them would drive the car out of the garage.

Laurie won the draw, so, she got behind the steering wheel, turned on the ignition, then after slowly releasing the clutch and pressing her foot down very slowly on the gas pedal, she held her breath as the car lurched forward, and then she began driving very slowly out of the garage.

She drove down the slope, applied the brake, then turned off the ignition, and then Scott and Alfie ran down the slight incline to the car, and they laughed. Scott then got behind the steering wheel, and backed the car up into the garage.

"It works great!" cried Alfie.

"Yeah, it does, but I was so worried that the brakes suddenly wouldn't work, and the car would keep going right across the road and into that pond over there!" exclaimed Laurie.

"Yeah, then you would've squashed all the shadow people under the water in *that* pond, too," said Scott.

"Who are the shadow people?" asked Alfie.

"Laurie thinks that the shadows of the trees in all the ponds around here look like people's shadows with long, black fingers, and they're reaching up to grab hold of her."

"Well, that's what it reminds me of."

"Talk like that'd give me nightmares! Boo!" exclaimed Alfie.

"Aw, stop trying to scare her! Come on, guys! Help me close the garage doors in case someone sees them open!" cried Scott.

They helped him close the garage doors, then they peered out from inside the garage through a partly smudged window to see if anyone had seen the doors open, and the car.

"Okay, *now* all we gotta do is start bringing more jars of gas here, then pour them into those big containers, and then after they're all filled up, we'll put them in the trunk of the car," said Scott. "It'll take us maybe a month to do that, but as soon as we get the gas containers full, we can make sure the old road's clear all the way to the gate near the local highway."

"We can sneak over this way to the old road every day, and then start working at getting that gate to open so that the car'll be able to get out onto the local highway," said Alfie. "After we clear all the brush and other stuff away from the gate, we can start clearing it off the road all the way over here to the old house. But don't forget we can only do that for fifteen minutes a day, okay? Or else somebody might wonder what we're doing. So, no longer than that, okay?"

"We know," said Laurie. "Guess we better get back, huh? We've been gone for almost an hour."

"Yeah, okay. Let's hope nobody comes around here and sees the car all fixed up because then they'll stop us from driving it without one of them in the car with us to make sure we don't go out on the highway with it," said Scott.

"Okay, let's go back upstairs, guys," said Alfie.

"Just a sec. I rubbed the soap off the glass on that part of the window over there, so we could look around to see if anyone was near here, so, I gotta smudge it again so nobody can look in and see the car," said Scott.

He rubbed a bar of soap over the small portion of the window pane they'd peered out from, then after Scott hurried upstairs, they climbed out the window, placed the boards back on it, and then they ran down into the ravine.

After they'd climbed out of the ravine, they began running through the trees, and then they slowed their pace as they neared the pond that was across from a street.

Scott and Laurie picked wild flowers before coming out of the forest, and as Laurie held his hand while they waded through the pond, she tried not to look down at the water.

Alfie met them on the other side of the pond, and then before they said goodbye, they promised to meet each other after supper for ice cream and soft drinks.

•   •   •   • • ◇•••••◇★◇•••••◇ • •   •   •

"I'm here!" shouted Scott, walking in the front door.

"Dinner will be ready in forty minutes! Oh, Scott! Did you pick those flowers for me?" asked Cynthia.

"Yup! You like them?"

"They're lovely! I'll put them in a vase, right away!"

"Hi, Scott! I hope you had fun playing with your friends! Let's have a swim before dinner, okay?" said Jim.

"You bet! I'll run upstairs and put on my bathing suit!"

"Meet you at the pool!" shouted Jim, laughing.

Scott rushed upstairs, undressed, put on a swimsuit, ran back downstairs, and then outside to the pool. He jumped into the water, then after resurfacing, he and Scott began tossing the beach ball back and forth to each other.

While playing in the pool, Scott thought about the car, and hoped that when they had the gas containers filled, nobody would see him,

Laurie, and Scott driving the car from the old house to the two-lane county road that led to the big highway.

After dinner, Scott told them that he was meeting Laurie and Alfie, then they were going to Bob's garage to pump gas for an hour, and do a few other chores for him, and then after that, they were going to the restaurant to have ice cream.

Jim said he felt proud of him for always helping Bob at the garage, then after he gave Scott two dollars, he reminded him that he had homework to do before he went to bed.

While Scott, Laurie, and Alfie ate their ice cream sundaes, they'd sometimes whisper excitedly about the car. The waitress smiled as she said that she hoped they weren't secretly planning to play a prank on somebody because they were whispering.

They laughed and told the waitress that they were planning to sneak up behind people on Halloween, and then scare them by suddenly shouting: "Boo!"

They left the restaurant for the school playground, and then after an hour of playing on the swings and other fun recreational structures, they said goodbye and left to do their homework before going to bed.

Scott finished his homework, put on his pajamas, then set the alarm clock, and got into bed. The next morning, he rushed to the bathroom, then got dressed, ran downstairs to the kitchen, and sat down at the table just as Sarah was turning off the stove.

"Oh, boy! Crispy Cornies and scrambled eggs!"

"Your favorites! Do you want some apple juice or some orange juice, dear?" asked Sarah.

"Apple juice, please!" exclaimed Scott, smiling.

"Harold? Breakfast! Here he comes. He's going to be late for breakfast *and* work. He's so slow in the mornings."

"Good morning, Scott. Finish all your homework before you went to bed?" asked Harold.

"Yup! Didn't have much, and it was sorta real easy!"

"Wait'll you start getting algebra."

"What's ajabra?"

"Brain twister," replied Harold, smiling. "It's much harder than the math you're doing at school now. Well, at least *I* thought it was when I took it at school, but with the fairly good marks you've been getting lately, you might find it easier than I did."

"Oh, and Scott? How's that school project coming? The one you've been working on all summer?" asked Sarah.

"It's okay. Well, not really, because when I put gas down the funnel, the little motor sputters for a bit, and then it stops. Mr. Wilson won't let me fill a bigger bottle with gas from the pumps because he said he's worried that some gas might spill on my clothes while I'm carrying it, and then my clothes might catch on fire somehow."

"He's right about that, son. Gas is dangerous because it doesn't take much to ignite it," said Harold, smiling.

"Yeah, I heard that can happen. The little jar *you* let me fill up is okay, but I wish I had a bigger one, so that I wouldn't have to keep running back here to get some more, and then running all the way back again to pour it in my project," said Scott, pouting.

"Hmmm, yes, I see what you mean. Well, you've been very careful handling gas while you've been working on your project, so, I'm sure it'll be okay to let you start helping yourself to more gasoline whenever you need it. I'll put a big container of gas in the garage beside your project, but only if you promise me you'll make sure the lid is screwed back on tight. Okay?" Harold told him.

"Yeah? Really? Gee, thanks a lot! Wow! Now I can keep testing it and testing it, and when I work all the bugs out of it, then I can take my project to school and surprise the teacher with it! Y'didn't tell her I was making something *real* secret to surprise her, did you?"

"No, we didn't, dear. I'll bet you'll get special marks in school for building your project," said Sarah, smiling broadly.

"You know, I built an airplane when I was your age, boy. But it burned so much gas, and it only flew about half a block before it crashed. I spent a week repairing it, but I didn't care because it was so much fun," said Harold, grinning.

"It sounds like you had lots of fun," said Sarah. "But I'm glad you didn't decide to become a pilot instead of a grocer, because you would've been away from home for weeks at a time in far away places, and your plane could've crashed."

"Not with all the special gadgets they have on planes these days, hon. They're very safe. Hey, Scott? Maybe you and I could build a model airplane together for your next project. Would you like that?"

"Sure! That'd be really, really great! Y'really mean it?"

"I sure do," replied Harold, grinning and winking at Sarah.

"Wow! Gee, thanks!" exclaimed Scott.

"Hurry up and finish your breakfast, Scott, dear, or you'll be late for school," said Sarah.

"I finished my cereal, so, I'm going now! I'll eat this toast on the way to school! Bye!" yelled Scott, running to the front door.

"Bye, Scott!" Sarah and Harold shouted in unison.

At morning recess, Alfie, Laurie, and Scott agreed that on their lunch hour, they'd ride their bicycles to the dirt road near the old abandoned house, and yank up some weeds that blocked the entrance gate to the local two-lane highway.

They planned to spend half an hour, twice a day, clearing that area of the dirt road, then start clearing weeds, brush, and rocks from that road all away from the gates to the old abandoned house to ensure that the tires of the car they'd been working on wouldn't be punctured by a sharp piece of rubble.

"Scott! Don't shove so much food in your mouth at one time! And don't gulp your milk!" exclaimed Judy.

"Sorry. I wanna finish lunch in a hurry because I wanna meet Laurie. Betty, the Shelton's cat, had kittens, and they had to stay inside the house 'til they were old enough to go outside, so, now Laurie and me are gonna give them all names."

"Oh, I see. How many kittens are there?"

"I think she said six. Is that a lot of kittens for all at once?"

"No, dear," replied Judy, smiling. "Some cats have more at one time. Sometimes there's up to eight at one time."

"Eight? Wow! Dolly only had four puppies! Can she have eight puppies at the same time, sometime?" asked Scott.

"Perhaps, but I don't think she'll have more puppies for a long time, dear."

"Okay, I'm finished eating! Hope I can think up some good names for the kittens! I already thought that maybe I'd give 'em names for Halloween 'cause it's not too far away before it'll be Halloween. Right? So, I was thinking up names like Ghost if there's a white kitten, and Goblin for a gray one, and...Well, I forget the other names I thought up, but I'll maybe remember the other names when I see the kittens, and maybe Laurie can think of some Halloween names, too. Okay, I'm gonna go, now! Bye!"

"Bye, dear! Give my love to Laurie!" shouted Judy.

Scott ran down the street and saw Laurie sitting on the grass with a cardboard box beside her, and she was staring away from the kittens that were crawling around on the lawn. He sat beside her, and she seemed to barely notice him when he said hello to her.

"What are you thinking about?" asked Scott.

"The nightmare I had last night. I dreamed that the shadows in the pond reached up and grabbed my legs, and when I tried to struggle away from them, I fell into the pond and they began dragging me under the water. Gawwwd! It was so terrifying! I could feel them grabbing at my ankles!"

"Aw, don't be scared. That'll never happen. Not even in the dark, so, try not to think about it, okay?"

"It's just that it's getting closer to Halloween and some stores and houses've got paper ghosts and skeletons hanging in their windows."

"Just keep talking to Alfie and me, and we'll keep your mind off that, okay? Okay, Laurie?"

"Yeah, okay. Thanks. Cute kittens, huh?"

"Yeah, they're so tiny and soft, aren't they? I like that little black and white one."

"When I look at it, I keep thinking that it's like a white kitten with black shadows on it. As if the spooky shadows I think I see in the pond had crept up and grabbed onto the kitten."

"Laurie! Stay cool, okay? You gotta stop thinking like that!"

"Yeah, I know. So are we ready to go? Help me pick up all the kittens. Sorry for sounding so scared again."

"It's okay. Quick! Get that one over there! Aw, hi, there, pussy-kitty! Hah! Good, you got that one! I'll get that orange kitten that's over by the bikes!" cried Scott, laughing.

They put the kittens back in the box, then after they put the box on the porch, Laurie and Scott sped away on their bicycles to meet Alfie at the old gate.

"Look how big some of these weeds are!" exclaimed Alfie.

"Yeah, and with really long roots. Okay, let's grab the same big weed, then we'll pull it together, okay? Laurie, you pull as many of the smaller ones as you can, okay?" said Scott.

"Okay. We have to make sure we all keep looking at our watches because we have to leave here in about fifteen minutes, remember. I sure hope all these weeds and things don't take us a long time to clear. We still have to pull so many weeds down the road and clear any sharp stones and rocks away, too."

"Yeah, I know. Man, it's a good thing we got the car finished already, because it gives us a lot more time to clear the way. Don't worry, Laurie, we'll have lots of time, okay? We've got the road almost cleared now," Scott told her.

"Yeah, guess you're right," she said with a slight smile.

"Even though the sun's shining just on my face and arms, my feet feel like they're burning!" exclaimed Alfie.

"Stop thinking about things like that or else you'll start having nightmares just like Laurie sometimes does. Okay? Just keep pulling at these weeds, okay?" said Scot, then he tugged a big weed out of the ground. "Whew! That was a really big one! Big, long roots, huh?"

"Yeah, really, man. I sure hope there aren't any with longer roots than that one. Hey, Laurie, you're doing great. Scott and me can pull out all these big ones in maybe two days."

"It's Scott and I, not Scott and me! This little kid thing is getting to both of you. You're not toddlers," she said, smirking.

"Yeah, sorry. I wouldn't talk like that if I was still at the...Well, I guess I better not think about that, right?" said Alfie.

"Golly, gosh and gee whiz! Stop picking on us, Laurie! After all, we're only thirteen!" exclaimed Scott, then he laughed.

"Get real, dummy! Keep working!" Laurie told them.

"Yes, mother!" exclaimed Alfie and Scott, laughing.

"Hey! Don't swear! Mother's a dirty word!" cried Laurie.

"A *real* dirty word around here, man," said Alfie, scowling.

"So's 'father.' Like, they're always telling us we can't do this, and we can't do that. And they're always watching us to make sure we don't go into the forest and get killed by something, or climb up something high, like a big tree, and then fall down. They think we're still little kids and we can't take care of ourselves," said Scott.

"Hey, you guys! Stop talking and keep working!"

"Yes, moth...Oops! Sorry, Laurie," said Alfie, smiling.

"Huhnnff! Some of these small weeds've got long roots, too! Look at the roots on this one!" she exclaimed.

• • • • • ❖•••••❖ ★ ❖•••••❖ • • • • •

They hopped on their bicycles, sped back through the trees along the edge of the ravine, and then they stopped at the pond, and washed their hands before riding their bikes back home.

The following day, they had lunch, then rode back to school on their bikes, and they still had fifteen minutes before they had to go inside to their classroom, so, Scott took out a folded piece of paper, and showed his calculations to Laurie and Alfie.

"So, I figure if at least one of us can sneak an empty apple juice bottle out of the house every day, then we can fill it with gasoline, and bring it to the old house. I'm sure we can have those two gas containers filled in maybe three weeks. I wish it could be a lot sooner that that, but if that big container I've got now, is emptied too quickly, then somebody might offer to help me correct my project so that it won't burn so much gas. This way, if we use up just one container a week, we'll still have those big containers filled so we can put them in the trunk of the car, and then we can drive it out to the highway around the beginning of the last week of October," Scott told them.

"It'll feel so great, zooming along the highway. That's if the old car can get up to a fast speed, or if the motor doesn't conk out after five miles," said Alfie.

"Naaa, I'm sure it won't. Right, Laurie?" asked Scott.

"Yeah, I don't think we have to worry about anything going wrong with the car when we start driving it because we've checked over everything it said in the manual, so, I'm sure we won't run into any problems. But I sure wish our apple juice jars were bigger, and that we could sneak more than one empty one out of the house every day, or maybe every other day if we're unlucky. I'm sure glad we can work together on that project of yours, Scott, but I don't see why we can't just tell them we threw the cloths away after I almost burned my fingers when I tried to light them when they had a tiny bit of gasoline on them."

"Because then they'd look everywhere for the cloths to make sure we didn't throw them away somewhere they'd start a fire. Right?

We've got to make them think that we've used up the gas after we've accidentally spilled it when we lit the wicks on my project. Right? So, the cloths've gotta disappear or else they'd wonder why they're not soaked with gasoline, and that's why we have to tell them that the cloths caught fire and burned up before we could put out the fire. It's *hiding* the cloths that's more of a problem. We've been wrapping so many cloths around rocks, and sinking them in the stream, that I bet if someone found some of them, they'd think it was some sort of art stuff done by an artist many years ago," said Scott, smiling.

"Naaaa! They'd think there were elves doing it, when the tiny guys weren't busy making shoes," said Laurie.

"I wish there really *were* elves because then after we drive the car away, everybody'd be busy looking for little elves to join the big Halloween party, instead of us. Right?" said Alfie. "Hey, y'know, that's not a bad idea! We could tell them we've seen elves under some bushes and sitting on tree branches, okay? People believe there's ghosts and goblins, and all sorts of weird, big and little creatures running around at Halloween, so, maybe they might also believe there's elves running around, too."

"Dream on, man!" exclaimed Scott, laughing.

"Well, I thought it might be a great idea," said Alfie.

"They wouldn't believe we saw any elves running around, but they must think we're apple juice junkies because we keep asking for apple juice with breakfast every morning. But it sure is a great cover for carrying gasoline in apple juice jars. Gas is about the same color as that," said Scott.

"Yuk! Apple juice, apple juice, and more apple juice. Every morning for weeks and weeks just so I can try sneaking an empty bottle out of the house. But almost every time when I'm finished drinking a bottle of apple juice, it gets snatched off the table as soon as I set it down. That's why I'm lucky if I can sneak just one empty apple juice bottle out of the house in a week. I'm so sick of apple juice, that I'll never drink it again," said Laurie, scowling.

"Aw, stop whining, little, big girl!" Scott said as he grinned.

"I've got to whine to *somebody* because no one else'll let me do it, okay? I always try never to complain about anything, but I'm so glad you're not complaining about helping me find homes for the kittens. It's a great excuse to be out late to take the car out to the highway, but I didn't mean it was going to be fun using the kittens as our excuse to do that. Okay? I'm sorry, Scott. Really. I'm just as scared as you are, and I'm so sorry you have to be the one to do it."

"It's okay, Laurie. I...I, um, yeah, I'm really scared, but I'll be okay. I know someone has to do it. So, um, the kittens are really cute, aren't they?"

"Yeah, they sure are," said Alfie. "I'm glad they were born now, because the kittens are our alibi. No one'll know we're really driving a car instead of knocking on doors, and asking people if they'd like a kitten. I can hardly wait 'til we drive the car to the local highway, and then drive it to the big highway, and then after that we can...Um, I guess just getting ready to go is going to be the hardest part, and the scariest part, too. I'm so sorry, Scott. Are you going to be okay?"

"Uh, yeah, sure. Sure, I am. I, uh, I know it's the only way, so, I'll do it. I have to, right?" he said, frowning.

They fell silent for over a minute as they thought about the kittens, the car, and what they knew Scott had to do before they'd be able to drive the car.

"I just hope nobody's driving along the local highway when we get the car past the gate," said Alfie.

"Stop worrying about it, okay?" Scott told him. "You can see way over two miles in both directions from where the gate is, so, we'll be able to see if a car's coming, and if there is, then we back up the car through the gate again, and wait 'til the car passes, and then we drive as fast as we can to the small road going up to the Kirby's farm, so, we'll be okay."

"If we *do* see a car, I hope they won't look over at the gate, and see us. But I guess they won't be able to because it'll be really dark, and the car's black," said Alfie.

"Yeah, and if we see someone driving toward us, we can jump out of the car, and close the gate so they won't wonder why it's open. But I bet they wouldn't notice the gate, anyway, because of all those big bushes at both sides of it. Right? Besides, they'll be looking at the road ahead of them while they're driving, right?" said Scott.

"Yeah, I'm sure you're right. I feel a bit nervous, but I know this'll work out okay because it'll be so dark when we leave," said Alfie. "Well, it's time we headed back to the classroom and be so amazed by Mrs. Gorrel. Acting dumb is worse than being an apple juice junkie, man. It's also so boring, trying to make a few mistakes when we're doing our homework, isn't it? But it sure does impress them that we need their clever minds to explain things to us. Hey, and don't forget to suck your thumb when we get back into the classroom, little Laurie."

"Get real, y'jerk!" she exclaimed, then she laughed.

• • • • • ❖•••••❖★❖•••••❖ • • • • •

Mrs. Gorrel told Laurie that sucking her thumb might cause her to eventually have deformed teeth, and then Laurie apologized to her, and said that she'd try to stop the habit. Alfie snickered when Laurie said that, so, Mrs. Gorrel told him to stand out in the hall until she called him back into the classroom.

She had to tell Laurie three times to stop sucking her thumb, then seeing her pout, Mrs. Gorrel smiled and told her that she, herself, had also sucked her thumb when she'd been a little girl, but that Laurie's habit would end right after the orange fairies fluttered out of the trees on Halloween.

At afternoon recess, Scott, Laurie, and Alfie laughed as they ran outside and over to the playground to use the swings. They played for ten minutes, then Laurie jumped off the swing, walked over to a tree, and after leaning back against it, she looked down at her shoes.

Scott and Alfie realized that she was very nervous, and that it was imperative to cheer her up, so, they hurried over to her, and then Alfie told her: "Your head's bowed and y'look sad."

388

She raised her head, forced a smile, then curtsied and jumped up and down a few times before exclaiming: "See? Little Laurie's a happy girl!"

"Good for you," said Scott, smiling at her.

"Sorry. It won't happen again."

"We know that. You're great, Laurie," said Scott.

"Yeah, you are," Alfie said as he smiled.

"I'm going to think about the kittens before I fall asleep every night, and then maybe I won't have any more of those nightmares. Hey, how about we see who can climb that tree the fastest, okay?"

"Yeah, okay. We can look inside the classroom window, and see if Mrs. Gorrel's changed back into a witch by turning around three times to make the B change to a W," said Alfie, grinning. "You know, take away the W in witch, and replace it with a B, and it shows her other side."

"Oh, you're terrible! Mrs. Gorrel doesn't do silly things like turning around three times to do that because she's a bitch even when she's a witch!" cried Laurie, laughing.

They laughed as they ran over to the tree, and after they'd climbed high enough so that they could look into their classroom, Mrs. Gorrel hurried to the window, and shouted at them to get down from the tree before they fell and hurt themselves.

After recess, she made Scott, Laurie, and Alfie write: "I won't climb a high tree, ever again," twenty-five times on the blackboard.

· · · · · · ◇••••••◇★◇••••••◇ · · · · · ·

After breakfast every day, either Laurie, Scott, or Alfie had been able to sneak an empty apple juice jar out of the house, then after filling the small jar with gasoline, they took it to the old abandoned house, and then a week before Halloween, they had filled the two, metal gas containers.

In the late afternoon of the day that the metal gas containers had been filled, Scott, Laurie and Alfie were laughing and talking as they walked along the street after they'd had milkshakes at the restaurant. When they reached the end of another street, they stopped walking to look over at the town square.

They saw that the circle made of logs had been completed, and over a dozen of their neighbors were pulling big branches down off the back of a big truck, then dragging them over to the log circle, and then stacking the branches around the perimeter of the circle.

There were already many branches stacked densely about three feet high around the perimeter, so, Laurie, Alfie and Scott knew that the work was almost completed. In the center of the circle, were three, tall poles that had many different symbols carved into them.

They knew that those three, tall poles represented winter, spring and summer, then at ten o'clock on Halloween night, the enormous bonfire would burn away those seasons, and then the beginning of autumn would be celebrated.

On that night, the adults wore black, hooded robes and skeleton masks to signify the passing of the previous three seasons, and children wore white robes to signify both purity and the coming snows of winter.

Three hours before the bonfire was lit each Halloween, music began playing from loudspeakers, then whenever the adults weren't dancing, they'd be drinking wine and liquor while enjoying all the food that would be set out on a long table decorated with garlands and wreaths of colored leaves.

Laurie, Scott and Alfie hated the old fashioned music and everything else about the town's gala Halloween celebrations, and they hoped that yearly tradition would cease.

They walked along the street leading away from the town square, while talking about how awful the Halloween celebrations always were. An hour after they'd said goodnight, and gone their separate ways, Laurie clenched her teeth and tried to look enthusiastic while standing on a chair, and having her white Halloween robe hemmed.

· · · · · ❖•••••❖ ★ ❖•••••❖ · · · · ·

The old road from the abandoned house to the rusty gate had been cleared of weeds and sharp stones, and Scott, Alfie, and Laurie had agreed that on the day they would drive the car to the highway, they'd tell everyone that they wanted to take the kittens door to door in the neighborhood after dinner, and that they'd do their homework when they returned.

Two days later, they were elated when they received permission to try to find new homes for the kittens, and now that Laurie had the kittens ready to take from door to door, she told Scott that she'd be sitting by the bedroom window, waiting for him to wave up to her from the sidewalk in front of the house.

Scott knew it was now time for him to carry out the first part of their plan that they knew was absolutely necessary. When he awoke the following day, he felt scared about the decision they'd made, however, he knew, that he had to work up the courage to do it.

That first and most important part of the plan had to take place after dinner when it was dark outside, and when Scott felt sure that almost all the neighbors would be sitting in their living rooms, watching television.

After breakfast, Scott met up with Alfie and Laurie, then they ran through the woods to the old dirt road that led from the abandoned house to the gate, and then they hurried along the dirt road, making sure they hadn't overlooked a sharp stone that could cause damage to one of the tires on the old car.

While they were checking the dirt road for sharp stones near the gate to the two-lane local highway, a man on a motorcycle appeared out of a side road farther down the highway, and before they could run and hide behind some bushes, the man saw them, and he waved and shouted to them.

Laurie, Scott and Alfie began quickly discussing ideas for an excuse to give the man about why they were at this area of the two-lane highway.

The man drove toward them, stopped his motorcycle, then smiled as he explained that'd he'd been low on gas while driving along the main highway, then he'd seen a billboard, advertising a gas station that was situated just over a mile down a side road from the highway.

He told Alfie, Laurie and Scott that after driving about halfway along that side road, another similar side road curved into it, and the two roads became one. He'd had his gas tank filled, then on his way back from the gas station, he'd come to the junction of the two roads, and then mistakenly chosen the other side road.

The man told them that he hadn't known that the other side road had led away from the main highway, and then he'd started coming across other, small side roads leading off the one he was driving along. He'd eventually decided to take one of the other side roads that he'd hoped would take him back to the main highway, however, the side road instead had led him out to the small local highway, and now he wasn't sure which direction to take to get to the main highway.

He asked Laurie, Scott and Alfie for directions back to the main highway, then after he introduced himself, and they felt sure that Steve wasn't a resident of the area, they kept looking in both directions of the road to see if a car was coming as they told him how to get to the main highway, and they also told him about themselves.

They then started telling him about their plan to drive the old car to the city. Steve had taken a pad and pen out of his jacket, and then after he'd stopped writing, he told Laurie to get on the motorcycle, and he'd take her with him to the city. But she told him that she wouldn't leave without Scott and Alfie.

Steve asked her a few more times, however, Laurie kept refusing, then he wrote down his address in the city, gave it to Alfie and Scott, and told them that they could meet Laurie at his home.

But she remained adamant about staying with Alfie and Scott, and going to the city with them. Steve had felt quite worried about them, and he'd tried to insist that at least Laurie come with him, however, when they saw a car approaching in the distance, Laurie, Alfie, and Scott ran away, and ducked down behind bushes.

They had shouted to Steve that they'd meet him that night at his home in the city. Steve had seen the car coming along the highway, so, he'd shouted to Laurie to wait until the car passed, then she could get onto his motorcycle with him.

She shouted back to him from her hiding place behind the bushes, that he could never persuade her to leave without her two best friends. Steve had watched the car driving slowly toward him, then he'd shouted to Laurie, Scott and Alfie to be very careful sneaking away to the main highway in the old car.

The car was less than half a mile away from him when Steve started his motorcycle and sped away. Scott, Laurie, and Alfie peered out from the bushes, and watched Steve drive out of sight, followed a couple of minutes later by a neighbor's slowly moving car.

The children then slapped hands and whooped in celebration of their tremendous luck in meeting Steve on the very day they planned to drive away from town in the old car.

Scott finished washing the dishes and putting them away in the cupboards, after they'd had dinner at five o'clock, as usual. He then left the kitchen, walked past the small den, and then after he'd stood by the entrance to the living room for half an hour, he turned around, and looked into the den.

"Can I please watch a bit more TV?"

"Have you finished doing the dishes?" Cal asked him.

"Yup! All of them! Honest! So, can I? Please?"

"Hmmm, oh, all right, but only for an hour, okay? And I'll keep the volume down because I want to finish this book I'm reading. It's hard to concentrate with all kinds of cartoon characters shouting and laughing so loudly at each other. Okay?" Cal told him as he smiled.

"Gee, thanks! You're the greatest, ever! Really!"

"Why, thank you, Scott, and *you're* a very good boy."

Scott kept glancing up at the clock on the wall as he watched television, then twenty minutes later, he walked into the den where Cal was reading a book. He knew that Cal liked to have a mug of hot chocolate every evening around this time.

"I'm going to put the kettle on and make some hot chocolate. Can I make you some, too?"

"Why, that's a great idea, Scott! Would you put some of those tiny marshmallows on top of my hot chocolate, too, please? Oh, and why don't we have cookies with it, okay? Would you like that?"

"Oh, yeah, I sure would! I'll get out those ones with the cream centers. They're *your* favorites, too, aren't they?"

"Yes, they are," replied Cal, smiling. "Be careful you don't burn yourself with the hot water, now."

"I'll be real careful. I haven't spilled the kettle, once."

He went to the kitchen, put the kettle on the stove, then got the hot chocolate and cookies out of the cupboard. Scott felt sweat beading on his forehead as he sat at the table, waiting for the kettle to boil, and then he went to the stove and held his breath as he poured the hot water into one of the mugs.

He put the mug and a small plate of cookies on a tray for Cal, then he walked slowly to the den. Cal was sitting in his chair at the desk, engrossed in his book.

"I did it! And I didn't spill anything!" exclaimed Scott.

"Good boy! Mmmm, mmmm, this smells great!"

"Is that enough little marshmallows?"

"Perfect," replied Cal, smiling. "Now you go watch television. This book's very exciting, so, I want to see if I can finish it before I go to bed. I'm close to the end of it. You can watch TV for another half hour, and then you'll have to come upstairs to bed. Okay?"

"Okay. You're the best of all the best," said Scott.

"Aw, thanks. Now, you go sit down and watch that nice TV show, okay? That's a good boy."

"Gee, thanks! Oh! I forgot to make some hot chocolate for me! Golly, I'm stupid. I'm gonna make some now, and then I'm gonna sit at the kitchen table to drink it with my cookies, and then maybe I might watch TV. But maybe I won't. Hmmm, I'll think about it while I'm drinking my hot chocolate. Yeah, that's a good idea."

"Okay, Scott. Whatever pleases you."

Scott poured hot water into the mug, sat down at the table, sipped on his hot chocolate, nibbled on a cookie, and watched the clock. Fifteen minutes later, he walked over to the kitchen counter, opened a drawer, and then he walked very slowly back to the den.

Cal had turned off all the lights in the den, except for the small reading lamp on the desk, and he was happily engrossed in reading his book. Scott felt perspiration trickling down over his ribs as he slowly moved toward him, and he felt so thankful that Cal had his back to him, and that the carpet was so thick that he could get close enough to Cal without him hearing any footsteps.

Scott clenched his teeth as he gripped the handle of the butcher knife in both of his hands, then raised his arms, sucked in his breath, and then swung the knife down as hard as he could into Cal's back.

Cal gasped, threw his arms out to his sides, and started struggling up out of the chair. Scott yanked the knife out of Cal's back, and then kept stabbing him until Cal gave out a weak wheeze, staggered sideways, and crumpled to the floor.

His thoughts whirled as he stood looking down at Cal's body for a few moments, then Scott knelt, removed the braided twine with the keys on it from around Cal's neck.

He fumbled with the keys as he sorted through them, then he felt so relieved when he found the right one. His fingers then trembled and he tried not to look at Cal's body as he turned the key in the lock, and then Scott stood up, and rushed over to the library cabinet.

He quickly sorted through the drawer of the cabinet, looking for other keys, trying each one until he'd found the key to the cabinet doors. He unlocked the doors, grabbed the gun, and then he began sorting through the small drawers below the book shelves.

Scott blew out a big sigh when he found several boxes of bullets, then he rushed back to the kitchen and dropped the gun and two boxes of bullets into a black plastic bag.

He slowly turned the lights off from room to room downstairs, climbed the stairs, turned on the light in his bedroom, then in Cal's bedroom, and then he turned on the bathroom light. Fifteen minutes later, Scott turned off the light in his bedroom, and then waited another five minutes before turning off the bathroom light.

Ten minutes after turning off the bathroom light, he turned off the light in Cal's bedroom, knowing it would appear that they'd gone to bed, and of course, Cal's bedroom light going off last meant that anyone who might have been looking over at the house for some reason, wouldn't be suspicious.

Scott went back downstairs to the den to make sure that Cal was dead, then he waited ten minutes before he left by the back door, gripping the bag with the gun and bullets in it, and feeling the sweat on his hands and the blood soaking the front of his shirt.

He had instinctively wiped his hands on his shirt, and then gasped when he'd realized his mistake, so, he hoped that no one would notice his bloodied shirt before he had a chance to change out of it.

He crouched down as he ran along the grass in the backyard, then he began hopping fences all the way down the street, and his heart suddenly began pounding faster when he heard a dog barking inside one of the houses.

When he was behind the house Laurie was in, Scott walked out onto the street, and sat on the curb to wait for her to appear at the bedroom window.

Whenever he saw a neighbor walking along the street toward him, he'd bend over and pretend that he was tying his shoelaces so that they wouldn't see the blood on the front of his shirt, then he'd grin and say hello to people as they passed by.

Laurie looked out her open bedroom window, and whistled to get his attention. She saw Scott pointing to the blood on his shirt, so, she left the bedroom, tiptoed quickly along the hall to the next bedroom, and removed a clean T-shirt from a drawer.

She folded the shirt until she felt sure it wouldn't be too noticeable in her hand, and then Laurie hoped no one would see her, and ask her what she had in her hand when she went downstairs, and through to the kitchen.

She put the T-shirt in a plastic bag before she made two trips back and forth from the kitchen to the front door, carrying the kittens and setting them down inside a cardboard box on the seat of the platform swing on the porch.

Laurie then carried the box of kittens down the porch steps, and put it on her little wagon, and then she pulled it along the front walkway to the sidewalk.

They began walking slowly along the street, then Laurie reached into the box, picked up the bag containing the clean T-shirt, and after giving the bag to Scott, he looked around to make sure he wasn't seen, and then he hurried up a driveway between two houses.

He changed into the clean shirt, put the bloodied one in the bag, then he walked back, and stuffed the bag back under the blanket in Laurie's wagon, then she began pulling the wagon while they walked slowly down the street.

Alfie met them at the corner of the street, and Laurie kept telling him and Scott to walk faster because they only had another two hours before bedtime.

They knocked on a few doors along streets leading to the ravine, asking neighbors if they wanted a cute little kitten. Only one neighbor wanted a kitten, so, Scott, Alfie, and Laurie placed the box of kittens at a neighbor's back door.

They then covered the kittens with the small, baby blanket that had been in the box, then they ran back out to the street, ran across it, hopped the fence, and then ran down into the ravine.

Ten minutes later, they'd reached the old, abandoned house, then Laurie and Alfie pulled open the garage doors. Scott held his breath as he started the engine while hoping the car wouldn't backfire, and then he felt so relieved when the engine ran smoothly as he drove it out of the garage.

Alfie and Laurie jumped into the car, then Scott drove along the dirt road toward the old, rusty gate. They stopped the car near the gate, then Laurie and Alfie got out of the car, pulled open the gate, and then they looked in both directions along the two-lane highway.

"Okay! C'mon!" shouted Alfie, then after Scott drove through the gate, Laurie and Alfie got back into the car, and then Scott began driving along the local highway.

Spread out for two miles along the two-lane, local highway, were ten houses near the road, and the last of those houses was about ten miles from the three-lane highway.

Laurie, Alfie and Scott had worried that they might be seen driving by those houses, therefore, they'd worked out a plan to avoid that problem.

Just over a mile from the first of those ten houses was the private side road leading to the Kirby farm, and Scott, Alfie and Laurie's plan was to drive a mile along that side road until they were halfway to the Kirby's farmhouse.

They'd then drive off the road, across the Kirby's cornfield to the barbed wire fence that bordered the part of the local highway that was about three miles past the last of those ten houses.

Scott drove fast to the side road leading to the Kirby's farm, and they were relieved when they hadn't seen another car by the time they turned onto the private road.

A few minutes later, they reached the beginning of the cornfield, then Scott turned off the road, and they held their breaths as the car rocked up and down as it went down into the ditch, then up out of it.

The corn was higher than the car as Scott drove along the edge of the cornfield toward the barbed wire fence at the end of the Kirby property. Scott clenched his teeth when the car tilted slightly sideways after the right front wheel went down into a deep rut, then he felt so thankful that the tire wasn't damaged.

He'd turned off all the car lights from the time they'd started out from the old abandoned house, and Scott knew he couldn't turn the lights on until they were driving away from the Kirby's farm.

He drove very slowly along the side of the cornfield while Laurie and Alfie walked in front of the car, and guided him past boulders and anything else that could hinder the car's progress.

Scott was becoming more excited while driving nearer to the high, barbed wire fence, then he stopped close to it, and got out of the car. Alfie had been able to get a pair of wire cutters, so, as he snipped strands of barbed wire, Laurie and Scott pulled the loose wire away.

"I've cut all the barbed wire lines high enough, so, the top of the car should get through now," Alfie told them.

Scott rushed back to the car, drove it closer to the edge of the property, and then after stopping at the top of the incline to the local highway, he said: "Okay, you guys go down to the bottom of the hill, and clear away any sharp rocks."

"Okay," said Alfie, looking down the incline. "It's not too steep, so, you'll make it okay. I sure hope nobody's driving along this part of the road, but I guess nobody'll be heading toward the other highway at this time."

He and Laurie checked to make sure there weren't any sharp rocks at the bottom of the incline, then they ran back up to the car, got in, and Scott held his breath as he started the car again, and drove down the slope.

The car bounced slightly a few times when it reached the bottom, then they cheered when Scott drove the car out onto the local highway. He then turned on the car's lights, and began driving toward the big, three-lane highway that led to the freeway.

Five miles along the three-lane highway, Scott increased his speed, but not enough to draw attention to them. They panicked when they saw a patrol car behind them, then it slowed down for a moment before continuing on past them.

When the patrol car had slowed down, Alfie had held his breath, Scott had clenched his teeth, and Laurie had gripped the gun with one hand and held a throw cushion over it with her other hand.

They began feeling less tense after the patrol car had kept driving along the highway, and they hoped that they could get by any other patrol cars just as easily.

To make themselves appear older than thirteen, Scott and Alfie had put on fedoras, and Laurie, who was seated in the back of the car, had managed to get a veiled and flowered, woman's hat. The night and the darkness inside the car had also helped to disguise them from close scrutiny by the patrolman.

Twenty minutes later, they reached the main highway, then Scott increased the car's speed a little more, and then after driving a few more miles, he drove faster.

They'd surreptitiously packed lunches the day before, and taken them to the old, abandoned house. Now that he felt hungry, Scott pulled off the highway at the entrance to a side road with many trees lining the sides of it, and then moments later, he stopped the car.

"Whew! So far, so good," said Scott. "Okay, let's eat! We'd better put more gas in the tank before we start driving again."

"Oh, man!" exclaimed Alfie. "That patrol car slowing down like that! I thought he was going to ask us to pull over! I was so scared!"

"I'm glad there was only one guy," said Scott. "I don't think we'd have had a chance with two, because by the time Laurie shot one guy, then the other guy would've seen him fall, and then he would've started shooting at us."

"Yeah, but if there had've been a second patrolman, he might've been in shock at first, then by the time he reached for his gun, I could've shot him. Right?" said Laurie. "Then we could've got rid of their bodies and the patrol car, somewhere. But I was worried that they might've had to use their car radio to call in and report that everything's okay. If they didn't call in after the time they were expected to, then another patrol car would've come looking for them to see why they hadn't used their car phone. I'm sure glad I didn't have to kill that one patrolman because hiding him and his car would've taken us a lot of time."

"Yeah, I know. Okay, Alfie, start driving because by this time, people are beginning to wonder where we are. Thank God there's not many phones in town, and right now we're supposed to be doing our homework, but in maybe an hour, if for some reason or other somebody wants to ask Mr. Morgan something, and they see his body, it'll sure cause a lot of squabbling, man," said Scott.

"Yeah, and a lot of scrambling to get in their cars and come look for us," said Alfie. "That's only if they've looked everywhere else for us. I wish we could've killed them all before we left, because then they wouldn't be squabbling about anything."

"Gee, Alfie the serial killer," said Laurie, then she and Alfie started laughing as Scott scowled.

"Yeah, sure, laugh you guys, but there was only one gun that we knew about," said Scott. "Let's hope we can get more guns in the city, and then maybe we'll be able to come back here, and then kill off everyone in town."

"Well, you couldn't've used a gun to kill mean, rotten Mr. Morgan because all of his next door neighbors would've heard the shot. But I'm so glad *I* didn't have to do it, especially by using a butcher knife," said Laurie.

"So am I. You're really brave, Scott."

"Not really. I had to do it, right? It was the only way to get the gun and the bullets. I sure hope we don't get too tired to drive because I don't wanna sleep anywhere near here in case they find us in the morning."

"Gosh!" exclaimed Laurie. "Wouldn't that be scary? They'll be so mad at us because of what we've done. How much longer before we get there?"

"I think about another two hours if we keep driving at the speed we were at before we stopped here to eat, and if we don't run into any problems, like another patrol car. Just in case we *do* see one, keep your gun handy," said Alfie.

They finished eating, then Alfie got behind the wheel, and slowly backed up the car along the side road. He felt very nervous as he turned the car around, and then began driving down the highway again, as Laurie and Scott looked out the back window to see if they were being followed.

When Alfie had driven another fifty miles, he looked for a side road, then he pulled off the highway, stopped the car, and they added more gasoline to the tank. Five minutes later, they were back in the car, heading down the highway, then Alfie drove faster.

. . . . . ❖•••••❖✦❖•••••❖ . . . . .

Just over an hour later, their excitement grew when they saw the sky lit up in the distance, and highway signs indicating that they were nearing the city they'd wanted to go to for the past two years.

They were quite worried that there might be faster cars in pursuit of them, and that they'd be caught before they got into the midst of the city, then they became slightly less tense when Alfie steered the car into the lane that led to the downtown area.

He began driving slower when he was surrounded by other cars that were also driving into the city, and then ten minutes later, they'd reached the downtown area.

Alfie parked the car on a street that was crowded with people, restaurants, and many houses with lights on, and then he felt so relieved that they'd made it all the way to the city.

They passed around sandwiches and munched on them as they watched people passing by, then Laurie picked up the pistol, opened the chamber, to look at the bullets, then she said: "I'm sure glad I didn't have to shoot that patrolman, and maybe another one if he'd been with him in that patrol car, too, then that'd mean I would've been a murderer," she said, frowning.

"No way! It'd be self-defense because they'd have guns, too! It's not murder, okay? So, get over it!" exclaimed Alfie.

"Don't worry, I would've killed them," said Laurie. "But no matter what we think about them, I'd still be having awful nightmares for months after I'd killed them. Maybe *years*."

"We're lucky you didn't think that way when the patrol car slowed down alongside us," said Scott. "But I knew you would've killed him, or them, Laurie. And if Alfie and I had been as good a shot as you are, then *we* would've carried the gun. That's something else they'll be mad at us for, like, when they find Mr. Morgan's body. Right? Man, I'm still sorta scared from doing that. It's really lucky I didn't get a lot of blood on me when I stabbed him like that. Like, I was really shaking before I killed him, but I knew it was the only way to get the gun and the bullets. Hey, and I sure don't feel like a murderer now."

"I'm more worried about those kittens. I just hope one or two of them don't crawl out of the blanket because it's pretty cold out tonight, and they might freeze to death."

"Aw, don't worry about the little kittens, Alfie. They'll be okay. I'm sure somebody'll find them in that box when they're out searching for us," Laurie told him.

"Yeah, I guess so. I wish the kittens and their mother didn't have to live with those people. I sure wish Mr. Morgan had've had a silencer for that gun! Then I would've killed off as many of them as I could! Especially Mrs. Orton! She's a real, rotten cook!"

"Alfie! You're so crazy! That's all you ever think about! Your stomach, and how to cram it full!" exclaimed Scott, laughing.

"Well, I would've killed her, for sure," he said, smiling.

"Now that we're all feeling happier, it's time to make our next move. Laurie, give me the gun and I'll put it back in the plastic bag, okay? Wait! Don't hold it up like that! Put something over it before you pass it to me. Somebody passing by might see it," Scott told her as he looked out at the street.

"Oh, okay. I never thought about that, but if a policeman saw it, he'd probably just think it was a toy," she said.

"No way! If he saw us with that gun, he'd start shooting at us! Then more cops'd come to help him, and then they'd shoot the car full of bullets. Okay? So, we don't want any more trouble 'til we get more guns, okay?" said Scott. "I bet Steve's got lots of guns here in the city. Hmmm, y'know what I'm thinking? I bet when we meet up with him, he'll tell us we can't go back there with more guns, and kill off the rest of the people in town. He said he was gonna make sure they didn't come after us, so, I bet he'll kill 'em all, but I sure hope we can talk him into taking us with him when he does it."

"I just hope they get it, and good," said Laurie, pouting.

"Look. There's a phone booth at the end of the street, so, you guys stay here and I'll go call Steve and tell him we're here in the city. Okay?" said Alfie. "I've saved up about a pound of coins in case

I had to call long distance if we were being followed. Now try to smile while I'm on the phone, okay? Hey, and Scott? If you see anyone from town while I'm in the phone booth, then shoot them in the head, okay?"

"You bet. The minute they bend down to look in the car."

. . . . . . ❖••••••❖★❖••••••❖ . . . . . .

Alfie hurried to the phone booth, then Laurie and Scott watched him talking to Steve on the phone, and then they grinned when they saw him returning to the car with a confident smile.

"Okay, it's all set," said Alfie after he got back in the car. "I told him we're okay, and then he asked me the names of the two streets where the phone booth was that I was calling him from, and what color the car was, and how old it was, and other stuff about it. After that he told me how to get to Alcorn Street, and then after we find number 226 Alcorn, we buzz apartment number 425. Okay? That's where Steve lives. He said he was really worried we'd get caught when we started driving away in the car."

"Not as worried as we were, man," said Scott. "I sure hope he can get us more guns because one isn't going to help if they come looking for us here."

"Get real!" cried Laurie and Alfie.

"Aw, shut up! Okay, tell me what street to take, Alfie."

"He said to go along this street to Taylor, then make a left, go along to...hmmm, I think he said, Gordon. No, I think it was Glen something. Glengordon? Just a sec, I'm sure I can remember it."

"Never mind, I got the map, okay? Let's see now...hmmm, man, there's so many folds to these things. Okay, we're on Landon, and we're supposed to go along it to Alcorn, so, if I find Landon on this map, then I'll see how far it is from here to Alcorn. Hmmm, Alcorn. Can't see it. I'll look under 'L' in the index, okay? Looking. Hmmm, still looking. Okay, it says here in the index that it's somewhere in the G12 square and the T6 square. Right. Okay, here's the G square, now if I...Yeah, this is the T square, so, Alcorn's gotta be around...hmmm, aw, darn it! I can't follow all these lines to..."

"Give me the map! Gawwwd!" exclaimed Alfie.

"Hey! I almost found it!" Scott insisted.

"Get real!" Alfie and Laurie exclaimed in unison.

Alfie began examining the map, and then a few moments later, he said: "Okay, I found the street we're on now, so, we have to go down this one, and then we turn right at the next street to...Yeah, okay, I got it! Okay, now we know exactly where we're going. Hey, Scott! What are y'doing? Put that gun away! We don't wanna leave a trail of bodies on the way there!" he exclaimed, then he grinned.

"Well, I'll shoot the first person who looks at us too long, man. You bet I will."

"Wow! Clint Eastwood in the front seat!" cried Laurie.

"And you're Clint Eastwood's kid sister," Alfie told her.

"But I haven't had the chance to kill anyone, yet. Oh, well, you never know," said Laurie, trying to smile.

As Alfie drove the car, Laurie and Scott felt very nervous while looking out the back window to see if they were being followed by anyone's car they recognized from town. They needn't have worried because less than five minutes after they'd phoned Steve, an unmarked police car began closely following the car that Laurie, Scott, and Alfie were in, to make sure that the children didn't get lost on their way to Steve's apartment building.

· · · · · · ✧•••••✧★✧•••••✧ · · · · · ·

Alfie parked the car two blocks away from the apartment building, then they walked to it, and rang the buzzer to Steve's apartment. They took the elevator up to the sixth floor, and when the elevator doors opened, they saw Steve and a beautiful young woman, whom he introduced as his wife, Erica.

She hugged Laurie, Scott, and Alfie, and then told them to hurry into the apartment and sit on the couch. Steve immediately made a phone call to say that the children had made it safely to his home, then he took the gun away from Scott before they left the apartment.

He drove them to a large building, led them to an office where another man made some phone calls, and then after he hung up the phone, he smiled while telling Scott, Laurie, and Alfie that everything would be taken care of.

Erica then hurried the children back out of the building, and drove them back to her apartment where she ordered them to undress, leave their clothes out in the hall, take showers, and then go to bed.

After they'd showered and put on fresh clothes that Steve and Erica had bought for them, they returned to the living room, and then Laurie, Alfie, and Scott sat on the couch.

Erica winced as she listened to Scott tell her how he'd stabbed Cal Morgan to death because it had been the only way he could get the gun and the bullets.

"Oh, Scott! His body might've been discovered before you got away! I think it's so awful that you had to kill him, but then I suppose you had to do it, considering. Was he the only person that the three of you killed?" Erica asked them.

"Yeah, but if we had to kill more, we would've. At least I'd've tried to," replied Laurie. "I was going to shoot the patrolman if he'd tried to stop us. I'm tougher than I look."

"Spoken like a true lady," said Erica, forcing a smile.

"So, do you think Steve and the others'll kill more of them? Maybe lots of them?" asked Alfie.

"I'm not sure. They might have to," Erica told him. "I just hope Steve doesn't get hurt. I told him not to go, but he insisted. I'm so glad he saw you kids, and stopped to ask you for directions, and thank God that patrol car didn't stop you. It must've been absolutely terrifying for you. It's too ghastly to think of what might've happened if you hadn't had that gun with you."

"Yeah, I know," said Scott. "We were so scared a long time before we left. My fingers kept shaking every time I poured a bit of gasoline into the funnel to start up my fake project, and also when we were filling up the gas cans. And Laurie was having nightmares, and she kept seeing shadows in just about everything, then while we were clearing the road to the gate to get the car out on the local highway, Alfie said he could feel his feet burning! That was so scary! We were starting to get more and more scared because it was getting so close to Halloween!"

"Yeah, and then Scott had to kill him so that he could get the key to the handcuff around his ankle, and the one for the lock on the cabinet where Mr. Morgan kept his gun and the bullets," said Alfie.

"The chain on the handcuff was long enough so I could go into the kitchen and his den, but not into his living room, so, I could only stand or sit down at the living room door to look in at the TV. Mr. Morgan always kept me chained up, and he chained me to the bed upstairs before he went to his bedroom. He wouldn't let me go out when I told him I was going to try getting homes for the kittens, so, I had to get the keys he always kept around his neck."

"But wouldn't the other adults have become suspicious if they'd seen you outside his house?" Erica asked him.

"Nope. I didn't tell any of them that he always kept that chain on my ankle when I stayed with him, so, none of them would've called him or come to his house to ask if he let me go out for an hour to help Laurie and Alfie get homes for the kittens," Scott told her.

"I was so scared because it was getting closer and closer to Halloween! I hoped they didn't find out that Mr. Morgan was dead before we were far away in the car!" exclaimed Laurie. "The patrol car would've stopped us, and taken us back there! We had to go to a different house for breakfast, and then for lunch, and then for supper every day, and we had to keep pretending we were their own kids, and that we were only about seven years old! Ohhhh, I keep thinking about all those other kids! We were the only ones left!"

"Naw, they would've got more kids from the orphanage near town if the kids were under thirteen," said Alfie.

"Yeah, I know. If some people had've adopted us, like, *nice* people who didn't live anywhere near the town, then we could've...Well, that's just wishing and dreaming. All those other kids they took from the orphanage! They killed them all! And all their own kids, too! They kill kids when they turn thirteen! They made them wear long, white robes and have flowers in their hair, and then they tied them to the three posts, and then they lit the bonfire! I was so scared! The gun! I might've had to...I didn't want to, but...Oh, I was so scared and I...I..." exclaimed Laurie, and then she began sobbing.

"Aw, Laurie. You're safe because it's over now. There are so many policemen on their way up there, and many of them are already there because they left here hours ago. Aw, don't cry, honey. You're safe, now. All three of you are. They can't hurt you now. Shhhh, you're safe," said Erica, hugging her as Laurie wept.

The End

Hey, Like Barbara!

By John A. Reid

Hey, Like, Barbara!

Barbara's most striking feature was her voice, which made people cringe because she shouted out every word she spoke, and her demeanor was often quite shocking. Her parents had learned to tolerate her shouting, but sometimes they still winced when she spoke to them.

Her mother, Dora, often almost jumped off the floor whenever Barbara suddenly appeared either in front, beside, or behind her, and then yelled: "Hi!"

Dora had baked a cake, iced it, and then she began decorating the top of the cake. She mixed several different colors of icing sugar, and then fashioned little roses with the pink icing.

She then made leaves with the green icing, and used the brown icing to form thin, brown stems. After studying her icing sugar artwork, Dora decided that the flowers and leaves would look even lovelier if she put a dozen or so tiny, silver, candied balls on them, and then it'd look like dew on the roses and leaves.

She was using a pair of tweezers to set tiny, silver balls on the icing sugar roses and leaves, therefore, she'd been unaware that Barbara was sneaking up behind her.

Suddenly, she grabbed Dora's waist, and shouted: "Gotcha!" Dora was so startled that she accidentally ruined her icing sugar floral arrangement by ramming the tweezers down into it.

"Barbara! Oh, diddle and darn! I wish you wouldn't sneak up on me like that! Now I've smeared the flowers!"

"Aw, sor-reeeeee! Anyway, it's just a cake for Mrs. Gorland's black, black, *real* black party!"

"Now Barbara! That's not very nice of you to call it that!"

"Well, everybody's going to be dressed in black! There's no way I'm going if I have to wear black!"

"But that's all you ever wear."

"Yeah, but this is a funeral party, so, because everyone's going to be wearing black, I wanna wear my old, red dress! He was stabbed to death, so why not wear red? It'll look like my dress is all covered in blood! Blaaaa-aaaaaaaa!"

"Oh, Barbara! That's an awful thing to say!"

"Why? I bet more than half of the people that are going to be there, hated him! He was always walking around and bragging about his good looks! Yuk! And I'll just bet Carol'll be standing there beside his mother, bawling her eyes out! She was bumping almost every guy in school! She's such a phony! And she's a huge whore, too!" cried Barbara, grinning.

"Now you don't really know that. Carol is a very pretty girl, so, there are a lot of boys interested in her, but that doesn't mean she cheated on Tony. Why, they were going steady for years. All through high school, and I know they had plans to marry. I feel so sorry for Tony's family."

"Bet Carol gets a lift home in the back of some guy's car! She's been in the back seat of every car in town!"

"Now that's enough talk like that! I certainly hope you don't say anything like that at the wake!" cried Dora.

"Oh, yeah? Ya mean, like, Tony's going to wake up? Wow! *That'll* shock everybody even more than they already are!"

"What an awful thing to say! I just...Oh, never mind! My nerves are jangled! Now would you please leave? Do something else! I don't care what, but *something*! *Anything*, so I can finish decorating this cake in peace! Please, Barbara! And please don't think about wearing that red dress to the wake! Oh, shoot! Look at this mess! Now I have to make *more* leaves for the cake!"

"Bye! Hey, mom! Make a coffin outta icing!"

"Honestly! You can be so morbid at times!"

Barbara stomped upstairs to her bedroom, slammed the door shut behind her, then went over to her closet, and began tossing clothes onto her bed.

She scrutinized the clothes for a few minutes, and then she thought, 'If I can't wear that red dress to Tony's, then...Yeah! I'll go to Frills and Frock Stock and buy black veil stuff! Yeah, I'll buy tons of it so it'll hang from the top of my head down to my feet! I gotta look like I'm sorry Tony's dead because I sure wish he wasn't dead, even if I never liked him! Hope there's enough leftover veil that mom can use some of it! Yeah! Whack on!'

Barbara counted the coins in her wallet, then stomped back downstairs, then grinned while she tiptoed up behind Dora, and then shouted: "Bye, mom!"

Dora was so alarmed that when she whirled around to face Barbara, she lost her balance, and when she reached out to support herself on the tabletop, she shoved her hand down into the cake.

"Barbara! Oh, no! Ick! I've squished the cake! Oh, now it's completely ruined! I wish you wouldn't do that! You never talk! You always shout out every word!"

"Sor-reeeee! I'm going down t'the store! Y'want anything?"

"What? *Now* what am I going to do? Look at this mess! Oh, well, I suppose I'll just have to *buy* a cake."

"Yeah? I'll go by the bakery and see if they make cakes with black icing on 'em! If they do, then I'll order one and ask 'em if they can make one real fast!" shouted Barbara.

"No, just ask for a chocolate cake. No, any cake with white icing on it, and have them put a sympathy message on it."

"Y'don't want a chocolate cake, huh? So, what'll I ask 'em for? Vanilla? Strawberry? *Frankenberry*?"

"Barbara! Honestly! See if they've got any type of cake that has at least four layers and is large enough for...Oh, hmmm, say, I suppose a dozen people. Wait'll I wash my hands, then I'll get my purse. I'm sure I've got about fifty dollars in it."

"Y'had forty, but I took ten of it t'buy black veils for us!"

"I've already got a black hat with a veil on it, dear."

"Yeah, but that veil only comes down to your forehead! The ten bucks I got is for a deposit on lots of veil! You'll have enough for veil down to the floor! Okay? And then Mrs. Gorland'll think you're *amazingly* sorry!" yelled Barbara, grinning.

"Don't be ridiculous! There's no way we're going over there with you looking like some kind of medieval witch!"

"Better than a *bitch* like Carol! Okay, okay! She's a nice, nice, *really* nice girl! Okay? She just makes big, big, *really* big boo-boos! Yuk! I just bet she'll be wearing a black veil at the wake, and a smaller one for a blouse, so that's why I want us to wear ones even bigger, okay? I mean, like, we're sorry for Mrs. Gorland, right? Hey, and besides, I've seen people going to funerals wearing black veils right down past their shoulders, so, like, this'll be a new fashion style, maybe!"

"Well, maybe you're right, dear. But promise you'll lower your voice when we're there. You shout out every word. It rattles my nerves sometimes, and besides, people are always staring at you."

"Yeah, but that's because of my flat breasts!"

"Barbara! Really! First blood, then breasts! What next?"

"You're shouting. Naughty-naughty," whispered Barbara.

"I'm sorry, but sometimes, I...Oh, never mind. Will you try to hurry back? If the cake's a little too plain, I can lift a few of the leaves off the cake I squished almost flat. I think some of them are salvageable. Oh, and tell Doris the cake has to be delivered here by six at the latest, okay? Now, we have to leave here around six-thirty, so, I'm planning an early supper. Will you try to be back soon, please?"

"Why are we eating? There'll be tons of food at the black party or wake at Mrs. Gorland's! Jif told me she's been to over three funeral parties and they had tons of food at those parties! So, like, why are we eating first?"

"Hmmm, yes, you're right. How silly of me. That reminds me. I should take some sort of food, as well, to the wake, so, could you stop by the deli and ask for a fair-sized container of meat and pasta? Like a casserole thing, and tell Lou you want it delivered here before six, okay? I was going to make pork chops for supper, but if we're not having supper, and if I wanted to make up something to take to the wake, it would take me too long to cut the meat off the bones, then slice the meat small, then oh, perhaps adding some macaroni or some sort of little noodles to it. Then I'd have to add some chopped onions and vegetables to the mix, too. That'd take too long to do that. But then I suppose if I'd thought of it earlier, I could've had it all done by...Barbara? Barbara! Oh, well. Hmmm," muttered Dora.

· · · · · ◆•••••◆ ★ ◆•••••◆ · · · · · ·

Wearing a shin-length, black coat with the collar turned up, and a pair of black sunglasses and heavy, black boots, Barbara stood at the corner of the street, leaning back against the wall while grinning across the street at the bakery.

She hoped that she'd now lingered long enough to cause the people in the store to stare back at her and wonder if she was a serial killer, then she stomped across the street, shoved open the door and shouted out: "I need a death cake!"

"A *death* cake? Oh, hello, Barbara. What is it exactly that you wanted, dear?" asked Doris.

"Y'know Tony Gorland's dead, right? So, mom wrecked the cake she was trying t'make, so, like, I told her I'd come by here and buy one of yours! Anything that's got white icing on it! Can you write something on top of it that says we're really, *really* sorry that Tony was murdered?"

"Yes. Yes, I see. Something sympathetic," said Doris.

"Yeah, that's the word I meant, man!"

"You're in luck because we have two left. One chocolate, and one lemon. So which one would you..."

"Is the lemon one sour?" asked Barbara.

"No, it's sweet. Would you like that one?"

"Naaaaaa! If it's not a *sour* lemon cake, forget it, man! Like, a sour one'd make their tears run, like, maybe! *Somebody's* gotta cry at Tony's wake! Hey, just bootin' your bum, there. Hold the chocolate one, okay? I just came in t'see what y'had! Gotta bop on over t'Frills and Frock Stock t'get a black veil! It's a *death* thing, right? It was really a *murder* thing! But whatever! So, I'll be back! Got it?" asked Barbara, grinning.

"Will you be paying for it now?"

"Yeah! I'll pay now! Oh, and mom needs it delivered before six, so, I hope Joey doesn't fall off his bike on the way to our place and wreck the cake because if that happens, we won't have time t'buy another one before you're closed! Right?"

"I'm sure Joey won't fall off his bike, Barbara," said Doris.

Barbara paid for the cake, then almost shattered Doris's nerves and the glass of the door when she left, then she dollied on down to Frills and Frock Stock to buy the veil material.

$$\cdot \quad \cdot \quad \cdot \quad \cdot \quad \cdot \quad \diamond \cdots \diamond \bigstar \diamond \cdots \diamond \quad \cdot \quad \cdot \quad \cdot \quad \cdot \quad \cdot$$

Evelyn and Judy stood watching Barbara throwing reams of black tulle over herself while checking out whether she'd be able to see through the material.

She tested the visibility of black tulle by staggering around the store with her arms out, and bumping into annoyed or frightened customers. Barbara then held up reams of black tulle that she liked, and then she shouted to Evelyn: "Hey, Ev! How deep's the slash on this stuff?"

"Huh? Oh, yes! That's fifteen, eighty-nine a yard."

"A *yard*? Yeah? I want something that's gonna *scratch* my budget, not hit a main vein, man! So, like, have y'got something else this thin, but cheaper?"

"Judy?" asked Evelyn as she quickly walked away.

"Well, we *do* have a lower-priced material that's just as transparent," said Judy. "But the quality is rather inferior, so, I'm afraid it won't stand up to much laundering."

"I don't think I'm going to *another* wake for Tony! So, show me the other black stuff! Please!"

"Yes, of course, Barbara. Right this way, please."

Barbara asked if she could leave a two dollar deposit on the material, and then she told Judy that her mother would drop by the following day to pay the balance, and Judy readily agreed.

On the way to the deli, she stopped at the tattoo store to pay another dollar toward the total cost of all the tattoos she wanted, then she made him promise again not to tell her parents. Hank Carlson, the tattoo artist, put the dollar into his shirt pocket instead of the till because, as usual, he'd be giving the dollar to Dora the next time he saw her.

Barbara then lurched toward the deli, and then reaching it, she grinned as she threw open the door.

"Ahrrrrrr! My God!" cried a woman customer.

"Sor-reeee!" shouted Barbara. "But, hey, man! Your big toe was sticking so far outta that hole in your shoe and I didn't see it!"

"Yes, Barbara? I'll serve you, first," said Lou.

"Please do!" exclaimed the customer with the sore toe.

"Thanks, ma'am! Beauty before age, huh? Hey, Lou! My mom wants t'take something y'can nuke for Tony's party, okay? *Wake!* Whatever! She said she needs enough of it for about a dozen people! Like, I hope y'got something with a lotta garlic in it! Y'never know! He wasn't stabbed t'death by a wooden knife! Ha-ha-ha-ha! Hey! It was a joke, okay, man?" Barbara roared.

"Of course," said Lou. "I have a beef, pasta, and broccoli casserole, a chicken, onion and noodle, and a rather spicy one made of sausage, red and green peppers, with onions."

"Yeah? I hope that's not *blood* sausage! Like, there was a lotta blood, and I mean a *lotta* blood on Tony's body when they found him, man! So, if it's a blood sausage casserole, it might make Mrs. Gorland throw up! So, is it?" asked Barbara, concerned.

"My God! How disgusting!" exclaimed the woman customer with the sore toe.

"Yeah? Y'saw it?" Barbara asked her, wide-eyed. "Awesome! Did y'throw up?"

"Barbara, we're a little rushed, so, please tell me which casserole you'd like," said Lou, smiling.

"Aaaaaa! O-o-o-o-o! Chicken!"

"Fine. That'll be twelve-fifty. It should serve a dozen."

"It's gotta be ink, Lou! Mom'll pay y'tomorrow!"

"Yes, of course, Barbara."

"Mom wants you to deliver it before six because we're leaving the house at six-thirty, okay? So, I hope Bobby doesn't fall off his bike on the way to our place and wreck the casserole because if that happens, we won't have time t'buy another one before you're closed! Right?"

"Yes, that's right, but I'll make sure the casserole's delivered well before six, and Bobby's very careful with his bike, so, there's no need for you to worry about him or the casserole, Barbara. Goodbye now," said Lou, smiling.

"Thanks, man! Bye! Hey, you! Yeah, you with the toe sticking outta your shoe! Better be careful, okay? Watch where y'point your big toe, man!" cried Barbara on her way out of the deli.

· · · · · ❖••••••❖★❖••••••❖ · · · · ·

Lorraine Gorland's hands were trembling, and she only lifted her head when she heard somebody give her their condolences. She felt that the only thing left inside her, was an empty void.

Sometimes, however, a gust of anger swept through her, then she'd feel her fingernails cutting into her hands, and then more tears ran down her face. She wondered how she was able to still weep because she'd thought that by now, she wouldn't have any tears left to shed.

She thought that Carol was so brave as she watched her chatting with friends who had come to pay their last respects to Tony. Lorraine tensed up when she heard a sudden bang, and she jerked her head up to see Dora Wallace standing in the vestibule.

Dora was holding a large foil container in one hand, and she'd used her other hand to lift the front of a very long veil up above her forehead so that she could look around at the guests. She then let the veil drop over her face again, and then the veil fell the rest of the way down below her knees.

Lorraine had gaped when she'd seen that the veil was the same length as Dora's dress. She looked at the figure standing beside Dora, covered from head to toe in black veil, then Lorraine smiled when she realized that Dora's companion must be Barbara.

Barbara was holding a box that Lorraine hoped had a cake inside it, but she was aware of Barbara's odd sense of humor, so she knew that inside that box, there could be a plastic head that Barbara had bought at a joke store. Barbara carried the box containing the cake, and Dora carried the casserole over to the table that had plates of food on it.

"Hi, Mrs. Gorland!" Barbara shouted as she smiled. "*We* brought some food, too! Bet you're really, really sad, huh? Too bad about Tony, man! I'm gonna go talk to the other guys, and ask 'em how they feel, too! So, see ya!"

Lorraine watched the long-veiled Barbara making her way through the crowded room, then she and Carol greeted Dora.

"I'm so sorry for your loss, Mrs. Garbland," said Dora.

"Uh, you...Please, call me Lorraine, and thank you for your condolences. It was so nice of you to come. Are...*Will* you be staying long? Oh, uh, would you excuse me, please? Carol, would you be kind enough to show Barbara the garden? It must be stuffy in here for her, with such a long, heavy veil. May I help you tie *your* veil behind you in some way, Dora? They *do* get in the way, don't they?" said Lorraine, gaping at all the material.

"Oh, yes. I'm sorry I lifted some of it away from my face, but with the length of it, well, I was sort of suffocating under it. I wasn't sure about wearing a veil so long, but then, when I saw how it was the same length as my dress, I had to agree with Barbara that it was rather chic-looking. I don't know how she can wear all that veiling all the way down to the floor like that, but she's always been one to try a new fashion trend. It's so terrible about Tony, Mrs. Gur...I mean, *Moraine*. You must be devastated. If something like this happened to my Barbara, well, oh, I just can't even think about it. It's nice that Tony was so popular, isn't it? Well, obviously not with *one* person. May I get you something? A plate of food? Have you eaten anything, today? How about a little bit of..." Dora started to say.

"Dora. Would you excuse me, please? I see a close relative over there, and I haven't had a chance to greet...Them. I'll speak with you later. I'm sure you must know many of the visitors here, so, please help me make them feel comfortable, would you? Thank you so much," said Lorraine.

"Why, certainly, Mogain. And again, I'm so sorry for your tragic loss," said Dora, frowning and pouting. "Oh, there's Nan Clithwell. I'll go talk to her."

Meanwhile, out in the back garden, Carol hoped that her sneer wasn't too blatant as she stared at the black apparition in front of her. She wished that somebody would accidentally spill a few gallons of gasoline over Barbara, because then Carol could accidentally hold her lit cigarette against the veils for as long as it took until they caught on fire, and then she'd be able to grin and shout out to everybody in the house: "Barbie-cue, everyone!"

Barbara swept away to the far end of the garden, then swirled around and lifted one of her draped arms, and it seemed that she'd started beckoning Carol.

Carol felt that if she didn't walk to the end of the garden to talk with her, then Barbara would shout out her why nots as she followed her into the house, which would irritate Mrs. Gorland, even more.

Feeling sure that would happen, Carol clenched her teeth as she walked slowly to Barbara, and then she forced a smile as she asked: "What do you want...Barbara?"

"Nothing! I was just seeing how this stuff blew in the wind! Great, huh? So, who y'going home with? Hitching a ride to hitch your skirt, or what?"

"I beg your pardon?" Carol exclaimed.

"Hey, chill out, man! Like, Tony's dead, right? So, why are y'mad at *me*? Get mad at whatever guy won't get in the back seat of his car with you on the way home from here!"

"You're disgusting! Tony was going to marry me! I don't know why you came here! I just...I don't understand how you can be so...Oh, why talk to you!" exclaimed Carol. "Why don't you go home and leave us alone! I'm going back inside the house, and I'd advise you to stay out here!"

"Okay! See ya!" yelled Barbara, swinging her veiled arm.

She liked the way the breeze lifted the black veil, and as she watched it wafting and lifting, Barbara started to wonder why Carol was putting on such a big performance of being so sad because Carol would be bumping with any one of the willing guests when she left the wake.

Barbara knew that the only thing that really upset Carol was a guy with no money, and now she'd have to find another guy with as much money as Tony and his family had, now that Tony was out of the picture.

Tony could have given Carol anything she wanted because he was so wealthy, but now he was dead, and Carol was more angry than sad.

Barbara knew that because she thought that Carol was such a huge whore. Everybody had called her disgusting for saying that, but Barbara was only telling it like it was, man.

If most people took the time to peek behind that wall of seemingly rude exclamations, they'd see that Barbara was really quite sensitive and very nice.

She simply had a different sense of humor from most people. But her best pal, Jif, understood her, and they were quite close because they had similar views of the world around them.

Views such as who was a huge whore, who played or sang the best music, and they liked the same styles of clothes, and they liked watching the same gory movies.

Now here she was at Tony's wake, and she'd been rude to Carol, however, she knew that Carol was really more insensitive than her.

Jif and Barbara had seen Tony being admired by girls, and they'd nudged each other and laughed at Tony and the girls, but they'd made sure that they hadn't been seen doing that.

Barbara felt that Tony wouldn't be dead today if he hadn't driven up to the top of the hill behind her house, and I mean, like, *right* behind her house, man.

That's where on many occasions, other whores, but not really huge ones like Carol, went with some of the guys to do it. Barbara thought it had been rather stupid of Tony to have driven up there that night, and Tony had seen her with her knife.

She had had been practicing her knife-throwing, and getting better at it with every passing month; often hitting the edge of the target she'd painted on the wall of an almost demolished, old wooden house.

Tony had laughed at her as he'd slowly driven by her, and Barbara had stuck out her tongue at him. She had continued throwing her knife, while thinking about what a stupid jerk Tony was for coming all the way up here to bump when he could easily have paid for a sleazy motel room where people did it all the time, for sure, man.

She thought that most romantic entanglements were boring, especially when she'd been near enough to Carol and Tony to hear them yelling at each other, like so many couples often do when they get so deeply involved.

Carol had always been so jealous and possessive about Tony, but Barbara knew that Carol had bumped with so many other guys while she'd been dating him.

Barbara knew that too, because many times when she'd been practicing her knife throwing, she'd seen Carol being driven past her in other guys' cars to do, like, whatever, for sure, man. Blah! Carol hadn't seen her those times because Carol had always had her head on some guy's chest, smearing all her makeup on his shirt. Yuk!

Barbara also knew that Carol had spent so much of her time hoping and trying to be Mrs. Tony Gorland. Blah! And any threat to that very wealthy union would cause Carol to become even more of a bitch.

Barbara had always thought it would've been rather funny if Tony had ever found out about Carol's bumpings with so many other guys. She thought it had been even funnier when she'd seen Tony driving by her with somebody other than Carol in his car, and he'd done that many times, too.

Barbara grinned while lifting first one, then the other of her veiled arms, and then she went back into the house to stare at the people who had come to Tony's wake.

Barbara stood by the long table with all the plates of food on it, eating little, fancy sandwiches by slipping them up under her floor-length veil.

"Barbara, dear. You'll get food all over your veil," said Dora.

"It adds texture!"

"Pssst! Did you do what you said you'd do to Carol when you were outside in the backyard with her?" Doris whispered to her.

"Nope," whispered Barbara. "But I got her really, really mad at me, so, now I'm gonna do it later."

"*When* later, dear?"

"Like, I'm leaving in like maybe a coupla minutes, okay? Then after I leave here, I'm gonna count to ten, and then I'm gonna come back in the front door, and then I'll get her even madder at me, then after that, I'll go over to Jif's house. Okay?"

"I still think this is much too..."

"But I told you fifty times I was gonna get her really, really, *really* mad at me. Right?"

"Yes, I know, but it's just that...Oh, well."

"Okay, now I'm gonna make sure she stays really, really mad at me. Here goes," whispered Barbara, then she shouted: "Hey, mom! I don't think Carol likes me! I think she hates me just as much as I hate her! Hey, Carol! Is that guy you're with giving you a lift somewhere after y'leave here? Carol? See what I mean, mom? She hates my guts! Hey, Mrs. Gorland! Sorry I'm not staying! Gotta go and see Jif! Maybe I'll drop by in a coupla days, okay? Bye, Mrs. Gorland! Bye, mom!"

"You should've invited Jif here so you'd have somebody your age to talk to," said Dora.

"So who likes Jif around here, anyway? Naaaa! No way! She would've booked two seconds after she walked in the door, after she saw Carol! She hates Carol, too! And Carol *really* hates Jif! Don't ya, Carol? Yeah, I know ya do! Okay then, I'm outta here! Bye again, Mrs. Gorland! Hey, and check out the guy Carol's juicing, man! Bye, mom!"

"Oh, have you had enough to eat, dear?...Barbara? Oh, well, hmmm, I wonder if Nan's in the bathroom?" Dora mumbled. She then smiled and began walking among the guests, then suddenly, the front door flew open, and Barbara shouted to Carol: "Hey, like, Carol! I forgot to ask ya! Y'going out t'the hot spot later? Might see y'there! I use my knife there! Just thought I'd ask, man! Seen y'there every time you've been there, man! Get it? *Every* time? That guy you're with there'll like it out there, too, huh? Maybe he might wanna throw my knife! Bet he's not as good with a knife like me, man! Hey! Just asking, man! Thought maybe y'might wanna see how good I toss my knife, Carol! Y'wanna have a contest? See me hit the target with my knife? Do you? Carol? Okay, ignore me, then! I don't care! See what I mean, mom? Y'try and y'try, but Carol just stares and stares at me! She hates me! Man! Okay! Bye again, mom!"

"Oh, Barbara! Wait! Oh, darn. Hmmm, now I'm sure Carol's so mad at her. I'll glance at her in a few seconds and see if she's calmed down. Yes, she keeps taking quick looks at me while she's talking to her friends. I'd better not try looking at her again or else Carol'll think I'm curious about what she's saying to her friends. Hmmm, I wonder what's in those little sandwiches. I'll try one and see what it is. Mmmmm, it tastes interesting. Maybe a mixture of tuna and marmalade? With a bit of some...Is it cinnamon? No, I think it's...."

"Excuse me, Mrs. Wallace. How are you? It was so...well, *nice* of you to come. It's too bad Barbara had to leave so soon."

"Oh, hello, Carol, dear. How *are* you? Sad about Tony. I hope Barbara didn't upset you by saying that she thought you didn't like her, or that she might have called you a huge whore for having so *very* many dates. She didn't, did she?" asked Dora.

"Uh, no, she's never called me that, Mrs. Wallace. Not to my face. It's unfortunate that she thinks I don't like her. It's just that I don't understand her, sometimes," said Carol. "I noticed you were chatting with Mrs. Clithwell. She babysat Tony when he was a little boy, you know, and I think she's..."

"Has Nan gone?" Dora interjected. "I thought she had, but I wasn't really sure, and I wanted to ask her if she made that casserole, or if she bought it at Lou's deli, and...Oh, well."

"She made it. I asked her. I tasted it. But I suppose she has so many *other* talents, though."

"I'm so glad you enjoyed it, Carol! I was going to ask Mrs. Gul...I mean, Moraine, if I could take a bit home with me, but I don't think I will, now. Nan might've made up two batches of it, and if she has, well, then I'll ask her if she'll give me a bit to take home to warm up for supper tomorrow night. I'll get the recipe from her tonight when I see her. We play bridge twice a week, and tonight's one of the nights we play, and we have such fun. That's why I was hoping that while Barbara's alone at home for the few hours that her father and I'll be playing bridge at Nan's, that she won't turn on the oven for some reason or other, then leave it on with some sort of thing in it that'll start smoking up the house."

"Oh, I'm sure you can trust Barbara not to cause any damage to your house while she's alone in it, Mrs. Wallace. I'd be worried about her doing something awful in *my* house if I left her alone in it for less than five minutes, but I'm sure she wouldn't do bad things at her own home," said Carol, forcing a smile.

"That's so nice of you to say that, dear, but then, Barbara's made that mistake before, you know. The oven thing, I mean. Oh, and talking about talent, you're right, Carol. Nan's quite clever with cards, and she can crochet so well, and she knits a bit, too, besides doing..." Dora was about to say.

"Besides doing casseroles, right? You were going to ask Mrs. Gorland if she didn't mind you taking home a bit of that casserole Mrs. Clithwell made, so, I'll ask her to put most of it on a paper plate, then you can leave right away. Okay? You *are* leaving *very* soon, aren't you? I imagine you want to change before you go to Mrs. Clithwell's. The dress you have on now is lovely, too, and of course, the veil's a nice touch. Barbara's veil was lovely, too. Well, I must get back to one of my friends, Mrs. Wallace. Perhaps we'll chat again, someday."

"I'd love that, Carol, and I don't think you're a huge whore, dear. Are you, Carol? Carol? Oh, well, hmmm, yes, odd girl. I'll tell Barbara that Carol likes her. I'll bet Jif would like her, too, if she got to know her a little bit better. But then, I suppose they're determined not to like her. So sad. Oh, well, I suppose appearances can be deceiving. Carol's such a pretty girl, and so pleasant too. It's a shame her mind is so messy. She said she liked Barbara, but of course she doesn't mean that. Hmmm, thank heavens so many people came to offer their condolences. Such a sad occasion. Tragic. I'm so worried about going to Nan's tonight, and then waiting for Barbara to call me, but I'm sure she'll be on the phone most of the time talking with Jif. I'm so relieved that she'll be very well-taken of tonight while Bill and I are playing bridge at Nan's. Hmmm, yes, I think I'll try a bit more of that casserole. Nan has such a gift. I wish I...' "Oh, hello, Thelma. Sad, isn't it? Awful way to die. Nice that so many of his friends came by to..."

· · · · · · ◇·······◇★◇·······◇ · · · · · ·

Ten minutes after Barbara's parents had left to play bridge at Nan Clithwell's home, Barbara had been driven home after visiting Jif, then she'd immediately rushed to the phone.

She always spent quite a bit of time every day, chatting to Jif on the telephone, which sometimes irked Dora whenever she wanted to use the phone, too.

Barbara wished that her mother would let her have her own phone with a different number, especially a cordless phone, because she had to keep telling Jif to hold on while she went to the bathroom, or when she had to run downstairs to the kitchen to get a soft drink out of the fridge, or sometimes when she took a bath or a shower, or whatever, as Barbara would say.

Instead of using the phone in the living room, Barbara was using the extension phone in her parents' bedroom because there were big windows that overlooked the backyard.

She'd turned off the lights in the bedroom, and as she talked to Jif, Barbara peered through the slats of the Venetian blinds that were almost closed.

"Hey, Jif, man! Tell me the time! If y'don't, then I'll have to go downstairs to look at the clock on the kitchen wall!"

"It's almost ten! So? Still nothing?" Jif shouted.

"Uh-uh! Not yet! I'm looking through the curtain slats!"

"Hey, like, Barbara! I saw a movie where a stiff sat up and, like, it's caused by something! Man, like, that'd really scare me if I saw a stiff do that! Wonder if Tony's sitting up, right now?"

"Maybe! But he didn't do it while I was there, man!"

"That's why I didn't wanna go over t'look at him!"

"It wouldna bothered *me*, man!" Barbara shouted.

"Hey, don't forget I want your mother's veil if she doesn't want it, when you ask her! Okay? It's gonna look great over the Christmas tree, man!"

"The one outside, or the one inside?"

"No! Like, the one outside's too tall! So, like, it'd only come down halfway, man!" exclaimed Jif.

"Oh, yeah, that's right! How many chains has your dad got in the garage?"

"Some! But I can ask somma the guys for more!"

"They won't let *me* decorate the tree with chains!"

"Hey! Y'can scrape mosta the needles off the branches! That'd look cool, man!"

"Hey, like, Jif! Why are we talking about Christmas? It's not for another twenty months, man!"

"Oh, yeah, right! I forgot! So what're y'drinking?"

"Beer and ginger ale! Any guy who hooked up with Carol at Tony's is gonna pick up a disease from her! She'll bump anybody, man! Like, my mom says it's what's inside y'that counts! There's nothing inside Carol, though! Like, I'd never marry any guy who bumped with her!"

"Hey, like, Barbara! By the time y'marry Mick Jagger, y'might get something from him, anyway, man! He marries at least fifty chicks a year! So, like, who knows what kinda bad thing y'can get from him if ya..."

"Shhhhhhh!"

"Yeah? Y'see something? So?" asked Jif in a whisper.

"Yeah. Keep whispering, okay? I'm looking. I saw something move, man," whispered Barbara. "Have y'got the other phone right beside you?"

"Yeah. We're sure lucky we got two different phone numbers because I can talk on one phone while my mom talks on the other phone. Or my dad can talk on the other phone while I'm..."

"Shhhhh! You've told me that a million times, okay?"

"Okay, already. I was just saying...Oops! Sorry. So, y'want me to start calling on the other phone now?"

"No! Shhhhhhhh! Gotta make sure it's not a dog or a cat, or something like that, man."

"So? What is it? Hey, like, Barbara? Wouldn't it be a blast if it was an alien?"

"An alien? What are you on, man? Toss your E.T. tape. I don't know, Jif, but y'get spacey sometimes, man. Wait! Oh, yeah.

Moving. Getting closer. A bit more closer. Past that tree. Yeah."

"Now? Barbara? Now, huh?"

"No! Shhhhhhh! Closer. Closer. Stops. Moves again. Stops. Looks around," whispered Barbara as she peeked through one of the slats of the Venetian blinds. "Get ready, Jif. Almost there. Getting closer to the back door. Okay, *now*."

"This is wild, man. Y'scared yet?" asked Jif.

"Naaaaaa, I got my knife ready. One slash to the throat, and lots of blood, man. Is their phone ringing yet?"

"Yeah, I'm waiting for them to answer it. Still waiting. Yeah, hi! It's me, Jennifer Logan! Yeah! Barbara's going to die soon if y'don't boogie on down here, now, man! They are? Hey, like, Barbara! It's all set, man! He said there's enough help, already!"

"Shhhhhh! Okay. Hey, Jif, I see 'em coming. Yeah. Moving slowly. Running now a bit. Closer. That's it. Yeah, now I can hear something downstairs. Maybe a door being shut. Wow, man, this is so great," she said in an excited whisper.

"Y'scared yet?"

"Naaaaa, I saw the others coming closer and...Yeah! We're on, man! Shouting and yelling! Like, wow!"

"Great! I'm coming right over!" Jif exclaimed.

"Yeah, c'mon over fast! I hope there's some blood, man! Lotsa blood! Blaaaaaa-splat! Run, Jif! Bye!"

"Bye!" yelled Jif, slamming down the phone.

* * * * * ❖•••••❖★❖•••••❖ * * * * *

Jif ran down al the streets to Barbara's house, but she got there too late. She hurried into the house to see if there was lots of blood everywhere, and then she felt very disappointed when she couldn't see any.

She rushed back out of the house, then saw Barbara chatting with a policeman out on the front lawn, and she was wearing her very big, black sunglasses over the long, black veil.

Barbara was holding her knife in her left hand and holding a lit candle in her right hand, so, Jif stomped over to say hi, and to hear what was going down.

"Thank you...I'm sorry, I've forgotten your name."

"Call me Barbara! What's *your* name, man? Like, your first name! I mean, like, after this, we sure don't have to call each other by our last names! Right?"

"Uh, well, I, uh, I'm Joel," he said, suppressing a grin.

"Hey, Jif! Meet Joel, man! Cute guy, huh?"

"Yeah! Y'date younger?" Jif asked him.

"No, I don't. Sorry," he replied.

"Y'like Barbara's veil, man? She wore that to look at Tony's body today! But I didn't go!"

"Oh, I see. There's no reason to yell. I can hear you."

"So, who's yelling?" shouted Barbara.

"Yeah, man! If y'don't speak up a bit, then people might miss something y'said!" yelled Jif.

"Well, uh, perhaps you two should go back inside the house because it's all over," said Joel.

"All over? Yeah? I didn't see any blood all over *anything*! Hey, like, Barbara? Is there lotsa blood on some of the walls inside the house? Somewhere I didn't see? Wow! Awesome! I'm gonna go look! Nice meeting you, Joel! Y'give good face, man! Like, really! Hey! Y'coming in, Barbara?"

"Just a sec! Hey, Joel! This crime we just had on Tony! Is this what y'call a gay bashing? Is it?" asked Barbara.

"Huh?" Joel asked, looking bewildered.

"Tony getting stabbed to death, man!" yelled Barbara.

"No, it's called a homicide," he explained.

"Sounds like the same thing t'me, man! Hear that Jif? I told ya! It *was* a gay bashing! Like, it's politically correct t'call it a homo...Y'said *side,* right, Joel? Got it! I'm cool, man! I don't call people queer, either! Don't call 'em fags, either! If I ever did, then my parents'd kill me! See y'Joel! Stay cool, man!"

"Yes, uh, goodnight. Oh! And thank you again for your help, Barbara. Your parents are on the way here, all right? Did you call them like they asked you to do?" asked Joel.

"Naaaaaa! They're playing bridge! Don't like me calling unless it's important! So, like, bye, Joel!"

"Goodnight, girls," he said, grinning.

Jif and Barbara slapped hands with him before they began walking back to the house.

"Wow! I hope Carol hasn't touched Joel, man! Y'missed all the action, Jif! I loved it! Wanna beer and ginger ale? Hey! Wave at Joel! He's looking back at us!"

"Great! I like cops! Hey! I'll have a beer and ginger ale! Like, how much beer did y'put in it, man?" Jif asked her.

"A whole half an ounce! I used the jigger! But I can still taste it, and I put it in the biggest glass I could find! That's why after I have another beer and ginger ale next week, I'm gonna go for the cure, man! Might take me a year t'get all the beer outta my body, but I bet I can kick the habit, and be real okay again! That's why I used the jigger, man! Gotta be careful!"

"Yeah? Half an ounce? That's all? I drink at least fifty bottles of beer an hour! Like, you're never gonna be a wino if y'don't drink more beer, man!" roared Jif.

"I changed my mind! I wanna be a junkie for a few weeks, or like, whatever!" yelled Barbara.

"Carol sure was a huge whore!"

"Hey! Like, we already knew that, man! Guess she'll be giving her diseases to her jailbird roommates, now! Naaaaa! I bet they spray whores like that with bug spray before they let 'em go near anybody else in jail!"

"She came close to killing y'Barbara!"

"I played her, man! I knew what I was doing! I had t'go and see Tony or else I couldna told that bitch that I saw her! Man! Y'shoulda seen the look on her face when I kept talking about seeing her up at the hot spot, and when I kept telling her about my knife, too! She clued in, man!"

"Yeah? Awesome!" cried Jif, agape.

"She stared at me like I was an airhead like her! I knew she'd come after me! Good thing I told the cops about her after breakfast this morning, man! She got mad because she figured Tony wasn't going t'marry her! I knew that before *she* did, man! He was, like, bumping Lloyd Dalton, so, Carol thought Lloyd was going to marry Tony! I don't know why she didn't kill Lloyd, instead, man! Go figure, huh? I wouldna married Tony even if he *was* gay! Carol loved the green, man! She was such a huge whore, man! Like, all she wanted was Tony's money! She was bumping so many guys that she coulda had Tony's money and not have t'bump him 'cause he'd be bumping Lloyd! Carol's a *stupid,* huge whore!"

"Yeah! I hated her! Let's have a beer and ginger ale! Hey! Wanna see if they'll let us go to her trial?" asked Jif.

"Why? I don't wanna even *look* at her, anymore! She kills everyone! Maybe her killing Tony'll make my mom see what a real bitch Carol was! And a huge whore, too! Like, my mom wanted me t'talk to her! Amazing! I told mom ten million times that I hated that huge whore!"

And Barbara hated babysitters, too. I mean, like, she was ten years old, right? So, she knew that she was old enough to take care of herself. Like, she just proved that, right?

Besides, all the cops were hiding in places all around the outside of her house, waiting for Carol to make her move, man. But even with two more cops inside the house, Barbara still wanted Jif to call for more backup, just in case Carol was stronger than all the cops who were there waiting for her.

When Carol had been trying to sneak into Barbara's house, she'd been carrying the knife that she'd killed Tony with. But Barbara had been sure that Carol's knife wasn't as big as hers, so, she could've protected herself and all the cops, too, man. Yeah!

The End

452

The River

Lydia ran out of the house, down the street, then through the forest to the river. She liked walking along the edge of the river and watching tiny fish swimming near the surface, away from the strong pull of the current in the center of the river.

She picked a handful of wild flowers, then began wading in the shallowest area of the river, giggling each time she felt a little fish brush against one of her calves or ankles.

She noticed that the flowers she held in her right hand were beginning to wilt from the heat, so, she waded back out of the water, and ran home to put the flowers in a vase.

Lydia sometimes stood on a chair while opening all the kitchen cupboards, looking for a vase, then finding one, she filled it with water, put the wildflowers in it, and set the vase down in the center of the kitchen table.

She then stood by the kitchen door, looking into the dining room at her mother playing cards with three friends. She'd often watched her mother playing cards with friends, but Lydia still didn't understand how to play any of those card games.

The guests always ignored her whenever she walked slowly around the table to look at the cards they were holding, so, Lydia would just sit in a chair, listening to their conversation until she became bored and looked for more fun things to do.

When her mother got up from the table to make tea for her guests, Lydia decided to run down the street to her best friend's home, and ask him to come play with her at the river.

$\diamond\!\!\cdots\!\!\diamond\!\!\bigstar\!\!\diamond\!\!\cdots\!\!\diamond$

She knocked on the front door of Gary's home, waited a few moments, knocked again, then not getting an answer after knocking on the door for the third time, she tried the door and found it unlocked, so, she went inside and upstairs to his bedroom.

Lydia peeked into Gary's room, and saw that he'd just returned from taking a shower, and he was starting to get dressed. She stared at his naked body, fascinated by his pubic hair, and she wondered if hair would grow down there on her, too, someday.

He was now thirteen; four years older than her, and they'd often skinny-dipped together at the river, but Lydia couldn't recall ever noticing that he had pubic hair, and she wondered how she could have forgotten seeing something as obvious as that.

She thought about asking him when that hair had suddenly appeared, and then she decided to wait to ask him later, when they were skinny-dipping at the river. Lydia stood close to his partly open bedroom door, waiting until he'd finished dressing, and then she smiled, pushed open the door wider, and walked in.

"Oh, no! Not you, again!" exclaimed Gary.

"Aw, you always say that, but I know you don't mean it. Wanna go play down by the river? We can maybe find a turtle."

"Turtles don't hang around the river. You find them where the water doesn't move so fast. Like at that little creek past the dam."

"Oh. Well, anyway, we can find something else, then."

"Okay," he said, smiling. "My parents don't like me talking to you, so, we better go before they get home."

"Great! You've always been my very best friend. None of the other kids'll talk to me."

"That's because you're really different."

"But everyone's different in some way, though," said Lydia.

"Yeah, but you're really, *really* different."

"But you still like me, though, don't you?"

"Yeah, you know I do. It's just that...Aw, forget it. We've talked about this lots of times before," he said, smiling.

On their way down the street, Gary waved at the other kids and shouted: "Hi!" to them, but although they greeted him, they ignored Lydia, as usual, so, she was glad that Gary wanted to be her friend.

She presumed that because she'd been away from the neighborhood for awhile, the other children now felt that she didn't fit in with them anymore. Her mother had once told her that sometimes children forgot their friends when they hadn't seen them for a long time, so, Lydia hoped that eventually she'd have more friends again.

"Let's go up the river to the dam, okay?" said Gary. "You always like swimming there with me. Okay?"

"Okay. I hope some of the other kids aren't there."

"So what if they are? Don't let that bother you. If they ignore you, then you should just ignore *them*. Okay?

"That's a great idea! I never thought of that before. Yeah, I'll just pretend I don't even see them," said Lydia.

Twenty years earlier, there had been a three-storey factory half a mile from the river that flowed into a bay of the ocean, but the factory had been razed when the company moved to a new location.

The foreman of the wrecking crew had seen the swift river current, and he'd decided to have his work crew use bulldozers to lift and carry huge pieces of the factory's concrete walls over to the river.

The concrete slabs were then stacked over the river to form a dam which created a safe area for the children of the town to swim in. The water burst through a few areas near the bottom of the concrete slabs at one side of the river, but where the children played, the water was a calm pool that slowly drained away through narrow openings between the massive concrete slabs.

In some places near the dam, slabs of concrete had been laid haphazardly over the river, creating shallow pools that Lydia loved to wade in to look for small frogs that basked in the sunshine gleaming down on the white, concrete slabs.

When Lydia and Gary reached the dam, they undressed and waded into the water. She loved seeing him playing and swimming, and especially diving off high concrete slabs, then resurfacing and spouting water.

Gary swam toward another huge slab of concrete, climbed out of the water, and laid out in the sun to deepen his tan. Lydia sat beside him, staring at his pubic hair, then she asked him: "Does everybody get hair down there when they're older?"

"Yeah, they do," he replied. "All the other guys my age have got hair down there, too. It's called puberty when you start growing hair down there."

"Oh, I see. *Puberty*. Do girls have puberty, too?"

"Uh-huh, but it's different for girls because they also start getting breasts when they have puberty."

"Oh. Why don't boys grow breasts? You've got nipples."

"Yeah, but I don't know why guys have nipples. We've got penises, too, and girls don't."

"Yeah, I know, but I don't care."

"Another way girls are different from guys, is that they can have babies after they have their puberty."

"Hmmm, do you know how that happens?" asked Lydia.

He explained how girls got pregnant, which astonished Lydia, then Gary went swimming again before climbing back onto the concrete slab, then laying out to bask in the sun.

Lydia wondered whether she'd have a new brother or sister if her mother and father did what Gary had just told her. She'd often walked into their bedroom during the night, but she had never seen them doing what Gary had explained to her, therefore, Lydia supposed that her parents didn't want another baby.

Gary got dressed after he'd laid in the sun for almost half an hour, then they walked back downstream. He saw some of his other friends, and then he told her that he wanted to play with them before he went home, so, after they said goodbye to each other, Lydia sat by the river and watched Gary walking away with his friends.

She became bored sitting by herself, and she decided to run over to the cemetery because she was always fascinated by the many different shapes and sizes of the gravestones, and by the names and dates engraved on them.

* * * * * ❖•••••❖★❖•••••❖ * * * * *

Lydia walked slowly through the cemetery, stopping occasionally to read tombstones, and discovering names that were the same as some of her neighbors.

She'd overheard other kids saying that the cemetery was spooky, however, Lydia liked all the white, stone angels at the top of many of the gravestones, and the huge, old maple tree at on end of the cemetery that turned bright orange in autumn.

Lydia like how peaceful it was in the cemetery, with only the sound of twittering birds, the buzzing of bees, and the sparkling insects slowly gliding by in the sunlight.

What she liked best of all, was watching people come into the cemetery sometimes, all dressed up in their best clothes to place fresh flowers on graves of family or friends.

Thinking about people coming into the cemetery, all dressed so nicely, made her recall her recurring dream of seeing quite the opposite, such as Seth wearing plain, gray clothes, and seated in a concrete room.

He would glare at her as she skipped around the room, then after a few moments, he'd try to reach out and grab her, but at that point, Gary always suddenly appeared outside the room, and then Lydia would laugh and run outside to play with him.

A butterfly fluttering close to her face caused Lydia to smile and dismiss the recollection of her dream about Seth in the concrete room. She watched the butterfly land near a little green frog sitting close to her, and she giggled when she and the frog kept slowly blinking their eyes at each other.

An hour passed by, then Lydia left the cemetery, and began walking back to the river while hoping that Gary had decided to go swimming again, but when she got there, she didn't see anyone so, she sat by the river and let the water rush over her bare feet.

When the sun began setting, Lydia heaved a big sigh and decided to go back home.

Late that night, she stood looking out the window of her bedroom, watching lights going out in houses near her home, then she looked up at the sky, hoping to see a shooting star.

It was quiet in the house because her parents had gone to bed hours ago, so, Lydia went downstairs, out the front door, then walked along the street, and then through the forest to sit by the river again.

She could hear what seemed to be over a thousand crickets singing to the fireflies drifting above them as she made a small bouquet from the wild flowers she'd picked while walking upstream toward the dam made from varied lengths of concrete slabs.

Lydia stopped walking, then bent back her head to gaze up at the countless stars, and then she began turning around and around while giggling from the dizziness she felt while watching the stars swirling high above her.

She fondled the petals of the wild flower bouquet as she walked closer to the great abstract pattern of concrete slabs leaning at many different angles in the river.

Lydia wasn't sure if it was just her imagination, but she watched wide-eyed as slabs of concrete began slowly rising from the river, then slowly slide together in midair to form tall, broken walls of a phantom room.

She then remembered that she had seen this happen in other visions she'd had. The slabs shifted into what seemed like four walls, although they never abutted each other, so there would be a narrow space between each slab of the strange, dreamlike room.

The openings at the sides of the concrete room weren't wide enough for anybody to pass through, but they were wide enough for her to see Seth, whom would always be shouting from between the openings of the concrete slabs because he was trapped inside the slowly turning, concrete, fantasy room.

Lydia closed her eyes tightly, and when she opened them again, she saw that the huge, concrete slabs were again laying at angles in the river. She felt slightly uneasy from seeing that strange illusion again, so, she walked back in the direction she'd come from.

Once in awhile, she'd look over at where she'd often laid to look up at the clouds, then after an hour she went over to that area again, and laid on her back to look up at the stars.

Time passed, and Lydia slowly closed her eyes, thinking about all her neighbors lying asleep in their beds, and missing the sound of the owl she could hear in a tree near her.

· · · · · ❖•••••❖ ★ ❖•••••❖ · · · · ·

She opened her eyes, and instead of laying on her back in the long grass near the river, Lydia found herself standing at the far end of a room that was dimly lit by a lamp on a small table beside a rumpled bed.

Seth was seated on the bed, wearing a gray shirt and gray pants, and he seemed shocked as he stared at her, and exclaimed: "How did you get in here?"

Lydia cowered back from him as she raised her left hand, grabbed the doorknob, opened the door, and just before she ran out into the hall, she shouted at him: "I know where you hide your gun! I saw you hide it, and now I'm going to tell the police! I'm going to tell them you're hiding the gun here!"

"You're a liar!" shouted Seth, leaping up from the bed.

She ran along the dark hall to the staircase, and as she began running down the stairs, she could hear Seth's pounding footsteps close behind her.

Seconds later, Lydia ran out of the house, then after running halfway down the street, she stopped, looked back, and saw Seth running toward her, and he looked very angry.

She reached the end of the street, ran into the trees, then stopped again to look back to see how close Seth was getting to her, then she waited until he was just entering the woods before she waved at him, and then Lydia turned and ran along the path to the river.

The night shadows seemed to gather into a dense mass, the farther she ran through the forest, but no matter how dark it would get, she knew that Seth would try his best to find her.

Lydia saw the moonlit surface of the river, then darting away from the path, she hurried through the trees and around bushes that were almost as tall as her.

She stopped rushing through the trees, then began walking after she felt sure that Seth was running in a different direction, and then a few minutes later, she sat by the river's edge.

She felt so sure that she'd had this dangerously exciting dream before about being chased by Seth after she had spoken to him somewhere.

Lydia stood up, and as she walked slowly away from the river, she looked around at the dark forest, wondering if she would suddenly wake up in her bed, then she thought that if she closed her eyes tightly again, she'd awaken far away from Seth.

She leaned back against the tree, closed her eyes, and then she became drowsy, and fell asleep.

      · · · · · ❖•••••❖★❖•••••❖ · · · · ·

Lydia slowly opened her eyes again, and saw that the sun had risen, and a branch of a dew-covered bush was hanging close above her face as she laid on her back in the tall grass.

A drop fell from the tip of the dew-covered branch, then splattered on her forehead. A bumblebee buzzed near her left ear, then she sat up to look around at the trees, listening for any sound of footsteps, and then she laid back down in the tall, damp grass.

Her body stiffened when she heard a branch snap, then moments later, the sound of bushes being shoved aside. Lydia slowly turned over onto her side, peered through the long grass, and saw Seth walking toward the river.

He was carrying a small bundle in his right hand, and when he reached the edge of the river, he leaned out over the water to reach for a big boulder. There was a moment when Lydia thought he would lose his balance and fall into the river, but Seth managed to keep his balance when his right hand touched the top of the boulder.

He repositioned his feet to make sure he wouldn't slip off the edge of the riverbank, then he put his left hand on the boulder and tugged hard on it with both of his hands to tilt it back, and then he put the bundle under the boulder. He then began shifting the boulder back and forth and side to side to ensure that it pressed the bundle down tightly beneath it, and then he almost lost his balance again when he quickly leaned up and away from the river's edge.

Lydia waited until she saw Seth disappear back into the bushes and trees before she moved stealthily toward the big boulder in the river. She waded into the swift current, looked down into the water, and then saw a small part of the plastic bundle protruding from under the boulder.

She tugged the bundle out from under the boulder, and then hurried back to her hiding place in the tall grass. Lydia opened the plastic bag and saw that something inside it had been wrapped in a few sheets of plastic.

She carefully unfolded the plastic sheets, and saw a gun, which she then held up with both of her hands and pointed the barrel of it at the boulder in the river. She fired the gun twice before tossing it over to the spot where Seth had appeared from out of the forest.

Moments later, Seth came rushing back out of the trees after he'd heard the gunshots. He saw the gun on the ground, then he leaned over, picked it up, looked around, and his eyes widened when he saw Lydia kneeling in the tall grass.

He ran over to her, grabbed her arm, yanked her up to her feet, then he shouted: "So, you saw me hide this, did you?"

"Yes."

"Then that means I have to kill you!"

"But I won't tell anyone I saw you."

"No, you won't!" he exclaimed, sneering at her.

He began strangling her as Lydia kicked him and pounded him with her fists. When she stopped struggling, Seth let her limp body drop to the ground, then he stared down at her for a moment before picking her up and carrying her to the river.

He held her above his head, threw her out into the river, and watched the swift current carrying her downstream. The deep river became broader as it rushed toward the ocean, and Seth hoped that her body would be swept out far enough in the ocean that nobody would know where he'd killed her.

Lydia bobbed up and down in the swift river, bumping gently against and over big, smooth rocks, then nearing a big bush that had some thick branches drooping out over the water, she raised her left hand and grabbed onto a branch.

She pulled herself out of the river, struggled up the bank, then smoothed out her drenched dress, and then hummed as she walked through the trees toward a clearing.

Lydia undressed, spread out her wet clothes on the grass, and then laid on her back to look up at the clouds while relishing the luxurious warmth of the sunlight on her tingling, drying body.

She thought it was strange that Seth hadn't recognized her, but then she supposed that was probably because it had been rather dark four years ago, when they'd first met.

She felt her clothes, saw that they were dry, and then after she dressed again, she began walking back up the river toward the place Seth had discovered her, almost an hour earlier.

Lydia looked down at where she'd been lying in the tall grass, then she decided not to lie there again because Seth might see her, then put her through another frightful ordeal.

This was the very place Seth had laid her body when he'd carried her away from her home after he'd killed her the first time, and that was probably why he'd looked over in that direction and seen her in the tall grass.

She wondered how often Seth would continue to find her, and force her to go through the same thing again. Lydia wasn't sure how many times she'd stood in Seth's bedroom, told him she knew where he kept his gun hidden, and then run away, with him in pursuit of her.

Those odd, recurring dreams always took place at night, and yet he always strangled her in the daylight, close to the river after she'd watched him hiding the gun, wrapped in plastic, then in a plastic bag, which he always stuffed under that boulder that stood a few feet away from the riverbank.

Her dreams seemed to become clearer each time they occurred, and as Lydia thought about them, she knew there was a purpose to her dreams. She concentrated as hard as she could, then remembered why she had been taunting Seth.

She'd been trying to make him feel insecure about having the gun hidden in his home, and Lydia desperately wanted him to hide the gun where it could be found. Now she knew that she'd only imagined

Seth hiding the gun under the boulder after she'd lured him to the river, then he'd kept seeing her, then murdering her, and then throwing her into the river.

Lydia could sense that very soon, he would really think about wrapping the gun in a plastic sheet, then seal that bundle in a plastic bag, and then hide it under that boulder near the river's edge. She could also sense that she had to find a way to have somebody find the gun soon after Seth had hidden it under the boulder.

For some reason she couldn't understand, Lydia had never been able to mention to Gary, nor to her parents, what Seth had done to her, and continued to do. She felt sure, however, that the time had come, along with her sudden sense of inner strength, to have Gary help her bring Seth to justice.

• • • • • ❖••••••❖★❖••••••❖ • • • • • •

As she waited for Seth to return to the river in another dream, Lydia began recalling her recurring dreams, and then she suddenly realized a solution to her dilemma.

Seth was much taller and heavier than her, and when he leaned over the bank of the river to tilt back the big boulder in every dream she'd had, Lydia recalled that he always almost lost his balance.

That vision prompted her to decide that if she saw Gary later that day, she'd ask him to dig away under the bank, then Seth would fall into the river.

She couldn't do something like that herself, and even though she somehow couldn't tell Gary that Seth had murdered her, she realized that she could ask him to dig beneath the edge of the bank.

Lydia could sense the panic in Seth, and envision him looking for some plastic sheets and a plastic bag for the gun, and she felt certain that instead of just dreaming about him hiding the gun under the boulder in the river, he would really do that within hours.

◆•••••◆★◆•••••◆

She walked through the trees, looking out at the area of the riverbank where she sensed that she'd soon see Seth begin hiding the gun again. Lydia wasn't sure how much time had passed before she saw him appear out of the trees, and start walking along the edge of the river.

She watched him hide the gun beneath the boulder, and then after Seth tilted it back, he almost lost his balance when he took his hands off the boulder while quickly leaning up and away from it.

She waited until he'd walked out of sight, and then Lydia hurried to Gary's home while hoping that he'd returned from school, and then she went upstairs to his bedroom, and pleaded with him to come to the river. Gary finally gave into her anxious pleas, and ran down to the river with her.

"Okay, now what?" asked Gary, impatiently.

"You see how the ground sticks out over the river? Well, I'd like you to dig away underneath it for me, but in a way that nobody can notice it. So, would you do that for me? Please?"

"Oh, I see. Y'wanna play a joke on somebody, huh?"

"Yeah, but you gotta dig right where I say, okay?"

"Okay. I got a bit of time before I meet up with the guys."

"Thanks, Gary. You're my best ever friend."

"I always *will* be. So where do you want me to dig out underneath the side of the river?" he asked, smiling.

"I'll show you. C'mon!"

They ran to the spot where Seth always leaned over the river to tilt back the boulder in Lydia's recurring dreams, then she pointed to where she wanted Gary to dig.

He took off his shoes and socks, rolled the cuffs of his pants up to his knees, stepped into the river, and began digging and scraping at the underside of the bank with a thick, sharp-ended stick.

While Gary was doing that, Lydia stepped into the river and waded over to the big boulder that Seth had put the plastic bag under, and she saw that the river current had exposed part of the bag.

Her plan to make Seth fall into the river, then be swept away by the current, suddenly vanished when a new idea took its place as she looked down through the water at the slightly exposed plastic bag.

"Gary?"

"Yeah?"

"I just sat on this boulder and it almost toppled over, and I almost fell off it and in the water."

"So, don't try sitting on it again."

"I tried to wiggle it around to see if I could make sure it won't topple over so I can sit on it, but it's too heavy. I bet you can't wiggle it around, either."

Gary turned around, looked at the boulder, and then he turned back around and resumed digging and scraping away the underside of the riverbank.

"It doesn't look that heavy," he said.

"Oh, yeah? Then prove it. I bet y'can't move it even a little bit. Gary? C'mon. See if you can do it, then I can sit here watching you dig away at the riverbank. Okay? Please?"

"Okay, already! Man, you're so weird sometimes."

He set the stick down on the grass above the area he'd been digging away, then Gary turned around, gripped the boulder, and wiggled it side to side, then he tilted it back and forth until he was sure it wouldn't wobble when Lydia sat on it.

She felt so pleased when she saw that while he'd been shifting the boulder around, much more of the bag had been exposed, and although shifting the boulder around had caused clouds of muddy water to rise up around the boulder, she knew that Gary would notice the plastic bag sometime after the water cleared.

Lydia sat on the boulder, watching Gary scraping away the underside of the riverbank, then she smiled when he stopped digging, threw away the stick, dipped his hands in the river, and began washing the damp earth off them.

"I dug out a lot underneath the riverbank, and I'm sure nobody'd notice that I did that. Now, if somebody stands near the edge, the ground'll give way, and they'll fall in the river. Who are you playing this trick on, anyway? Lydia? Hey, you're starting to fade again! I can hardly see you, now!"

"Am I fading again? Gary! Come back later! Promise? Right here where we're standing, you'll see a plastic bag under the water by the boulder! Get the bag, but don't open it, okay? Gary! Promise me you won't open the bag! Please? Promise me!"

"Okay, I promise I won't open it! Okay? What should I do with it? Lydia! Your voice is fading, too!"

"Take the bag to the police station, and tell them where you found it! But don't open it, Gary! Wait! Now I know! Yes! Now you don't have to promise me you won't open the bag! You won't *want* to open it! Somehow you'll be scared of it! You don't have to promise me, now! Take the bag to the police, Gary! You have to! Please! Do it for me! Gaaaaa...reeeee–eeeeeeeeee!" her voice echoed.

"Lydia! Lydia! Why did you go away? Why would somebody hurt you? I'll always love you! I'll always remember you! Awwww, no! I can't see you, anymore! Lydia? Lydia!" He looked around, but of course nobody was there because he hadn't really seen anyone since he'd arrived at the river.

Gary looked down at the water and laughed when he realized that he was standing in the river, close to the edge of it. He slowly shook his head as he smiled and wondered if he'd been daydreaming when he'd unknowingly walked into the river.

He waded back out of the water, and started to walk upstream while muttering to himself: "The guys said they'd meet me here, long ago. Wonder what's keeping them? Maybe they decided to play baseball, instead. Aw, to heck with 'em! I'm going swimming, anyway. Darn it! I forgot my socks back there."

Gary walked back to where he'd waded into the river after he had left school, then as he picked up his socks, he noticed that a part of the riverbank had caved in while he was gone.

He looked down into the water, and saw what looked like a plastic package stuffed halfway under a big boulder that stood about two feet away from the riverbank.

He stepped down into the water, leaned over, reached below the surface, and tugged the plastic bag out from under the boulder, and then he turned the bag over in his hands as he examined it.

Gary then had a sudden, strange, almost frightening, cold feeling throughout his body, and he shuddered. He felt cold perspiration on his forehead as he looked down at the plastic bag in his hands.

Suddenly, he thought he heard a faint voice somewhere close to him, and he wondered if it could be one of the guys yelling on his way to the river, but after waiting about ten seconds, and he hadn't heard anyone calling out to him again, Gary felt somehow that he should take the mysterious plastic bag to the police station.

There was something heavy wrapped in plastic inside the clear, plastic bag, and he had an odd, scary feeling that it was something very dangerous and very important, too, therefore, he began walking away from the river, and his hands trembled as he carried the bag.

He felt paranoid about every sound he heard and everything that moved around him, so, he quickened his pace while thinking that he was being surreptitiously watched from somewhere among the trees.

When he saw the streets ahead of him, Gary began running, after he felt more frightened. His heart was pounding faster as he ran, then he started to recall his closest friend, Lydia, whom he'd played with years ago, and then he felt much anguish as he remembered how people had found her body by the river.

Visions of Lydia flashed through his mind as he pictured her laughing and playing in the river with him, and he could vaguely recall many people crying as they stood around a big mound of earth, covered with flowers, and he remembered again how he'd cried when they'd told him that his best friend had died.

Gary started weeping as he ran. He stopped several times, and sobbed, then the terrifying feeling swept over him again, and he resumed running toward the police station.

He ran up the stairs to the door of the police station, rushed inside, put the plastic bag down on a counter, then Gary lifted the bottom of his T-shirt to wipe tears off his cheeks.

He stammered out where he'd found the strange, plastic bag, and how scared he was of it, then a policeman picked up the bag, came around the counter, and held him, as Gary wept.

An hour later, his parents came to the police station to take him home, and Gary sat in the front seat of the car, hugging his father. The police examined the gun they'd found in the plastic bag, then a few days later, they told Gary's parents that they'd found Seth's fingerprints on the gun, and it had been used to murder little Lydia, four years ago.

His mother asked Gary if he remembered saying that he often saw Lydia, but Gary said he couldn't recall seeing her since the day before Lydia had died. She sighed, and felt relieved that Gary had finally passed through his immense grief, and then she decided not to mention to her son again, how he used to tell her that he often saw and talked with his once closest friend, Lydia.

• • • • • ❖••••••❖★❖••••••❖ • • • • •

Seth was arrested, then sent to an institute for the criminally insane. For years, his mind had been deteriorating because he kept seeing Lydia, week after week, standing in his bedroom late at night, telling him that she knew where he'd hidden the gun, and that she was going to tell the police.

He had chased her so often out of his house, and then he'd always lost sight of her somewhere in the forest. Seth had also seen her many times during the day at the river, then he'd kept killing her in the same spot where he'd laid her body four years ago.

He'd felt that he had to keep strangling her, then throwing her body into the river so that she wouldn't tell the police that he had murdered her when she'd awakened one night and come downstairs to find that he'd broken into her home.

Lydia had been so frightened when she'd seen Seth pointing a gun at her as he moved toward her, that she had only been able to barely whisper: "No! I won't tell anyone I saw you!"

He had shot her, then run out of the house, carrying her body, and he'd felt safe because nobody had seen him, but he started dreaming about seeing her at the river. The last time he'd dreamed about being at the river, he'd hidden the gun under the boulder, and then the riverbank had crumbled away, and Seth couldn't swim, so, he'd almost drowned while being swept away by the swift current.

He recalled that in his nightmare about almost drowning, he'd snatched at branches of heavy bushes hanging over the river until he was finally able to grip onto one of them, then he had climbed out of the river, pulled off his sopping-wet clothes and laid them out on the grass to dry before he had dressed and returned home.

Seth had thought that his dream about hiding the gun under the boulder close to the river's edge had been an omen. An omen that erased his dread of the gun being found in his home, and that's when he'd decided to hide it under that boulder in the river so that the police would never find it.

But now he knew that Lydia had been in his bedroom at the time he'd dreamed about hiding the gun under the boulder, and she'd heard him muttering that plan in his sleep, and then after watching him hiding the gun under the boulder, she had taken it to the police.

Seth realized that the next time he strangled her, he had to make sure he bound her body with rope, then tied heavy boulders to it, so that Lydia could never resurface again, and then tell the police that he'd murdered her.

Every day, he sat in his small, concrete room, glaring at Lydia skipping back and forth, but every time Seth tried to grab her, then strangle her, Lydia called out to a boy, and then she laughed and ran away to play with that boy.

Through the years, Lydia's face faded slightly from Gary's memory, but sometimes he'd walk through the cemetery to lay flowers on her grave.

He would then try to remember what Lydia had looked like that last time they had played together at the river when they had both been nine years old.

The End